ers

The Women's Press

science fiction

The Women's Press science fiction series features new titles by contemporary writers and reprints of classic works by well known authors. Our aim is to publish science fiction by women and about women; to present exciting and provocative feminist images of the future that will offer an alternative vision of science and technology, and challenge male domination of the science fiction tradition itself.

We hope that the series will encourage more women both to read and to write science fiction, and give the traditional science fiction readership a new and stimulating perspective.

Tanith Lee has forty books of science fiction and fantasy in print, including books for children. She has also completed a novel on the French Revolution. She has written numerous short stories and is a contributor to the anthology *Despatches from the Frontiers of the Female Mind* (The Women's Press, 1985). Two of her short stories, 'The Gorgon' and 'Elle Est Trois', won the World Fantasy Award, and her novel *Death's Master* won the 1980 August Derleth Award. *Night's Sorceries* was shortlisted for the 1988 World Fantasy Award for Best Collection. Her two most recent novels are *The Book of the Damned* and *The Book of the Beast*.

Women as Demons

The Male Perception of Women through Space and Time

Stories by
Tanith Lee

The Women's Press

sf

First published by The Women's Press Limited 1989
A member of the Namara Group
34 Great Sutton Street, London EC1V ODX

The following stories have been published previously: 'The
Demoness' in *Years' Best Fantasy 2*, 1976; 'Deux Amours d'une
Sorciére' in *Swords Against Darkness 4*, 1979; 'The Unrequited
Glove' in *Weird Tales*, 1988; 'Gemini' in *Chrysalis 9*, 1981; 'Into
Gold' in *Isac Asimov's Science Fiction Magazine*, March 1986; 'You
are My Sunshine' in *Chrysalis 8*, 1980; 'The One We Were' in
Elsewhere 3, 1984; 'The Truce' in *Daw Science Fiction Reader*, 1976;
'The Squire's Tale' in *Sorcerer's Apprentice Issue 7*, 1980; 'Winter
White' in *Years' Best Horror 6*, 1978; 'Written in Water' in
Perpetual Light, 1982; 'Mirage and Magia' in *Hecate's Cauldron*,
1982; 'The Thaw' in *Isaac Asimov's Science Fiction Magazine*, June
1979; 'Northern Chess' in *Amazons*, 1979.

British Library Cataloguing in Publication Data

Lee, Tanith, *1947–*
  I. Title
  823'.914 [F]

  ISBN 0-7043-4169-7

Typeset by AKM Associates (UK) Ltd,
Ajmal House, Hayes Road, Southall, London
Printed and bound in Great Britain by
Hazel, Watson & Viney Ltd, Aylesbury, Bucks

Contents

Preface

She is in the bothy, and through the dim fire-glow, he can see her strange shadow flung up on the wall. She may only be cooking that night's meal, turning the raw meat into something tasty and nourishing . . . or she may be making magic. He will not go in for a while. He will stay to talk with the other men, about the hunting they have had, and the raiding they will be going on. That will be best.

She is with child, the woman. Her body is different. Her long shining hair seems half alive. She sings with words he cannot hear, is singing now.

She has told him, the child comes from the goddess. That she is to bear a child is the pact between her and the female Power of the earth. Though the priests say now it is the male seed quickens a woman's womb, yet the women still murmur in this fashion. Without the goddess and the women and the womb, there would be an end to all things.

Her strange shadow flickers on the wall.

Yes. Better to wait. And not to listen to her song.

There are many submissions as to why there has been built about the female a mythology of darkness, corruption and the uncanny. Her offerings of blood, and her ability to bear children out of her own body, have jointly made of woman a creature 'pure' and 'unclean', a human hampered by seemingly irrevocable laws, chained; subsequently a being clandestine. She moves to primal music, and is therefore perhaps possessed of fundamental powers, and whims.

I do not propose to debate such causes here, though I will be found to have debated them here, and there (and not always overtly), in the stories which follow.

I must say at once that I, in common with countless women, have drunk up the Demon Woman mythology, and by now carry it in my bones. The mysterious and fascinating world which I entered at the age of nought, subtly and sweepingly fed me all the glimmering tales and all the jewellery lies. It was, and is, the *glamour* of the wicked lady that endears her to me. A heroine may be unattractive and cloying. The villainess, with her dashing carelessness and accoutrements of sin, she turns the head. An equation evolves: bad is beautiful. And the same may be said of men, if it comes to it. Satan, Dracula . . . the myth of the Man as Demon also exists, nurtured by the fantasies of women, and the hero-model wish-fulfilment of the male. A woman may find the demonic but powerful anti-heroine a welcome extension, the powerful demonic man desirable and challenging. Just so may a man find the image of the anti-hero liberates him from certain gender ghettos – *false* courtesies, imposed roles – while becoming ensnared by the dangerous female, be she Countess Bathory or Morgan le Fey. There is nothing inherently wrong in any of that – except where it loses the true nature of the game or the experiment, and begins to cloud visions of the real – that is the *lived-in* – world.

As a writer my means – I can hardly say method – is to allow the story, its nuances, characters, purpose, to shape themselves. I am the instrument. This evidently supposes that I do not, save rarely, interfere during the stages of production. And, when writing in the first person, I become, as an actor does, the character her- or himself.

Why or how one is able to do this, those who can are rarely able to explain. I am inclined to believe myself that it is an avenue open to everyone of reasonable intelligence and sympathy. Not merely to understand – but to *become*, if only for a moment, another person, regardless of sex, origin or creed, renders to us a compassion of a form for which there is no proper word. But too it gives into our hands valuable weapons of insight and thought. These rewards may not last, but at least we shall have had a brief possession of them.

If writing as a man, then, I do not recall in any way that I am a woman. I am able to put down what my character feels and knows. And drawing back, in the intervals, I have been occasionally shocked at what I have been party to. That does not mean, however, that I would deny a single word. Far from it. I am not a censor, but a recorder. My passion for what, as a writer, I can do, is bound up for ever in my faith that even the fiction I write is real, in some inexpressible way.

Because I am writing from a powerhouse of human genes, the very fact that I permit an inner voice to speak, should, I insist, conjure nothing that violates integrity. Aside from my paper people, *I* am a woman, and *I* do not think that woman has any more of the bestial or the demonic in her than has her masculine opposite.

Writing inside fantasy, with its parallels of those primitive societies where the female position was that of goods, valued or un-, the writer is obliged to concoct female characters who fit their era and element. Whose situation is therefore a frank nullity (given the framework of Action and Adventure), unless leavened by some psychic and/or devilish ability. When writing as a male, I am next able to explore 'first hand' some of the responses to the superstition of the Demon Woman. I have indeed begun to see, inside those bearded, weaponed skins, a spark of what may have started the fear. And, with luck, thereby demonstrated something of it, on the page. Also, inevitably, I have been struck by the revelation that women, under this relentless pressure, can become the accomplices of their own downfall. They too may credit themselves with grim undercurrents unique to their gender, shadow-powers that set them apart in hidden rituals that men dare not look on, offering a chance to 'win' by underhand practice: purely the philosophy of the slave.

Nevertheless, that said, inside the context of fantasy, where psychic powers and magic of all types really do work, a woman who draws up from herself these same forces, dark or bright, is attaining a strength entirely legitimate and self-expressive. In those climes there will be plenty of men gifted with sorcery and employing the art to exact pleasures and vengeances. A woman, *there*, who uses her own talent and gift to do the same or worse, is merely achieving her majority, proving her equality. That her unhappy life has made her into an evil person is another matter, having to do with morals. She is fighting with a genuine arsenal. And that is *not* the philosophy of the slave, but of the warrior.

The only danger arises out of a misconception *here*, amidst the everyday distresses and injustices. Here a woman should not fight by imagined means. Although personally I believe in the possibility of psychic power and its affiliations, it will probably not work with the drum-roll efficiency it offers the witch in the story. Certain things therefore should not be borne with self-consoling delusory promises of dark mental retributions, curses of the backstairs. *Here* the warrior must use the ordinary (s)word.

And I do think that most of us cannot fight an unseen enemy, even if we have been given an excellent description of it. The case needs constantly to be examined, and part of that examination must entail a grasp not merely of where and when the myth began, and was perpetuated, but of where it has sunk its roots into the bedrock of heart and brain. I am aware, as I have said, that I am not immune to the male perspective on women. Obviously I have been influenced. This I understand and accept in myself. However, the tendency, where it occurs, need not be used to prolong the damaging nonsense that sometimes has been told about Woman Strong and Woman Wise. By retelling the myth it seems to me I have tried to investigate and pin-point the issue, rather than uphold the sham. The structure of *The Demoness* for example, for me rests upon its final line. *Into Gold* makes a quavering double-take feasible. *You are my Sunshine* is a black burlesque that *surely* defies unqualified acceptance. *Deux Amours* and *Mirage and Magia* are outcries from that last ditch wherein even the gifted and vital woman can find herself. As is *The Unrequited Glove* – although this carries too the caveat: man, beware. In creating this terror you may bring it down upon yourself.

These, or coexisting patterns, can be detected in each story. Except perhaps in the very last, *Northern Chess*. There a solution is presented at least to the problem of female oppression by a male partner, and the restrictions of the female 'persona'. A proportion of women, casting aside the real or invented mask and mirror, know too well that this will be their station. Woman not as demon, or adjunct, but as hero – distinct, self-responsible, uncompromised, veritable – and alone.

Tanith Lee

Women as Demons

The Demoness

She waited in her high tower.

Day in, day out she waited.

The tower was white and stretched beneath her, far, far, to the sweep of the bleached dunes and the gray glister of the sea.

Her world was all gray, all white, half-tones, glitterings, without shape. A world colourless, and abstract. And she too was white, her foamy dress, her feet, her narrow hands – all white as the chalk hills that ran distantly above the sea. But her long, long hair was red, blood red, red as an eruption of magma out of the white volcanic crystal of her flesh. She did not look at her hair; obscurely she feared it. She bound it on her head in braids.

She was waiting, and not certain why she waited, or for whom, or for what.

She did not think of her past or her future, or really of any particular thing. She had no memory, or so it seemed, only an empty page from which words had faded. She watched the gulls dip in on the wind, screaking in their wind voices. She came out of the tower at certain times, and went in again at certain other times. Like a figure on a clock. She had no ambitions or yearnings, nor any hope. She was, in the sense that she existed. She was, but that was all.

Time passed, but time had no meaning. It might have been yesterday or tomorrow when she saw him.

He was riding up the beach in the dawn, a man in gold on a golden horse, its mane like blowing corn, scarlet reins and golden bells on them, its hooves striking up the sand. He dazzled her eyes. He wore a kind of armour that was either too antique or else too recent for her to recognise it. Tassels swung from his shoulders, his hair was ragged and bright like the ripped-out strings of a golden harp.

She felt a quickening as she leaned down from the length of the white tower. *Am I waiting for this man*? He was a burning ant on the beach, but soon he rode under the arch of the tower. An echo came, and then his feet loud on the stairs. She heard him pass through room after room, stopping sometimes. She imagined him examining certain things. But all the while he was drawing nearer. She turned to face the door through which he would come. Her heart beat. Without thinking, she reached up and let down her hair.

He stood still in the doorway looking at her. He was stern; she wanted to make him smile. He stared in her face.

'Where is Golbrant?' he asked her.

She put her hand to her mouth. She shook her head.

'He that passed by here, thirty days gone, riding to Krennok-dol. He that had a harp on his back and a scar like a cross on his brow.'

She shook her head once more, and her heart beat fast and she put her hand on her throat and waited.

'Golbrant,' he said, his eyes narrow and very bright, 'my brother by vow, not blood. He to whom the Sisters said, "Beware the white woman waiting for death in the tall tower by the sea." '

He came forward and seized her by the hair, and twisted it around his hand until the pain filled her skull like a silver cloud.

'*Where is Golbrant*?' he hissed, and then he met her eyes.

This was how it was to her. His eyes were like a summer garden. She wanted to draw from them those vistas of amber shades and yellow darts of sun, she wanted those hopes, those ambitions and yearnings she saw in them to fill her emptiness, her darkness, with their purpose and their light. She was hungry and thirsty for his reflected life as the fish for water, the wings of the bird for air. And her eyes began to breathe, to drink like beasts at a pool, and she put out her hands to his neck and drew herself against the hard armour, and clung to him tight. He spat a curse at her, and tried to shake himself free of her hands, her eyes, but could not. There was a kind of pleasant deathly heaviness in her embrace, her gaze, like sleep, except where it filled and curdled in his loins. She drew him down. She drowned him in her eyes and her body. He swam in the current of her flesh, and the tide took him away, and he was lost in the tunnel of the pleasure she had to give him. Such pleasure it was no woman before or since had been, would be. It was the whole store of her pleasure, held for him. She was the jar that contained the oceans, the fountainhead; he strove to reach the source and cried aloud to reach it.

But at the last his body checked itself. Out of desire came a great numbness, and then a revulsion of the pale thing wriggling beneath him. He understood then what he would have given her along with the life that ran out of him.

And then he twisted aside. He pulled his body free, and he turned his head, shielding his eyes as if from a dreadful and consuming glare.

'So, what they said of you is true, white woman,' he muttered in sick cold anger, more to his own self than to her. 'You devour the brain's knowledge and the mind's reason with your look and your womb. Yes, I felt it leaving me, and I would be hollow after as the bone of marrow when the wolf has had it. Is this then how you dealt with Golbrant?'

Her gaze was darkening, dimming, going out. She lay on the ground. She did not understand. And yet there was a faint memory, a memory like a dream, of a man on a dark horse, dark-haired, with a harp on his back with a woman's face, and a jagged criss-cross above his eyes. She had waited for him too, she remembered now, and he had come, across the long rooms, up the stairs of the tower. But he had not flinched aside, the light had passed from him to her. She looked up at the man whom she had almost possessed, for she recollected now, abruptly, what it meant when she lay with men. It was neither a shock nor a surprise, and not abhorrent. It seemed natural, for what did she know of the natural order of things to make this one thing that was hers seem strange and dark and evil?

'He is dead,' she said softly, an explanation only.

The golden man drew his sword, swung it to lop her head from her shoulders, but it was not the habit of the warriors of Krennok-dol to kill women, however great their anger. So he halted, and after a moment he sheathed the sword again.

'Live, vampire,' he said, his eyes now blind with hate, 'but never practice on a man again to take his wits, or I'll see your head on a pole yet.'

It could make no sense to her; she was not quite human, human values and laws had no meaning. Yet she stared at him, and she loved him, because he had won free from her and had no need of her any more.

He strode from room to room, searching for his vow-brother,

Golbrant, but Golbrant had staggered from room to room when his self and his sanity had gone from him, and had fallen down from the high place into the sea. The waves had carried him off like sour green vinegar dogs, and the vulture gulls had picked at him, and the fish, so that now he was ivory on the ocean floor, with no mark on him any more to say who he was, except the gold harp turning green in the sand at his side.

While the warrior searched, the woman followed him. She could not tell him where Golbrant had gone, could not remember, though no doubt he guessed. She stared at his back, stared at his face when he turned. Her love was all-devouring; she would have eaten him if she could. Her love was like that.

But he thrust her aside, and went down the stairs of the tower, away from her and away. He found the horse and rode it off up the sea road into the chalk stacks that margined the shore.

For three days she wandered in the tower. She did not bind up her long, long hair. She did not go out above the bleached strand. She was no longer waiting. Golbrant and all the other men who had sunk like ships in her deadly embrace, lost their wills and their minds in her eyes and her womb, were quite forgotten again, shadows at the back of her thoughts perhaps, no more. But him she remembered, the warrior on the grain-yellow horse, his narrow bright eyes, his flax hair, his anger and his going away.

On the dawn of the fourth day she went down the stairs of the tower, and out, and up the sea road after him.

She had never left the tower before, not in all her years since she had become what she was. There had been no desire before; now there was a compulsion.

The sun cracked open the gray sky, and the sun and her blowing hair were two bright dabs of scarlet in the colourless land she was leaving.

After some days the land changed colour. It changed from white to black. Hills like black crouching crows stood guard on either side of the road. The sky was dark with storms. Now her feet were red as her hair because the sharp black stones bit them like snakes. She was one of those who had no need to eat or sleep, so she simply walked day and night. She followed the hoofprints of the horse, and sometimes there were droppings; here and there a piece of his cloak might have caught on brambles, or she would come to the cold ashes of a fire and run her fingers through them and touch the ash with her tongue because he had lain by them for warmth when they were alive three nights before.

Then there was a black river in the twilight. There was a round blue moon overhead that looked almost transparent, and great clouds beating by like angry birds. And there was an old devil-woman crouched by the rushing water tending a bluish fire and a cauldron of death over it. She was wrapped up in something black, only her eyes showed and her skinny hands stuck out, all bone. When she saw the white woman walking along the river bank she screamed out:

'Krennock-dol lies that way! That way! Over the river.'

Then the devil-woman left her brew and went up to her, and turned her to look out across the river.

'No way for you to cross. The bridge is down – he did it, knowing you followed after. He was afraid, the horse leaped and struck sparks from its iron feet, knowing the vampire girl came behind them. I gave him a charm to protect him from you, but it will do him no good. Look at you, all hunger. Is this your love then, to follow a man who runs in terror, a man who hates you in his loins and sword arm? Didn't you drive to death his vow-brother, Golbrant the Good?' Here the devil-woman spat. 'What is it makes you hurry after the sword stroke which is all he wants to give you?'

But the white woman was already wandering down the bank away from her, searching, searching for a place to cross, though there was none at all, and anyone could see it but her. The devil-woman ran after her, skipping like a ghastly black goat, for she had goat horns on her head, being what she was. She tapped the woman's shoulder.

'Do you know his name even? No. Well, there's too much of him in the world. If you want him, walk into the water and it'll carry you over, unless you're afraid to do it. A long search you will have, but when you find him, he will be yours. Only remember the price he pays for it. Witless he will be then, but what a joy to you – if you keep him from the tall crags and death. Like your child and your man, all in one, for ever and ever.'

She heard, and though it was only a shadow on her thoughts, yet she understood. At the brink of the river the devil-woman whispered:

'If you let him go free, you will be dust, for a sword will strike off your head. Let nothing and no one come between. Remember.'

Then she thrust with her bony hands, pushing the woman down into the water. The white woman had no fear. Her hair and her dress floated her up, the current bore her downstream, her hands trailed like drowned flowers, and she thought only of him she sought. All night, under the blue-ringed stars, the river pulled her between the hills by silver ropes. Near dawn it cast her up like a white fish-maid on the icy quays that lie below the dol hill.

Six or seven river fishermen found her. They thought she was a suicide and crossed themselves, but before they could run for the priest, she got up and walked away from them up the stone path to the hill, not seeing them.

The hill was green. Things grew on it that were not rank or poisonous in any way, and behind lay a forest. The land of Krennok was a land alive between the dead lands, north, south, east and west. High on the green hill the king's house stood, made of wood, stone and brass. Two hundred pillars upheld the roof in the king's great hall, pillars carved like trees of green marble. Fountains played and pools lay clear as glass, and white birds fluted in the gardens where round fruits grew in clusters under the yellow sky. This was Krennok-dol. At the great gate of bronze hung a bell the size of a warrior, with a tongue the size of a girl-child ten years old.

She had no means to strike the bell; it would take a tall man on a tall horse, striking with his sword, to do it. So she knocked, till her hands bled like her feet, on the bronze door panels.

It was the law in the king's hold that whoever came asking for mercy or justice, or any other kind of boon, should at least get a hearing from him. Consequently the porter came at last and let her in. Her dress and hair were still wet from the river, and she walked over the threshold trailing black river weed from her skirt. She frightened the porter a good deal.

She went up the great stairways into the hall with its forest of pillars. The king and his warriors had come from their dawn prayers, and were sitting eating and drinking at long tables. The king himself sat on his high seat of hammered gold, as he had sat three days before when a warrior came galloping from the sea with red-rimmed eyes and a horse frothing with fear. The king had risen to welcome and embrace him; he loved this warrior perhaps better than the rest, though possibly he had loved Golbrant the Good even more than this his Alondor, that women called the Gold behind their hands.

But Alondor held away from the king.

'There is a curse on me,' he said. 'God forbid I give it to you like a contagion.'

He told them of Golbrant's death in the high tower by the sea. He reminded them of the Sisters, those five dark witches who had come to Krennok-dol five months ago to wail prophecies of death for five warriors. When he spoke of the woman in the tower and what he had done with her, he went white with shame. Later he made confession to the priest. The priest prayed hard, understanding very well what Alondor feared. Having lain with her but given nothing, having failed to kill her when he was able, he had left with her those powers of his pleasure and his hate he had renounced. And she had come after him, still came, relentless as winter with her cold white desire. If again he stood in her presence he knew he, in turn, would have no power. The succubus would entangle him and destroy him, draining his brain of its life. Such was the shadowy magic of her sexual vampirism, the oldest and most terrible of all the demons in the world. He had not known all this till he was three days on the road and sensed, by a prickling of his skin, a coldness and a frenzy in his loins, what followed and with what ability.

Alondor fled out of Krennok-dol a day before she came there.

As she stood in the king's hall, she looked about for him, and her heart beat. When she saw he was not there, a deadly misery made her falter. Yet only for a moment. Then, forgetting it, remembering only him, she turned to leave the king's house the way she had come.

The king sprang up with an oath and three warriors ran into her path. They raised their swords to strike her down, but again the old stigma caught at their hands. They had never killed or harmed a woman. It came hard to do it now. Then she walked by them with her pale blind eyes.

'Go after!' shouted the king. 'Do as he should have done. Remember her foulness and her sorcery! Not a woman but a *thing* under your blades.'

They followed her out. On the stairway one looked in her face. He shrank back and could do nothing. Farther down another reached her. He swung her about and the sword swung, but at the last instant she seemed so pitiful, only a poor madwoman.

This is some mistake! he cried to himself, and let her go in an agony of bewilderment.

The third ran for his horse. He followed her across the court, out of the gate, grinning with fury. It seemed to him he was out hunting; he heard the dogs snarling ahead and glimpsed the running white deer leaping down from the green dol hill. When he was near enough, he snatched her on the horse, and rode with her limp in one arm into the forest beyond the hill. There he flung her down and himself over her in an unbearable ecstasy of need. The sword he used on her was flesh, and soon she slid from under him and walked away, barely conscious of what he had done or had become. Days later the king's warriors found him, a wandering madman screaming for his hunting dogs under the thick-leafed boughs.

She walked through a year. For a year Alondor the Gold fled before her. He became a mercenary, hiring out his war skills to many kings whose causes seemed good. Never did he stay long in any one place. He dreamed of fear and lust, and of Golbrant, his vow-brother, whom he had loved better than any man or woman.

The seasons changed. Red leaves fell into her red hair and over her scarred, misused, unnoticed feet, also into the bloody battlefields where he rode. Snows came and went, frost and rain. Beyond the land of Krennok, in the gray dead lands with their twisted trees and tall-spired mountains, he ran, she followed, drawn by instinct and desire, seeing and hearing only him.

In the barren steeples of the north he came at last to the pile of a solitary hold. It was dark and it was gloomy as were the crags around it. A green moon watched as he hammered at the gates. He was sick with the wound a battle two months before had given him, and he was sick of himself and his compulsion to fly the unknown thing which followed. He still had his looks; he was a man to be stared at, but there were white strings in the gold harp hair now, and his eyes ran back deep into his soul, the eyes of a murderer, a victim, or a man possessed by devils. Such was the penalty of an unstruck blow in a tower by the sea.

In a hall where flickering torches burned, he spoke with the lord of the place, but a ringing noise came and went in his head. Finally, from the corner of his eye, he saw a pale shape in the arch of a door. From over the white face to the white shoulders and beyond fell a blood-red curtain. He thought she had found him, she who came after, and terror rose up in his belly and choked him, and struck him, like all enemies, from behind. He fell down in the kind of faint that is an outpost of death.

Yet the woman in the door was not the one he thought. She was the daughter of the hold, her name Siandra, and she wore a scarlet shawl over her head because the hall was cold. She was beautiful as an icon. Her skin was white but her mouth was red, and her hair as black as Golbrant's hair when he rode with the harp on his back toward Krennock-dol. She might have been indeed a sister to Golbrant, for she resembled him very curiously, but she knew nothing of the warriors of the green-growing hill. She had her own kind of waiting, did Sian. When she saw the gold-haired man with nightmares in his eyes, she felt a quickening too. If he had chosen at that time to win her love, he could have done nothing better than fall down like a dead man a few yards from her feet.

She took it on herself to nurse him, and did not find it irksome in the least. Opening his eyes on her face, he felt life turn for him like a page. Love grew up between them as easily as a child will grow.

As the spring drew on, a night came and took her with it into his chamber. She brought sweetness with her, if not the full draught of the cup. But then, he had known the pleasure of demons, and it was almost good that with this human girl it must be less. Towards dawn he kissed her and said:

'Tomorrow, Sian, I must be gone from you and here.'

Tears filled her eyes. She thought the immemorial thought of the discarded.

'No,' he said, 'not for that. There is a doom on me. I am pursued. If I remain, I die.'

'Then let me go with you,' Siandra said.

'No. What gift of love is that from me to your sweet self, to make you wander the world homeless at my heels?' His face was pale and he had shut his eyes. 'Let me go alone, and have your peace. There's none for me. I have already stayed too long.'

If she was sweet, she was strong too, this girl in the north land. She took his hands fast and asked him for the truth, asked him again and again, until he thrust her from him as if he hated her, and told her everything, and then wept on her breast like a child.

'Let her come,' Siandra whispered, and her eyes burned.

He was so tired. The year had tired him out. He stayed, for her woman's strength seemed more than any shield or sword in the wide world.

Nights passed. Spring lay on the land, but nothing grew save bright weeds at the door, and birds made nests in the crags of the mountains and the hold. Alondor was the lord's man now. He fought a battle for him and came back with the heads of enemies. The feast ran on into the dark, but for all the wine and meat, he felt a growing cold and uneasiness on him, like a fever coming.

In the close room he paced about while Siandra lay asleep. The moon rose late, the colour of yellow bones, and he looked with a turmoil in his belly along the causeway, and saw something standing there, ice-white, holding back its blowing scarlet hair with long white narrow hands on which the nails had grown to talons. She had had no change of garment; her white clothes hung on her like the tatters of a shroud, her feet were carved over with scars. Her face looked up, yearning, her eyes like pools holding only his image. Her love had lasted, was still all-devouring; she would have eaten him if she could. Her love was like that.

Alondor fell on his knees and prayed, but no words came into his mind, only the woman. He felt her draw nearer and nearer across the rocky road, he felt her drift through the gates like white smoke, while the sentries dozed or did not see. He heard her soundless feet on the stairs, and how doors sprang silently wide at her touch.

Siandra woke and sat up in the bed. She looked at him crouching to pray, and heard how his prayers grew weaker and weaker.

She felt terror – *She* is here.

At that instant he got to his feet and the prayers left him altogether. He was a man deprived suddenly of everything – except that one thing which drew him and drew him. Like an automaton, he turned and crossed the room, went out through the door, and his eyes were very bright, his cheeks flushed. He went cheerfully, eagerly, the blood hot as fire in him, lusting, forgetting, caught up in the spell of the white woman who waited, this time, below.

When he was on the stairs, Siandra slid from the bed. If he looked burning and alive, she looked like his death. She snatched up the sword he had left behind and walked trembling, yet soft as a cat, after him.

She was in the house, the woman from the high tower by the sea. She was in a passage, and sensing that now at last he came to her, she had stopped quite still. Her heart beat. She put up her hands to her hair to let it down; finding it loose, she let down her hands instead. She thought she was in the tower, but it had no meaning for her. She thought she heard the sound of the sea sweeping in against the shale beaches; perhaps it was the sound of her own blood, the tide of her body moving in and out. A gull screaked, but it was a stair under his foot. Rounding a corner he came into sight for her. Her heart lifted in her body as if it had no weight or purpose except to lift in her like a bird. A warmth and gladness filled her up like the empty vessel she was, and for the first time since she had become what she was, her lips parted and she smiled. She held out her arms, and he was eager enough to come into them. He had forgotten.

But Siandra was just behind him, holding the sword. She also had the knowledge of old things, old ways – the oldest and most indisputable magic. Even as Alondor reached out to take his own death, Siandra ran between them. She lifted and swung the heavy sword as though it were a grass stem. She knew nothing of Krennok-dol and the warriors, and the chivalry of men who did no harm to a living thing with breasts and a womb, which called itself a woman. She struck for all she held dear and needful, with a selfish, careless, passionate stroke.

What she felt, the woman from the sea, was a long white pain, and then a long scarlet pain. Her head fell from her shoulders in an instant of time, but time had no meaning for her. Her agony lasted many ages. After the passing of these ages, she lay scattered, deaf, dumb, blind and in a million fragments. She knew what it is to be a million separate things, and still to be one.

Siandra shrank back against Alondor, looking away from what she had done, and he held to her, waking from the trance. She had been Golbrant, his vow-brother in that instant, rising out of the sea intact, green-gold harp on back, black hair strings on the strings of the harp, wielding the blow Golbrant had never thought to strike in the tower. This was how Siandra finally took his love, more by becoming the past than by ending it.

While they held together, the white woman fell apart like the petals of a blossom. She blew up into their faces like white flour. She was dust as she had been promised she would be by the devil-woman in the blue moonlight. All dust.

The dust circled and pulsed, falling in on itself. Grains disbanded into grains, millions became millions upon millions. Soon there was no more of her to see, neither white nor red.

Yet she was aware. In every minuscule atom her hunger persisted, unassuaged.

Now she is blown here and there, endless varieties of place suck her down and fling her away. She is in everything, her hunger everywhere.

Long after Alondor and his Siandra will be dust of another sort, she will be blown about the world. Into the eyes to cause tears, into the fingernails of murderers, into the crannies of broken hearts to seal up the hurt with more hurting. She has no name. She is in every deed and dream and thought. She is all things and nothing. She is still waiting, and will wait forever, over every inch of the world.

Strangers come and go unharmed up and down the steps of the tall white tower. Gulls build in the ruins. One day every stone will have fallen bit by bit across the sweep of the bleached dunes and into the gray glister of the sea. One day the cliffs too will have fallen. After them, the land. The sea will shrink and drain away, the sky will tumble and the stars go out. And in that last or intermediary dark, she will remain. Still waiting.

Pity her.

Deux Amours d'une Sorcière

It was a time when Parys was new, immature and beautiful. It was a season of pinks and of blues. Turrets of blue slate pencilled on deep summer skies; roses like sugar-paste in the little walled gardens of rose brick. Pale rose wine, with blue eyes gazing across the cup. Blue dusks with a pink quarter moon. Sapphires and a girl's blush. Dawn falling into love-beds with canopies of blue velvet. Candle smoke. Flamingoes.

It was a time of love. Of a needing to be in love. Of the ground loving the feet which passed over it. The pointed towers loving the soft clouds they seemed to uphold. Flowers loving to be plucked, and the air loving to be full of the songs which filled it. Everything was in love, loving, loved. All but one. All but Jhane.

She would stand at her window, with her light fine hair bound about her head, with pearls the colour of her own mouth glowing in it. She dressed for the season, for she was aware of such things. She dressed for it, she understood it. But she had no part in it.

Once, long ago, she had been poor. Now she had a protector, a man who had ended her poverty. This man was an old man. He did not want anything very much from her. To sit and look at her. To walk with her in the garden of the house he had given her. Sometimes he liked to caress her, but nothing more. He was gentle and courteous, foolish only in his cleaving to a woman's youth. He did not expect her to be faithful to him. He imagined she would occasionally take lovers, young men. Sometimes he hoped vaguely for a child to be born, a girl child, with clear-water skin and great clear-water eyes. Then he might bathe his spirit in a child's youth also. But Jhane did not take

13

lovers. Her protector's position had raised her to the outer circle of the court. She saw the king's chevaliers, but she did not see them frequently, and those she did see she beheld as strangers. Sometimes handsome, sometimes not, none of them was for her. It was the age when a man might be everything together: fighter, artist, horseman, poet, musician. But a woman might be only a woman. Or, there was something else, which, in secret, she might be: a sorceress.

It was easy for a woman to become a sorceress in those days. She could slip into it, as if into silk, or a swoon. Sitting before a mirror combing her hair, the play of the lamp on hair, on comb: she could become a sorceress at such moments. Or in the tender morning, the fragrant evening, her feet on grass, leaves flooding her ears and eyes: then. She would find the magic in the earth, in light, in shade, so in herself. At these periods, a spell might radiate from her, like breath, and a flower would open that had been closed, a nightingale sing where there had been no nightingale. Or a hand knock on the garden's door . . .

But while there was no necessity, such powers went unrecognised. Jhane sensed, as every woman did, the well-spring within herself, yet did not think to tap the source.

Until there was a dawn, and under the dome of rouged crystal sky, horses' hoofs on cobbles sharp as daggers flung at the window. And then, in the square beneath, where the fountain put out its whorled unicorn spike into the basin, silence; punctuated by the scrape of a cup on stone.

It was a summer of sleepless nights, all Parys sleepless for one reason or another. Jhane had read, by candle-shine, and next by the dawn which dyed the pages with madder. Now she left her book for the window, that other living book in which she might read the romance of the street.

There by the basin were two horses trimmed with bullion. A young man stooped to drink from the basin. Another was in the act of pouring over the drinker's head the water collected in a cup of beaten gold. As Jhane watched, the water encountered its target, and with a shout the drinker sprang around. The gold cup sang on the cobbles. The two men seized each other as if for combat, and then desisted, laughing. One had hair nearly as gold as the cup he had performed the anointing with. His blue garments had the tint of a noon sea and the gold embroidery the noon sun would make on it. All of blue and gold he was, even the eyes. But it was the other that the dawn had brought

Jhane to her window to see. His was a darkness left behind at sunrise – clothed in a blue so dense as to be almost black, hair like dark honey, gilded only where the light touched it. His eyes were black, and perfectly shaped, like the eyes of saints in pictures. An icon. Jhane's lover. Formed by her heart and her solitude. Who did not know she lived in the world.

She had an impulse to fling wide the casement and cry out to him. But only harlots were so free; she dared not. This she could tell from their dress, and the accoutrements of the horses, that both men were chevaliers of the king. It had happened that she had never before seen them, or, if she had, blindly, at some other season not of love.

She watched from her window as they ended the business with the fountain and mounted up again. With a quicksilver pang of her vitals she watched them ride away. To the very last, she fixed her gaze on his darker head. She thought: 'It is impossible that we should ever meet. And if we do not, how shall I bear it? I have been alone so long. But here is my life's reason. Here is my soul. And it cannot be. I must live on, without life.'

The air was altering to day-bright air and birds swam in the clouds above the towers. To look at heaven brought thoughts of God or Fate; or hope, at least.

The moment evolved.

She thought: 'If I cannot live alone, I must bring him to me. There is my only answer.'

Jhane had become a sorceress.

At the noonday of Greece, it had been the fashion to accord visual immortality to the mighty, the famous and the fair, to carve them in marble, cast them in bronze, paint them on the plains of amphorae. In the shining morning of Parys it was also the fashion, but in another mode. There were certain shops beneath wide white airy studios. Here you could see twenty or so current faces and forms upon oblongs of hemp, ovals of wood, and burning jewel-like in cameos. An idyll of a lady with a dove, or a goddess with a basket of pink grapes, these might be the king's sister, or his mistress. And here those canvases, each titled 'Portrait of a Young Man' – the chevaliers of the court, its princes of love.

Such a shop Jhane entered, veiled in blue lace. She sought him up and down the rows of the beautiful and young. She found him, as in the dawn she had, beside his friend. It might be that they were lovers, too.

But at that season most trees bore the double fruit. As with the ancient gods, the statute was: Love Is, and not 'Love must be thus and so'.

Seeing a lady was in the shop, the master of the studio had come down. He bowed to Jhane and spoke to her gently of how the paint was brushed on the ivory.

'But who,' said Jhane, 'is this? And this?'

'You joke with me,' the master said. 'All Parys knows these, the young lions of the court. He who is golden haired, that is Nicolin Solat, who has come to be called Le Soleil for his goldness, much like the sun. The darker man is Bernard de Cigny. Notice, if you will, how excellently my student has caught the glint of the sapphire drop in his left ear.'

'Yes,' said Jhane, 'I will have this one, for the glint of the sapphire pleases me.'

Her protector, who poured coins into her coffers and trusted she would take a lover, now unsuspectingly paid for the picture of a lover.

She placed the simulacrum in a niche beside her bed where formerly only a holy relic had stood in a vessel of silver. By the niche hung a curtain. She drew it closed, and hid his face from the daylight.

She did not eat; she sent the dishes away untouched. The servants her protector had given her did not suppose her to be sick. Or rather, they guessed the sickness – *mal de coeur*.

The city entered the dusk like a vast ship, her towers her masts, her silken canopies her sails; floating on blueness, her candles and her fireflies lighting windows, walks and gardens. The sweet melancholy of evening drifted in a smoke, and bathed Jhane as she let down her hair at her mirror like fine warm summer rain.

A lamp burned low before the niche with the two holy things inside it. As Jhane turned toward the curtain, outside, a song spread its wings on the twilight:

> *Un peu d'amour, un peu de vie*
> *– Mais j'ai perdu mon amour*
> *– Pourquoi vivre?*

She smiled, for a sorceress must, on all occasions, be aware of portents. Then she drew the curtain and kneeled down, as she would do to pray.

In the cathedral of the night, bells sounded, marking the hours. The carriages came and went, the torches and processions. The moon passed over and sank under the river of sky. And all the while Jhane kept her vigil before the painted likeness, her eyes on his painted eyes, and sometimes she murmured his name very low . . .'Bernard . . . Bernard de Cigny . . .' For a name uttered often, in love (or hate), must eventually be heard, though spoken at the ends of the world.

And she half fancied he could sense eyes upon him, might glance about to see who called to him. And the spell wove on the loom of the night, until at length it filled the house.

Dawn came, and Jhane rose, still and chilled and sightless, to sleep a little.

But she felt her power, the seed planted in soil.

Night after night, she did this thing. When the sun lifted she slept a short time. She took meals which had no substance, water fruits and dishes of wafers and soups made from honey, whirling and frost, and slender colourless wines. When her protector visited her and saw how she had become, pale, exquisite and translucent as what she fed on, his vanity ached, but he put it aside. He invited her to stroll in the gardens of the city, and her hand on his arm was like a feather. She conversed with him and laughed, but she was not with him in fact, merely in person. Sometimes she would gaze at a particular item – sun on a piece of dark gilding, the burnish of a gem, and he would know that now she saw another's hair or eyes, his walk, the manner of his gestures. And her protector was curious to behold for himself who the young man might be. And so he resolved to bring Jhane more into the happenings of the fringe of the court, where the great came and went like meteors and the lesser great ones hovered like dragonflies.

He brought her a white greyhound with cochineal eyes. She paced with it in the gardens as if she trod on crystals, and the old man watched her. He grew ashamed, and said to her finally: 'I fear, demoiselle, you are in love.'

'No. You mistake me.'

They paused by a tree like a fountain, while riders went by on the path. And the old man perceived how Jhane flinched toward them as each approached.

'I have assured you I shall not mind it,' said the old man. 'Now tell me who it is.'

'It is no one, monsieur,' said Jhane.

Then his curiosity seemed to him to become insupportable. He went away and let others do the work for him. He set some on, by devious means, to question her in his absence, and himself began to listen to gossip.

Women came to Jhane's house or approached her on the street or in the shady walks of the gardens, where she moved in a gown of powder blue with strawberry sleeves, with her hound on its leash.

'You are remarkable this summer, Jhane. Who is the lover that has inspired this mood in you?'

Jhane's face was a traitor, and her heart shook, wanting to unburden itself of everything. But she replied:

'You know the man who has befriended me.'

'No. Not the old protector. The new.'

'I entertain no one else.'

'If not lover, then beloved. Who is it, Jhane, that you love?'

But Jhane was a sorceress. She comprehended she must not speak. The power in the spell was kept by secrecy, contained and made potent by her silence. And at dawn today, her lids falling shut, she had caught a glimpse, without sight, not of the painted simulacrum of Bernard de Cigny, but of the man himself, as at that instant he must have been. A girl slept beside him, but he was not aware of her. His dark eyes were lamps in darkness. It seemed he might look straight through the insubstantial fabric of distance, locality, and all the walls between, and see Jhane looking back at him. And though the picture perished, still she was reassured that the flower was taking root in the soil and putting out its leaves and buds. No, she would not speak to crack the jar and let the magic potion seep away.

But the women swarmed to her like bees to syrup and would not leave her alone. And her face, that wished so much that they should learn the truth, lost its pallor. At this, the interrogators began to name names to her, observing her carefully as they did so. And eventually a woman cried: 'It is one of the king's two favourites, the young lions of the court.'

Suddenly Jhane thought of what the master of the studio had described to her, and said at once: 'You have discovered me. My longing is for the chevalier who resembles the sun, Nicolin le Soleil.'

The women laughed and clapped their hands.

Jhane, having deceived them, permitted the game.

When the women came to her afterward it was always of Nicolin le Soleil they whispered. They informed her of how marvellously he rode and fenced, of his cunning with alchemy, with music, and whom he couched with and whom he no longer couched with. When they glanced up for Jhane's sighs or her frowns or her joy, she offered them unstintingly. Sometimes, the narrators touched upon the friend of Le Soleil, virtually by accident.

By night now she would fall asleep at her vigil, and dream of Bernard de Cigny. She would feel a fine thread stretched between them through the myriad twinings of a labyrinth. She was certain that he had begun to follow the thread which would bring him to her. Twice she heard hoofs under her window. The second night she heard them, she rose and stared down, and he was in the square, alone, mounted on his horse, hesitating only a moment before riding on. Not suspecting she had drawn him there and would draw him there again and yet again, to her very door, and to her very self.

Spiders spun on the roses in her garden. Conscious of portents, she was disturbed and quickened by their webs which captured and retained.

Jhane's protector underwent advancement at the court. He visited Jhane and told her of a jousting and that he would take her to witness it. He held her pale hands and stared at her eyes that had changed to strange enchanted ponds and her hair like a halo about her head.

'Demoiselle, you are more lovely than ever I saw you. And now I know why and for whom, and perhaps you will see him at the jousting. Perhaps, indeed, very likely you will.' And then, smiling, he shielded his brows from the sky. 'Such a bright sun today,' he complained. 'So much sun scorching my poor ancient skull.' And she realized he too believed she yearned for Nicolin le Soleil.

In the enormous meadow of the joust, the grass was hidden by blue flowers. A hundred shades of blue and cramoisi, the banners floated on the summer wind, thick with golden lilies, snowy leopards, rampant black basilisks. And the tents to right and left were sugar plums, upended daisies, many-tiered hyacinths.

Jhane's protector had procured a place for them at the forefront of the stands, opposite, though across forty yards of turf, the royal canopy, the king and queen. But Jhane had no interest in them. She sat there, dumb and motionless as if she had been blown from glass. The bones seemed to show through her hands as she waited, and concentration, like a shadow, through her eyes.

The trumpets blew, and all the banners shifted, passing and repassing each other like figured cards shuffled in a pack.

The king's chevaliers rode out on the meadow over the blue flowers. Arms and armour dazzled; Jhane looked through fires and could not recognise the one she sought. And then, straight from the dazzle, a man came riding. Blue and gold, as the banner carried behind him. Preoccupied, she did not guess until the gasping and the laughter swelled all about her, and turned aside from the field, and found Nicolin le Soleil seated at ease in the saddle, directly before her.

Apollonian, he sat there. His expression was of interest, but not kindness. She realised too late he too might hear rumours, and meant to humiliate her in some sort before the crowd. But she met his scrutiny, for she recalled that, at its depth, the jest was really hers. And by swift beautiful degrees, his expression was transfigured. He turned slightly and bowed insultingly to her protector, and then to Jhane he said: 'I have no equal here today and shall win. Lend me your favour, demoiselle, and I promise you the couronne.'

All about was silence, now. Beside her, her protector filmed the air with bitter disapproval, but Jhane could do no other than her part. She did not need to feign blushing; a thousand eager gapings had seen to that. She untied the blush-coloured ribbon from her waist and extended it without a word to Le Soleil, who accepted it, nodded, and rode away to win the tournament.

Events were not as she had reckoned. Presently she puzzled out, from casual chat and remembering Le Soleil's dismissal of the other chevaliers, that Bernard de Cigny was from court that day. Her vitality grew wizened, and the rich dyes faded on the stands and the pavilions and from the sky and from the morning itself. She did not have the soul left to her to care that her protector was pained and incensed at so immediate a discourtesy offered him. But she perpetuated her role, and when Le Soleil took the field she made herself all eyes. She held her breath when the lances shivered, and when the poniards and the halberds smote and clove she breathed fast so her heart beat strongly. Dimly she noticed that there seemed always about Le Soleil a kind of golden mist, blinding to his opponents. He made her afraid. She wondered what extra measure he would wish to add to the jest, or if crowning her the Queen of Beauty would suffice.

Finally he was the champion of the joust, and had looped the colours of twenty chevaliers on the haft of an unbroken lance.

He strode to her across the forty yards of turf now rutted and wrecked. He brought her the chaplet of roses, tinted like their name, and silver wire and pearls, and set it lightly on her hair.

'I will keep the ribbon,' said Nicolin Solat. 'It shall be the marker in my memory of you, Jhane la Fée.'

She lowered her eyes and her protector grunted sullenly.

'Demoiselle,' he said, 'we are going home.'

Nicolin le Soleil did not glance. He bowed to Jhane and said:

'I return you then, to your father's care.'

Jhane's protector came to his feet. Coldly he said: 'I am not madame's father.'

Le Soleil was contrite. 'Humbly on my knee your pardon. Her grandfather then, monsieur.'

Jhane felt the thunder in the air and longed only for solitude, longed for night, the low-burning lamp, the picture in the niche. Longed for Bernard de Cigny whose face, by this time, was also painted on her brain.

And in the carriage she paid small heed to her protector, or to his hands plucking at his garments restlessly. A man, foolish only in his cleaving to a woman's youth, he had not expected her to be faithful, had hoped vaguely for a clear-water child in which to bathe his spirit. But he had complacently pondered abstracts. Jhane had not taken lovers, had not borne a child. Now the reality, the public degradation, the taste of his own silliness sickly in an old man's mouth. Jealousy without a salve.

And in the streets they sang: *Mais j'ai perdu mon amour* . . .

A sense of shame hung over Jhane. She was too glad to shut herself away, to observe night re-enter Parys with a panther's tread, night to mask the countenance, the dreams, the deeds of love.

And then swiftly, as she kneeled before the portrait, one of those bizarre sorcerous glimpses bubbled up from the well of her inner mind. Half vision, half deduction, formed by the thread she had spun between them: Bernard was at his sister's house in the north. Candles flamed and there was a celebration, for the woman had given birth that noon to a child. Yet, while the cups rang and the wine glowed in them, Jhane perceived he was impatient to be gone, back to Parys, for what reason he could not quite express. So much she beheld in a few seconds, and the dark turning of his head with the candles blood-gold on it, and the black saint's eyes.

In swirling elation she raised her lids – to torchlight on the wall, and music thrown in dancing notes, against her window.

She abandoned her vigil, unable to keep it. Lowering the lamp further, she ventured to the window. In the street below five players made their harmony. They wore the livery of Nicolin Solat.

Jhane went from the room. She summoned her porter and sent him to the door. 'Be off!' she heard him shouting. 'My mistress would sleep.'

And – 'This is no night for sleeping,' one of the players answered. 'Look at the stars. Do they slumber?'

She identified the tones of Le Soleil, with a dreadful clutching at her heart. She flung wide the casement and deliberately threw out a handful of gold. 'Take my coins and leave me my privacy.'

'You are too winning to be private, demoiselle,' he said.

And easily he slipped by the stupefied servant and was in her house.

She met him on the stair. Alarm made her bold.

'You have joked enough,' she said.

'Begun in joke, ending in earnest,' replied Le Soleil. He snapped his fingers and a page ran to her and kneeled. The entire troupe seemed bursting into the house after the master and Jhane despaired. The page held up to her an open coffer. On damask, an imperishable rose wrought of mother-of-pearl and gold.

'You cannot buy me,' Jhane declared, 'I am not a harlot.' But this was not quite the case, for her protector had bought her.

Le Soleil only regarded her, and coming up the stair he gently clasped her hand. 'I thought it was for love you would have me. The jewel is but a token.'

'Who spoke to you of my love?' said Jhane. 'Was it I?'

'Oh,' he said. 'I see I have overshot the mark.' He dropped her hand and turned and moved down the stair scornfully. She hated his pride, which she had hated from the beginning. He thought her a fool that she did not desire him. He thought all men forgave his transgressions, out of love, all women, too. The anointings of cold water, the insults and the mockeries – healed by his caress, his smile.

He was at the door again, this time going out.

'Be sure I shall remember you hereafter, Jhane,' he said.

He left her the rose.

The house was empty.

She returned to her room above, and she wept. But the tears of a sorceress are valuable; voluptuous and purging. She dedicated her tears to the man in the picture. She drifted into sleep and dreamed of Bernard de Cigny's arrival at her house. How she would welcome him, how he would be uncertain of himself, not cognizant of what had brought him to her, yet bound already, mind and spirit, as he had bound her from the first.

When she roused, the air was cool and soft with dawn, the scent of flowers and trees stole through the window. But no birds sang, as if all birds had died in the night. And suddenly a sound of lamenting went up far away along the streets, a stern bell tolling, and human throats crying.

Jhane was filled with fear. She gazed from her window. The pastel light was beginning in the sky and a fresher voice wailed something shrilly over and over, drawing every instant nearer as it did so. Soon a boy raced into the square beside the house.

'What is the matter?' Jhane called to him. 'Stop and tell me what it is.'

The boy halted wild-eyed. 'Twelve footpads in a band,' he shrieked. She could barely make him out. 'Twelve footpads, and they were only five and a little page. Instruments of music, torches, and but two swords between them. He was coming from a woman's bed, they say. But now descending to a bed of earth, alone. Cut in pieces as if by butchers. No longer beautiful. No longer alive. He is dead, madame.'

'But who is dead?' Jhane whispered.

'Nicolin Solat.'

Jhane's protector came to her house an hour later.

'I have been unable to sleep,' he said to her. He seemed not to see her blanched face, her stony immobility – she had not moved from the window when the boy had run away. This lack of interest in her appearance on her protector's part need not have been surprising. He had surely been told of the death of Nicolin le Soleil. He would expect Jhane's distraction. Yet he did not attempt to console her, either, or even to exult in her loss. Presently she herself became aware that her protector was unquiet. He paced the room, and once he glanced uneasily at the curtained niche, as if he felt the painted eyes of his true rival upon him.

'Jhane,' he said at last, 'I have urgent business in the south. Certain estates you have heard me mention . . . I cannot be sure how long I must be away. I have left provision for you in my usual fashion.'

'If it is necessary,' she answered faintly. Life and observation were returning to her body. She deciphered his look now. It was of consternation and nervousness, oddly mingled with a curious satisfaction. 'Monsieur –' she said.

'No questions, demoiselle,' he said quickly. 'I have no leisure. To reveal the secret somewhat, I think I have incurred the disfavour of the king. Adieu. Remember me sometimes in your prayers.'

But – 'Nicolin Solat was slain,' said Jhane, 'yesternight, slaughtered by twelve footpads on the street.'

'Indeed? I regret that for your sake, demoiselle. For my own, I cannot.'

'Had no one spoken to you of it?' she insisted.

At this he smiled, a grey, terrified, malevolent smile.

'I am old,' he said, 'but I have my honour. You should not have loved an upstart puppy, Jhane. Ask nothing else.'

So she waited in silence till he was gone, knowing he had borne his insults ill, that he had hired twelve men, who, hunting under the unsleeping stars, had murdered, according to the old man's instructions.

And then she thought: 'If I had not played this game, had not revealed Le Soleil, wrongly, as my lover, he would live.' And then again she thought: 'If I had not denied him, he would not have left my house.' And she recalled his brightness in the morning, his brilliance at the tournament, the touch of his hands when he set the chaplet on her head; how she had feigned love, but not loved. How she had denied him and he had died.

She wondered what she must do now. Finally, she understood. She had mimicked loving; now she must mimic lamentation.

She dressed herself in a black gown slashed with vermeil – the colour of a prince's blood. She veiled her hair and face with indigo gauze and took a sable rose in her hand – the colour of a dying coal.

All up and down the city the bells were tolling. The birds, mute, hung heavy on the air.

Twelve had killed him; he had twelve thousand mourners. The men stood like blind statues, the women wept and laid their flowers on the closed casket until it became a mountain of flowers, the most sombre of the blues and pinks, the carmines and the azures of that summer.

The priests chanted. The music towered up and pierced the roof of the sky. But the bells seemed to ring that other song: *Un peu d'amour, un peu de vie.*

The women wept on. Sorrow filled the cup and ran over. Jhane wept, too. She had wept because of Nicolin Solat before.

Weeping, she forgot to look for Bernard de Cigny.

The dregs are darker than the wine. So the summer season was drained to the dregs, darkening, intensified, mysterious.

Jhane's vigil that night was different. As her protector had done, she paced the room. The curtain remained undrawn. Yet she heard the bells marking the hours, and far off the funeral bell, a great mass which went on and on, priests replacing each other, candles burning down, orisons murmured for a man's soul. For surely, a prayer uttered often must eventually be heard, though spoken in the youth of Parys on a summer night.

After midnight, it began to rain. Even the sky it seemed, would weep. And through the rain, a noise of hoofs in the street, pausing, not resuming. And then a knocking on the door of the house.

Not a soul but Jhane was awake, or if they were, something kept them from rising. Perhaps a superstition of ghosts, a golden-haired man, patterned by blood, his clay-cold hand fumbling for the catch.

But Jhane knew. And strangely without any stirring in her, she went down and unbolted the door.

The storm streamed across the night. Under the lash of it, not noticing, his hair nearly black with rain, his black eyes like pools the rain had filled, Bernard de Cigny, close to her as life.

'Madame,' he said, 'you will think me mad, but something drew me to your house, as if to a church.' These were the phrases she had visualised for him. Her spell had brought him to her. 'I was away in the north,' he said. 'I had a friend who died here in my absence. Now I wander the streets like a lost child. You will think me mad.'

Jhane put out her hand into the night and the rain dashed it. He took her hand. She thought of another's touch.

'Enter my house,' she said. But the words meant so little to her.

Was it that, acting to convince the world, she had convinced herself? Or was it that she had mistaken love from the first, as one recollects in error the melody of a song, setting one note in place of another?

Too late she saw how the golden thread which had bound them was broken and torn away. Bernard and Jhane, with nothing left save rain and dark, nothing left but the comfort they might transmit to each other, in the absence of happiness. But the summer was gone, and the sun had descended into earth.

Hand in hand they stood in the chill sunless night.

And still the bells rang their plaint: A little love, a little life.

And well might they answer: But I have lost my love. Why live?

The Unrequited Glove

Jason Drinkwood had many advantages. He was both young enough and old enough, and good-looking enough, and well enough off, that nothing very much need lie very much out of reach for very long. During the Amerenglish season along the coast, he was generally known by sight, and by name, for at that time 'Jason' was an uncommon appellation, particularly augmented by such dark wavy hair, bright blue eyes, expensive garments and ice-cream-coloured car. His code of conduct, none the less, was quite decorous. He did not belong to the artist or poet caste whose seasons sometimes ran in tandem with the Amerenglish one. He was seen to drink, but never drunk, to gamble a little, but never recklessly. He would dance, and he would dine, but with the air of one only performing a natural duty naturally well. Though the ice-cream car might sometimes be spotted swimming home along the palm-lined roads in the dusk of dawn, it was never anything but tidily driven. In other words, Mr Jason Drinkwood was not a man of passions. And so, though there had at first been some speculation in the caravanserai of the colony as to what his intentions and inclinations might be, they were, when noted, of a very ordinary and discreet kind, and in the order of three: female, sophisticated, *brief*.

It was something of a surprise, therefore, when Jason Drinkwood was sighted with Alys Ashlin.

Miss Ashlin was a painter, partly American it was believed, and rather more than partly something else, something fey and foreign, which had afforded her a slender and unreal quality, two large and gazing eyes, and wispy ash-blonde hair. That she should be an artist was no more than one would expect, that she had some money also was, admittedly, an oddity, but since she did not 'mix' very much, it was supposed she might go on as she wished. There had, of course, been some curious rumours now and then, but it was the age of the rational, and one had only to look at the girl to know her for a hopeless romantic, who would probably drink herself to death on cocktails before she was thirty-five.

Certainly, she was not Mr Drinkwood's type, not at all. Presumably he had met her at some gallery. Presumably her moth-like attractions had for some reason piqued a jaded palate. Whatever the cause, the colony observed that they lunched together, and took picnics to the hills in the pale car, and drank white *fine* and Russian Blushes at Co's, and danced at The Balconies, and all other fashionable spots.

Then, quite as suddenly as it had begun, the affair ended. A dark lady was seen to occupy the ice-cream chariot, and a dark lady was seen to be dining with Mr Drinkwood at Piccaletta's. No one was in the least surprised, nor expected any more of the matter, except perhaps news of Miss Ashlin's abrupt illness in the morning gazette.

The sigh which escaped the chiselled lips of Jason Drinkwood had nothing to do with the seraphic and cloudless day, the cuisine of a just-completed breakfast, or any of the prospects before him, save only one. Putting down the small blonde card, he said, 'Very well. You can bring her up here.'

Thereafter Jason rose to his feet, and prepared to put another cup of coffee into his lean and graceful frame.

It was, he believed, inevitable, that this final confrontation would have to come. Unfortunately, that was the trouble with these unusual women. Though they might be entertaining for a while, they soon became merely irritating, and then, when one wanted to finish it, they simply did not know how to behave. Had he not, he now asked himself, done everything perfectly and with utter good manners? He had cancelled their last meeting giving plenty of notice, and using the most courteous and apologetic address, with just the hint of terminus he had felt necessary in Alys's case. And had he not sent her a box of white roses, three dozen of the things? What more did she want from him? But he knew only too well. *She* wanted a *Scene*. That was what all her tribe required.

It was true, he had met her at a gallery, her own to be precise. She had been looking very chic that day and he had mistaken her for an idler come to buy. Something in her quality had given him an urge to investigate her, and by the time he had invited her to lunch and she had accepted, it was too late to back out when he realised she was The Alys of the paintings. He knew nothing about art, had never had much time for it. He cared for pictures and ornaments as he cared for fine weather, for he liked and appreciated pleasant surroundings. Her feelings on the subject, which began to be displayed almost as soon as the entrée was brought to the table, were both alien and unalluring. However, Miss Ashlin (all those A's, S's, L's and I-Y's seemed quite overdone) was shy. She preferred not to talk about herself, but liked to listen to him. He therefore set out to amuse her, poor little thing. Her vulnerability did rather appeal to him, even while he knew it was a mistake to like it. He could not bear stupid women, but had a deep distrust of clever ones. Alys did not fit either of those niches, though she was destined to represent both to him by the time he sloughed the liaison. Her trust and her simplicity in the matter of the male initially filled him with a desire to protect her. Later, of course, every frailty demanded of him that he pierce the weak place with a honed stiletto. Though he would not so have qualified it to himself, he was drawn to Alys Ashlin by the instincts of the tiger for the tethered lamb. Perhaps the tiger too has moments of enjoying the lamb's charm and the music of its bleat. Perhaps, if not too terribly hungry, the tiger also will delay the ultimate seconds when he falls on his prey and tears out its entrails.

When he had caused enough damage to her, and she, trying equally to protect herself and appease him, had lain at his feet gasping: But what have I *done*? Jason had sensibly withdrawn, cancelled the next meeting – there was no fun in killing a dead sheep – and sent a box of a dozen or so white roses to mask the stench of spilled blood.

However, now, incredibly, the lamb – having already written to him on three occasions in the most aggravatingly mild of terms – had arrived at his lair. To have it out with him, he concluded with dread. To make her *Scene*.

The door opened, and she entered the sunlit room, a wisp of ashes and fainting blonde violets.

'Oh. Hallo,' said Jason, with slight astonishment, as if he had been expecting anyone but she. 'Will you have some coffee?'

'Thank you. I don't think so.'

'Do. It's very good.'

Previously, she had always done exactly as he told her. But now she said again, 'I don't think coffee is appropriate.'

'Really? Why ever not?'

'Jason – I may still call you that?'

'Don't be so absurd,' he said, harshly.

She lowered her wild eyes – they truly were wild, as if she had come straight from the hills and the old pagan altars there, instead, plainly, from off the manicurist's couch.

'Jason . . . I'm very obtuse about these things. I'm afraid I don't understand at all. Is it that you're finished with me?'

He poured some more coffee and tried to check a not unpleasurable surge of rage.

'Well. What an ultimatum. When do the tanks arrive, and the air-cover?'

'Please, be serious, Jason. I should like to know.'

'Oh should you? Like to? I don't think so. Or you'd be quite well aware of the facts already.'

'I see. I think I see.'

'Good. Splendid.' He shot her a look as he lit a cigarette. She did not smoke, she had said it affected her eyes. Certainly something had done so. They were larger than ever, and though not exactly reddened, the pre-dawn greyness of their depths was bluer and more saline. 'You know really, young woman, you're making an awfully big issue out of this, aren't you? I mean.'

'What do you mean?' she inquired softly. He saw with dismay that she was pulling off her mauve gloves, a signal of intended temporary permanence.

'For God's sake,' he said, 'we spent some time together. An interlude. It was delightful, Alice. Thank you so *very* much. But now. What can I say? I hope you won't force me to be rude.'

'You mean that it is over, absolutely over. Between us.'

' "It." What is there supposed to have been? Over? Obviously.'

'Yes, obviously.'

'For heaven's sake, Alice,' (he had always insisted on pronouncing her name in a straightforward way, none of that *Aleez* ridiculousness) 'for heaven's sake. You're acting as though we've been Romeo and Juliet. Good God, woman. Try to grow up.'

'But,' she said, 'I love you.'

He turned his back on her at once. Oh Christ, much worse than he had thought. Of course, he knew, but even she, surely, should have had the tact not to use this idiocy. After a moment he mastered himself and said, 'I'm very sorry.' Then, when there was only a silence, he added,

'Look, I have to be over the other side of the bay in about ten minutes' time. You'll have to excuse me. I must go.' He had visions of her weeping or swooning on the sofa, being unable to rid the room of her – but when he flung round, to his genuine surprise on this occasion, he saw she was silently gone. All that remained was one of the faint violet gloves, the left one, lying *évanouissement* by the coffee pot. He fired a look of hatred at it, for she might use it as a pretext to come back. He would have to send it to her, bloody woman. But *later*. For now he was getting out.

He ran down the villa stair with a feeling of release and exultation, as if he had just won some sort of race. And for once he drove the car rather fast along the coast road.

In the small hours of the following day, when he returned, Jason noticed, vaguely, that the glove too had gone. He put this down to the tidiness of his domestics, or to a miraculous display of common sense by Miss Ashlin, in returning to retrieve her property during his absence.

About a week after these events, Gerard Caul, an intermittent friend of Jason Drinkwood's since their first meeting in the caravanserai, received a message at his hotel. Responding to it, he called Drinkwood's villa. The conversation was short. 'Caul? Thank God. I'm glad. Can you come over? No, I mean now. Come to lunch. Well as soon as. Five o'clock? All right. But you'll be there. Wrong? Oh . . . Probably nothing. No, nothing's wrong at all. Five o'clock. Till then.'

Gerard, a prosaic but easy-going man, not without wealth or influence, arrived at the proper station which was, in the current parlance of colony etiquette, five minutes late. Driving up to the villa, he was rather startled to see that something was slightly amiss with its façade. His first thought was of birds, or geckos, but when next he came across the famous car, drawn up between the flower-beds and an old fountain, Gerard rejected the notion. The peculiar marks had a symmetrical nastiness about them that suggested manic human rather than faunal activity.

Presently, meeting Jason on the lower of the two terraces, Gerard waited until the drinks had been served and they were alone to remark, 'Well, and who have you fallen foul of, my boy?'

At which Jason started, spilled some of his drink, and retorted with a careless laugh, 'What on earth do you mean?'

'*Absit omen*,' said Gerard, and refilled Jason's glass himself. Even if he had not by now been searching for signs, he might have noticed that Jason's face appeared rather dirty, rather colourless, and that his hands had developed a nervous tremor. 'Someone, patently,' said Gerard, 'has it in for you. The car, for example.'

'That was very unfortunate,' mumbled Jason. 'It seems to have found a supply of something in the kitchen, I'm not sure what, some kind of molasses, or glue . . . Very difficult, you know, to get off. I apologise for my face. That's simply writing ink. I'd forgotten how damned resistant it is to soap and water.'

'Ah, yes,' said Gerard. He opened his cigarette case and offered Jason the beautiful snow-white cigarettes. And watched Jason take and try to light one with his tremblous hands. 'But who is this ingenious enemy, and why haven't you gone to the police? I know they can be difficult. Is that the problem?'

Jason laughed again. Dropping the cigarette, he lowered his ink-stained face into his hands and shuddered.

'My dear fellow,' said Gerard, immovable.

'I'm quite all right. I shall be splendid in a moment. It's just the – frankly the bloody hopelessness of it. I don't know what to do. At first, when it only ran about, and moved things, I tried to laugh it off. Then I thought I was going mad. But I'm not the only one to see – that boy ran off, you know. Scared to death. I think the woman's caught a glimpse, too, but she just accepts it. Well, she knows *she's* safe enough. But the worst of it is, I feel such a fool. I mean, look at me. I tell you I'm afraid to go to sleep. The days are bad enough. All I can do is move out, but – I did try sleeping at – well, somewhere else, you understand. But somehow, and this is the positively horrible part, *somehow* it followed me. It must have got into the car – I don't know how, I'd been so careful – but in the morning I woke up – in this state, *patterned*, you could say. But much worse. My – companion was rather put out. One could hardly blame her. There was ink all over the sheets. She thought it was some schoolboy prank of mine.'

'Yes,' said Gerard. He extinguished the stub of his cigarette, folded his arms, and gazed upwards at the line of balconies above. The sun was beginning to touch them now to a languid mellowness, while the green of the oleanders shone like torches as the light drove through. It was an exquisite hour, made strangely, like the chill first dawn, always for strange revelations.

Suddenly Gerard found Jason almost at his feet, gripping him and whimpering: 'You have to help me, Gerard, you have to help me –'

It was just at this moment that Gerard became aware of a different note of colour in the vine that grew about the balconies. It seemed to him the leaves contained a flower of palest mauve, or perhaps even a mauve bird, for surely it had only just appeared – but his attention was now distracted.

'Drinkwood, I'm quite prepared to do all I can. But you must tell me first –'

A large ball of mud-clay, about the consistency of setting tempera, hurtled down from the direction of the balconies. It landed on the drinks tray, splattering the soda siphon and sending Jason's glass flying. Jason gave an uncharacteristic shriek and leapt to his feet. At that instant a second mud-ball, rather larger and rather more glutinous, struck him squarely in the chest.

Instinctively the eyes of Gerard Caul had risen once more to the vine. He had the impression of a capricious nymph, casting missiles from a slender hand gloved in softest mauve. At the same time, Gerard realised and comprehended no flesh and blood nymph, however svelte or small, could hang there in the tenuous foliage. And then, *then*, he caught sight of something, something definitely mauve and capricious and definitely operating entirely alone, scrambling lightly away, up the creeper, over the balustrade and into the house.

'Whatever was that?' inquired Gerard, with the disarming fascination of a man who knows that all things have a reasonable explanation.

Jason Drinkwood, sitting in his chair with the face of ink-stained death, told him.

'Oh come now,' said Gerard.

An hour and a half later, Gerard Caul took his leave. He had offered to do a great many things, but most of them had involved the summoning of doctors. Since Jason insisted, with ever-increasing hysteria, that no human agency was at work against him, Gerard was forced to concur that at least no *external* human agency was. Which left only Jason himself as the psychopathic culprit. Gerard had no desire to be included in such a fiasco, even on behalf of a friend. Besides, the atmosphere of the house was beginning to bother him. It felt positively booby-trapped. After he had explained to Jason for the twentieth time that mud might be come at near to the roof and that birds had been known to drop portions of it in the past on undeserving persons below, enervation began to steal a march. The last straw was then presented to him as Jason, now drunk, postulated a search of the house culminating in the laying of ambushes. At this juncture Gerard rose to his feet. In a weak moment he had offered Jason sanctuary at the hotel, but this had only resulted in Jason's frantic mirth and avowals that he would be 'followed'. Gerard left the villa. Like every true realist, he knew that in certain areas of life, all one could do for a friend was to desert him.

That Mr Drinkwood seemed to be suffering from some form of illness or mania was quickly the talk of the colony. As the days of liquid honey spilled themselves over and over into each other, as the blue seas poured ceaselessly to and fro and the blue skies answered them with their equally ceaseless immobility, the talk rose and fell along the boulevards, over the café tables, and in the fashionable shops of the Monte d'Oro. Even at the Casino they might sometimes be heard to remark that Drinkwood was never seen there now; and the great dinner parties that splatter the turn of season with champagne corks and fireworks, also deplored his absence. It was a fact, he had been a social asset. He was so eligible and so unobtainable, so dashing, and so completely safe. What a pity it was, they said, whatever it was. But what was it, precisely? He had taken to the drink after all, they said. Or someone had thrown him over that he had cared for – no, not anyone here, some mysterious one in London, or Boston, or New York, or Paris . . . Or it was some hereditary ailment. Or he had lost all his money. Yes, that seemed the most likely. Some kind of financial crash. These things happened constantly, even to the young and the beautiful.

Of Miss Ashlin nobody thought to ask, or to whisper. They had all forgotten her quite. As far as anybody knew she was painting somewhere, and running her petite gallery, as she had done for years. Now and then, even, a picture might be bought from her. But she did not figure in the drama of Jason Drinkwood. She had never been suited to him, wan, wispy little thing in her dilute purples and blondes. Pressed against his bronze, his vivid eyes, his white teeth and suits and car, she had been seared to cinders. But one never saw his car now, did one? There had been some sort of an accident, one thought. Those who had applied to Gerard Caul had formed the impression that Mr Jason Drinkwood was suffering from hallucinations, and had been strongly advised to seek medical aid. Mr Caul did not visit Mr Drinkwood. They were not seen together in the bar at Co's, or on the tennis court at The Balconies.

It must be fairly serious, if such old friends now avoided contact. It must be rather unsavoury.

Night had fallen, and the villa lay plastered in a black stucco of darkness. At its heart sat Jason Drinkwood, drinking gin to keep awake, and to keep fear at bay. His servants had been sent forth days ago, since they had become mere witnesses to his humiliations. Besides, they facilitated disasters by those things they brought into the house in the way of foodstuffs and cleaning fluids, long after his ban on more dangerous substances. It was true, had it wanted to, his foe might already have murdered him, with one of a selection of knives, with some heavy object pushed on to his head, by fire or poison. Even the time in the car when the mauve silk hand, weightless and bodiless yet firm as flesh, had flown up at him, it was not his throat it had gone for, or even the wheel. No, it had merely perched there, on the dash, gentle and elegant, and he had stared at it, stared at every line and angle of it, every little crease in the material of its gloved life, every little stain and mark that it had acquired in the processes of its hounding him. And, staring, he had run the car – in some ghastly evocation of a pun – off the road and into a palm. When he came to, dazed and groaning, the glove had hidden itself again. It was always shy when it had had its way with him. It would conceal itself, in a closet or a drawer, or behind a curtain. Sometimes he caught it peeping at him around a piece of furniture.

Several times, before the incident with the car, he had attempted to destroy the glove. Once he had almost got hold of it, but as he struggled to retain his grasp, it seemed to go all to nothing, not even to cloth but to air – and then he had lost it. He had lain on the polished floor where he had that time fallen, and watched it hurry upstairs, running on its fingertips.

He had even allowed Gerard Caul's doctors to look him over. Jocund and reassuring, they had nevertheless wanted to remove him from the villa to costly nursing establishments in which they took an interest. But by then he had realised the glove would follow him wherever he took refuge. Even as they tested his heart and shone lights into his eyes, he had been aware of the glove sidling round the room, now and then pausing behind the physician's back, as if to examine something, a plant or an ashtray. It was very careful with all the doctors, the glove. It never once played at revealing itself, as in the case of Gerard it had. Gerard, naturally, had refused to believe that any such thing was possible, it had been safe to flirt with him. Even he, Jason Drinkwood, did not properly believe in the glove's animation and life, and perhaps that was what gave it its power over him. He constantly expected them to stop, the silly endless puerile awful tortures. He would constantly be thinking, on some level, that it was all nonsense, such things did not happen. And all the while the glove would be scuttling about behind the chairs, coming down from the picture-rail to tweak his hair, to upset salt into his food and dash his wine glass to the ground, to break and to despoil, or merely to flutter, sweetly as a butterfly, about him, until he broke down himself and cried like a child.

After the car, he gave up all hope.

Now he sat, with his broken wrist arrested across his chest, idly tapping the gin glass over and over against his teeth, looking sightless on darkness.

He knew the glove was near. It always was. He knew also that, if he should get up, it would pursue him. He made an experimental shift in his chair, and heard, in the huge cricket-sewn rhythm of the villa's silence, a dim slim rustle, over near the windows.

'I'll tell you what I'll do,' said Jason Drinkwood coldly to the mauve glove that haunted him, 'I'm going to go out now. I'm going to go out and walk across to the Monte. I'm going to go along to the gallery. Yes. Her gallery. I'm going to go straight up and knock on her door. That's what I'll do.'

He wondered if the glove could actually understand words, if, as it were, it spoke English. And if that should be so, he puzzled a moment, would it try to stop him? When he got up, he flinched as he heard it lisp across the floor. But there was no assault, and by the time he stepped out on to the plains of night, he sensed that it was only going to shadow him, weaving independently along in the blue-black, avoiding the lamps, keeping under the trees, probably disappearing just before he reached his destination, the gallery on the Monte, where Alys Ashlin had her being and painted her pictures and worked her febrile magics of the night.

When he arrived at the gallery, which located itself on the oldest side of a picturesque small square, it was almost three in the morning. Yet, looking up from the street, he perceived there was a soft light in the upper storey. By using a tiny courtyard at the back and climbing the outer stair, he attained her studio door and jangled the bell. There was usually a porter, but he might be in bed by now. In fact, it was she who answered, appearing not at the door but on the balcony, and he gazed up at her in dismay, wondering how he could have allowed himself to be so foolish as to come here. For she was so slight a thing, so irrelevant to him, surely he had imagined it all? But then the veiled glow of the summer moon, sailing high above the hill, caught in her eyes. They were like opals, colourless, changeable, unlucky.

'Will you let me in?' he said.

'It depends what you want,' she said.

'You know that,' he said. He no longer felt foolish, only desperate, looking up into those cold moon-opal eyes. 'I've come to tell you, to ask you – to make it – stop.'

'What are you talking about?' she said.

Was she enjoying it, this power, or afraid of what he might do, maddened by all the tricks? She sounded only very tired.

He pointed to the sling which contained his wrist. He did not bother to show off his decoratively soiled clothing, the tiny holes sliced in its fabrics.

'Do you see this?'

She nodded, he thought, but he was not sure. Her eyes flashed oddly as she lowered them to his arm.

'That's enough, isn't it?' he asked. 'Isn't it?'

'I'm afraid I don't understand.'

He found he could not speak about it directly, just as it seemed she refused to. He said lamely, 'It's a bit unfair, you know. What did I do? I hardly *wronged* you, you know. For God's sake. I've had enough.'

She sighed then. The sigh was like a leaf, sweetly fluttering down. The moonlight touched her hair, her white face and her slender white hands on the balustrade, above the pots of vermilion dorisa, black by night as old blood.

'Mr Drinkwood,' she said slowly, looking past him across the roofs of the Monte to the implication of the distant bay, 'I can only tell you this. Our first duty is to ourselves. To protect ourselves. There are things I must do, and obligations I must fulfil. I can't let you get in the way.'

'For Christ's sake,' he exploded, 'what are you saying?'

'I told you once that I loved you. My emotion was very strong. You don't understand about such things, it would be fruitless to explain. But you hurt me very much, very deliberately, and there were only two things I could do. Either let the hurt eat into and perhaps destroy me, or turn it away. Turn it back. The gift of pain you gave me, I don't want it, Mr Drinkwood. Return to sender. If it was to be you or me, it must be you.'

'You're mad,' he said. He felt quite sick, and cold sweat had broken out all over him. In avalanching terror he added, in a withered, dying voice, 'If I – do you want me to come back to you?'

'No thank you,' she said. And then, 'I'm very sorry. Good-night.'

'Wait, you bloody bitch!' he screamed, and a door opened sonorously in the storey below. Out into the moonlit yard stepped the porter, a large faceless obsidian shape, staring up at him. Jason was a moment stupefied, looking down at this apparition, as the balcony doors were drawn to above him. *Romeo and Juliet*. Well, he had said that.

He came down the stair unsteadily, and the porter towered in his path.

'Get out of my way,' Jason mumbled. The porter obeyed him, without haste, but when Jason had negotiated the courtyard gate, he heard it being locked behind him.

He stood deflated in the alley, tears streaming down his face, in rage, in fear, in utter embarrassment and futility. As he did so, there came a soft rustling close by, like a small mauve sigh blowing through the shadows.

The letter, which was delivered by hand to Mr Gerard Caul's suite at the Hotel Fleuris, did not especially delight him. It was in a version of Jason Drinkwood's formerly entirely readable, if slap-dash, hand-writing. It began,

Dear Caul,

You can still help me, if you will. I take this opportunity, since at the moment I'm not being observed, rather I do the observing, for I can see it sitting in a strawberry tree outside the window. It keeps watch on me, and I on it. Of course, how can it read? But maybe it can, by some peculiar means, do so. I can't take the chance. So, when I lose sight of it, I shall hide this letter on my person, next to my very skin.

Getting so far, Gerard Caul was inclined to throw down the letter, but, since the remainder was brief, he resolved to finish it.

My plan is to get out of the place – not just the villa, the whole country. The first steamer to the first homeward port. Spells don't travel over water. I remember hearing that. It may not be correct, but it's the only hope I've got. And no luggage, nothing it can stow away in. Just the garments I happen to be standing up in, and whatever essential cash and documents. And – it mustn't know what I'm up to. This is where you come in, Gerard, if you'll see me through. I won't waste your time with obvious details. You've got all the pull that's necessary. Use my funds, you know how to get at them. Just simply book me on the first boat out, with some kind of reference of your own – it may be needed. Say I've been ill, under a strain, am really quite a decent fellow, etc: I rely on you. I'm at your mercy. If you won't, I tell you I'm through, I'm lost. Yours, J.D. P.S. If you can see your way to doing this, don't telephone me, write me just one word: Y E S. And then, later, date and time, only the numbers. Oh Gerard, for God's sake, do it.

Gerard Caul was offended by the whole project, but, in default of anything else, old strangle-hold ties of friendship presently forced him to pick up a pen, and write, aloofly, in a firm hand: '*Yes. G.C.*'

About the middle of July, a curious occurrence overtook the passenger steamer *La Sebastienne*, as she was en route for open water.

The majority of the passengers had dispersed from their departure posts along the ship's rail, and were heading for their cabins, or the saloon. A few still at large on the landward decks were engaged to see a young man, who was in the process of removing his shoes and socks. These he then hurled away into the kohl-blue water, in the manner of offerings. They were shortly joined there by a shirt, a tie and a jacket.

The acute had already noticed that the dress of this individual young man, while of excellent material and cut, had none the less undergone some weird farewell rituals, prior to embarkation. These were felt, however, to be insufficient grounds for dispensing altogether with social dictates in the matter of modesty. As bit by bit, piece by – and by now intimate – piece of apparel was jettisoned, the volume of comment on the decks increased to a roar. Presently assistance was applied for. The ladies either turned their heads or did not turn their heads as a bevy of ship's personnel swarmed over the madman and bore him off. He was by this time completely naked, his face a study in triumph and anguish. Though generally it was not his mood which drew most attention.

By the cocktail hour, it was reported that the mad passenger lay sedated in his cabin, to which replacement clothing had been taken in the spirit of encouragement. It transpired that he had been rather ill, under rather a strain, that he was very sorry for his outburst, that everything was taken care of. For the remainder of the trip he was not seen again, though frequently looked for. At landfall he was smuggled ashore. The air resounded to the twang of pulled strings.

Thereafter the occurrence merely entered the lists of those travellers' anecdotes which are seldom believed and yet which tend to become the myths of other places, any places where one has never ventured, the lands of Unreal, the islands of Elsewhere.

For the sea, it swallowed Jason Drinkwood's clothes and presumably anything else that might have attached itself to them. And when the wake of *La Sebastienne* faded from the water, nothing at all was revealed there, but the sunlit currents and the ghostly palmate shapes of fish.

For his part, Gerard Caul – to whom the ship-board episode had filtered – would have been happy to hear no more of the subject which signed itself J.D. Gerard was of that estimable order of men who are able to leave behind all waste items, among them wasted friendships, with only the neat arm-movement normally required in such disposals.

However, in the ensuing months, a letter arrived, a letter warm with gratitude, acidulous with proper self-mockery, and bright, ah so very bright, with relief. A letter, that is to say, from Jason Drinkwood, who, from his flat near Kensington Gardens, in the ancient city known to itself as London, now revealed that business was as usual. Indeed the letter, for all its warmth, acidity and brightness, cautiously skimmed the past, cautiously *hinted* at what would seem to have been an era of sickness, some bad dreams, an involvement with a silly and unstable female person, a revolt against summer heat and foreign climes. Only the postscript was a trifle odd. It requested that Mr Caul would please omit to reply. Nothing, it turned out, that came from Mr Caul's present part of the world, was being permitted access to Mr Drinkwood's London life.

Gerard, who had not a wish on earth to reply, was gratified by obliging.

It happened a week later that Gerard saw Alys Ashlin, as he was driving up across the Monte d'Oro. It was the swiftest viewing, a vague momentary sight, recognisable only because of Jason's agonies of description. She was standing outside one of the patisseries, buying flowers from a woman who sat there under her sunshade on the pavement. Pale violet flowers they were, the whole image a pastel, the whites, blues and lavenders of the merchandise, the dry old woman, the mild amber shade above, the contrasting blonde of the girl's hair and the little hat, the cool hands taking the clear wild mauve of the spray in a stream of blanching sun. Ah, yes, not at all displeasing. Gerard thought Miss Ashlin rather charming, a type of woman somewhat neglected now, like certain kinds of art, out of her time, delicate, fragile and too easily crushed, a gauzy thing. Then she was gone from his vision and his awareness. At no other hour of his life did he ever see her, and seldom heard of her again, and that only in the way of her work.

But it was less than a year before he heard something else of Jason Drinkwood.

'But surely, surely he must have loved her quite terribly. Oh, I do wish you'd tell me who she was.'

Gerard, who, if he had needed it, had used the interruption of lighting a cigarette to mask any shock he felt at the news of Jason's suicide, now answered, 'My dear Cecilia. So far as I know, there was no one at all. That was just a foolish piece of gossip.'

'But you're so wrong,' said Mrs Cecilia Hanson.

'Well, that may occasionally happen.'

They were seated in the Long Room at Co's, overlooking the lawns, the bougainvillaea, and the bay. The summer had come back as if it had never been gone, the distressing fire-wind of the early months was over, everything was set for another colonial season. Mrs Hanson, whose husband had for years had business dealings with Gerard, and who, intermittently, had had her own dealings with him, now continued silkily, 'Of course, I know you and Jason Drinkwood lost touch – of course, you had *heard* he was dead?'

'Oh, naturally,' lied Gerard.

'From the window,' said Mrs Hanson, in such a way that he suspected her of testing him. 'Six floors. And the railings,' added Mrs Hanson. 'Simply awful. I can never understand it. I mean, I can understand a man might feel driven to take his own life. But the method. An impulse, it must have been. He was so sunny the day before, quite himself. Not that I knew him well, ever.' Her voice sharpened a little, grated a fraction, before she smoothed it over, 'But

Harry had just had lunch with him, at the London place, that good one. For heaven's sakes. But there you are. Brooding over this mystery woman you tell me never existed. And suddenly, unable to bear it any longer. So, the window. I blame the oranges myself.'

'The oranges?' said Gerard, wondering, rather more than what she was talking about, how soon he could slip away. A vicious woman, he did not want to antagonise her unduly, but it was too hot for seduction as it was too hot for Cecilia Hanson's toiling complexion.

'Harry ordered oranges at lunch. They came from the hills here. He told me, Jason seemed quite distrait about it for a minute or two, then just broke out laughing, and ate two of them. But I can only conclude it was a sad reminder. Good lord. Three hours after he flings himself from a sixth-storey window.'

Something tugged gently at Gerard's memory. It said: *'Don't write, my boy. Nothing from your neck of the woods, not for a while.'*

'Oranges,' said Gerard. He stubbed out his cigarette.

Cecilia Hanson sensuously licked the olive from her drink, a habit he disliked. There was a gleam in her eye he did not care for, and this harping on lost love . . . Well, in the interests of fair trading with Harry, after all, he might have to take her along the coast to that dreary little shack of an hotel, chase her through the frothy waves as she giggled girlishly, overpower her in the dark room thick with scent and mosquitoes. Good manners. It did not do to offend such women.

'Now Gerard, you will tell me, won't you? Or am I going to have to do something reckless to get it out of you? What would you like?'

'Ah, Cecci. You shouldn't tempt me this way.'

She snuggled closer. She wore a new perfume he liked better than the previous one, although probably, by the end of the endless afternoon, he would have come to loathe it utterly.

'Well, who was she?'

'Now, Cecci, I've said I have no idea. There was no one.'

'Yes there was. Or why would he have kept her glove?'

To a man as prosaic, as easy-going, as influential, as efficient and modern and jaundiced as Gerard, his own reaction to this statement was an unwelcome, threatening thing. He turned cold, as if a wave had rushed up on him, from his feet to his skull, a cold cold icy comber from the depths of some unremembered, non-existent sea.

'What do you mean *her glove*?'

'Well, don't snap at me for goodness sakes. I only know what Harry told me – you know they called him and he had to – well, he said there was a glove, a woman's glove, lying there on the – right by Jason's body, under his hand. He must have been clutching it when he – as he – And Harry said it was such a pathetic little glove, all worn and torn, almost colourless, all wrinkled – it looked as if it had been through just about everything, and he must have been always wringing it in his hands or something.'

Gerard's mind slipped suddenly away from Mrs Hanson. It slipped away and saw a pale mauve fish swimming, and a pale mauve spider crawling, and then a pale mauve five-fingered wisp of silk scrambling, running on tiptoe, up rocks, over stones, thorough bush, thorough brier, over park over pale, thorough flood, thorough fire – And finally falling, fainting, from a crate of oranges. Dragging itself, poor crushed, sodden, rent and ruined fragile tinsel thing, through all the by-ways of London, and up the steps, under the door –

'Why Gerard,' said Mrs Hanson, 'Gerard? Oh Gerard, I truly have missed you so.'

Gemini

The Bell

By the oval window a bell rings.

'Nine seven,' I say, because it keeps me a unit still, and not a person. Who knows? This might be a wrong number.

Beyond the window, the glass city stretches away.

'Hallo?' asks a voice, 'is that you, Geminna?' it asks me.

And the turquoise hills, and the blue hills.

'Yes. This is Geminna,' I say, and inside me, *It* stirs.

'Why, Geminna, we haven't seen you for so long. We're going to the sea, Geminna. Come with us.'

And the pale blue hills, like hyacinths.

'I can't,' I say. 'I'm sorry.'

And the palest blue hills, like sky.

'Oh, but, oh, Geminna – I know there's your reading and your studies – can't you study with us at the beach, by the sea? Can't you, Geminna?'

'Another time,' I say, 'it would be wonderful.'

'Oh.' Rebuffed, the voice of a forgotten friend hangs adrift in the wires. I don't have many of these calls now. Soon they will stop forever. 'If you're sure, then. Some other time.'

And the pale silver sea.

But I can't go out.

It won't let me.

The House

This is an old house, stone and brick and stucco, a long ramble of a house, with many rooms and inner courts, and a long, wild garden with a high wall. Here I may do what I want. As long as I am alone. In the garden are mulberry trees and twisted hawthorn, and tall pines, and old stone urns from which spill beautiful rank weeds. Half-way, a river runs, several feet across, where fish glitter. A stone bridge crosses the river, and on the other side the wilderness rises in terraces to a faded white summerhouse. Beyond the summerhouse is the tower. This is the highest point, and from the tower roof, ringed by the crumbling parapet, I can see all the city, the hills, even the sea, restless in the distance. Above, the stars turn and burn. In winter everything is white, and the sea opaque with ice-floes.

The Sea

Sometimes *It* will let me go to the sea, for a little while. Then I walk barefoot in the cool water and the sand, smelling the old fish smell that the sea carries with it. I bring back shells and stones, and pictures I have drawn, or clicked with the eye of my little camera. Once a big dog found me, and we played by the sea's edge, in the salty froth. We ran backwards and forwards, laughing, until a man came.

I thought I would stay and speak to the man. He was young and handsome and the dog loved him, but *It* wouldn't let me. So I went away.

Dawn is the best time for the sea, or early in the morning, before the moon sets. There are not many people then.

The House

There is a lot to do in the house. It cleans itself twice in every ten days, and I help it. I like to cook from the deliveries that are brought to the service door. There's no problem there, of course. The door takes in what I need and pays the men, who then go away. They mutter and look up at the windows, blind with sunlight. Does anyone really live here? Books come, too. I have already a vast library; poetry, drama, novels, works of science and philosophy and magic. I don't always understand, but I try. My mind is opening little by little, like a rusty flower. I can play five instruments, the ancient pianos of the house, the harp, all the range of guitars which hang from mahogany pegs in the music room, the reed flute whose sound is uneasy, green, and my own voice which I have trained now to an extensive range. I also paint and sculpt, embroider, study the stars – I have much to do.

Often, very late or early, I walk through the city.

I have seen drunks lying in the road, or lovers in the parks. In winter the parks are empty except for the swans.

But people still remember me.

If only people would leave me alone.

Before

When I was a child, before *It* came, I knew many people, and children, but I was always more adult than child, and had no understanding with my own kind. They were like wild animals to me, but without the beauty of wild animals. They had to grow before understanding came between us, and then it was too late.

I was a born child, but my mother soon tired of me.

I don't remember her, only my guardians, who were kind and did not stay long. And, of course, I remember the name she chose for me. She called me Geminna, after the golden twins of the Zodiac, but she didn't know how apt that name would be.

At sixteen I received this house, an ancestral possession, and my citizen's pension, enough to keep me. I have all I need, and more.

Service

But there is no complete escape.

Every three months come the ten days of Service, my duty to the city.

It is my spring fear, my summer terror, my autumn horror, my winter despair.

This is where I meet these people who linger and cling.

I seem to fascinate them because I am remote.

They want me because I am always moving away.

The Bell

The bell rings.

'Nine seven.'

'Ah, yes. Am I speaking to Sol. Geminna Mavern?'

'Yes.'

'Sol. Mavern, I am to inform you that your three-monthly period of Service is due.'

'Thank you.'

'We have on record your request for isolated labour. This time we suggest you report to the Library of Inanimate Beauty. This is more or less a solitary post, where your studies may be continued and also used to profit the establishment.'

'Thank you.'

'You will commence Service the morning of the day after tomorrow. The twenty-fifth of the month. Your stated working time will be ten in the morning until sixteen hours. Your instructor will meet you in the outer hall.'

I have often wanted to visit the Library of Inanimate Beauty, but I couldn't. And now – fear.

Darkness.

The Day is Here

The day is here.

I rise, bathe and dress in inconspicuous pale black, a dress reaching almost to my ankles, and a wig to hide my hair. The wig is a dull but pleasant brown. My own hair, the golden hair of the golden Twins, attracts too much attention.

Hypnotised by the pale green of the breakfast grapefruit, I can hardly eat it. I drink wine with my coffee, and then more wine without coffee. And then . . .

And now I must go.

I leave the house.

The succession of old doors clang to behind me, shutting me out. Will I be able to return?

There is never this panic when I leave for my lonely walks. This panic is only because I am going where *It* does not like me to go.

The streets surge with people.

Their teeth glint like eyes; their eyes, like teeth, bite my peeled face. A river rushing nowhere sweeps me along. The crowded public cars, the dust, and morning slapping the city across the face. I look back. On the hill, an old mansion. Mine.

There are cascading trees in Palmer Street which leads to the Library of Inanimate Beauty. I think I have come this way before.

White steps, tall slender Martian pillars, each wound round with a bronze snake.

The doors, having recognised me from my Service card, slip open and close behind me.

Now.

Now *It* begins. How can I explain what happens, this intangible terror, the great waves of thick silence beating at my head.

But my instructor is coming.

'Good morning,' we say to each other.

He guides me, gliding through the roaring chasms of fear he does not see.

'Sitting room . . . garden . . . food is brought in . . . these books . . .'

He is telling me all manner of things I shall have to discover for myself, later.

He is a big man, like an overfed dog, but plain. Because of this, *It* does not torture me too much. Any sense of quickening at a new presence, and *It* would wring me from end to end with agonised jealousy.

Half an hour has passed.

We drink thin delicate tea, and now he is going.

He is gone.

A Sort of Peace

It washes back into *Itself* but I can feel *It*, waiting, watchful. *It* will never let me be completely at ease in this new place. There is no guarantee that others may not come, even though I have been told I shall be alone.

But compared to what I was before, now I am liberated. I take off the hot wig and *It* pangs in me:

'Be careful.'

I wander from room to priceless room, among the ice-limbs of statues, the turning harps, playing, the mosaics and paintings, glass and books. Today people will not come in until fourteen in the afternoon, and by then I will be in my own apartment with my work. Tomorrow the Library will be shut, and mine all day. After that it will be open all the time, and I shall hide, quite safely, but out of reach of this beauty.

There is a golden sun, inside the sun a crystal, inside the crystal a lion of some black glossy material. It sings at the touch of a switch.

The apartment where I am to work is cool and lofty, lined with books, and looks out on to a small walled garden. My instructor has left me a list of instructions, despite our meeting.

I catalogue the books and the music tapes, reading some and listening to some. It is leisurely and enjoyable work. I have been very lucky this time. On the great plaster sheet, four feet by six, I plan the painting they have suggested I might try for them. It will be a panel in one of the walls of the Library, something rich for the whiteness of the room.

Of course, I will make it the Twins.

Slight, muscular, white-bodied beauty in yellow robes, their long hair like marigolds. They are so alike that it is only their sexes, male and female, that makes the slight difference between them, but her breasts are very small, and he has no beard. Around them are paler yellow leaves and darker ochre leaves, copper flowers, and the enormous limbs of old trees. Geminna and Geminni, in their mind forest, hand in hand, a golden incest of the soul.

My meal break comes, an optional hour – shorter or longer if I wish. I sit in the garden, hot with sun, eating a peach. I am almost, almost at peace. It is still. Quietness.

A Voice

A bell rings.

I look up, and see it singing in a niche in the garden wall. I stare at it. It rings and rings. It occurs to me that I must answer.

I answer.

'L.I.A. three five.'

'May I speak to Sol. Mavern? I believe she's working there.'

'Yes, this is Sol. Mavern.'

'Geminna!' The voice tells me a name, and says she met me three months before, when I worked in the Gallery of Light. 'May I come to see you? Now, perhaps.'

'I have a lot of work to do,' I say.

'Oh, now, Geminna. You know no one expects you to work *hard* at anything. You always were so conscientious. I shall be there at fifteen, after the Library opens.'

The Trap

I put on the brown wig and wait, in my trap, as the sun slants down the sky. At fourteen the doors open, and people wander in. Distantly I hear the extra activity as things whirr and sing, shapes dance, and colours musically change. I put away the books and continue with the Geminni, but my hands are trembling.

She comes early.

Her dress is a scarlet that hurts my eyes, her movements, fluttery and agitated as a bird's, hurt my eyes. *It* hates her. She flickers into a chair. I summon tea for her and slices of orange, and she smokes long silver cigarettes which make her an aura of silver perfumed smoke.

'Ah, yes . . . So long . . . The party, a simple thing – you never came . . . You promised us you would. This place . . . Old . . . Boring for you . . . Dinner . . . You must come then. Oh, you *must*. So many men, dying to meet you. It *is* a *man* that you'd be interested in? I have other friends . . . Such a recluse! Geminna, you are so *elusive*!'

I say, I think, the correct things. I hope she will go soon. She does not. She is suggesting that we walk to a café or wine-house at sixteen to celebrate our reunion.

'I'm afraid I can't,' I say. 'It's impossible.'

'Oh, it always is!'

She laughs. *I* am impossible.

At last sixteen comes and we leave together. My apartment locks itself behind me. She walks beside me in the open street, where every shaft of sunshine is too brilliant, brittle like glass (we may crack the light by moving through it too quickly), and her voice is splintering the air.

At a corner she leaves me, amused sourly at my rejection. I am white and drained. But I am going home. I seem to run the last yards. My doors fly open, shut fast behind me.

The vice *It* held me in all day relaxes.

I

I am looking at my face.

It is looking at my face.

Small, pale, tapering, all colour drawn out of it into the gold hair. Sometimes plain, sometimes ugly, sometimes beautiful. A changing face, a face like a year, with seasons, days and nights. When I am beautiful, *It* feeds on me, staring out of my own eyes into my own eyes. I have sat half an hour before a mirror, hypnotised, till *It* has had enough.

This is the morning of my fifth day of Service.

Tomorrow and the day after are my rest period, and I may stay at home if I want. After that, another five days and then freedom. Until the next time. It has not been so terrible after all. The girl in scarlet rang me again, but she didn't come to see me.

The Intruder

I walk through the streets, half shut against the noise and movement, and come to the Library of Inanimate Beauty.

Inside I find my instructor. A brief shock. *It* grasps me hard as if I had betrayed *It* and must be punished – as though this unexpected intruder were my fault.

'You look surprised, Sol. Mavern,' I hear him saying. 'Don't be alarmed. Your work is excellent, I must say. The mural-panel is – ' he spreads his hands – 'I wish we could attach you to our staff permanently.'

In the book-lined room, he summons tea which we drink. He is talking and talking. I wonder why he waits. Suddenly he takes my hand. The touch is electric but horrifying. Alien contact. As if he had burnt me, I snatch away, and *It* writhes in me like a serpent.

He laughs, uneasily.

'A quiet dinner,' he says, part of a sentence I have missed.

'No,' I say.

I think he has seen *It* in my eyes, hating him. Now it is his turn to recoil. He clears his throat, gets up.

'Someone else will be joining you this afternoon, Sol. Mavern. I hope you'll be kind enough to show them the work that must be done.'

Icebergs are splintering and clashing in my head as he goes.

Always I have hated to be touched, because *It* has hated it, furious at my violation. Now I cannot be calm. *It* will not let me be. Once a man, long ago in one of the periods of Service . . . He pulled me to him. He was a handsome man, and *It* detested him more than most. The dark room was red with blood colour as he forced my mouth towards the chasm of his mouth, and *It* was a cobra smashing my spine. If I cannot get away, *It* will kill me, kill me rather than let another being have me, even for an instant. I am not very tall or particularly strong, but I thrust the man away from me. *It*'s strength worked through me.

Now *It* would like to kill the instructor, and cannot, and so *It* hurts me instead.

When calm comes back, I recall what he has said.

Another one is coming.

Another outsider, another alien.

And I must –

The Young Man

I am painting now, and while the colour and the pattern absorb me, I can almost ignore *It*'s iron grip, tightening, as we wait.

I look into the face of Geminni. He looks at me. His face is beautiful and cruel. He holds Geminna tightly by the hand, his other hand stealing towards her breast; claiming her and holding her tight.

The brown wig is very hot. I can't take it off.

Outside, the hum as people move between the statues and the music.

Another sound.

The door of my apartment slides open.

I can't turn. I stare into the face of Geminni, who lashes me with thorns across the old scars of other lashings.

'Can I come in?'

Almost the voice of Geminni, young, male, a beautiful voice.

'Of course.'

I must look round now.

I look round.

Damn them, damn them. They have sent me a handsome man.

No, a beautiful man. Young, sapling, lion's hair, eyes like blue knife blades.

It leaps. Like a sea-dragon *It* leaps.

I see him staring at me, this young beautiful man. He looks – delightedly amazed.

'I'm sorry,' he says, 'I expected an old hag. A woman working alone among books and *objets d'art* – I'm not sure how I formed such a ridiculous impression. And you're not.'

He flushes slightly, giving so much away at once to my silence. His skin is clear, pale, the tough, gold, male hair along his jaw a surprise after the smooth hard softness, almost metallic, across his cheek bones.

I consult the name on his Service card.

Sol. Cyprian.

I can't see the name, but I have memorised the name previously.

'Sol. Cyprian?' I ask him.

He grins.

'Oh yes. Very formal. Try David.'

It is eating me alive as I tell him I am called Geminna. He looks from me to the panel, but I whisk him towards the books and music-tapes. I have learned my lines for two hours. Now I am word perfect. I see him staring at me as I explain the work he must do. He is puzzled by me. Friendly and attractive, he is used to any response but this. He looks curious, quizzical. When I finish, he wanders back towards the Geminni, wanting to talk to me about it. But I go away. I close myself in the rest room, and sit on the long couch, and the beating sea retreats, leaving me cast-up like a dried-out shell on the beach of despair.

Far off, unreal, I hear a flight of planes pass overhead.

Later

Later, it comes to me I must go back. I walk into the room, every sure step the creeping of a terrified insect. I cannot seem to focus as I balance before my painting. I am aware that he sits reading, looks up at me from time to time, still curious. He does no work at all. Ignore me, grow bored with me. You are so beautiful I cannot be quiet. The whole room is full of your presence as if of the sound of the sea, or of some incense burning. I am burning. My hands, my lungs, my eyes are scorched out.

What is the time? Tension has stretched minutes into a thin bright sharpened stake to pierce me. Only fourteen. I cannot bear two more hours of sharp crystal. Where is escape? There must be escape. Sea waves gurn and turn and roar through the hollows of my body, until I am blind, deaf, numb, defeated, caring for nothing except release. I do not even question *It*'s cruelty any longer. I accept all, all, only find me some way to obey you, and so be free.

'Tell me,' he says. I hear him from a great distance. It occurs to me that he is not real, a nightmare only. 'Do you disapprove of me as much as you seem to? I mean, if you like, I can really do some work.'

'Please do what you want,' I say.

He smiles, gets up, takes his book into the little walled garden. The sun shines on him. Golden. He is no longer in the room. The transparent doors close softly, dividing us. I will go now. Nothing matters. Excuses can be made later – I am ill, perhaps, or have forgotten some vital personal errand . . . I slip out of the room, make a way through the people in the Library. The streets are full. Sunlight bursts on the white glass towers of the city, the million windows. There is so much *light*.

The House

Evening purples the oval windows of the house into stained glass. Cool garden darkness hangs over the river. I watch the fish and think of nothing. There is a great calm in me, like the sweet cool peace which follows the cessation of great physical pain. Deliberately, I do not think back over the afternoon, or forward, ahead of the next two days which are mine, for both these avenues of thought are sharpened to hurt me. My image evolves like a ghost on the dark water, disturbed a little by the fish. This is how it is with me, to stand forever, disturbed a little, wavering, distorted, forming again, but always transparent. But there is a reason. There must be a reason. Am I special? Yes, yes, *It* whispers in me. Unique, singled out from the rest – the ones who run in herds. Am I? For what purpose then? The purpose is myself. Why then? There must be some answer, hidden – where? And what?

Dreaming

I am dreaming. I know I am dreaming, because when I am asleep, *It* is no longer with me. Asleep, I am often with people, and it does not seem strange or impossible then, neither am I afraid. David Cyprian is waiting for me in Wilton Square, before the marble portico of the airport. I see very clearly the blue and white flagstones laid out in patterns under our feet. He takes my hand. His touch is familiar yet wonderful. My hand is delighted at its contact with his hand, which is so much larger, dry and cool as a leaf. We walk under the portico. My hair is the colour of his, though lighter. I see our reflection in the long mirrors of the walls and, though we are different, we are similar, like brother and sister. Music tinkles through the airport, as I have heard it sometimes, awake, standing outside in the star-frosted dark. A page of the dream turns. Now we are in a little plane, lifting straight into the blue air above the city, rising and rising. He turns and kisses me on the mouth and his mouth is like the world all brought together and given to me in one moment.

I open my eyes and am awake. *It* grips me at once, strongly, fills me and bursts me open. Betrayed, vengeful, *It* rips every memory of pleasure from me, and leaves me empty in the silence.

The House

Two days pass very swiftly. I have done many things, played much music late into the night, finished the embroidered hanging that I shall put up on this wall which faces the garden. Dusk brings uneasiness. I wander across the lawns, the river, the terraces, around the summerhouse. I climb the steps of the old tower. The city stretches to the hills, a net of neon stars spread over it.

Tomorrow.

I will not think about tomorrow.

Morning

It is morning. I rise, linger over bathing, linger over breakfast without eating. Now is the time to leave. I do not leave. I walk from room to room. An ivory clock-face shows itself, threatening eleven o'clock. I will not think.

Now it is almost twelve. It is impossible that I should see him again. The very *thought* of seeing him again – is impossible. I go to the wall and touch the bell. I ask for the Committee. I explain. I am ill, but very willing to complete my period of Service when I am well once again – in ten days, perhaps? They agree, are sympathetic. I will have to sign a form, of course, which they will send me. But I must not distress myself. They will arrange for my duties to be resumed once I am completely recovered, and everything is perfectly all right. Relief is wonderful. Breathtaking. It was so easy, I am suddenly ashamed. I will not think of this. I am safe. This is all that matters. And whoever else will be there in ten days' time, it will not be him. He will be gone, his Service over. It was so easy.

Will he wonder where I am? Will he wonder why I am not there? Will he remember me at all?

I

The day of unexpected freedom is full of an exciting refinding. I read a great deal, and it seems to me my progress is accelerating. In the sunset I dress in the long white dress with its winding embroidery of yellow flowers which are the same shade as my hair. We stand before the mirror. I touch my own hand in the glass, and seem to feel the contact of flesh. We are one. I am whole. *It* lights up my heart like a warm flame. What does anything else matter?

The Door

There is a sound. I recognise the sound as the noise which the door makes when someone comes to it to be admitted. The noise is rare yet full of menace. I sit frozen among the white roses, the candles, the wine glass frozen into my hand. Seconds skitter away. The noise comes again. The core of me holds itself tightly. Go away, whoever you are, go away. I wait. The noise comes. I rise, look about me. Will they stare in at the windows? Will they see the lower rooms where I have sat and walked and lived? Will they climb the walls by some incredible means, stare through into this room and see me imprisoned here in the vivid candlelight, a fly in amber? The door sounds again. So persistent. Who is it that is so persistent? Anyone else would have gone away, thinking me out. I wait.

The door is silent. I count the seconds, then the minutes, standing still at the centre of the room. Slowly the core of me relaxes. My hands unfreeze from the glass which breaks in pieces on the floor. They have gone.

It comes to me suddenly that I must check the lower doors of the house – particularly the glass doors to the garden. I cannot remember that I have locked them – these doors which in this old house must still be bolted and barred. And yet, how seldom it is that I forget . . . I take a candlebranch, afraid of the harsh revealing ceiling lights. I go down the stairs, across the hall, into the room where the candles touch gold on the embroidered hanging. I go to the glass doors, and beyond them, in the dusk garden, I see a man's figure.

The Visitor

He has climbed the garden wall after all, its dilapidation providing dangerous but successful footholds. He is dusting himself down after his jump from the top into the patch of purple weeds at the side of the house. He looks up and meets my eyes, and comes to the doors. He opens them before I can move, and is in the room with me.

'I really am sorry,' he says. 'God knows what you must think. You don't even remember who I am, do you? David Cyprian – we met three days ago – look, when you didn't come back, I thought something might be wrong. Then this girl arrived – she said she was a friend of yours. She mentioned where you lived, and it's an out-of-the-way sort of place, isn't it? I dropped by after work – just on a sudden impulse – to see if you needed anything – you're on your own, aren't you? Then you didn't answer the bell. I thought, well, I thought you might be ill. Hence the rescue act over the wall.' Suddenly he stops explaining. He takes in my appearance. 'But I can see you're quite all right,' he says. His eyes narrow slightly. 'My apologies. I'll be going then. Can I use your front door, or would you rather I went back the way I came?'

I shut and lock the doors behind him. My hands are trembling; the situation is so strange I don't know what to do with it. I walk out of the room and he follows me.

In the hallway I hear him stop behind me. I too stop, as if at a signal.

'Tell me,' he says, and his voice has changed again, 'you *are* all right, are you?'

He is young and he is concerned. Unafraid of his own kind, he has an interest in them, an affection for them; he does not even understand that I am *not* of his kind. I turn to him, and become all pain and terror as

It lashes *Its* serpent coils into my heart and brain. I stand and look up at him out of the vortex of my individual and special agony.

The Word

'No,' I hear myself say.

One word. One word of betrayal for which *It* will never forgive me. There is nothing more *It* can do to me than *It* will do to me now, for now *It* will kill me. And yet. I am looking into his face still, seeing in his face the lost world drifting away, out of my reach forever, which is foolish, for how can one lose that which one has never possessed? And then I am angry. Anger comes like a biting howling thing; never before have I experienced this madness which exalts in its own extremities.

I run towards the stairs, up them, and he runs after me.

'Wait!'

I run into the music room. The candles smoke. He stands at the open door. I run to the pianos and my fingers sparkle over the decaying keys like scurrying diamond rats in the erratic light. I pull the guitars from their pegs and break their hearts open in brief insanities of song. I run out, and he lets me past. I run into the library. I pull the books in showers of white and scarlet from the shelves. Science and philosophy, poetry and magic lie like severed flower-heads at my feet. I turn and look at him, and I see he is startled, afraid almost of what I have become. It gladdens me. Now *I* am fear also. And the fear in me, the never-slackening vice, becomes his fear, not mine, so that I glory in it. I run out, down the stairs, across the house. My fingers fumble at the locks of the glass doors, and then I am running in the silent darkness of the garden. Pines, the tortured hawthorns, over the stone bridge, the river below me. The summerhouse – a white clock-face deprived of hands – timeless, is for ever. The terraces, the tower. And then comes stillness, for there is nowhere else to run.

Below, the city. Beyond, the hills fading into the sea. Stars blink at the brightness of the city's stars beneath.

By the Parapet

I stand by the parapet, listening. He is gone. No. I hear him come out on to the tower roof behind me. He is afraid of me. Why has he followed me?

He comes to stand beside me. Why is he here? He is at a loss. I can't grasp his sense of obligation. If only he would leave me alone. In that moment he reaches towards me. A second later I understand that he only meant to touch my arm, guide me back from the edge of the tower roof. But in the moment when I feel the pressure of his hand, I am certain that he will kiss me, and his mouth will become the world. And *It* leaps in me. Like a sea-dragon *It* leaps. Always I have hated to be touched, because *It* has hated it. Once, a man, long ago . . . If I cannot get away, *It* will kill me, kill me rather than let another being have me, even for an instant. I am not tall or particularly strong, but I thrust him away from me. *It* thrusts him away from me.

And, losing his balance, the crumbling parapet is all that can support him. And the parapet does not. In an incredible little burst of snow-white breath, the old stucco-work falls apart like the mummy-dust in the violated tomb.

Death

I accept because I must.

I accept my difference. Understanding follows acceptance. Understanding of the defences I must not allow to be breached. Nothing else matters. Preservation is the foremost instinct. Ultimately, we kill to survive. Even so, the responsibility is not mine, could never be mine. *It* knew the threat against *It*self. *It* acted. The blade, the bullet, the bomb are not assassins, it is the hand which uses them. I also have been put to use. *It* did what *It* must.

When I think of death, it does not offend me. Death can be beautiful. There need be no stigma of any kind attached to it. Grass and rank flowers, the powder of old stone, the silence, hold all the elements of the wreath, the grave, the monument, the requiem.

The garden reclaims all things into itself.

I put the books back, and the guitars on their pegs. I have begun a new embroidery, larger than the last. Soon I shall have to complete my period of Service, but not yet. There is a lot to do. I shall have no time to go to the tower for many weeks, but the stars are very patient and enduring.

The house is full of peace.

The Bell

By the oval window a bell rings.

'Nine seven,' I say, because it keeps me a unit still, and not a person. Who knows? This might be a wrong number.

Beyond the window, the glass city stretches away.

'Sol. Mavern?' asks a voice.

And the turquoise hills and the blue hills.

'Yes,' I say, and inside me, *It* stirs.

'Sol. Mavern, I'm speaking on behalf of the Committee. We're making inquiries about a young man – a David Cyprian. I understand you worked a Service period with him quite recently?'

And the pale blue hills, like hyacinths.

'It's possible,' I say, 'but I don't remember. I'm sorry.'

And the palest blue hills, like sky.

'I see. In fact, it was your last Service period – I think you left some days early because you were unwell?'

'Yes. Perhaps that's why I don't remember. There was a young man, I believe. I can't recall his name.'

'Then you wouldn't have seen him at all since the third of the month?'

'Oh, no,' I say. 'I didn't really know him.'

'I see, Sol. Mavern. Well, I'm sorry to have troubled you.'

And the pale silver sea.

But I can't go out.

It won't let me.

Perhaps *It* will never let me again.

Into Gold

I

Up behind Danuvius, the forests are black, and so stiff with black pork, black bears, and black-grey wolves, a man alone will feel himself jostled. Here and there you come on a native village, pointed houses of thatch with carved wooden posts, and smoke thick enough to cut with your knife. All day the birds call, and at night the owls come out. There are other things of earth and darkness, too. One ceases to be surprised at what may be found in the forests, or what may stray from them on occasion.

One morning, a Corn-King emerged, and pleased us no end. There had been some trouble, and some of the stores had gone up in flames. The ovens were standing empty and cold. It can take a year to get goods overland from the River, and our northern harvest was months off.

The old fort, that had been the palace then for twelve years, was built on high ground, scanning out across a mile of country strategically cleared of trees, to the forest cloud and a dream of distant mountains. Draco had called me up to the roof-walk, where we stood watching these mountains glow and fade, and come and go. It promised to be a fine day, and I had been planning a good long hunt, to exercise the men and give the breadless bellies solace. There is also a pine-nut meal they grind in the villages, accessible to barter. The loaves were not to everyone's taste, but we might have to come round to them. Since the armies pulled away, we had learned to improvise. I could scarcely remember the first days. The old men told you that everything, anyway, had been going down to chaos even then. Draco's father, holding on to a commander's power, assumed a prince's title which his orphaned warriors were glad enough to concede him. Discipline is its own ritual, and drug. As, lands and seas away, the centre of the world caved in, soldier-fashion they turned builders. They made the road to the fort, and soon began on the town, shoring it, for eternity, with strong walls. Next, they opened up the country, and got trade rights seen to that had gone by default decades ago. There was plenty of skirmishing as well to keep their swords bright. When the Commander died of a wound got fighting the Blue-Hair Tribe, a terror in those days, not seen for years since, Draco became the Prince in the Palace. He was eighteen then, and I five days older. We had known each other nearly all our lives, learned books and horses, drilled, hunted together. Though he was born elsewhere, he barely took that in, coming to this life when he could only just walk. For myself, I am lucky, perhaps, I never saw the Mother of Cities, and so never hanker after her, or lament her downfall.

That day on the roof-walk, certainly, nothing was further from my mind. Then Draco said, '*There* is something.'

His clear-water eyes saw detail quicker and more finely than mine. When I looked, to me still it was only a blur and fuss on the forest's edge, and the odd sparking glint of things catching the early sun.

'Now, Skorous, do you suppose – ?' said Draco.

'Someone has heard of our misfortune, and considerably changed his route,' I replied.

We had got news a week before of a grain-caravan, but too far west to be of use. Conversely, it seemed, the caravan had received news of our fire.

'Up goes the price of bread,' said Draco.

By now I was sorting it out, the long rigmarole of mules and baggage-wagons, horses and men. He travelled in some style. Truly, a Corn-King, profiting always because he was worth his weight in gold amid the wilds of civilisation. In Empire days, he would have weighed rather less.

We went down, and were in the square behind the east gate when the sentries brought him through. He left his people out on the parade before the gate, but one wagon had come up to the gateway, presumably his own, a huge conveyance, a regular travelling house, with six oxen in the shafts. Their straps were spangled with what I took for brass. On the side-leathers were pictures of grindstones and grain done in purple and yellow. He himself rode a tall horse, also spangled. He had a slim, snaky look, an Eastern look, with black brows and fawn skin. His fingers and ears were remarkable for their gold. And suddenly I began to wonder about the spangles. He bowed to Draco, the War-Leader and Prince. Then, to be quite safe, to me.

'Greetings, Miller,' I said.

He smiled at this coy honorific.

'Health and greetings, Captain. I think I am welcome?'

'My prince,' I indicated Draco, 'is always hospitable to wayfarers.'

'Particularly to those with wares, in time of dearth.'

'Which dearth is that?'

He put one golden finger to one golden ear-lobe.

'The trees whisper. This town of the Iron Shields has no bread.'

Draco said mildly, 'You should never listen to gossip.'

I said, 'If you've come out of your way, that would be a pity.'

The Corn-King regarded me, not liking my arrogance – though I never saw the Mother of Cities, I have the blood – any more than I liked his slink and glitter.

As this went on, I gambling and he summing up the bluff, the tail of my eye caught another glimmering movement, from where his house wagon waited at the gate. I sensed some woman must be peering round the flap, the way the Eastern females do. The free girls of the town are prouder, even the wolf-girls of the brothel, and aristocrats use a veil only as a sunshade. Draco's own sisters, though decorous and well brought-up, can read and write, each handle a light chariot, and will stand and look a man straight in the face. But I took very little notice of the fleeting apparition, except to decide it too had gold about it. I kept my sight on my quarry, and presently he smiled again and drooped his eyelids, so I knew he would not risk calling me, and we had won.

'Perhaps,' he said, 'there might be a little consideration of the detour I, so foolishly, erroneously, made.'

'We are always glad of fresh supplies. The fort is not insensible to its isolation. Rest assured.'

'Too generous,' he said. His eyes flared. But politely he added, 'I have heard of your town. There is great culture here. You have a library, with scrolls from Hellas, and Semitic Byblos – I can read many tongues, and would like to ask permission of your lord to visit among his books.'

I glanced at Draco, amused by the fellow's cheek, though all the

East thinks itself a scholar. But Draco was staring at the wagon. Something worth a look, then, which I had missed.

'And we have excellent baths,' I said to the Corn-King, letting him know in turn that the Empire's lost children think all the scholarly East to be also unwashed.

By midday, the whole caravan had come in through the walls and arranged itself in the market-place, near the temple of Mars. The temple priests, some of whom had been serving with the Draconis Regiment when it arrived, old, old men, did not take to this influx. In spring and summer, traders were in and out the town like flies, and native men came to work in the forges and the tannery or with the horses, and built their muddy thatch huts behind the unfinished law-house – which huts winter rain always washed away again when their inhabitants were gone. To such events of passage the priests were accustomed. But this new show displeased them. The chief Salius came up to the fort, attended by his slaves, leaning on his staff, and argued a while with Draco. Heathens, said the priest, with strange rituals, and dirtiness, would offend the patron god of the town. Draco seemed preoccupied.

I had put off the hunting-party, and now stayed to talk the Salius into a better humour. It would be a brief nuisance, and surely, they had been directed to us by the god himself, who did not want his war-like sons to go hungry? I assured the priest that, if the foreigners wanted to worship their own gods, they would have to be circumspect. Tolerance of every religious rag, as we knew, was unwise. They did not, I thought, worship Iusa. There would be no abominations. I then vowed a boar to Mars, if I could get one, and the dodderer tottered, pale and grim, away.

Meanwhile, the grain was being seen to. The heathen god-offenders had sacks and jars of it, and ready flour besides. It seemed a heavy chancy load with which to journey, goods that might spoil if at all delayed, or if the weather went against them. And all that jangling of gold beside. They fairly bled gold. I had been right in my second thought on the bridle-decorations, there were even nuggets and bells hung on the wagons, and gold flowers; and the oxen had gilded horns. For the men, they were ringed and buckled and roped and tied with it. It was a marvel.

When I stepped over to the camp near sunset, I was on the look-out for anything amiss. But they had picketed their animals couthly enough, and the dazzle-fringed, clink-belled wagons stood quietly shadowing and gleaming in the westered light. Columns of spicy smoke rose, but only from their cooking. Boys dealt with that, and boys had drawn water from the well; neither I nor my men had seen any women.

Presently I was conducted to the Corn-King's wagon. He received me before it, where woven rugs, and cushions stitched with golden discs, were strewn on the ground. A tent of dark purple had been errected close by, its gilt-tasselled sides all down, shut as a box. A disc or two more winked yellow from the folds. Beyond, the plastered colonnades, the stone Mars Temple, stood equally closed and eyeless, refusing to see.

The Miller and I exchanged courtesies. He asked me to sit, so I sat. I was curious.

'It is pleasant,' he said, 'to be within safe walls.'

'Yes, you must be often in some danger,' I answered.

He smiled, secretively now. 'You mean our wealth? It is better to display than to hide. The thief kills, in his hurry, the man who conceals his gold. I have never been robbed. They think, Ah, this one shows all his riches. He must have some powerful demon to protect him.'

'And is that so?'

'Of course,' he said.

I glanced at the temple, and then back at him, meaningly. He said, 'Your men drove a hard bargain for the grain and the flour. And I have been docile. I respect your gods, Captain. I respect all gods. That, too, is a protection.'

Some drink came. I tasted it cautiously, for Easterners often eschew wine and concoct other disgusting muck. In the forests they ferment thorn berries, or the milk of their beasts, neither of which methods makes such a poor beverage, when you grow used to it. But of the Semites one hears all kinds of things. Still, the drink had a sweet hot sizzle that made me want more, so I swallowed some, then waited to see what else it would do to me.

'And your lord will allow me to enter his library?' said the Corn-King, after a host's proper pause.

'That may be possible,' I said. I tried the drink again. 'How do you manage without women?' I added, 'You'll have seen the House of the Mother, with the she-wolf painted over the door? The girls there are fastidious and clever. If your men will spare the price, naturally.'

The Corn-King looked at me, with his liquid man-snake's eyes, aware of all I said which had not been spoken.

'It is true,' he said at last, 'that we have no women with us.'

'Excepting your own wagon.'

'My daughter,' he said.

I had known Draco, as I have said, almost all my life. He was for me what no other had ever been; I had followed his star gladly and without question, into scrapes, and battles, through very fire and steel. Very rarely would he impose on me some task I hated, loathed. When he did so it was done without design or malice, as a man sneezes. The bad times were generally to do with women. I had fought back to back with him, but I did not care to be his pander. Even so, I would not refuse. He had stood in the window that noon, looking at the black forest, and said in a dry low voice, carelessly apologetic, irrefutable, 'He has a girl in that wagon. Get her for me.' 'Well, she may be his – ' I started off. He cut me short. 'Whatever she is. He sells things. He is accustomed to selling.' 'And if he won't?' I said. Then he looked at me, with his high-coloured, translucent eyes. 'Make him,' he said, and next laughed, as if it were nothing at all, this choice mission. I had come out thinking glumly, she has witched him, put the Eye on him. But I had known him lust like this before. Nothing would do then but he must have. Women had never been that way for me. They were available, when one needed them. I like to this hour to see them here and there, *our* women, straight-limbed, graceful, clean. In the perilous seasons I would have died defending his sisters, as I would have died to defend him. That was that. It was a fact, the burning of our grain had come about through an old grievance, an idiot who kept score of something Draco had done half a year ago, about a native girl got on a raid.

I put down the golden cup, because the drink was going to my head. They had two ways, Easterners, with daughters. One was best left unspoken. The other kept them locked and bolted virgin. Mercurius bless the dice.

Then, before I could say anything, the Miller put my mind at rest.

'My daughter,' he said, 'is very accomplished. She is also very beautiful, but I speak now of the beauty of learning and art.'

'Indeed. Indeed.'

The sun was slipping over behind the walls. The far mountains were steeped in dyes. This glamour shone behind the Corn-King's head, gold in the sky for him, too. And he said, 'Amongst other matters, she has studied the lore of Khemia – Old Aegyptus, you will understand.'

'Ah, yes?'

'Now I will confide in you,' he said. His tongue flickered on his lips. Was it forked? The damnable drink had fuddled me after all; that, and a shameful relief. 'The practice of the Al-Khemia contains every science and sorcery. She can read the stars, she can heal the hurts of man. But best of all, my dear Captain, my daughter has learned the third great secret of the Tri-Magae.'

'Oh, yes, indeed?'

'She can,' he said, 'change all manner of materials into gold.'

II

'Sometimes, Skorous,' Draco said, 'you are a fool.'

'Sometimes I am not alone in that.'

Draco shrugged. He had never feared honest speaking. He never asked more of a title than his own name. But those two items were, in themselves, significant. He was what he was, a law above the law. The heart-legend of the City was down, and he a prince in a forest that ran all ways for ever.

'What do you think then she will do to me? Turn me into metal, too?'

We spoke in Greek, which tended to be the palace mode for private chat. It was fading out of use in the town.

'I don't believe in that kind of sorcery,' I said.

'Well, he has offered to have her show us. Come along.'

'It will be a trick.'

'All the nicer. Perhaps he will find someone for you, too.'

'I shall attend you,' I said, 'because I trust none of them. And fifteen of my men around the wagon.'

'I must remember not to groan,' he said, 'or they'll be splitting the leather and tumbling in on us with swords.'

'Draco,' I said, 'I'm asking myself why he boasted that she had the skill.'

'All that gold: they didn't steal it or cheat for it. A witch *made* it for them.'

'I have heard of the Al-Khemian arts.'

'Oh, yes,' he said. 'The devotees make gold, they predict the future, they raise the dead. She might be useful. Perhaps I should marry her.

66

Wait till you see her,' he said. 'I suppose it was all pre-arranged. He will want paying again.'

When we reached the camp, it was midnight. Our torches and theirs opened the dark, and the flame outside the Mars Temple burned faint. There were stars in the sky, no moon.

We had gone to them at their request, since the magery was intrinsic, required utensils, and was not to be moved to the fort without much effort. We arrived like a bridal procession. The show was not after all to be in the wagon, but the tent. The other Easterners had buried themselves from view. I gave the men their orders and stood them conspicuously about. Then a slave lifted the tent's purple drapery a chink and squinted up at us. Draco beckoned me after him, no one demurred. We both went into the pavilion.

To do that was to enter the East head-on. Expensive gums were burning with a dark hot perfume that put me in mind of the wine I had had earlier. The incense-burners were gold, tripods on leopards' feet, with swags of golden ivy. The floor was carpeted soft, like the pelt of some beast, and beast-skins were hung about, things I had not seen before, some of them, maned and spotted, striped and scaled, and some with heads and jewellery eyes and the teeth and claws gilded. Despite all the clutter of things, of polished mirrors and casks and chests, cushions and dead animals, and scent, there was a feeling of great space within that tent. The ceiling of it stretched taut and high, and three golden wheels depended, with oil-lights in little golden boats. The wheels turned idly now this way, now that, in a wind that came from nowhere and went to nowhere, a demon wind out of a desert. Across the space, wide as night, was an opaque dividing curtain, and on the curtain, a long parchment. It was figured with another mass of images, as if nothing in the place should be spare. A tree went up, with two birds at the roots, a white bird with a raven-black head, a soot-black bird with the head of an ape. A snake twined the tree too, round and round, and ended looking out of the lower branches where yellow fruit hung. The snake had the face of a maiden, and flowing hair. Above sat three figures, judges of the dead from Aegyptus, I would have thought, if I had thought about them, with a balance, and wands. The sun and the moon stood over the tree.

I put my hand to the hilt of my sword, and waited. Draco had seated himself on the cushions. A golden jug was to hand, and a cup. He reached forward, poured the liquor and made to take it, before – reluctantly – I snatched the vessel. 'Let me, first. Are you mad?'

He reclined, not interested as I tasted for him, then let him have the cup again.

Then the curtain parted down the middle and the parchment with it, directly through the serpent-tree. I had expected the Miller, but instead what entered was a black dog with a collar of gold. It had a wolf's shape, but more slender, and with a pointed muzzle and high carven pointed ears. Its eyes were also black. It stood calmly, like a steward, regarding us, then stepped aside and lay down, its head still raised to watch. And next the woman Draco wanted came in.

To me, she looked nothing in particular. She was pleasantly made, slim, but rounded, her bare arms and feet the colour of amber. Over her head, to her breast, covering her hair and face like a dusky smoke, was a veil, but it was transparent enough to see through it, to black locks and black aloe eyes, and a full tawny mouth. There was only a touch of gold on her, a rolled torque of soft metal at her throat, and one ring on her right hand. I was puzzled as to what had made her glimmer at the edge of my sight before, but perhaps she had dressed differently then, to make herself plain.

She bowed Eastern-wise to Draco, then to me. Then, in the purest Greek I ever heard, she addressed us.

'Lords, while I am at work, I must ask that you will please be still, or else you will disturb the currents of the act and so impair it. Be seated,' she said to me, as if I had only stood till then from courtesy. Her eyes were very black, black as the eyes of the jackal-dog, blacker than the night. Then she blinked, and her eyes flashed. The lids were painted with gold. And I found I had sat down.

What followed I instantly took for an hallucination, induced by the incense, and by other means less perceptible. That is not to say I did not think she was a witch. There was something of power to her I never met before. It pounded from her, like heat, or an aroma. It did not make her beautiful for me, but it held me quiet, though I swear never once did I lose my grip either on my senses or my sword.

First, and quite swiftly, I had the impression the whole tent blew upward, and we were in the open in fact, under a sky of a million stars that blazed and crackled like diamonds. Even so, the golden wheels stayed put, up in the sky now, and they spun, faster and faster, until each was a solid golden O of fire, three spinning suns in the heaven of midnight.

(I remember I thought flatly, We have been spelled. So what now?

But in its own way, my stoicism was also suspect. My thoughts in any case flagged after that.)

There was a smell of lions, or of a land that had them. Do not ask me how I know, I never smelled or saw them, or such a spot. And there before us all stood a slanting wall of brick, at once much larger than I saw it, and smaller than it was. It seemed even so to lean into the sky. The woman raised her arms. She was apparent now as if rinsed all over by gilt, and one of the great stars seemed to sear on her forehead.

Forms began to come and go, on the lion-wind. If I knew then what they were, I forgot it later. Perhaps they were animals, like the skins in the tent, though some had wings.

She spoke to them. She did not use Greek any more. It was the language of Khem, presumably, or we were intended to believe so. A liquid tongue, an Eastern tongue, no doubt.

Then there were other visions. The ribbed stems of flowers, broader than ten men around, wide petals pressed to the ether. A rainbow of mist that arched over, and touched the earth with its feet and its brow. And other mirages, many of which resembled effigies I had seen of the gods, but they walked.

The night began to close upon us slowly, narrowing and coming down. The stars still raged overhead and the gold wheels whirled, but some sense of enclosure had returned. As for the sloped angle of brick, it had huddled down into a sort of oven, and into this the woman was placing, with extreme care – of all things – long sceptres of corn, all brown and dry and withered, blighted to straw by some harvest like a curse.

I heard her whisper then. I could not hear what.

Behind her, dim as shadows, I saw other women, who sat weaving, or who toiled at the grindstone, and one who shook a rattle upon which rings of gold sang out. Then the vision of these women was eclipsed. Something stood there, between the night and the Eastern witch. Tall as the roof, or tall as the sky, bird-headed maybe, with two of the stars for eyes. When I looked at this, this ultimate apparition, my blood froze and I could have howled out loud. It was not common fear, but terror, such as the worst reality has never brought me, though sometimes subtle nightmares do.

Then there was a lightning, down the night. When it passed, we were enclosed in the tent, the huge night of the tent, and the brick oven burned before us, with a thin harsh fume coming from the aperture in its top.

'Sweet is truth,' said the witch, in a wild and passionate voice, all music, like the notes of the gold rings on the rattle. 'O Lord of the Word. The Word is, and the Word makes all things to be.'

Then the oven cracked into two pieces, it simply fell away from itself, and there on a bank of red charcoal, which died to clinker even as I gazed at it, lay a sheaf of golden corn. *Golden* corn, smiths' work. It was pure and sound and rang like a bell when presently I went to it and struck it and flung it away.

The tent had positively resettled all around us. It was there. I felt queasy and stupid, but I was in my body and had my bearings again, the sword-hilt firm to my palm, though it was oddly hot to the touch, and my forehead burned, sweatless, as if I too had been seethed in a fire.

I had picked up the goldwork without asking her anything. She did not prevent me, nor when I slung it off.

When I looked up from that, she was kneeling by the curtain, where the black dog had been and was no more. Her eyes were downcast under her veil. I noted the torque was gone from her neck and the ring from her finger. Had she somehow managed her trick that way, melting gold on to the stalks of mummified corn – No, lunacy. Why nag at it? It was *all* a deception.

But Draco lay looking at her now, burned up by another fever. It was her personal gold he wanted.

'Out, Skorous,' he said to me. 'Out, now.' Slurred and sure.

So I said to her, through my blunted lips and woollen tongue, 'Listen carefully, girl. The witchery ends now. You know what he wants, and how to see to that, I suppose. Scratch him with your littlest nail, and you die.'

Then, without getting to her feet, she looked up at me, only the second time. She spoke in Greek, as at the start. In the morning, when I was better able to think, I reckoned I had imagined what she said. It had seemed to be: 'He is safe, for I desire him. It is my choice. If it were not my choice and my desire, where might you hide yourselves, and live?'

We kept watch round the tent, in the Easterners' camp, in the market-place, until the ashes of the dawn. There was not a sound from anywhere, save the regular quiet passaging of sentries on the walls, and the cool black forest wind that turned grey near sunrise.

At sun-up, the usual activity of any town began. The camp stirred and let its boys out quickly to the well to avoid the town's women.

Some of the caravaneers even chose to stroll across to the public lavatories, though they had avoided the bathhouse.

An embarrassment came over me, that we should be standing there, in the foreigners' hive, to guard our prince through his night of lust. I looked sharply, to see how the men were taking it, but they had held together well. Presently Draco emerged. He appeared flushed and tumbled, very nearly shy, like some girl just out of a love-bed.

We went back to the fort in fair order, where he took me aside, thanked me, and sent me away again.

Bathed and shaved, and my fast broken, I began to feel more sanguine. It was over and done with. I would go down to the temple of Father Jupiter and give him something – why, I was not exactly sure. Then get my boar for Mars. The fresh-baked bread I had just eaten was tasty, and maybe worth all the worry.

Later, I heard the Miller had taken himself to our library and been let in. I gave orders he was to be searched on leaving. Draco's grandfather had started the collection of manuscripts, there were even scrolls said to have been rescued from Alexandrea. One could not be too wary.

In the evening, Draco called me up to his writing-room.

'Tomorrow,' he said, 'the Easterners will be leaving us.'

'That's good news,' I said.

'I thought it would please you. Zafra, however, is to remain. I'm taking her into my household.'

'Zafra,' I said.

'Well, they call her that. For the yellow-gold. Perhaps not her name. That might have been *Nefra* – Beautiful . . .'

'Well,' I said, 'if you want.'

'Well,' he said, 'I never knew you before to be jealous of one of my women.'

I said nothing, though the blood knocked about in my head. I had noted before, he had a woman's tongue himself, when he was put out. He was a spoiled brat as a child, I have to admit, but a mother's early death, and the life of a forest fortress, pared most of it from him.

'The Corn-King is not her father,' he said now. 'She told me. But he's stood by her as that some years. I shall send him something, in recompense.'

He waited for my comment that I was amazed nothing had been asked for. He waited to see how I would jump. I wondered if he had

paced about here, planning how he would put it to me. Not that he was
required to. Now he said:

'We gain, Skorous, a healer and deviner. Not just my pleasure at
night.'

'Your pleasure at night is your own affair. There are plenty of girls
about, I would have thought, to keep you content. As for anything else
she can or cannot do, all three temples, particularly the Women's
Temple, will be up in arms. The Salius yesterday was only a sample.
Do you think they are going to let some yellow-skinned harlot devine
for you? Do you think that men who get hurt in a fight will want her
near them?'

'You would not, plainly.'

'No, I would not. As for the witchcraft, we were drugged and made
monkeys of. An evening's fun is one thing.'

'Yes, Skorous,' he said. 'Thanks for your opinion. Don't sulk too
long. I shall miss your company.'

An hour later, he sent, so I was informed, two of the scrolls from the
library to the Corn-King in his wagon. They were two of the best,
Greek, one transcribed by the hand, it was said, of a very great king.
They went in a silver box, with jewel inlay. Gold would have been
tactless, under the circumstances.

Next day she was in the palace. She had rooms on the women's side, it
had been the apartment of Draco's elder sister, before her marriage.
He treated this one as nothing less than a relative from the first. When
he was at leisure, on those occasions when the wives and women of his
officers dined with them, there was she with him. When he hunted,
she went with him, too, not to have any sport, but as a companion, in a
litter between two horses that made each hunt into a farce from its
onset. She was in his bed each night, for he did not go to her, her place
was solely hers: the couch his father had shared only with his mother.
And when he wanted advice, it was she gave it to him. He called on his
soldiers and his priests afterwards. Though he always did so call,
nobody lost face. He was wise and canny, she must have told him how
to be at long last. And the charm he had always had. He even consulted
me, and made much of me before everyone, because, very sensibly he
realised, unless he meant to replace me, it would be foolish to let the
men see I no longer counted a feather's weight with him. Besides, I
might get notions of rebellion. I had my own following, my own men
who would die for me if they thought me wronged. Probably that

angered me more than the rest, that he might have the idea I would forgo my duty and loyalty, forget my honour, and try to pull him down. I could no more do that than put out one of my own eyes.

Since we lost our homeland, since we lost, more importantly, the spine of the Empire, there had been a disparity, a separation of men. Now I saw it, in those bitter golden months after she came among us. He had been born in the Mother of Cities, but She had slipped from his skin like water. He was a new being, a creature of the world, that might be anything, of any country. But, never having seen the roots of me, yet they had me fast. I was of the old order. I would stand until the fire had me, rather than tarnish my name, and my heart.

Gradually, the fort and town began to fill with gold. It was very nearly a silly thing. But we grew lovely and we shone. The temples did not hate her, as I had predicted. No, for she brought them glittering vessels, and laved the gods' feet with rare offerings, and the sweet spice also of her gift burned before Mars, and the Father, and the Mother, so every holy place smelled like Aegyptus, or Judea, or the brothels of Babylon for all I knew.

She came to walk in the streets with just one of the slaves at her heels, bold, the way our ladies did, and though she never left off her veil, she dressed in the stola and the palla, all clasped and cinched with the tiniest amounts of gold, while gold flooded everywhere else, and everyone looked forward to the summer heartily, for the trading. The harvest would be wondrous too. Already there were signs of astounding fruition. And in the forest, not a hint of any restless tribe, or any ill wish.

They called her by the name *Zafra*. They did not once call her 'Easterner'. One day, I saw three pregnant women at the gate, waiting for Zafra to come out and touch them. She was lucky. Even the soldiers had taken no offence. The old Salius had asked her for a balm for his rheumatism. It seemed the balm had worked.

Only I, then, hated her. I tried to let it go. I tried to remember she was only a woman, and, if a sorceress, did us good. I tried to see her as voluptuous and enticing, or as homely and harmless. But all I saw was some shuttered-up, close, fermenting thing, like mummy-dusts reviving in a tomb, or the lion-scent, and the tall shadow that had stood between her and the night, bird-headed, the Lord of the Word that made all things, or unmade them. What was she, under her disguise? Draco could not see it. Like the black dog she had kept, which walked by her on a leash, well-mannered and gentle, and which

would probably tear out the throat of anyone who came at her with
mischief on his mind – Under her honeyed wrappings, was it a doll of
straw or gold, or a viper?

Eventually, Draco married her. That was no surprise. He did it in
the proper style, with sacrifices to the Father, and all the forms, and a
feast that filled the town. I saw her in colours then, that once, the
saffron dress, the Flammeus, the fire-veil of the bride, and her face
bare, and painted up like a lady's, pale, with rosy cheeks and lips. But
it was still herself, still the Eastern Witch.

And dully that day, as in the tent that night, I thought, So what
now?

III

In the late summer, I picked up some talk, among the servants in the
palace. I was by the well-court, in the peach arbour, where I had
paused to look at the peaches. They did not always come, but this year
we had had one crop already, and now the second was blooming. As I
stood there in the shade, sampling the fruit, a pair of the kitchen men
met below by the well, and stayed to gossip in their argot. At first I
paid no heed, then it came to me what they were saying, and I listened
with all my ears.

When one went off, leaving the other, old Ursus, to fill his dipper, I
came down the stair and greeted him. He started, and looked at me
furtively.

'Yes, I heard you,' I said. 'But tell me, now.'

I had always put a mask on, concerning the witch, with everyone
but Draco, and afterwards with him too. I let it be seen I thought her
nothing much, but if she was his choice, I would serve her. I was
careful never to speak slightingly of her to any, since it would reflect
on his honour, even to men I trusted, even in wine. Since he had
married her, she had got my duty, too, unless it came to vie with my
duty to him.

But Ursus had the servant's way, the slave's way, of holding back
bad news for fear it should turn on him. I had to repeat a phrase or two
of his own before he would come clean.

It seemed that some of the women had become aware that Zafra, a
sorceress of great power, could summon to her, having its name, a
mighty demon. Now she did not sleep every night with Draco, but in

her own apartments, sometimes things had been glimpsed, or heard –

'Well, Ursus,' I said, 'you did right to tell me. But it's a lot of silly women's talk. Come, you're not going to give it credit?'

'The flames burn flat on the lamps, and change colour,' he mumbled. 'And the curtain rattled, but no one there. And Eunike says she felt some form brush by her in the corridor –'

'That is enough,' I said. 'Women will always fancy something is happening, to give themselves importance. You will know that. Then there's hysteria and they can believe and say anything. We are aware she has arts, and the science of Aegyptus. But demons are another matter.'

I further admonished him and sent him off. I stood by the well, pondering. Rattled curtains, secretive forms – it crossed my thoughts she might have taken a lover, but it did not seem in keeping with her shrewdness. I do not really believe in such beasts as demons, except what the brain can bring forth. Then again, her brain might be capable of many things.

It turned out I attended Draco that evening, something to do with one of the villages that traded with us, something he still trusted me to understand. I asked myself if I should tell him about the gossip. Frankly, when I had found out – the way you always can – that he lay with her less frequently, I had had a sort of hope, but there was a qualm, too, and when the trade matter was dealt with, he stayed me over the wine, and he said: 'You may be wondering about it, Skorous. If so, yes. I'm to be given a child.'

I knew better now than to scowl. I drank a toast, and suggested he might be happy to have got a boy on her.

'She says it will be a son.'

'Then of course, it will be a son.'

And, I thought, it may have her dark-yellow looks. It may be a magus too. And it will be your heir, Draco. My future Prince, and the master of the town. I wanted to hurl the wine cup through the wall, but I held my hand and my tongue, and after he had gone on a while trying to coax me to thrill at the joy of life, I excused myself and went away.

It was bound to come. It was another crack in the stones. It was the way of destiny, and of change. I wanted not to feel I must fight against it, or desire to send her poison, to kill her or abort her, or tear it, her womb's fruit, when born, in pieces.

For a long while I sat on my sleeping-couch and allowed my fury to sink down, to grow heavy and leaden, resigned, defeated.

When I was sure of that defeat, I lay flat and slept.

In sleep, I followed a demon along the corridor in the women's quarters, and saw it melt through her door. It was tall, long-legged, with the head of a bird, or perhaps of a dog. A wind blew, lion-tanged. I was under a tree hung thick with peaches, and a snake looked down from it with a girl's face framed by a flaming bridal-veil. Then there was a spinning fiery wheel, and golden corn flew off clashing from it. And next I saw a glowing oven, and on the red charcoal lay a child of gold, burning and gleaming and asleep.

When I woke with a jump it was the middle of the night, and someone had arrived, and the slave was telling me so.

At first I took it for a joke. Then, became serious. Zafra, Draco's wife, an hour past midnight, had sent for me to attend her in her rooms. Naturally I suspected everything. She knew me for her adversary: she would lead me in, then say I had set on her to rape or somehow else abuse her. On the other hand, I must obey and go to her, not only for duty, now, but from sheer aggravation and raw curiosity. Though I had always told myself I misheard her words as I left her with him the first time, I had never forgotten them. Since then, beyond an infrequent politeness, we had not spoken.

I dressed as formally as I could, got two of my men, and went across to the women's side. The sentries along the route were my fellows too, but I made sure they learned I had been specifically summoned. Rather to my astonishment, they knew it already.

My men went with me right to her chamber door, with orders to keep alert there. Perhaps they would grin, asking each other if I was nervous. I was.

When I got into the room, I thought it was empty. Her women had been sent away. One brazier burned, near the entry, but I was used by now to the perfume of those aromatics. It was a night of full moon, and the blank light lay in a whole pane across the mosaic, colouring it faintly, but in the wrong, nocturnal, colours. The bed, narrow, low and chaste, stood on one wall, and her tiring table near it. Through the window under the moon, rested the tops of the forest, so black it made the indigo sky pale.

Then a red-golden light blushed out and I saw her, lighting the lamps on their stand from a taper. I could almost swear she had not been there a second before, but she could stay motionless a long while, and with her dark robe and hair, and all her other darkness, she was a natural thing for shadows.

'Captain,' she said. (She never used my name, she must know I did not want it; a sorceress, she was well aware of the power of naming.) 'There is no plot against you.'

'That's good to know,' I said, keeping my distance, glad of my sword, and of every visible insignia of who and what I was.

'You have been very honourable in the matter of me,' she said. 'You have done nothing against me, either openly or in secret, though you hated me from the beginning. I know what this has cost you. Do not spurn my gratitude solely because it is mine.'

'Domina,' I said (neither would I use her name, though the rest did in the manner of the town), 'you're his. He has made you his wife. And – ' I stopped.

'And the vessel of his child. Ah, do you think he did that alone?' She saw me stare with thoughts of demons, and she said, 'He and I, Captain. He, and I.'

'Then I serve you,' I said. I added, and though I did not want to give her the satisfaction I could not keep back a tone of irony, 'You have nothing to be anxious at where I am concerned.'

We were speaking in Greek, hers clear as water in that voice of hers which I had to own was very beautiful.

'I remain,' she said, 'anxious.'

'Then I can't help you, Domina.' There was a silence. She stood looking at me, through the veil I had only once seen dispensed with in exchange for a veil of paint. I wondered where the dog had gone, that had her match in eyes. I said, 'But I would warn you. If you practice your business in here, there's begun to be some funny talk.'

'They see a demon, do they?' she said.

All at once the hair rose up on my neck and scalp.

As if she read my mind, she said:

'I have not pronounced any name. Do not be afraid.'

'The slaves are becoming afraid.'

'No,' she said. 'They have always talked of me but they have never been afraid of me. None of them. Draco does not fear me, do you think? And the priests do not. Or the women and girls. Or the children, or the old men. Or the slaves. Or your soldiers. None of them fears me or what I am or what I do, the gold with which I fill the temples, or the golden harvests, or the healing I perform. None of them fears it. But you, Captain, you do fear, and you read your fear again and again in every glance, in every word they utter. But it is yours, not theirs.'

I looked away from her, up to the ceiling from which the patterns had faded years before.

'Perhaps,' I said. 'I am not blind.'

Then she sighed. As I listened to it, I thought of her, just for an instant, as a forlorn girl alone with strangers in a foreign land.

'I'm sorry,' I said.

'It is true,' she said, 'you see more than most. But not your own error.'

'Then that is how it is.' My temper had risen and I must rein it.

'You will not,' she said quietly, 'be a friend to me.'

'I cannot, and will not, be a friend to you. Neither am I your enemy, while you keep faith with him.'

'But one scratch of my littlest nail,' she said. Her musical voice was nearly playful.

'Only one,' I said.

'Then I regret waking you, Captain,' she said. 'Health and slumber for your night.'

As I was going back along the corridor, I confronted the black jackal-dog. It padded slowly towards me and I shivered, but one of the men stooped to rub its ears. It suffered him, and passed on, shadow to shadow, night to ebony night.

Summer went to winter, and soon enough the snows came. The trading and the harvests had shored us high against the cruellest weather, we could sit in our towers and be fat, and watch the wolves howl through the white forests. They came to the very gates that year. There were some odd stories, that wolf-packs had been fed of our bounty, things left for them, to tide them over. Our own she-wolves were supposed to have started it, the whore-house girls. But when I mentioned the tale to one of them, she flared out laughing.

I recall that snow with an exaggerated brilliance, the way you sometimes do with some time that precedes an illness, or a deciding battle. Albino mornings with the edge of a broken vase, the smoke rising from hearths and temples, or steaming with the blood along the snow from the sacrifices of Year's Turn. The Wolf Feast with the races, and later the ivies and vines cut for the Mad Feast, and the old dark wine got out, the torches and a girl I had in a shed full of hay and pigs; and the spate of weddings that come after, very sensibly. The last snow twilights were thick as soup with blueness. Then spring, and the forest surging up from its slough, the first proper hunting, with the smell of sap and crushed freshness spraying out as if one waded in a river.

Draco's child was born one spring sunset, coming forth in the bloody golden light, crying its first cry to the evening star. It was a boy, as she had said.

I had kept even my thoughts off from her after that interview in her chamber. My feelings had been confused and displeasing. It seemed to me she had in some way tried to outwit me, throw me down. Then I had felt truly angry, and later, oddly shamed. I avoided, where I could, all places where I might have to see her. Then she was seen less, being big with the child.

After the successful birth all the usual things were done. In my turn, I beheld the boy. He was straight and flawlessly formed, with black hair, but a fair skin; he had Draco's eyes from the very start. So little of the mother. Had she contrived it, by some other witch's art, knowing that when at length we had to cleave to him, it would be Draco's line we wished to see? No scratch of a nail, there, none.

Nor had there been any more chat of demons. Or they made sure I never intercepted it.

I said to myself, she is a matron now, she will wear to our ways. She has borne him a strong boy.

But it was no use at all.

She was herself, and the baby was half of her.

They have a name now for her demon, her genius in the shadowlands of witchcraft. A scrambled name that does no harm. They call it, in the town's argot: *Rhamthibiscan*.

We claim so many of the Greek traditions; they know of Rhadamanthys from the Greek. A judge of the dead, he is connectable to Thot of Aegyptus, the Thrice-Mighty Thrice-Mage of the Al-Khemian Art. And because Thot the Ibis-Headed and Anpu the Jackal became mingled in it, along with Hermercurius, Prince of Thieves and Whores – who is, too, the guide of lost souls – an ibis and a dog were added to the brief itinerary. Rhadamanthys-Ibis-Canis. The full name, even, has no power. It is a muddle, and a lie, and the invocation says: *Sweet is Truth*. Was it, though, ever sensible to claim to know what truth might be?

IV

'They know of her, and have sent begging for her. She's a healer and they're sick. It's not unreasonable. She isn't afraid. I have seen her close an open wound by passing her hands above it. Yes, Skorous, perhaps she only made me see it, and the priests to see it, and the wounded man. But he recovered, as you remember. So I trust her to be able to cure these people and make them love us even better. She herself is immune to illness. Yes, Skorous, she only thinks she is. However, thinking so has apparently worked wonders. She was never once out of sorts with the child. The midwives were amazed – or not amazed, maybe – that she seemed to have no pain during the birth. Though they told me she wept when the child was put into her arms. Well, so did I.' Draco frowned. He said, 'So we'll let her do it, don't you agree, let her go to them and heal them. We may yet be able to open this country, make something of it, one day. Anything that is useful in winning them.'

'She will be taking the child with her?'

'Of course. He's not weaned yet, and she won't let another woman nurse him.'

'Through the forests. It's three days' ride away, this village. And then we hardly know the details of the sickness. If your son –'

'He will be with his mother. She has never done a foolish thing.'

'You let this bitch govern you. Very well. But don't risk the life of your heir, since your heir is what you have made him, this half-breed brat –'

I choked off the surge in horror. I had betrayed myself. It seemed to me instantly that I had been made to do it. *She* had made me. All the stored rage and impotent distrust, all the bitter frustrated *guile* – gone for nothing in a couple of sentences.

But Draco only shrugged, and smiled. He had learned to contain himself these past months. Her invaluable aid, no doubt, her rotten honey.

He said, 'She has requested that, though I send a troop with her to guard her in our friendly woods, you, Skorous, do not go with them.'

'I see.'

'The reason which she gave was that, although there is no danger in the region at present, your love and spotless commitment to my well-being preclude you should be taken from my side.' He put the smile away and said, 'But possibly, too, she wishes to avoid your close company for so long, knowing as she must do you can barely keep your fingers from her throat. Did you know, Skorous,' he said, and now it was the old Draco, I seemed somehow to have hauled him back, 'that the first several months, I had her food always tasted. I thought you would try to see to her. I was so very astounded you never did. Or did you have some other, more clever plan, that failed?'

I swallowed the bile that had come into my mouth. I said, 'You forget, Sir, if I quit you I have no other battalion to go to. The Mother of Cities is dead. If I leave your warriors, I am nothing. I am one of the scores who blow about the world like dying leaves, soldiers' sons of the lost Empire. If there were an option, I would go at once. There is none. You've spat in my face, and I can only wipe off the spit.'

His eyes fell from me, and suddenly he cursed.

'I was wrong, Skorous. You would never have –'

'No, Sir. Never. Never in ten million years. But I regret you think I might. And I regret she thinks so. Once she was your wife, she could expect no less from me than I give one of your sisters.'

'*That bitch*,' he said, repeating for me my error, woman-like, 'her half-breed brat – damn you, Skorous. He's my son.'

'I could cut out my tongue that I said it. It's more than a year of holding it back before all others, I believe. Like vomit, Sir. I could not keep it down any longer.'

'Stop saying *Sir* to me. You call her *Domina*. That's sufficient.'

His eyes were wet. I wanted to slap him, the way you do a vicious stupid girl who claws at your face. But he was my prince, and the traitor was myself.

Presently, thankfully, he let me get out.

What I had said was true, if there had been any other life to go to that was thinkable – but there was not, any more. So, she would travel into the forest to heal, and I, faithful and unshakable, I would stay to guard him. And then she would come back. Year in and out, mist and rain, snow and sun. And bear him other brats to whom, in due course, I would swear my honour over. I had better practise harder, not to call her anything but *Lady*.

Somewhere in the night I came to myself and I knew. I saw it accurately, what went on, what was to be, and what I, so cunningly excluded, must do. Madness, they say, can show itself like that. Neither hot nor cold, with a steady hand, and every faculty honed bright.

The village with the sickness had sent its deputation to Draco yesterday. They had grand and blasphemous names for *her*, out there. She had said she must go, and at first light today would set out. Since the native villagers revered her, she might have made an arrangement with them, some itinerant acting as messenger. Or even, if the circumstance were actual, she would have been biding for such a chance. Or she herself had sent the malady to ensure it.

Her gods were the gods of her mystery. But the Semitic races have a custom ancient as their oldest altars, of giving a child to the god.

Perhaps Draco even knew – no, unthinkable. How then could she explain it? An accident, a straying, bears, wolves, the sickness after all ... And she could give him other sons. She was like the magic oven of the Khemian Art. Put in, take out. So easy.

I got up when it was still pitch black and announced to my body-slave and the man at the door I was off hunting, alone. There was already a rumour of an abrasion between the Prince and his Captain. Draco himself would not think unduly of it, Skorous raging through the wood, slicing pigs. I could be gone the day before he considered.

I knew the tracks pretty well, having hunted them since I was ten. I had taken boar spears for the look, but no dogs. The horse I needed, but she was forest-trained and did as I instructed.

I lay off the thoroughfare, like an old fox, and let the witch's outing come down, and pass me. Five men were all the guard she had allowed, a cart with travelling stuff, and her medicines in a chest. There was one of her women, the thickest in with her, I thought, Eunike, riding on a mule. And Zafra herself, in the litter between the horses.

When they were properly off, I followed. There was no problem in the world. We moved silently and they made a noise. Their horses and mine were known to each other and, where they snuffed a familiar scent, thought nothing of it. As the journey progressed, and I met here and there with some native in the trees, he hailed me cheerily, supposing me an outrider, a rear-guard. At night I bivouacked above them; at sunrise their first rustlings and throat-clearings roused me. When they were gone we watered at their streams, and once I had a burned sausage forgotten in the ashes of their cookfire.

The third day, they came to the village. From high on the mantled slope, I saw the greetings and the going in, through the haze of foul smoke. The village did have a look of ailing, something in its shades and colours, and the way the people moved about. I wrapped a cloth over my nose and mouth before I sat down to wait.

Later, in the dusk, they began to have a brisker look. The witch was making magic, evidently, and all would be well. The smoke condensed and turned yellow from their fires as the night closed in. When full night had come, the village glowed stilly, enigmatically, cupped in the forest's darkness. My mental wanderings moved towards the insignificance, the smallness, of any lamp among the great shadows of the earth. A candle against the night, a fire in winter, a life flickering in eternity, now here, now gone for ever.

But I slept before I had argued it out.

Inside another day, the village was entirely renewed. Even the rusty straw thatch glinted like gold. She had worked her miracles. Now would come her own time.

A couple of the men had kept up sentry-go from the first evening out, and last night, patrolling the outskirts of the huts, they had even idled a minute under the tree where I was roosting. I had hidden my mare half a mile off, in a deserted bothy I had found, but tonight I kept her near, for speed. And this night, too, when one of the men came up the slope, making his rounds, I softly called his name.

He went to stone. I told him smartly who I was, but when I came from cover, his sword was drawn and eyes on stalks.

'I'm no forest demon,' I said. Then I asked myself if he was alarmed for other reasons, a notion of the scheme Draco had accused me of. Then again, here and now, we might have come to such a pass. I needed a witness. I looked at the soldier, who saluted me slowly. 'Has she cured them all?' I inquired. I added for his benefit, 'Zafra.'

'Yes,' he said. 'It was – worth seeing.'

'I am sure of that. And how does the child fare?'

I saw him begin to conclude maybe Draco had sent me after all. 'Bonny,' he said.

'But she is leaving the village, with the child – ' I had never thought she would risk her purpose among the huts, as she would not in the town, for all her hold on them. 'Is that tonight?'

'Well, there's the old woman, she won't leave her own place, it seems.'

'So Zafra told you?'

'Yes. And said she would go. It's close. She refused the litter and only took Carus with her. No harm. These savages are friendly enough – '

He ended, seeing my face.

I said, 'She's gone already?'

'Yes, Skorous. About an hour –'

Another way from the village? But I had watched, I had skinned my eyes – pointlessly. Witchcraft could manage anything.

'And the child with her,' I insisted.

'Oh, she never will part from the child, Eunike says –'

'Damn Eunike.' He winced at me, more than ever uncertain. 'Listen,' I said, and informed him of my suspicions. I did not say the child was half East, half spice and glisten and sins too strange to speak. I said *Draco's son*. And I did not mention sacrifice. I said there was some chance Zafra might wish to mutilate the boy for her gods. It was well known, many of the Eastern religions had such rites. The soldier was shocked, and disbelieving. His own mother –? I said, to her kind, it was not a deed of dishonour. She could not see it as we did. All the while we debated, my heart clutched and struggled in my side, I sweated. Finally he agreed we should go to look. Carus was there, and would dissuade her if she wanted to perform such a disgusting act. I asked where the old woman's hut was supposed to be, and my vision filmed a moment with relief when he located it for me as that very bothy where I had tethered my horse the previous night. I said, as I turned to run that way, 'There's no old woman there. The place is a ruin.'

We had both won at the winter racing, he and I. It did not take us long to achieve the spot. A god, I thought, must have guided me to it before, so I knew how the land fell. The trees were densely packed as wild grass, the hut wedged between, and an apron of bared weedy ground about the door where once the household fowls had pecked. The moon would enter there, too, but hardly anywhere else. You could come up on it, cloaked in forest and night. Besides, she had lit her stage for me. As we pushed among the last phalanx of trunks, I saw there was a fire burning, a sullen throb of red, before the ruin's gaping door.

Carus stood against a tree. His eyes were wide and beheld nothing. The other man punched him and hissed at him, but Carus was far off. He breathed and his heart drummed, but that was all.

'She's witched him,' I said. Thank Arean Mars and Father Jupiter she had. It proved my case outright. I could see my witness thought this too. We went on stealthily, and stopped well clear of the tree-break, staring down.

Then I forgot my companion. I forgot the manner in which luck at last had thrown my dice for me. What I saw took all my mind.

It was like the oven of the hallucination in the tent, the thing she had made, yet open, the shape of a cauldron. Rough mud brick, smoothed and curved, and somehow altered. Inside, the fire burned. It had a wonderful colour, the fire, rubies, gold. To look at it did not seem to hurt the eyes, or dull them. The woman stood the other side of it, and her child in her grasp. Both appeared illumined into fire themselves, and the darkness of garments, of hair, the black gape of the doorway, of the forest and the night, these had grown warm as velvet. It is a sight often seen, a girl at a brazier or a hearth, her baby held by, as she stirs a pot, or throws on the kindling some further twig or cone. But in her golden arm the golden child stretched out his hands to the flames. And from her moving palm fell some invisible essence I could not see but only feel.

She was not alone. Others had gathered at her fireside. I was not sure of them, but I saw them, if only by their great height which seemed to rival the trees. A warrior there, his metal face-plate and the metal ribs of his breast just glimmering, and there a young woman, garlands, draperies and long curls, and a king who was bearded, with a brow of thunder and eyes of light, and near him another, a musician with wings starting from his forehead – they came and went as the fire danced and bowed. The child laughed, turning his head to see them, the deities of his father's side.

Then Zafra spoke the Name. It was so soft, no sound at all. And yet the roots of the forest moved at it. My entrails churned. I was on my knees. It seemed as though the wind came walking through the forest, to fold his robe beside the ring of golden red. I cannot recall the Name. It was not any of those I have written down, nor anything I might imagine. But it was the true one, and he came in answer to it. And from a mile away, from the heaven of planets, out of the pit of the earth, his hands descended and rose. He touched the child and the child was quiet. The child slept.

She drew Draco's son from his wrapping as a shining sword is drawn from the scabbard. She raised him up through the dark, and then she lowered him, and set him down in the holocaust of the oven, into the bath of flame, and the fires spilled up and covered him.

No longer on my knees, I was running. I plunged through black waves of heat, the amber pungence of incense, and the burning breath of lions. I yelled as I ran. I screamed the names of all the gods, and knew them powerless in my mouth, because I said them wrongly, knew them not, and so they would not answer. And then I ran against the magic, the Power, and broke through it. It was like smashing air. Experienced – inexperienceable.

Sword in hand, in the core of molten gold, I threw myself on, wading, smothered, and came to the cauldron of brick, the oven and dropped the sword and thrust in my hands and pulled him out –

He would be burned, he would be dead, a blackened little corpse, such as the Semite Karthaginians once made of their children, incinerating them in line upon line of ovens by the shores of the Inner Sea –

But I held in my grip only a child of jewel-work, of poreless perfect gold, and I sensed his gleam run into my hands, through my wrists, down my arms like scalding water to my heart.

Someone said to me then, with such gentle sadness, 'Ah Skorous. Ah, Skorous.'

I lay somewhere, not seeing. I said. 'Crude sorcery, to turn the child, too, into gold.'

'No,' she said. 'Gold is only the clue. For those things which are alive, laved by the flame, it is life. It is immortal and imperishable life. And you have torn the spell, which is all you think it to be. You have robbed him of it.'

And then I opened my eyes, and I saw her. There were no others, no Other, they had gone with the tearing. But she – she was no longer veiled. She was very tall, so beautiful I could not bear to look at her, and yet, could not take my eyes away. And she was golden. She was golden not in the form of metal, but as a dawn sky, as fire, and the sun itself. Even her black eyes – were of gold, and her midnight hair. And the tears she wept were stars.

I did not understand, but I whispered, 'Forgive me. Tell me how to make it right.'

'It is not to be,' she said. Her voice was a harp, playing through the forest. 'It is never to be. He is yours now, no longer mine. Take him. Be kind to him. He will know his loss all his days, all his mortal days. And never know it.'

And then she relinquished her light, as a coal dies. She vanished.

I was lying on the ground before the ruined hut, holding the child close to me, trying to comfort him as he cried, and my tears fell with his. The place was empty and hollow as if its very heart had bled away.

The soldier had run down to me, and was babbling. She had tried to immolate the baby, he had seen it. Carus had woken and seen it also. And, too, my valour in saving the boy from horrible death.

* * *

As one can set oneself to remember most things, so one can study to forget. Our sleeping dreams we dismiss on waking. Or, soon after.

They call her now, the Greek Woman. Or the Semite Witch. There has begun, in recent years, to be a story she was some man's wife, and in the end went back to him. It is generally thought she practised against the child and the soldiers of her guard killed her.

Draco, when I returned half-dead of the fever I had caught from the contagion of the ruinous hut – where the village crone had died, it turned out, a week before – hesitated for my recovery, and then asked very little. A dazzle seemed to have lifted from his sight. He was afraid at what he might have said and done under the influence of sorceries and drugs. 'Is it a fact, what the men say? She put the child into a fire?' 'Yes,' I said. He had looked at me, gnawing his lips. He knew of Eastern rites, he had heard out the two men. And, long, long ago, he had relied only on me. He appeared never to grieve, only to be angry. He even sent men to search for her: A bitch who would burn her own child – let her be caught and suffer the fate instead.

It occurs to me now that, contrary to what they tell us, one does not age imperceptibly, finding one evening, with cold dismay, the strength has gone from one's arm, the lustre from one's heart. No, it comes at an hour, and is seen, like the laying down of a sword.

When I woke from the fever, and saw his look, all imploring on me, the look of a man who has gravely wronged you, not meaning to, who says – But I was blind – that was the hour, the evening, the moment when life's sword of youth was removed from my hand, and with no protest I let it go.

Thereafter the months moved away from us, the seasons, and next the years.

Draco continued to look about him, as if seeking the evil Eye that might still hang there, in the atmosphere. Sometimes he was partly uneasy, saying he too had seen her dog, the black jackal. But it had vanished at the time she did, though for decades the woman Eunike claimed to meet it in the corridor of the women's quarters.

He clung to me, then, and ever since he has stayed my friend; I do not say, my suppliant. It is in any event the crusty friendship now of the middle years, where once it was the flaming blazoned friendship of childhood, the envious love of young men.

We share a secret, he and I, that neither has ever confided to the other. He remains uncomfortable with the boy. Now the princedom is larger, its borders fought out wider, and fortressed in, he sends him often away to the fostering of soldiers. It is I, without any rights, none, who love her child.

He is all Draco, to look at, but for the hair and brows. We have a dark-haired strain ourselves. Yet there is a sheen to him. They remark on it. What can it be? A brand of the gods (they make no reference, since she has fallen from their favour, to his mother). A light from within, a gloss, of gold. Leaving off his given name, they will call him for that effulgence more often, Ardorius. Already I have caught the murmur that he can draw iron through stone, yes, yes, they have seen him do it, though I have not. (From Draco they conceal such murmurings, as once from me.) He, too, has a look of something hidden, some deep and silent pain, as if he knows, as youth never does, that men die, and love, that too.

To me, he is always courteous, and fair. I can ask nothing else. I am, to him, an adjunct of his life. I should perhaps be glad that it should stay so.

In the deep nights, when summer heat or winter snow fill up the forest, I recollect a dream, and think how I robbed him, the child of gold. I wonder how much, how much it will matter, in the end.

The Lancastrian Blush

> Sad and sooth sad, my heart lies dead,
> On Bosworth Field.
> Rent is the White Rose, bleeding red,
> On Bosworth Field.
> Who plucks the last flower from the bush,
> Bring it him woe and worse,
> From Bosworth Field.

He dreamed a dream of women, in the moon's round eye. They were shadows, yet he saw, not seeing, their faces and their narrow hands: One old, the Hag, moon at her wane, one Courtesan and Wife, a harvest, the moon at full. The last was a girl, a slim, summer crescent in her light yellow gown. They sang in a grove that was out of time. Their song chilled him for he was a man, though not the man on the sharp-baited line of their spell.

He woke with the sun at the brim of the window, to bird-song and vague anger, forgot the dream, and thought a moment of Black Richard in Leicester town.

The Lion days were passing into the shadier late August house of the Maiden, but little odds. The weather had been strange all summer. Master Cornelius had said, however, the sun would shine for the battle tomorrow. And that, one supposed, was a good omen for somebody. Today, there would probably be a storm.

He had paused on the brow of a hill, the young man still bearing the name of another man not his father. And from this vantage, of geography and confused lineage, he stared down the sweep of land that ran now before him in a rippling map, due south to Leicester.

Cloud came and went across the sky above Henry Dacey, and mirrored in purple banners, sheets of bleached amber light on the uplands and valleys. Armies massing in heaven, as on earth . . . Well, let that be for now. It was enough to get to the meeting-place by sunset, collect the batch of men who were to be his for a morning's work, and who had marched there under his father's orders. His real father, that was. Something of a problem there, or a jest, depending on how one regarded these things. When you had, actually, only known your 'father' was nothing of the sort for just three months. Remember the scene. Yes, that was easy. Your mother ashy to the lips, wondering if you would turn and yell *Whore* at her. Your not-father sheepish, waiting to see if you reckoned him a pander (and what else was he, by God?). And then this bloody brand-new father bursting from the undergrowth, strutting about the hall of his manor, this lord, prepared to like and claim you on a whim, and: 'Well, Harry, you've turned out a fine boy,' and 'Well, Harry, the Bend Sinister's no shame; plenty bear it with pride.' Because you had been judged, at eighteen years of age, worth telling at last. By God and All Angels.

For the rest of it, the allegiance had always been the wrong one, and now he was the lord's bastard it was still wrong. All Harry's life they had been factious for Lancaster, the Red Rose, while the dynasty of the White Rose of York held England in its snowy fist. Out of favour then, keeping quiet and careful, poor as mice. And now a Lancastrian lord's by-blow into the bargain. And then this – to top all. War tomorrow. War with the anointed King, Richard, the White Boar. And for whose sake? The lank lorn Welshman, Tudor, himself a Henry and himself out of a bastard line. Harry had had chances to watch that curd-colour mask-like face in France, and not like it.

Then again, Richard, a man who murdered young children, was not to one's taste, either.

There was a *Holla*! behind him. Harry turned and viewed Cat come galloping up on his rabbit-hued horse.

'I never thought to catch you yet, Harry. I'd thought you would get on faster far than this.'

Cat, fourteen but – soul-wise – older, scolded him. It was true, they were not making a proper pace. There had since setting out been a variety of minor excuses and necessities for stopping. Harry had availed himself of all. A few miles back, he had sent Cat on a detour to a farm for bread and fruit, and idled to let the lad come up. It should have been more of a helter-skelter course. Now they walked the horses down through the blown blown-rose cloud shadows, eating the berries and apples, drinking the wine, as on the way to a maypole or a wedding.

Cat gave up scolding on the third pippin. Harry was in a Harry Mood, fey and silly, only to be made worse by chivvying.

Harry himself knew it. He picked wild flowers and stuck them in his crimson hat. His clothes were part of the mood. A foolish notion at sun-up, but not to be denied – to dress all red for the Red Rose, when one had guessed that part of the battle plan was to be secrecy and desertion. The real father had commitments to the pack which had promised Richard its staunchest support, and meant to fling its power on to the other side at the most propitious moment. Not privy to the strategy, deducing it, Harry had winced. Now he had dipped himself in Lancaster's colour and rode like a blot of blood towards Leicester. Not that it definitely mattered. It was only a personal thing. Like hating one's true father and longing to push the teeth down the throat of the fake.

'Rain,' said Cat, as they trotted their horses up from the next valley.

'No.'

'Yes.'

'Yes,' Harry agreed as Heaven spat in his eye.

The wind lifted ten minutes later. They pushed the horses into a run and the wind thrust them, perpendicular, over a bumpy gorsy hill, long hair, horse-tails, all blowing back to front. The sky darkened to a bruise. The rain exploded; arrows, shot. They thundered through thunder and up and across the hill and down through walnut trees and into a copse of green may and out.

'God's Life, a sea!' called Cat, as they crashed through a mad stream that flashed to their knees, rain also falling back to front, and realised the rain itself, summer storm, was done.

'But look,' said Harry. And they looked and saw the storm rolling about them on four hill-tops around, and a lightning like a silver skewer, stabbing in and out.

Here, in the storm's cup, they sat in the may trees and the stream, the dry sun coming down to them through a tunnel in the cloud.

'Magic,' said Cat.

'And there, a magic castle.'

Beyond the trees and the water was a wall, but it was broken. The ivy and the flowers rioting over it and down into emerald moss at the water's edge, had made it partly invisible. Now it seemed to Henry Dacey that the more he believed the wall was there, the more postively there it became. And beyond the wall, the stand of willows with lights plaited in their branches. And through the willows glimpses, that a wish would make a garden and a house of fawn brick.

'Whose manor is this?'

'Someone's. Come on,' said Cat.

'No, no. It's some enchanted place –' the dreamer struck a pose.

'No time,' said Cat. 'Southward, my sir. No *time* for this.'

'All the time,' said Harry. And laughing, he sent the Lancaster-red roan horse flying at the broken wall and cleared it, and went between the willows and found the garden, where he should not be, and where dogs might be set on him for being. And let you wait, my daddy. And let the traitor Stanleys wait. And butcher-handed Richard, the Hog of York. And Master Cornelius astrologer's bright day for a battle. And Market bloody Bosworth.

The girl, standing at her mirror of metal, saw her own slender ghost – and little more. Familiar with herself intimately, she would not really recognise herself by sight. The ghost was all she had ever seen. By primal instinct, unvoiced, she sensed she might be fair. She did not know.

Her own white slenderness, however, this she did glance at, to appreciate in her own fashion, innocently. The slim pale hands and feet, the throat and breast smooth to the touch. Those near her had always told her, her eyes were large; grey eyes, perhaps the shade of the mirror itself. Unbound, her hair fell to her ankles, a great mass of hair but fine as mist, the colour of moonlight, or no colour. The colour of the chaplet of white roses the women had yet to weave, mysteriously smiling, to place on her head. Crowned for the Maiden, the imminent ninth station of the zodiac. And she, Elsabet, virgin, early-September born, fitting symbol of this time, the will and the way.

The whole manor secretly hummed and pulsated with its knowledge. It was like the drone of bees, permeating the summer days, once lazy, now stressed and poised, a bird in the instant before flight.

The analogy was apt. A white pigeon flew across the open casement. Elsabet and the women glanced at it. One of the women, glancing on into the garden, let out a cry.

Down there, in the dark green arteries between the hedges of box, a splash of blood. The dire augury spilled across the web the manor had been weaving, unconscionable.

'Who is it?'

'None of ours.'

'Some traveller – trespasser – my lord must be told – '

Already the door flung wide, a page sent scurrying to her father, footsteps, the whip of dresses on the stair down to the solar.

Not yet crowned with her diadem, the white girl almost still only that, leaned from her window. She watched the crimson creature as it hesitantly moved. Yes, it might seem strange to him, the stranger.

He was nearer now, staring about, but not upward to her window. She saw, unseen, his face.

He was handsome and young, tall among the carved green hedges, on the brink of the inner garden. He held his hat in his hand. Not only the garments red, but the hair, like red chestnuts. Tanned and vibrant in his clothes of blood, he must be kept from the white garden beyond the green. He must come no further.

But already he advanced, stepped through. He wounded the white garden.

The simmering vibrating peace of the manor stirred, and shuddered. The sorcerous bird fluttered a warning wing.

Or was it that her heart had stopped? (Silken, the drum of throat to her fingers, and the drum within hammering fast as if with terror.)

And Elsabet beheld her father's men run out through the door towards the wound of fire, to staunch it.

Yes, he was surprised. An enchanted castle? For sure. Beyond the wall and the willow trees, the pleasure walks through palisades of box, and the marchpane perfume of the flowers. And then the little gateway in the green and a garden of winter in the storm-ringed sunny August light.

There was a patch of pleached bleached stones. On either side, a lawn. These lawns were white. Clovers and daisy flowers made up the turf, so fantastically thick there was no blade of green to be found. Above the lawn the roses grew, white on black stems, like clumps of snow. Their leaves were gone. Behind the roses, white stone. The eyes blurred. Look away. There, a sundial, made of salt. At length, relief – tawny brick, a door of dark timber, but a white hound seated there, made of stone, or of ice; it did not move.

No, it was not uncanny, any of this. And yet, it was not worldly, either.

He entered it, open mind lured by unfriendly perfection, immaculacy, while the horse insolently ate the green lawn at his back. White enclosed Harry Dacey. He drowned in the scent of white roses, *white* scent, and expected to stifle or faint, or drop down at least, drunk and laughing-crazy. Then the timber door burst wide.

They poured around the white statuary hound, the five or six who ran at him. Now there would be trouble. Yet even trouble came fantastically.

Each man was dressed from crown to heel in – white. Shoes, hose, doublet, shirt – white. And the pale skin, winter skin, night skin. And fair-haired, every man. The splash of a jewel-drop in the sun was a pearl, a diamond. Albino gems.

Startled, he looked over his shoulder, back down the aisles of summer green, where the world was, and saw Cat coming at a scramble with the rabbit-hue horse. Your eyes ached when you put them again into the blanch of the inner garden.

But the men were close. They circled him. Pale hands to the hilts of paler swords.

A pale *rich* house. The blank jewels were many and the silver tracery abundant as frost.

Harry Dacey nodded.

'Your wall is down,' he said. 'I've no apology of worth. I'm a lout. Do you kill for discourtesy, here?'

'There's rebellion not fifteen miles away,' one of them said.

Rebellion. Ah, there was the clue.

'I'm on my way,' Harry murmured, 'to fight for the king.'

'Who is your lord?'

'Why, Richard Plantagenet.'

'Whose is your party?'

Careful now. They were York. By the Arms of God, what else could they be with the white roses thick as bog cotton, blinding the eyes, and the lungs with scent.

Harry named his true father. 'He is with the lords Stanley, for the present. But he mistrusts Stanley. As who would not, with such ties to the vile Tudor Dragon?' Neatly spoken, Harry. A silk purse made from a Hog's ear. But not out of the pickle yet, it seemed. They looked Hell at him, cold ice-hell. Harry let loose his charm, smoothed them with a smile. Said, engagingly, prepared to be a comrade, 'And do you go to fight with Dickon?' Silence. My, my. Surely not affronted by the use of Richard's pet name? Employed by the commons in every ale-house and brothel of the land. Those that loved him, named him like lover, brother, friend. (Dickon, killer of children, poisoner of frail women, *monster*.) There was already another name coined, Harry had heard it. A black imp, a devil, sat on Richard's shoulder, his familiar. This, setting its talons into him like roots, now grew there and must be hidden under his shirt, giving him, nevertheless, a deformed shape. So the name: Crookback. He was straight, of course. If there was an imp, it was invisible.

'Yes, we fight,' one of the white Yorkists said suddenly. 'Not on the ground you –'

And another rapped out: '*Garde*! He needs not know it yet.'

Harry stood, fascinated, annoyed, uneasy, drugged by roses, dizzying.

Cat had come near with the horses. One or both beasts would now defecate on the clover-lawn and daggers would be out, and God knew what.

The manor, the things, the persons of the manor, were insane. This one already knew.

They discussed matters. No, the visitor must not yet depart. He must meet the master of the house, take refreshment. (That had a sinister sound.) Cat caught his eye. Could they try a break for safety? *No, Cat.* Cat glared.

Presently boys came for the horses, and Cat was taken off, too. *Sorry, Cat.* Cat cast at him one final thirty-year-old scowl.

Harry grinned and bowed to his hosts as they ushered him in.

It had been irresistible. One could not be blamed, arrested by lunatic Yorkists, maybe to be dispatched, if one were not canny – no, they would never go so far.

But he would be late to the meeting tonight. Unless the manor were out of time, resting in some shell where a day lasted a hundred years, or only a single second.

Fate binds me, thought Harry, parody of a King's blazon.

The timber door closed behind him.

The manor's lord entered the solar and found his guest gazing, which was no wonder. One did wonder how sensitive might be this intruder, to the aura of the house. Had it even drawn him here in his red? Was this young knight some pawn of the chessgame that was about to begin, undreamed of, across miles of country, the axis of the board a battlefield, the prize: England, history, and peace?

'Good day,' said the lord. 'I see you mistrust our wine. There's no wolfsbane, no hemlock in it, I assure you. Nothing but the grape.'

'But not a red wine,' said Harry. 'Of course.'

He bowed again, courtly, magnificent. The adventure pleased him. He had needed it.

The solar had been no shock, it would have shocked Harry to find it otherwise. White draperies, a tapestry of silver and pastel, white stone for the fireplace – lucky they did not need the red heresy of a fire. Even the rushes underfoot were thick with white, sweet-smelling flowers. He had poured out a drop of the pale gold wine on them to see if it banefully sizzled.

This lord – they had offered no more title or name than that – wore his long white gown trimmed with white brocade of another tint, and an air of conscious humour, it must be added. His hair was faded black, unlike the hair of his blond liegemen. The face was hard with years and learning, but not with particular spite.

'You were on your way to the service of Richard, then,' said this lord and master. He took a cup of wine from the white-clad server, then waved him out. 'Let's drink,' said the white lord, 'to the triumph of the Boar.'

They drank to it.

(Do I perjure myself, invite the wrath of the battle-god? What do I know? Tomorrow I may turn my handful of men for Richard's banner after all. That would vex my *father*.)

'Sit down,' said the lord. Harry sat in one of the carved chairs and stretched his long red legs, his red feet, in the white petals. 'Now tell me why you came here.'

'To my disgrace, a schoolboy fit, a wish of my horse – we jumped the broken wall. No reason and no excuse. You treat me far too nicely in my fault.'

'No, we do not treat you nicely. I regret, sir, now you are in, you stay.' The voice had remained mild and courteous. There was no whisper of menace as the man appended: 'Our prisoner. Until tomorrow is well past.'

Harry laughed.

'A fair joke, my lord, and well-deserved by me.'

'No joke.'

Harry saw he must pretend to some strong emotion. Outrage?

96

'My lord, I'm bound for the battle. What of my men, my honour –'

'You dallied here. I think your command is small, nor do you hanker for it. No, I don't call you coward, sir, but I surmise, like many in this fray, you are uncertain where your power should be spent.'

'My father –'

'Yes. I know of your father. Though he will no doubt miss your person, the field will hardly miss the little captaincy he gave you. If any debts remain, they can be settled when war is done.'

Harry rose, strode about, slapped his gloves, spilled more wine.

'This will not do, my lord.'

'It will do very well. We shall see you comfortable, never dread.'

'And my honour?'

'What of it? In your heart you hoped never to get there. So, you will not. Be thankful.'

Henry Dacey sat down again. He stared into nothing and saw his wretched unfather at the burly crowing of his true sire. He saw the sour waxy sly murderer's face of Henry Tudor, and dark Richard Plantagenet, who did not have the face of a murderer at all.

'Well,' said Harry. His mind urged him: lull them, you may get away. His heart – found out – hoping *not* to get away, sighed as if sleeping. 'Well, but what goes on here?'

His lordly jailor watched him, a long while. Proudly now, rudely, Harry returned this scrutiny.

'Do you feel nothing of what goes on?' was inquired of him eventually.

Harry shrugged. Certainly he felt . . . something. Ever-present, permeating, yet distant. Like the sound of the sea. It had beckoned him in, perhaps, in to drown in waters of pearl and milk. The undertow. Witchcraft.

'Witchcraft,' said Harry quietly. 'Do I need to be a scholar to guess that?'

'Evidently, you need merely your own good faculties to guess. Trust your heart, it will guide you.'

'Ah, it guided me ill today.'

'That's possible. For I think our adversaries sent you, though you never knew it.'

'And who are your adversaries, my lord? I take it you don't refer to Tudor?'

'Tomorrow,' said the lord, 'that plain by Bosworth will be the battleboard. But we, sir, fight here, in this house, as hard as any fight there with the sword or axe. You may have heard, witchcraft is prevalent in England. That tribe of the Wydvilles and the Greys, ever the enemies of the King – ever witches, man, woman and child of them. Yes, even the daughter, Elizabeth, Richard's niece from his brother's loins.'

'I heard, too, after he poisoned his marriage-partner, Anne, the Boar would have had that Elizabeth unlawfully to wife,' said Harry boldly. 'Maybe she had some cause to strive against him.'

'Against him she did strive, but to have him, not to hold him off. She would be his queen and the Greys would have her queen, one of their own again in power. They, not he, moved to harm Anne, and killed her with their arts. A seduction followed. Yes, he fell from grace with Elizabeth. So they got their grip on him; it can be done by means of such. By love, even of that sort. And she a virgin, and beautiful, and close in blood. Yes, a great spell they made from that, like a spider's web. But they did not get back their hold on England's crown, he did not surrender that. So they would come to it another way, wedding their bitch to the Tudor dog when once they have helped him to the height. Through this night, and through tomorrow's sun, they will be at their work. And we, at work against them.' The white lord drew a long, noiseless breath. 'Who wins, is with God. But you, my firedrake, won't shake us from it.'

Stunned now, Harry said, 'I, how could I –'

'It may be the blind will of their sorcery sent you here, a leaf blown in the storm, some element of chaos. You see how our magic is laid, magic of image and symbol, the flawless white of the White Rose, that Richard of York may gain victory. And you, blood-red for Lancaster, and Tudor's scarlet Dragon.'

Harry stayed still. He remembered the sunrise in the window and the song of the birds, and the daft notion to dress all in red –

He faltered. Then he said:

'Keep me, then. I no longer know where my loyalty lies. Is Richard a fiend? Is a battle to depend on witches? God forfend.'

'Not the first battle to rest so. And Richard's no fiend. A slandered man is Richard.'

And Harry burst out, 'And those two children in the Tower – his brother's sons – the royal bastards –'

'Alive. Unless the Dragon sets his claws to them.'

Harry stood up again. Fear scuttled somewhere inside him. Not fear of detention, but fear that his world stood on its ear, had always done so, and only now did he notice the tilt.

'Well,' he said, frivolously, 'here's my sword. Confine me.'

They confined him. The guest apartment over the buttery became his prison, a light and an airy one. There were all the appurtenances for his comfort. The bed was white. The bed-curtains, tied back on the stout posts, white.

The window was generous, with crystal, somewhat wavered panes. It looked south, to Leicester town, where he would never get.

They locked the door, making no bones. He sensed the door was also sealed in other ways.

It was a time of symbols. To hem in and confine the red flower of a young man's strength and duty – a symbol too, and fair.

Food was left. White food. The breast of a chicken, wan bread, a syllabub of tinctured cream . . .

He looked out of the window to the combers of the hills which held this place in a cup, as the storm had held it. The storm was done. A mackerel sky with humours of gold, promising fine for the morrow, Master Cornelius, as you said. How my mother wept when I left home. She was afraid I would perish, now I knew all, and end loathing her.

Suddenly, he felt like weeping himself, did laughing Harry. He pushed the casement wide and breathed the still, warm air. The sun was low. Soon the west would all be red, red for Lancaster, and his shame – the men unmet, the die uncast. Culpable, if I willed it. What of witches, the perfidious Wydvilles, Greys; say it was only my dawdling undesire.

The Red Rose and the White. Blood and snow, fire and ice.

He drank the wine and dozed and dreamed of Tudor's scarlet Dragon bellowing on the hills.

Then, in the dream, turning, saw night, and women like shadows at some curious deed in a grove of leaden trees. All was grey, starlight and mist, and mantles, and the fall of an old woman's hair – grey for the Greys, the Wydvilles, the tribe of witches.

Born of the Wydville clan, the allies of Lancaster, one of these women had wed Grey, but Grey had died. Thereafter it was Edward, England's King, she married. But that marriage was a sham, the King being joined elsewhere. On Edward's death, this had taken the crown from her son, and given it to Richard. She, and hers, they had some cause to hate kind Dickon. And she was wise in hatred, it seemed. In the grove, the silver flicker of a knife, like the lightning on the hill, the shriek of some small thing as it died, presage of greater deaths.

Even in the dream, then, it seemed he had had the dream before.

Beyond the grove, through a fog of leaves, a girl was walking. Her gown was the colour of a yellow plum, a yellow summer moon, sweet in the sunlight there beyond the night. She held a skein of long black hair in her hand, man's hair – the hair of Richard her uncle – and she sang to it, telling it what would be. But Harry could not hear, and he was glad of that.

He turned again, from day, through night, to day, and saw the scarlet lizard rampaging – but it was only a cloud dyed in the sunfall, and he had woken.

When he woke, everything was changed.

He leapt up, cursing himself for a fool, swordless, witless. He flung himself on the door, rattling it, roaring. No one answered. The door did not give. He fell to pacing, speaking aloud. Not merely a fool, a dupe. Richard the Swine, due to be slaughtered, was owed no second thought. And these wild sorcerers must have spelled Harry Dacey, too, to make him docile such a while. His father would disown him once more. He would lose everything through this, all he might have had.

The sky was a ruby now in the open window. A shard of flame lay over the room, staining the ivory bed, flushing to fever the pallor of the walls.

He would not consider the dream. (Twice-dreamed?) There might have been drugs in the wine, if not poison.

He went back to the window for the air, fearing a miasma of enchantment. Bathed in red light, he looked at burning sky, and down the curve of the hills, into an orchard there below the house.

In the tree shadow, a girl was walking, seeming to sing . . . enough like the dream he would not consider, that he cursed again. But then, not like at all. This girl was part of the *waking* dream, dressed in white, her hair so pale and long he took it for a veil, then understood it was not, and marvelled. Fey, she was. Fey and beautiful. Unseen, he saw her, her whiteness in the red.

Then he thought to shout.

'Maiden,' he bawled, down the upper storey, over the buttery's slant, across the wall, to the apple trees. 'Damsel! Angel! Sweetheart!'

She caught the cry, and looked at once straight up at him. In an instant, then, from that swiftness alone, somehow he knew she had seen him earlier, (seen, unseen, crimson in snow), and that she had been thinking of him now, poor captive in his tower . . .

Who else might have heard the cry was moot. To shout again, too, would cost his throat something. He waved his hands: desperation. Rolled his eyes: passion.

She stood, pale and still. She did nothing.

'Help!' he shouted. And then, wasting lungs and voice, from France, an old song in mind: '*Hareu! M'aides, douce anemie!*' And laughed again, wildly, at the absurdity of all this.

To walk in the sunset and murmur songs of love, it should not be, on this eve. The colourless roses had been cut, were woven this very hour to crown her for the ritual. Maiden and new moon. Hope.

But Elsabet's mind had strayed, as her footsteps strayed. She did not know where they had lodged him. Perhaps reason had told her it would not be in the guest apartment, but deeper, in the store or cellars under the house, a proxy dungeon. Or, reason may have known they would not dishonour him so. The room above the buttery it would be, where, if he gazed out, he might see her pass.

She had not, though, imagined he would call to her. No, never that.

She turned, looked, saw his splendour of hair, and the merry, good, laughing face, gorgeous in male beauty, gilded – haloed – from the tumbling of the sun.

Henry, he was named. A lord's bastard. Due to be rich and landed, if, after tomorrow, he lived. But he would live. Mured up here he could not risk himself in battle.

And what now? Help, he cried, come to my aid, gentle enemy.

She stood in her portion of shadow, looking up at his light, as if the sun rose again in the window. She knew this must not be. This day, the night, the dawn to come, were sacred.

Yet, she did not really understand it. They had shown her what must be shown, lessoned her in her part. But it was like the metal mirror. The revelation was dim, and did not tell enough. She knew, and did not know.

This she knew, the happy days had already been chased away, the season without care, when she had been loved and fussed, sweet Betsi, pretty Bet, her father's doll, and herself all joy in everything, seeming free as the sky. Now this sombre season came, and she was grown, and they trained her in ice, cool, so cool now she seemed sometimes to herself a stone, like the white beast at the garden door. Even this training she had never questioned. Till today.

It was true, she had begun to dream of some lover, faceless and rare, her future. He had no name, no house. She was ignorant of him. Asleep, sometimes he had walked with her. Waking, she had sobbed for loss, not knowing what the loss might be. And her visions were abstract and pure, for she was innocent. There had never been lessons in love.

So, the first lesson was harsh. It slapped her heart and shouted *See!*

Still she stared up into his fire, the salamander in the window. But the glow and glory went from him. Anger clouded his face, then even as the sun itself went under the hill, the dusk of pain and misery put out his smile and his rage alike. He turned from day, from window, and from sight of her. She knew he had cursed her, bleakly, foully, though she did not hear the words.

Elsabet was smitten. Her heart at least fell to its knees. Her careful moulding kept her pale and quiet. She thought, *Ah, no, no, my lord, my gentle enemy. Do not judge me so.*

She walked through the orchard, she passed from tree to tree, under the arch of stone with its nets of ivy and untamed rose. She stood at the house corner as the shadows flowed like deep water over the hills, and night came in on a tide. She truly did not realise her goal until she passed on to the inner stair behind the buttery. Even then, amazement neither stayed her nor pushed her on. She walked only steadily as if some string reeled her in. She reached the heavy door, locked, garlanded with the by-now-familiar tingle of much subtler locks, the bounds of magic. No guard was set. No man could be spared, each one a part of the night's patterning. And she, already they would look for her on the far side of the house. There was little time to be disgraced.

Her fingers smote the door, so fragile he would never hear them. But he heard. She in her turn heard the stifled oath, one footstep clear, and then the voice – his, imperative with its anxiety: 'So you repent. Let me out then.'

'Alas,' said Elsabet, 'I may not.'

'Oh God!' he shouted. Again a laugh, again rage, these special for his dealings with her. 'You, the white maiden from the apples?'

'I am Elsabet,' she said. 'My father would quarrel with me, if he knew that I was here.'

'Your father, the lord –'

She heard now how he waited for a name.

'I shan't tell you that. Nor set you free. For this I came to ask forgiveness. It's cruel to pen you so –'

'Worse than cruel, lady. Everything I may get or be rocks on this venture.'

'A King's destiny rocks there, also.'

'Damn the King. What of me?'

Horrified, she caught her breath. Through timber and spell she felt him sorry for the abuse.

'Pardon me that,' he said. 'But my state is a sorry one. If I fail the battle I'll get nothing. I'll be penniless, landless, an oaf with no true name. No rescue, then. But at least, pity me.'

'I do,' she said. 'If the law in this house were mine, you should be let go, no matter what.'

Silence. Then words against the timber, warmer, at her very ear.

'*Douce* enemy. For that, my thanks. When I have nothing, robbed of it by your father, this untitled lord, who also robs me of my chance to fight for Richard – in the wretched aftermath, I'll have at least the comfort of your memory. Your beauty and your goodness, Elsabet.'

When he spoke her name, it became a thing of wonder. She leaned one side of the door, sensing the strength and heat of him that leaned against her, only the wood between, and listened to the echo of her marvellous name. She had had no lesson in love but this. But he, Harry Dacey, had had several. He knew, striving for survival now, how to speak a girl's name.

'Elsabet, Elsabet, *fleur de cœur* – I don't understand your work tonight, nor how it runs – but if you have space, visit me again. Give me that much solace in my ruin.'

'No, I may not.'

Ah, so soft you barely hear her now.

'Then, if your witchery lets you pray, spare me one orison.'

Elsabet closed her eyes. And sensed at once a sharp dark ripple cutting through the swooning pond of love, intention seeking her across the house.

'I must go,' she said. She tore herself with agony from the door, as if her flesh had grown to it and now was ripped.

'Promise – one prayer.'

'I – promise it.'

'And Elsabet?'

'Oh, what?'

'I ask only that you consider what imprisonment loses me. I suggest merely this: if, by first light, your sorcerous designs are sure, could there be harm to let me free? With my willing horse, I might be at the place by mid-morning. Join the rout of the Dragon's rabble. Undishonoured. Consider it, Elsabet; sweet Betsi, consider. And how I must – *love* you for your sympathy.'

He heard her run away, her small shoes like a patter of white hail.

And night shut the window.

Night, black night, holding the English earth. Summer almost done, autumn almost come. One time giving place to another. And on the loom, the thread, running, blood and snow, heat or coolness, Red Rose and White. Which way shall the garment finish and fall?

From over the water, the sallow Welshman, winged with his Dragon, so auspiciously red it stirs the old savour, the rose-red splendour of Harry the Fifth, Agincourt, France brought home in a sack. See just the banner, not the dry drab thing riding inland under it. Careful and cunning, Tudor like a beetle, slinking with his pack of Breton curs, the sweepings and leavings of another land, here to get him England whose tongue they do not speak.

Not lying soft or sound this night, this black night, Henry Tudor, on the plain that may tomorrow drink your watery blood. Bad dreams, my boyo, in your scruffy tent there, hard against the flank of destiny.

Bad dreams, but not so bad as Richard's dreams, troubled by witches to be set upon by ghosts. Dreaming of enemies slain in other wars, lipless, eyeless, crying round the dark, or those killed by policy since, living, they would have had your life instead, or lives of those you love, but they forget that. All these, a crowd, a *celebration mors* inside the cold pavilion of unsleep. There your traitor brother George, come wine-wet to upbraid you. There Hastings, second Judas, bloody-necked, his head set on askew in his hasting haste to visit you. And here two boys, your nephews, weeping that you murdered them in the Tower, though you have not, the figments of the popular myth – they live and thrive, yet here they are, smothered and stabbed, howling. And then, worst of all, the pangs of guilt, the lies, Anne in her silver shroud, her skin palest blue as moonlight, hair like embers. Oh, you did not love me enough, my Dickon, my love, to let me go down into the chill, still grave alone, and not to lie with me in death as in lust. You did not love me, love.

And so in the corner there, Elizabeth, your brother's child, sweet Eve, your fall, grinning as you sweat and writhe trying to wake, unwoken. And under her rosy body, the White Boar, the spear between its ribs.

And there, beyond all others, over the rim of night, the voices singing the lullaby obitus, the witches' incantation. Driven in like an iron nail, by force of repetition, in and in, and in and in –

> Richard, Richard,
> Bitter his bread.
> Richard, Richard,
> Despair his sup.
>
> Richard, Richard,
> Edgeless his sword.
> Richard, Richard,
> Death his hap.

Fractured and moiled, the night moans too, twisting to be free, be gone.

Tomorrow must come. The garment must fall finished. And a winter of red roses . . .

Cat, who had been struggling for some two hours, came on the knife, and curled by it, exhausted. He was too spent as yet to start in on the second exercise, that of sawing at his bonds. They had tied him well, if not painfully. Indeed, they were curious bonds, which, left to themselves, were little discomfort, but which, when struggled against, drew tight, gnawing and grinding to the very bone – magic. God's peace!

He might have lain all night where they had put him, luxurious enough with cushions, ale and bread to hand without stretching. There had seemed no choice. He had resigned himself with fortitude, only bothered for Harry's remorse, and Harry's person secured elsewhere.

Then, the girl came, lovely and weird, like some being from a star. Her face was whiter than her gown – from one of the long sleeves of which she took a sliver of metal and showed him. No words. She laid the tiny blade where he could come at it, with great and determined effort, rolling and contorting against the biting bonds, all across the storeroom. And next the knife she placed a key. Then she did speak.

'No man guards the stables. No man guards the room above the buttery.'

Cat stammered thanks and accusation, viewing the long agonised rotations he would have, past urns of flour and hills of spice.

'Is it a game, lady?'

'No. To delay you.'

'Oh, and it has.'

Now, his hands and feet squeezed numb, the blood thumping like hammer strokes in groin and temples, Cat lay retching and part dead, waiting just to be able to feel the knife, and the key, against his flesh, before he should use them.

Above, the house was full of soundless noise. Like a huge dumb church it seemed to pulse and hymn. Till this, on his progress of penance, he had scarcely noted it. Now it prickled his spine. Too much sorcery here. Best be gone. He set to chafing one foot, one hand, on its neighbour.

And that silver Virgo, on the steps . . . What had she whispered? *'Tell him it was I freed you.'*

Yes, mistress. Cat grit his teeth at the hurt of resumed blood. I *thank* you. There would be an hour's sawing yet to do.

The hall of the manor was white, whiter than the white garden, the solar, the guest-prison on the upper storey. By the white walls the white standards were upraised thick as a wood, the emblem of a white beast, maybe a hound, on a ground two shades darker white. White sand lay on the floor, there were no rushes, but mingled in the sand, the flowers, the Yorkist roses crushed so the air sang with their scent. In their sconces of silver, the fat cream candles bloomed, sun-tipped.

The company stood as it had stood since the hour after sunset, in its bloodless doublets, mantles, gowns, its starched rime veiling like the wings of frozen butterflies. Figures of chalk.

The vigil was kept. Their lord was its captain, standing before them all. He did not falter. At certain times he threw the incense in its silver bowl, he described the esoteric motions of the ritual. At other times he, or another, spoke. For any might speak, or cry out, at will, provided it were on one theme.

In the first three hours, a woman was faint, but revived. She returned to sustain her ground, and the fabric of will did not give way.

They knew their task and had long practised it. By now their concentration was quite tangible, thick as clear aspic in the wide room whose windows held ebony, the Moorish face of darkness – black as

Richard's hair, or black as Richard's hurt. His soul, clean as their whiteness, unspotted. So they said, and so they fashioned it.

What they willed and wanted – that was simple enough. Richard's life to continue, against the Dragon's failure. The dragon which was also a rose. While other sorceries toothed and mauled the night with malignant wishes for York's downfall into Hell, these here spun their web of snow, sympathetic magic, a wall against all such venomous waters, such barbs of jealous hate.

On the dais, last focus of this bastion, three women also stood, in the candles' shine.

One was old, a grandmother: the Crone. Another was winsome, bonny; under her high girdle was the lilted swell of life-to-come: the nubile Wife. Third was a Virgin, with hair to her shoes, hair like the candlesmoke. Elsabet, crowned with white roses. Elsabet, jewelled with her chastity, intact and closed, fount of a mystery, the better mirror of that other, sister – named, Elizabeth – whose seals were gone.

Elsabet, the inner centre of the weave. Little and lovesome and fair.

Her eyes were lidded, her will flowed out with theirs. She was their symbol, she the key that locked the chink of the white wall's door. She had not altered. No. She had not run to him, the crimson rose, the loud blood of sex and mortality ablaze in the icicle's core. She had given him nothing, save a dubious escape, its timing all delayed. The new symbol of Harry Dacey's red freedom would come too late to meddle with the Power of the White.

A little after three in the morning, as Cat scratched more frenziedly with his needle of blade in the storeroom below, the flies in white amber stood on at their woof and weft, and an ectoplasm rose out of the loom.

There was a sighing cry, that brought Elsabet from her trance. She gazed up and beheld, between floor and roof, the astral visitation of a host. Drawn in dark film there were the shapes of tents, the pickets with their horses, sentries, buglers, dicing men, and men unquietly asleep. There at the hub, the folded-out flower of the pavilion with its unmistaken arms. And so within the tent, visible as if in chrysalis, the half-broken psyche of Richard. The token of the golden broom, the Planta Genesta, floated like some Egyptian soul-fire in the air. But Richard lay, bound in the leaden chains of loyalty, a ghost himself, that died.

A long, long while she looked, and her heart was moved by pity, and to love. She was upborne by the surge about her. She wished to take that tired and noble face between the hands of her thoughts, to soothe, to console . . . Lifting like breath, the separated melded similar wishes of that room poured up to heal him, as he sank under the scourge of more than witches.

White lambency filled the phantom visitation of the tent. Like countless candles, their hopes crept in to repair his soul.

And in that instant, miles away, bonds frayed, steps stumbled, a key grated in a lock and shattered unseen fetters flew apart — all, all in one second, so it seemed.

The body and mind and will of Elsabet stood here, in her father's hall, her eyes and brain consumed by yearning for the vitality of one pale and black-haired man, about thirty-three years of age. But high in her skull another sprang up with a clamour of joy, two summers the senior of her span, and with salamander hair.

She had freed him. She. *Sweet Betsi, consider it*, he had said, his voice against her ear, his body leant on hers despite the door. *And how I must love you for your sympathy*.

Life, that should have succoured the force of Richard, the last Yorkist King, swirled in her veins.

It was a little thing, so little.

There, in that blanched company, Elsabet blushed.

Soft pink as dawn, no more, unnoticed yet. But the blood, alarmed at itself, rioted, sped. Her colour deepened. Now her cheeks, her brow, her throat, were red. Her breast took fire. (*Hareu! Hareu! Le feu. Le feu –*) Flame ran and caught. In that church of sorcery, each thing was sorcerous. The blush of ingenuous lust and pleasure and shame, like sunfall on white linen, spread and stained.

One by one, jolted from patient ecstasy, they saw, recoiled, let slip their hold.

There in the midst of the snow, Elsabet was burning. The blush had filled her like a vessel with reddest wine. Her icy gown, crossed at the breast with silver, was a gown of blood trimmed molten. Her hair blushed to the hue of claret in a cloudy glass. The roses of her chaplet blushed deepest, blushed crimson. The Rose of Lancaster she wore now, raw as a wound. She, the white virgin of the will and the way, a figure as if from a carnelian hell: their enemy.

And through this chink the torrent rushed, and blasted down the wall, the bastion, and everything.

Like smashed windows the image of the army of the Boar splintered apart. Reality gaped through. Broken again, expunged, put out, the ghostly dreamer, Richard Plantagenet, was cast from their protective light. Back to the mouths of the darkness.

Elsabet, her fire draining to ash, found she knelt alone in an empty hall. The dark was paved with weeping.

Bitter his bread. Despair his sup. Edgeless his sword. Death his hap.

More than a King died that day.

Harry Dacey, having fled an occult manor near cockcrow, pursued by terrible wails and laments, like those of ghouls (for sure the place was haunted), came to a battlefield before noon, stole a sword and shared the carnage, was brave, was sickened, and found after that a man well-pleased by general events forgives much. And so with his strutting father.

Later too, much later, in a tavern very drunk, Harry Dacey heard of Black Richard's death, hacked in bits by Stanley's righteous soldiers. The crown, flying off, lodged in a hawthorn bush. It was plucked and given, like a late summer flower, to the true King of England, God send him well and better, Henry Tudor. The monster was no more. The Golden Age began. Outside, Crookback's straight and bloody corpse rotted in the market-place.

And later yet, loaded with goods and gains and a new name and a Bend Sinister, Harry laughed in his sleeve when the Tudor Dragon wedded Elizabeth of the tribe of the Wydvilles and the Greys. And later yet, and later yet, Harry wept, not knowing why, thinking of shadows singing, thinking of a pale girl never seen nearer than a window's distance, of a garden like winter, of a sunset like a blush. But he was an old man and wiser, before he knew to weep for Dickon's body festering in the end days of the Lion sun, and for the death of the White Rose.

You are My Sunshine

(Tape running.)

– For the record: Day two, Session two, Code-tape three. Earth Central Investigation into the disaster of the S.S.G. *Pilgrim*. Executive Interrogator Hofman presiding. Witness attending, Leon Canna, Fifth Officer, P.L. Capacity. Officer Canna being the only surviving crew member of the *Pilgrim*. Officer Canna?

– Yes, sir.

– Officer Canna, how long have you been in the Service?

– Ten years, sir.

– That would be three years' service in exploration vessels and seven in the transport and passenger class. How many of those seven years with Solarine Galleons?

– Six years, sir.

– And so, you would know this type of ship pretty well?

– Yes, sir. Pretty well.

– And was the *Pilgrim* in any way an unusual ship of its kind?

– No, sir.

– Officer Canna, I'm aware you've been through a lot, and I'm aware your previous record is not only clear, but indeed meritorious. Naturally, I've read your written account of what, according to you, transpired aboard the Solarine Space Galleon *Pilgrim*. You and I, Officer Canna, both know that with any ship, of any class or type, occasionally something can go wrong. Even so wrong as to precipitate a tragedy of the magnitude of the *Pilgrim* disaster. Now I want you to consider carefully before you answer me. Of all the explanations you could have chosen for the death of this ship and the loss of the two thousand and twenty lives that went with her, why this one?

– It's the truth, sir.

– Wait a moment, Officer Canna, please. You seem to miss my point. Of all the explanations at your disposal, and with ten years' intimate knowledge of space, the explanation you offer us is nevertheless frankly ludicrous.

– Sir.

– It throws suspicion on you, Officer Canna. It blots your record.

– I can't help it, sir. Oh sure, I could lie to you.

– Yes, Officer Canna, you could.

– But I'm not lying. Suppose I never told you this because I was afraid how it would reflect on me. And then suppose the same situation comes up, somewhere out there, and then the same thing happens again.

– That seems quite unlikely, Officer Canna.

(*A murmur of laughter.*)

– Excuse me, but I don't think this thing should be played for laughs.

– Nor do I, Officer Canna. Nor do I. Very well. In your own words, please, and at your own pace. Tell this investigation what you say you believe occurred.

The girl came aboard from the subport at Bel. There were thirty-eight passengers coming on at that stop, but Canna noticed the girl almost at once. The reason he noticed her was that she was so damned unnoticeable. Her clothes were the colour of putty, and so was her hair. She had that odd, slack, round-shouldered stance that looked as though it came from a lifetime of sitting on her poor little ass, leaning forward over a computer console or a dispensary plate. Nobody had ever told her there were machines to straighten you out and fine you down, and vitamins to brighten your skin, and tints to colour your hair, and optic-inducers to stop you having to peer through two god-awful lenses wedged in a red groove at the top of your nose. Nobody had ever presumably told her she was human either, with a brain, a soul and a gender.

Watch it, Canna. A lost cause is lost. Leave it alone.

Trouble was, it was part of his job to get involved.

P.L. – Passenger Link – required acting as unofficial father, son and brother to the whole shipload; sometimes you got to be priest-confessor, and sometimes lover, too. It took just the right blend of gregariousness coupled to the right blend of constraint. Long ago, the ships of the line had reasoned that passengers, the bread-winning live cargo that took up half the room aboard a Solarine Galleon, were liable to run amok without an intermediary between themselves and the crewing personnel top-side. The role of P.L. was therefore created. Spokesman and arbiter, the P.L. officer knew the technical bias up top, but he represented the voice of the non-technical flock lower-side. He related to his flock what went on behind the firmly closed doors of the Bridge and Engine Bay. If he sometimes edited, he took care not to admit it. He belonged, ostensibly, to the civilians, and that way he stopped them rocking the boat.

To do this job at all you had to be able to communicate with your fellow mortals and they had to be able to communicate with you. In that department, Canna did excellently. Sometimes better than excellently. Dark, deeply suntanned as were all Solarines, and with a buoyant, lightly sardonic good humour, he had found early on that women liked him very well, sometimes too well. This had been one of the score of reasons that had driven him off the exploration vessels, where for one or two years at a stretch, you rubbed shoulders with all the same stale passions and allergies. The E.V.s took on no passengers to provide diversion, stimulus and, in the most harmless of ways, fair game. Conversely, the Solarines had a low percentage of female crew – since women had realised their intellectual potency, they tended to go after the big-scale jobs which pleasure-cruisers didn't offer. However, the passengers provided plenty of female scenery, women who came and went, the nicest kind. For the rest, Canna could easily stand the grouses of transient passengers, because next stop the grousers got off. Canna's trick was that he found it easy to be patient, appreciative and kind with all birds of passage.

So there was this little grey drab of a girl no one had ever been kind to, creeping into the great golden spaceship. Canna reminded himself of the story of the man who would go up to drab women on the street and hiss suddenly to them: 'You're beautiful!' For the strange ego-trip of seeing the dull face abruptly flare into a kindling of brief surprised loveliness: the magic a woman would find in herself with the aid of a man. Watch it, Canna. There were two day-periods and a sun-park of twenty before they turned for Lyra and this live cargo got off.

S.S.G.s operated, as implied, on stored solar power. Their original function was transport, and with a meton reactor geared into the solar drive, they had been the hot rods of the galaxy. The big suns, any of a variety of rainbow dwarfs, provided gas stations for these trucks. Parked in orbit round the furnace, shields up and Solarine mechanisms gulping, the truck became a holiday camp. The beneficial side-effects of S.S.G.s were swiftly noted. Golden-skinned crews whose resistance to disease was ninety-nine to a hundred per cent, gave rise to new ideas of the purpose of the galleons. Something about the Solarine filter of raw sunlight acted like a miracle drug on the tired cells of human geography. Something did you a world of good, and you might be expected to pay through the nose to get it. From transport trucks, S.S.G.s became the luxury liners of the firmament, health cures, journeys of a lifetime, the only way to travel. The Solarina sun-decks were built on, the huge golden bubbles that girdled the ship, wonderlands of glowing pools, root-ballasted palms and giant sunflowers, lizardia blooms and lillaceous cacti, through which poured the screened radiance of whichever sun the ship was roosting over, endless summer on a leash.

The sun between Bel and Lyra was a Beta-class topaz effulgence, a carousel of fire.

The third period after lift-off, the 'day' they settled around the sun, the little grey putty girl was sitting in the sun lounge that opened off the entry-outs of the Solarina. Not sitting precisely, more crouching. Canna had checked her name on the passenger list. Her name was Hartley. Apollonia Hartley. He had guessed it all in a flash of intuition, though if he was right he never found out. The guess was someone had died and left her some cash, enough to make a trip some place. And someone else had said to her: Gee, Apollonia honey. With your name you have to have a Solarine-cruise. Apollo's daughter, child of a sun god (they must have maliciously predicted she'd turn out this plain to crucify her with a name like that), could bask in the sun under the ballasted ballsy palms, and fry her greyness golden. Except that she wasn't doing that at all. She was sitting – crouching – here in the lead-off lounge, with a tiny glass of champazira she wasn't even sipping. A few people were going in and out, not many. Most of them were placed to grill like tacos within the outer-side bubble.

'Hi, Miss Hartley,' said Canna, strolling up to her. 'Everything okay?'

Apollonia jumped about ten centimetres off her couch and almost knocked her champazira over.

'All right, thank you,' she muttered, staring at her knees.

It was a formula. It meant, please go away, I'm afraid to talk to you.

That was a professional slight, if nothing else. People had to *want* to talk to Leon Canna. It was what he was there for.

'Had enough of the Solarina for today?' he asked.

'Oh yes. That is – yes,' said Apollonia. She must be seeing something about her knees which no one but she ever would.

He sat on the arm of the couch beside her.

'You haven't been out there at all, have you?' Silence, which meant go away, go away. 'Why's that?' Silence, which had become an abstract agony. 'Maybe you've got sun-fright. Is that it? It's quite common. Fears of strong radiation. But I can assure you, Miss Hartley, it's absolutely safe. Do I look sick, Miss Hartley?'

Inadvertently, she glanced at him. Her eyes got stuck somewhere on the white uniform casuals, the sun blaze over the pocket. Black hair and eyes and cleft golden jaw and the golden hands with their fine smoke of black hirsuteness, these she avoided.

'I'm not,' she said, 'that is, there are so many – people out there.'

She might have said lions, tigers.

'Sure. I know,' he said. He didn't know. People to him were a big fun game. 'But I'll tell you what, you know when it gets really quiet in the Solarina?'

'When?' Whispered.

He liked that. He understood what was happening. Fascinated by him, she was beginning to forget herself.

'Twenty-four midnight by the earth-clock below. Come back then, you'll get a good three or four hours, maybe alone.' She didn't speak. 'Or I might come up,' he said. Christ, Canna, what did I say to you? He could see her breathing, just like a heroine in an old romance, bosom, as they said, heaving. 'Why don't you drink your champazira?' he said.

'I don't – I only –'

'Ordered it for something to play with while you sat here,' he said. 'I didn't see you at dinner the last two night-periods.'

'I ate in my cabin.'

'Oh Miss Hartley – Apollonia, may I? – Apollonia, you'll get the *Pilgrim* a bad name. You're supposed to get something out of your voyage. Come on, now. Promise me. The Solarina at midnight. I have to make certain our passengers enjoy themselves. You don't want me to lose my job, do you?'

Startled, her eyes flew up like birds and collided with his jet black ones. Her whole face stained with colour, even her spectacles seemed to glaze with pink.

'I'll try.'
'Good girl.'
Good God.

He told himself not to go up to the Solarina after midnight. Of course, he'd met women out there before, who hadn't. But not women like Apollonia.

At twenty-four thirty by the earth-clock, he walked through the sun-lounge. The passenger section of the ship was fairly still at this hour, as he had assured her. The Solarina was empty except for its flora and its light. In the sun-lounge, Apollonia was huddled on her couch, without even the champazira to keep her company.

'I didn't think – you would come. I was,' she said, 'afraid to go through on my own. Is it – all right?'

'Sure it is.'

'Will the doors open?'

'I have a tab if they don't.'

'It looks so – bright. So fierce.'

'It's like a hot shower, or the sea at Key Mariano. You ever been there?' He knew she had not. 'Just above blood heat. The fish cook as they swim. Come on.' She didn't move, so he moved in ahead of her, into the glowing summer, sloughing his robe as he went. He understood perfectly what he looked like in swim trunks. If he hadn't, enough women had told him, using the analogies of Greek heroes, Roman gladiators. 'The harmful rays are filtered out by the Solarine mechanism,' he said. Encouraged, mesmerised, she slipped through, and the wine-water closed over her head.

She wore a long shapeless tunic. Probably just as well. She would be nearly as shapeless underneath.

'Will this do?' she said. 'I didn't know what –'

'That's fine. The filtered sun soaks through any material. The tan is all over, whatever you wear. I just like to get directly under the spotlight when I can.'

They folded themselves out among the palms, which threw down coffee-green papers of shade. The warmth was honey. You felt it osmose into you. You never grew bored with it. The walls of the bubble, sun-amber hiding the actual roaring face of the sun, pulsed very faintly, rhythmically, sensually, with Solarine ingestion. The Galleon was a child, given suck by a fiery breast. All this to fuel a ship. Man oh man.

'It's beautiful,' Apollonia said.

She lay on palm-frond shadows. Her eyes were wide behind the spectacles. Her putty-coloured hair was ambiguously tinged, almost gilded. Her lips were parted. He hadn't noticed before, she had a nice mouth, the upper lip chiselled, the lower full and smooth, the teeth behind them even and white. He leaned over her and gently lifted the spectacles off the red groove in her nose. He was completely aware of the cliché – Oh, Miss Hartley, now I see you for the first time without your glasses . . .

She made a futile panicky little gesture after the spectacles.

'Relax,' he said.

She relaxed, closing her eyes.

'I can see. But not so well. But I can see without them.'

'I know you can.'

'I never felt the sun, any sun, like this before,' she said presently. He saw it often, every journey in fact, how they grew drunken, wonderful solar drunks, with no morning-after.

An hour later, one-thirty earth-time, he looked at her again. There was something changed. Already, her skin was altered. Long lashes lay like satin streaks against her face. The red groove had faded, become a thin rose crescent. Okay Canna, so you're Pygmalion. But the Solarina sun had got to him also, as it always did. He leaned over again, and this occasion he kissed her lightly on the lips.

'Oh,' she said softly, 'oh.'

'Baby,' he said, 'I have to go back to my quarters and put on tape for my captain what nine hundred and seventy-six people find wrong with S.S.G. *Pilgrim this* trip.'

She didn't stir. He thought she'd gone to sleep, perhaps (fanciful) melodramatically passed out at the fragile kiss.

He left her to the Solarina, and when he closed the door of his cabin he found himself carefully locking it, and the sweat between his shoulder blades had nothing to do with the sun.

He didn't see Miss Hartley next day-period. This was partly deliberate and partly luck. There were plenty of things to do, reports to make, two hours' work-out in the gym. Then some crazy dame lost a ruby pendant. He took a late dinner in the salon – as P.L., he had a place at the co-ordinators' table, alongside his flock. The golden wash was spreading over them all, just as usual. Then he saw the girl.

Something had happened to the girl.

She was tanned, of course, enough tan that she must have been back to the Solarina during the day, or else she'd stayed there all night. Or maybe both. But it wasn't only the tan. What the hell was it?

He couldn't stop staring, which was bad, because any moment she might look his way. But she didn't look. She wasn't even wearing her spectacles. She finished the tawny liqueur she was drinking, got to her feet and walked unhurriedly out of the salon. She didn't move the same way, either.

'I don't remember that girl,' said Fourth Officer Co-ordinator Jeans. 'Apollonia Hartley.'

'Not the right mixture for you, Canna.'

'Help yourself,' said Canna.

After dinner there was the report to make on the rediscovery of the lost pendant. It looked like it was going to be one of those runs with a lot of desk-work. Around midnight there was cold beer and nothing much left to do except wonder if little Miss Hartley were on the sun-deck.

There were girls, and there were girls. Some girls you had to be wary of. Even birds of passage could turn around and fly straight back, and some had nest-building on their minds, and some had damn sharp claws. This girl now. She might be grateful. She might have taken it for what it was. Then again, she might not. And for godssakes anyway, what was there for him to be interested in?

At one o'clock earth-time, Canna went up to the Solarina. No robe and trunks now, but the rumpled uniform casuals he'd had on all day. The sun-lounge was empty. Canna went to the entry-out, and glanced through the gold-leaf tunnels of shine under the lizardia. Miss Hartley was lying face down on a recliner, about thirty metres away. Her hair poured over on to the ground. He couldn't see her that well through the stripes of the palms, but enough to know that, aside from her hair, she was naked.

He stepped away from the entry-out noiselessly, and walked soft all the way back to his cabin. Oh boy, Canna.

You're beautiful! he said to the plain woman. Her face kindled, she opened her mouth and swallowed him whole.

Ten o'clock next day-period, Jeans' jowly face appeared on the cab-com.

'Priority meeting, all officers non-Bridge personnel. Half an hour, Bridge-annex.'

'What's going on?' Canna asked.

'Search me,'

'No thanks.'

'Okay, funny guy. Usual spiel to the mob, okay?'

'Sure thing.'

'Usual spiel' was, as ever, necessary. Somehow, your passengers always knew when something was up, however mild, however closely guarded. Passing three groups en route top-side, Canna was asked what emergency required a Bridge-annex meeting. Usual spiel meant: 'No emergency, Mr Walters. *Pilgrim* always has an annex meeting third day of sun-parking.' 'But surely, if everything is going smoothly?' 'Nothing ever goes quite smoothly on a vessel this size, Miss Boenek.' 'Then there *is* an emergency, Mr Canna?' 'Yes, Mr Walters. We're all out of duck pâté.'

'Sit down, gentlemen, if you will,' said Andersen.

He had been captain of the *Pilgrim* since Canna had started with the ship, and Canna guessed he respected the man about as much as he'd ever respected any extreme authority. At least Andersen didn't think he was God and at least he sometimes got off his tail.

'Gentlemen,' said Andersen, 'we have a slight problem. I'm afraid, Mr Canna, yours, as ever, is going to be the delicate task.'

'You mean it involves our passengers, sir?'

'As ever, Mr Canna.'

'May I know what the problem is?'

'We have some excess radiation, Mr Canna.'

There was the predictable explosion, followed by the predictable dumb show that greets the distant tolling of that bell, about which ask not for whom. Spake, Bridge Engineer Galleon Class, waited for the ball.

'With your permission, sir? Okay, gentlemen, it's not big business. We have it under control. Every cubic centimetre of this tub is being checked.'

'You mean,' said Jeans, 'you don't know the hell where it's coming from.'

Andersen said: 'We know where it isn't coming from. The meton is sound and there's no bleed-off from the casings. That's our only source of internal radiation. *Ergo*, it can't be us. Therefore, it's coming in from outside. From the sun we're parked over. As yet, we don't know how or where, because every shield registers fully operational. According to top-side computer there's no way we can have a rad-bleed at all. So naturally, we're double checking, triple checking until we pin the critter down. Even if we can't figure it, and there's no reason to suppose we eventually can't, all we have to do is weigh anchor and move out of sun-range. Meantime (and here, Mr Canna, is the rub), the most obvious danger zone is the Solarina.'

Canna groaned.

'What you're saying, sir, is that we're going to put the Solarina off-limits to the passengers, and I have to find some reason for it that won't cause an immediate panic.'

'You know what passengers are like when radiation is involved,' said Andersen.

'Mention the word and they're howling and clawing for the life-launches,' said Jeans.

'What's the rad level?' Canna asked.

Engineer Spake looked at the captain, got some invisible go-ahead, and answered: 'At three o'clock this morning, point zero one zero. At nine o'clock, point zero two ten.'

There was a second round of expletives.

'In other words, it's rising?'

'It appears to be. But we have a long way to go before it reaches anything like an inimical level.'

'I guess that's top-side's hang-up, not mine,' said Canna. 'My hang-up is what story I tell lower-side.'

'Just keep it simple, Mr Canna, if you would.'

'The simplicity isn't what's troubling me, sir.'

'You'll think of something, Mr Canna.'

At noon by the earth-clock, when nine hundred-odd persons were shooed from the Solarina, Canna guided them into the major lower-side salon, and told them about the free drinks, courtesy of *Pilgrim*. Then, standing on the rostrum with the hand mike, gazing out at the pebbled-beach effect of cluster on cluster of grim, belligerent, nervous faces, Canna found himself reviewing the half a dozen times he had been required to make similar overtures; the time the number twenty Solarine Ingestor caught fire, the time they hit the meteor swarm coming up from Alpheus. A couple of those, and a point zero two ten radiation reading was a candy bar. And then he remembered the girl, and for five seconds his eyes ran over the crowd, and when he couldn't find her, he wondered why the mike was wet against his palm.

They were making a lot of noise, but they quietened down when he lifted his hand. He explained, apologetically, humorously, that *Pilgrim* needed to make up a fuel loss, caused by a minor failure, now compensated, in one of the secondary ingestors. Due to that, the ship would be channelling off extra power through the ship's main Solarine area, the sun-deck. Hence the closure.

'For which inconvenience, folks, we are truly sorry.'

Now came the questions.

A beefy male had commandeered one of the floor mikes. 'Okay, mister, how long's this closure going to last?'

'A day-period, sir. Maybe a couple of days, at most.'

'I paid good cash for this voyage, mister. The Solarina's the main attraction.'

'The beneficial solar rays permeate every part of the ship, sir, not only the Solarina. The sun-deck's function is mostly ornamental. But the company will be happy to refund any loss you feel you've suffered, when we reach Lyra.'

'If the goddam Solarina's only ornamental, how can closing it affect the ship's power?'

'That's kind of a technical query. The Solarine pipe ingestors run out over the hull, you recall, and the Solarina's banks are the nearest to outer surface.'

'Okay, okay.'

A pretty young woman miked from the other side of the room: 'Is there any danger?'

'Absolutely none, ma'am. We're just tanking up on gas.'

'Well, then, let's tank up,' someone yelled, and the free drinking began in earnest.

The *Pilgrim* had got off lightly, Canna thought.

He met Jeans near the bar, downing a large double paint-stripper. Grinning broadly for passenger benefit, Jeans muttered: 'Guess what the number game was ten minutes ago?'

'Thrill me,' Canna, also grinning.

'Full point one.'

'Great,' said Canna.

'And you know what?' grinned Jeans. 'Still climbing.'

Far across the room there was a sort of eddy, a current of gold, like a fish's wake in sunset water. He thought of a woman baking in the yellow-green cradle of the palms, her arms and her hair poured on the floor.

'The max is fifty, right?'

'Right, Canna, right.'

The woman with the ruby was approaching. Miss Keen? Kane? Koon?

'I think it's just lovely,' she giggled to Canna. 'These marvellous ships, and they still get caught with their pants down.' She tried to buy him one of the free drinks.

The golden current had settled, become a pool of molten air. Where the girl was. Apollonia. She'd dyed her hair, the colour of Benedictine. He couldn't be sure it was Apollonia, except there was nobody else who looked like her now, as none of them had looked like her before.

When he escaped from his flock and got back to his cabin, a slim sealed envelope had come in at the chute with the lower-side stamp over it. Canna opened the envelope.

I waited for you. That was all she had written, in rounded, over-disciplined letters. *I waited for you.*

Sure you did, baby.

He felt sorry for her, and disgusted. She'd improved herself. Perhaps he could palm her off on Jeans. No, he couldn't do that. He'd understood she was trouble the first moment. He should have left her alone. God knew why he hadn't been able to.

At four, Spake came through on the cab-com.

'Thought you'd like to hear it officially. The count is now point fifteen zero five.'

'Jesus. Got a fix yet?'

'Nothing. It's everywhere lower-side, from the Solarina to the milk bar.'

'Not top-side?'

'Sifting through.'

'Then the source has to be down here.'

'According to the computer nothing leaks, nothing's bleeding off. Unless one of your sheep has a stash of plutonium tucked in his diapers . . . It's got to be coming *in*, but the shields are solid as a rock.'

'Maybe you're asking the computer the wrong questions.'

'Could be. Know the right ones?'

'What does Andersen say?'

'He wants another meet, all available personnel, midnight plus three.'

'Three in the *morning*?'

'That's it, Canna. Be there. And Canna –'

'What?'

'Complete passenger drill tomorrow. Launches, suit-ups, the whole show.'

'That'll certainly lend an atmosphere of calm. I'll get it organised.'

Just then, the cabin lights faltered. The clear sheen of the Solarine lamps went white, then brown, steadied and flashed clear again.

'What the hell did that?' Canna demanded, but Spake was gone. Somewhere there had been a massive drain-off of power. That could mean several things, none of them pleasing. Already he was spinning a story for the passengers, a switch-over of batteries as the fabricated weak ingestor was shut down. You stood there with the smoke billowing and the walls red-hot and screaming people everywhere, and you told them: It happens every trip. It's nothing. And you made them believe it.

Canna went out of the cabin, strolling towards the lower-side salon, taking in the three TV theatres on the way. The flock came to him like filings to a magnet. He was amazed they'd noticed the lights faltering. It was only the spare ingestor shutting down. They believed him. Makes you feel good, huh, Canna?

But where was Canna when the lights went out? In the goddam dark.

He opened his eyes. It was half-past one, the cabin on quarter-lamp. Over by the tape cabinet, fastened to its stanchions, the grotesque survival suit stood, blackly gleaming, like a monster from a comic rag. He'd been checking the suit for the demonstration tomorrow and then lain on the bunk to snatch an hour's sleep before Andersen's meeting. What had woken him?

The door buzzer sounded again. That was what had woken him.

Two-thirds of the way to the door, he knew who it was, and hesitated. Then he opened the door.

There in the corridor stood Apollonia Hartley. But it was not the Apollonia Hartley who had come aboard at Bel. The whole corridor seemed to shine, to throb and glow and shimmer. Maybe that was just the effect of full light after quarter-lamp. Then she stepped by him into his cabin, and the throbbing, glowing, shimmering shine came in with her.

'I waited,' she said quietly. 'And then, when you didn't come, I realised you meant me to come here.'

'Did I?'

She turned and looked at him. Without her glasses, there was a slight film across her eyes, making them large, enigmatic. Not seeing him quite so well seemed to make it easier for her actually to look at him. Her Benedictine golden hair hung round her, all around her, and all of her was pure gold, traced over by the briefest swim suit imaginable. And she was beautiful. Shaped out of gold by a master craftsman, Venus on a gold medallion.

'You look fine,' he said. 'What have you done to yourself?'

'Nothing,' she said. 'You've done this for me, Leon,' she said.

He thought, Christ, no woman could make herself look like this in two days, not starting on the raw material Apollonia had started with. Not even with the Solarina.

'You,' she said, 'and the strange wonderful sun. No man ever looked at me before, ever kissed me. I've never been this close to a sun.'

As she breathed, regularly and lightly, planes of fire slid across her waist, her breasts, her throat. And the cabin gathered to the indrawn breath, spilled away, gathered, spilled –

'Can you let me into the Solarina, Leon?' she murmured. 'I can do it this way, but it's better there.'

He tried to smile at her.

'Sorry, the Solarina's out of bounds, Apollonia – Miss Hartley – until –'

'Leon,' she said.

When she spoke, the room was full of amber dust and the scent of oranges, peaches, apricots, and volcanoes blazed somewhere. Then she put her hand against his chest, flat and still on the bare skin. Here he was, Leon Canna, with the best-looking lady he'd ever seen, and he was holding her at arm's length. He stopped holding her that way and held her a better way and she came to him like flame running up a beach.

Over by the cabinet, the black survival suit for tomorrow's drill rattled dully, as if sex vibrated the cabin.

When he opened his eyes the next time it was with a sense of missing hours. He felt dizzy and the cab-com was bawling. The girl had gone.

'Canna!' For some reason no picture had come over to fit Spake's shouting.

'Yes. I'm sorry. I'm late for my very important date with the Bridge, right?'

'No, Canna. Canna, listen to me. The radiation count in your cabin is point forty two, and rising.'

Canna straightened himself, his eyes and brain focusing slowly.

'Canna, are you there, for Christ's sake?'

'I'm here, Spake.'

'We have a firework display over the panel here for the whole of lower-side, centralised on your level, and through to the B entry-out to the Solarina.'

Canna saw the suit, black as coal against the wall.

'I've got a demo suit with me, Spake.'

'*Good*, Canna. Get it on in two seconds flat.'

'Don't make any bets.'

'*Canna*, it's forty two point zero nine. *Forty three, Canna.*'

'Why no alarms?' Canna inquired as he shambled over to the survival suit, cracked it open and began to load its myriad pounds on to himself.

'The alarms are out, drained. This com is working on emergency. Get suited-up, then get as many of the passengers suited as you can. You've got about ten minutes to do it before it goes above fifty in there. Oh, and Canna, with the power shrinkage, half the auto-gears are jammed, including those of the Bridge exit and the seven lifts through from top-side. That's why you're on your own. That's why we can't unpark this truck. Something's just eating up the Solarine, and we're glued over the bloody sun.'

Now he was a black beetle. The casque clacked shut and he hit the suit shields and they came on all around him. Did he fantasise the sudden coolness. His skin felt tender, blistered, but he forgot it.

Beyond his cabin everything was quiet. Innocently, the lower-side of *Pilgrim* slumbered or fornicated, unaware that death lay thick as powder on every eye and nostril, every limb and joint and pore. Yet the lights were flickering again, and presently somewhere a dim far-off yelling arose, more anger than fear, the ship's insomniacs, God help them. He wasn't going to be in time. And then he ran at the door and it wouldn't shift.

'Spake,' he said, 'I'm suited-up, but I can't get the door open.'

But the com was beginning to crackle. Through the crackle, Spake said to him excitedly: 'There's something happening in the Solarina – (yes, I have it on screen, sir) –'

'Spake, will you listen, the door –'

'My God,' Spake said, in a hushed low reverent voice, 'it's a woman, and she's on fire.'

Canna stood in his cabin in the black coffin of the survival suit. He visualised Apollonia, her fingers in the pocket of his uniform casuals, the authorisation tab, the entry-out of the sun-deck softly opening.

He saw her, as the Bridge was seeing her, lifting her amber arms, her golden body into the glare of the topaz sun. And the sun was shining through her, and like the bush on the holy mountain she was burning and yet not consumed.

A shock of sound passed through the ship. From the suit it seemed miles of cold space away. And then he felt the wild savage trembling like the spasm of an anguished heart, and the tapes and papers on his desk were smoking. The whole cabin was filling with steel-blue smoke he couldn't smell, like the heat he couldn't feel.

The screaming seemed to come all on one high frozen note, two thousand voices melted into one, as the ship bubbled like toffee in a pan. And then the screaming became in turn one with a long roar of light, a blinding rush of noise, and silence, and the dark.

The third time he opened his eyes, he was in a black box with white stars stitched over it. A few bits of unidentifiable wreckage went by, lazy as butterflies. Vast distances below, *Pilgrim*'s charred embers fell into the pin-point of a sun.

Automatically, Canna stabbed on the stabilisers in the suit which had saved his life, anchoring himself firmly to a point of nothing in space. The suit could withstand almost anything, and had just proved as much. It had liquid food and water sufficient for several day-periods, air for longer; it could probably even sing him songs. He had only to wait and keep sane. Every time a ship died, a red signal lit up on every scan board from Earth to Andromeda. Someone would come. He only had to wait.

If he could have got to any of his flock, he'd have had company. They had suits on the Bridge, of course, but they'd had the jammed doors too. And Bridge was right over the meton reactor. Even a suit couldn't take that on.

He drifted about the anchor point using up any foul words he could think of, like candles. He started to hurt. As all survivors did, he stared at the stars and wondered about God. He thought about the pretty girl in the salon who had asked if there was any danger, and he cried. He thought about Apollonia Hartley, and then the pain came, and he started to scream.

When the search ship found him two day-periods later, his voice was a hoarse wire splinter from screaming, and he spat blood from his torn throat.

(*Tape running.*)

– Thank you, Officer Canna. I think we are all in the picture. I should now like to analyse this vision. Or would you prefer a short recess?

– No, sir. I'd like to get this finished.

– Very well. Whatever you wish. Officer Canna, I hope you'll forgive me when I say, once again, that this story is preposterous. Having heard your account firsthand, I fear I must go further. You've somehow managed to turn a naval tragedy into an exercise in masculine ego. This tale of yours, the man who tells the woman she's beautiful, at which she magically makes herself beautiful for him. Can it really be that you credit – and expect us to credit – the notion that the sexual awareness you brought to this pathetic, rather unbalanced girl, triggered in her an unconscious response so enormous that she attempted to make herself beautiful by absorbing and eventually fusing with a solar body, becoming a fireball which consumed S.S.G. *Pilgrim*?

– I don't know, sir. I only know what I saw and what I heard.

– But what *did* you see and hear, Officer Canna? You saw an ugly girl, who for some perverse reason attracted you, who then prettied herself for you, tanning quickly, as do all travellers on the Solarine Galleons, dyeing her hair, using a slimming machine. A girl who eventually offered herself to you. Coincidentally, there was a shield failure which the computer of *Pilgrim* failed to localise. The computer may already have been affected by the loss of power from the Solarine system, hence its inability to identify the source of the trouble. A vicious circle ensues. The shield break degenerates the Solarine bank, the bank is unable to supply sufficient power to stem the break. On the other hand, assuming your bizarre hypothesis to be true, the computer should surely have traced the source. Do you agree, Officer Canna?

– A computer can't think on its own. You have to feed the right questions. Bridge was asking the computer to check for a specific *leakage*, in or out.

– Very well. I don't think we'll split any more hairs on that, Officer Canna. My comments on this phenomenon are amply recorded. The other phenomena you describe are due to the experience itself, but seen in the retrospect of your guilt.

– Excuse me, I don't like what happened, but I don't feel guilty. There was no way I could guess. When I did, there was nothing I could do.

– Perhaps not, but you were wasting precious hours with a female passenger when you might have been able to help your ship.

– I didn't know that at the time.

– Lastly, the woman on fire in the Solarina, by which garbled fragment you seem to set great store. With the radiation level where it was, and so near the outer surface of the ship as the sun-deck, spontaneous combustion of tissue was not only possible but predictable. Er – Mr Liles? Yes, please speak.

– As the witness's counsel, Mr Hofman, I would respectfully draw your attention to the note appended to Leon Canna's written statement.

– This one? To do with the radiation burns Officer Canna received? But I would have thought such burns inevitable. After all, the exposure –

– The rad level in the cabin before Leon Canna suited-up was insufficient to cause burns of this magnitude.

– Well, I see. But what –

– Excuse me, Mr Hofman. Leon, are you sure you want to go through with this?

– I'm sure.

– Mr Hofman, I'm setting up here a view screen, and on the screen I'm going to present to this investigation two shots of Officer Canna, taken before he underwent treatment and tissue regeneration. Lights, please. Thank you. Shot one.

(*A faint growl of men unaccustomed to seeing raw human flesh.*)

– Mr Liles, is this strictly –

– Yes, Mr Hofman, sir. And I'd ask you to look carefully, here and here.

– Yes, Mr Liles, thank you.

– This is the frontal shot of Leon Canna's body. The second shot is of the hind torso and limbs.

(*Silence. Loud exclamations. Silence.*)

– I think you will take my point, gentlemen, that what might be a curious abstract in the first shot, becomes a rather terrifying certainty when compounded by the second.

(*Silence.*)

– Mr Liles – Officer Canna – gentlemen. I think – we must have a

recess after all. Someone please stop that blasted tape.
   (*Tape stopped.*)

Appendix: two photographs.
   First shot: a naked man about thirty-six years of age and of athletic well-proportioned build, badly burned by a class B radiation strike across the lower face, chest, arms, palms of the hands, pelvis, genitals and upper legs.
   Second shot: the same man, also nude; hind view. Burns of similar type, but small in area and fragmentally scattered across the shoulders and buttocks. Across the middle to upper region of the back, definitely marked as if with branding irons, the exact outline of two female arms and hands, tightly and compulsively pressed into the skin.

The One We Were

Eccentricity is a sort of talent, in some cases amounting to genius. Certain climates or orders in the human advance seem to facilitate it. And while money is not essential to the condition, it helps.

Claira Von Oeau, born to poverty, of mixed Austrian, Russian, Parisian, and perhaps Hebrew, extraction, had earned her considerable fortune by a florid success in the Arts. She was a popular writer of romantic historical novels. The kind of work is not unknown. Blood-red sunsets unrolled from her pen to match the spillages of the ancient Romans strewn among the pillars beneath; armadas met with the shock of war; beautiful heroines with streaming hair craned over the parapets of Carthage, Troy and Verona. The Black Death had ridden again through Europe at the whim of Claira, and Pompeii collapsed once more under lava. Though her researches were minimal and her scholastic bent rather slight, Claira's torrid literary gift tended to make nothing of everything, all of nothing. She had the knack of bluff. Despite evidence to the contrary, one felt, however briefly, that Byzantium *had* been Claira's way. Regularly castigated by the critics, Claira remarked that she was indifferent equally to praise or blame. And so she seemed to be. Even the wealth her work had brought her was treated with the casual brutishness of familiarity.

Of course, she suffered. She existed on the unshakable premise that all life proceeded from herself. As the centre of the world, perhaps the universe, she was aware that all things and persons took their being only in order to be of use to her. In this way, she had never been amazed at her lucky rise to fame and fortune. It was inevitable. When, however, the world or its inhabitants did not treat her as they were expected to do, she felt the conspiracy of the gods ranged against her. How can I endure this cruelty? (She would cry.) She would lie in bed and weep for days on end. Until some favourable omen – the earth is full of omens for those who believe they are the centre of it – roused her.

Claira was a small slight woman, not unattractive, with a long slender nose and dark sweeping brows, her fine eyes accentuated by mascara. As a general rule, one would not have taken a great deal of notice of her. But she was possessed of a tremendous, indeed an overwhelming personality. She was what is sometimes termed a 'vampire'. That is, her terrific energy, though spent frequently in the pursuit of her vocation, recharged itself almost instantaneously, and usually at the expense of others. Even her griefs were strong, and drained those who supported her through them. Her enthusiasms were tidal waves. Sitting quite still in a secluded restaurant, Claira could utterly exhaust her companions, who felt they had been running non-stop for hours, tied to the tails of several wild horses. She had a habit of relating the plot-line of her current book, pausing only to interpolate character-notes upon the *dramatis personae*. These recitals were normally incomprehensible to any save herself. And though she attempted to explain the in-jokes of the précis, few understood them. As a form of punctuation, she would exclaim, 'What a jumble all this must seem to you! But you're being so *helpful*. Just by letting me discuss it with you – invaluable. Have some more of the lobster.' In other words, fill your mouth and listen to *me*.

Invariably, Claira's close friends did not stay the course. They were sloughed from her over the years, and new models were adopted, only to be sloughed in turn, panting and shattered at the wayside. Some of the friendships, and usually the intimate liaisons, ended in uproar, mild violence and, naturally, suffering. 'No man will ever love me as I need to be loved,' Claira announced. 'Jealousy! I must give up my work or all hope of personal joy.'

Actually she had no intention of giving up either. Since the world proceeded from Claira, it had no choice but to supply each of her wants as they arose. If failed, she had the solace of loud clamour.

A small coterie of friends did remain, those who were able to tolerate Claira mostly by rationing the time they spent with her. Some, it seems, even felt a genuine affection for her, and a respect for her – for want of a better word – *extraordinary* talent.

The most consistent of these was a Madame Sarnot, who more or less inadvertently unleashed the following events.

* * *

To the Sarnot salon one evening had been invited the celebrated medium, Madame Q–. At this time she was the talk of half of Europe. A very tall woman, dressed in flowing antique silks, and most frequently escorted by a pet snake, she could have stepped straight out of one of Claira's Egyptian cave-temples. Under the circumstances, to exclude Claira from the action would have been unthinkable.

Madame Q– was an exponent of transmigration. 'The body is a house,' she had explained in her most famous thesis. 'The soul, like a bird, flits from life to life . . .'

Claira had always credited reincarnation. 'How else,' Claira had demanded, 'can I understand so well so many past civilisations? My research is negligible. And yet – I *know*. Why? Because I was *there*.' Her critics might (and did) take issue with this statement. If Claira had been there, then it must be a singularly bad memory which was to blame for such items as the mandolin a slave had so engagingly played in Pompeii, or the roast potatoes served at the court of Richard III.

On the fateful evening, Claira was late. About an hour after Madame Q– had made her statuesque entrance, complete with snake, Claira made hers, lacking reptiles but in no way else deficient. The most notable feature was possibly a hat, itself not large, but decorated with the bronzy-green, yard-long tail-plumage of a mythical bird. At each turn or inclination of Claira's head, the eyes of fellow guests were threatened, champagne goblets altered their positions, or fire attempted to break out.

From the moment of her entry, Claira had been noted by the medium (it was hard to do otherwise), who riveted her with gimlet eyes. Two sets of scarab rings, Madame Q–'s and Claira's, clicked ominously. Presently Madame Q– fed her restless snake an opium pellet and Claira, who, despite her merciless descriptions of chariot-races and whale-hunts, was a champion of all contemporary fauna, wondered aloud if this were not injurious.

'Not at all,' responded Madame Q–. 'Although, no doubt, mademoiselle, you are now over-cautious of the poppy, having abused it in your previous incarnation.'

A deep silence instantly descended. Claira grew rigid, and the flickering candles reaching eagerly towards her hat sank down.

'I see such things quite clearly,' Madame Q– continued calmly but inexorably, 'when the impression is very recent or very vivid. It is, you comprehend, as if a shadow walks at the left side. And at your left side, Mademoiselle Von Oeau, there is a fair-haired young man. I behold him perfectly distinctly. The burning eyes, the frock coat, the sheaf of manuscript in one hand. A little less light, if you please. I am prepared to enter trance. Such resonances are not to be ignored. Let us see with whom we are dealing.'

The lights were accordingly doused or moved further off. Madame Sarnot might have been observed glancing with amused concern at Claira. But Claira possessed all the inner strengths of the somewhat mad. Bolt upright, unblinking as a dark-eyed owl, she held Madame Q– in her sights. No quarter was now to be expected from either party.

After some mutterings, moanings and snorts, during which the snake tried drunkenly to escape and failed, Madame Q– fell back in her chair and began to speak in a baritone voice. Her, or its, comments were ponderous but to the point. The psychic echo of the gentleman observed at Claira Von Oeau's left side was the residue of a life lived a little more than a century previously, and in the same city – possibly hence the evocation. He was also a writer; another sure connection. He had been quite notorious in his day both for his poetry – which was on the affectionate side – and his riotous social tendencies. He had been bloodily murdered by his best friend in the English cemetery of Notre-Dame du Nord. 'But who is it?' someone – not Claira – cried. Madame Q–'s possession obediently rumbled out the name *Simplice de Meunier*. This might have been a disappointment. None of the guests had heard of such a person. Clearly Monsieur de Meunier, despite his riots, was on the obscure side. A pity. Claira, however, showed no sign of dismay. Rather, she sat for some minutes in a peculiarly galvanic stillness. She had, as it happened, introduced a minor character into a recent book, a minstrel by name – *Simplice*. This coincidence now struck her with all its awesome significance. What was a minstrel but a poet? And the name was identical. It seemed she too had been aware of pre-bodily echoes. This could be nothing but proof.

As Madame Q– revived and stretched out her claws towards the wine, Claira was at her elbow, in the way. Feathers dipped amid the caviar.

'Madame, you have given me a treasure beyond price.'

Madame Q– nodded imperiously. Claira, cutting off the refreshments entirely, embraced her. The snake escaped into an ice-bucket, and Claira's hat at last began to burn.

Madame Sarnot heaved a gentle sigh. 'I think I was wrong, Horace,' she remarked to her husband. 'How wrong, only time will tell.'

* * *

It was (for reasons too numerous and far too patently obvious to air here) a man's world. Claira, whatever her personal success, could not fail to be, if only subconsciously, aware of it. Nor, no doubt, had she evaded the ambient brain-washing. Though she considered herself no one's inferior, to learn that, little more than one hundred years before, she had been that most emancipated of all earthly creatures, a man, added a fillip of considerable burnish. To be male, fascinating, and romantically dead, filled Claira with an elation that is difficult to describe to those who have never felt it, worse, have never aspired to feel it. Being Claira, of course, a strange incestuous schizophrenia had begun instantly to work in her. Here she was a woman. There she was a man. What could they be to each other but – everything? At last, a masculine presence who was not a rival, who would not seek to destroy her genius, but was part of it, and, eternally, of herself. What else? They were one. Closer than husband to wife, than mother to son. 'My own,' Claira wrote in her journal, underlining in coloured ink. 'As no other man can ever be, or wish to be, or be wished to be. Simplice is *mine*.' Already, one perceives, she was on first name terms with him.

In the weeks which followed, Claira began to research her subject with a diligence never lavished on any of her novels. The chase was made all the more entertaining and emotional by Monsieur de Meunier's slight reputation. But Claira, in the tidal-wave mode, was easily a match for his obscurity. She tracked him down, she traced him; she was at all times in full cry. The libraries private and public grew to fear the sound of her footsteps. The countless messenger boys she dispatched in all directions waxed rich, and lean from running. From dubious basements and the sleep of decades, surfaced greenish cakes of paper that had once been books. These soon came to furnish every spare surface, stuff every neglected cranny, of the Von Oeau suite. So much for biography. The hunt for likeness came hard upon. The great galleries of the city did not possess portraits of Monsieur de Meunier, and so escaped unwittingly from Claira. The Musée Miramelle, which had two, was not so fortunate.

With a fiercely beating heart Claira had entered the gallery and searched out the first picture. What if, after all, her poetic self had been ugly, or – far more awful – plain? Presently she was gratified to discover an attractive male person leaning in his frame, a manuscript in one hand. His hair was very fair with amber highlights, but his eyes and brows, Claira at once decided, were her own. With these eyes he gazed out sidelong at her, with a mischievous expression. Here I am, you see, they seemed to say, loving and teasing, glad to be found.

The second picture was smaller, and less clear, and perhaps less flattering. When she returned to the larger work, a party of young ladies was in attendance on it, and Claira stood by regally, allowing them their perusal. After a while, one of the young women remarked, to no one in particular, 'How very elegant he was.'

'Thank you,' said Claira, an unaccustomed blush staining her cheeks.

The young ladies turned.

'I beg your pardon?'

'I said,' modestly reiterated Claira, 'thank you for your compliment.'

'But I –' said the young lady who had spoken.

'And I am sure,' Claira added, giving her a long, level look, 'that approval would have been mutual.'

It was now the young lady's turn to crimson.

There were to be several red faces that afternoon.

'I tell you, mademoiselle,' finally shouted the director, called in alarm from more important matters, 'that it is in no way possible for you to purchase this portrait. I do not care how much you are willing to pay, the Musée Miramelle does not conduct its business in this fashion. Good day.'

'Then I shall arrange for its theft,' Claira responded.

'Pierre, run to the corner at once and summon a policeman.'

'You have no grounds,' said Claira haughtily.

'You have made a threat.'

'I am entitled to make threats. The portrait is mine. Rightfully mine. How dare you attempt to keep it from me? Name the sum your wretched waxworks requires.'

'*Waxworks* – ! Mademoiselle, this is too much –'

'I shall not move. I shall, if necessary, chain myself to the railings outside, refusing food or water. I will *die* here to get what I want. Do you understand, Monsieur?'

'I am beginning to. Pierre? The corner, if you please.'

About five o'clock, the arrival of Madame Sarnot in a *fiacre* defused the situation. 'I shall return,' promised Claira. The horses, frightened by the commotion of three portly gentlemen shouting on the pavement, bolted as soon as a whip was cracked. Borne home so speedily, Claira was still voluble as she burst into her apartment on the rue Swanhilde.

'My dear,' said Madame Sarnot soothingly.

'How can you say this to me?'

'I don't recall saying anything very much, as yet –'

'I will *have* it. It's mine! Mine! As Simplice is mine. Each atom of that previous life, Sophie, I have every right to recover. Did I not *sit* for this portrait?'

'But Claira –'

'No. Will you speak to Horace? He can arrange something.'

'Yes, Claira,' said Madame Sarnot, with deceptive meekness. As Claira flung about the silken drawing room, her friend had paused to examine one of the numerous piles of books. 'Why, how interesting. There is a volume here which is growing a most unusual fungus. It's spreading up the wallpaper. Some kind of mushroom, probably. Don't forget to pick them before the sun shines on this wall or they will be quite spoiled.'

Claira had passed into the bedroom. Her latest hat, winged like a vulture, came off, and Madame Sarnot noticed that what she had taken for a clump of hirsute anemones pinned beneath, was in fact something else.

'My goodness. Claira, your hair has been peroxided!'

'You speak as if some hairdresser crept up on me and did it while I slept. I'm quite aware my hair is bleached. The shade is completely wrong. Now I've seen the portrait, I shall have it adjusted.'

Madame Sarnot, stepping over more books, sat down in an armchair. 'But why is it necessary –'

'Why? He is a part of me. I mean to be as close to him as I can. It's essential. I feel it to be so. The experience is extraordinary. I wake in the night and I – am *him*!'

'For how long?' Madame Sarnot perceptively inquired.

Claira did not reply. Instead she launched into a sort of psychic carousel, a circle which revolved about and about itself, and showed no signs of stopping. This, now, had replaced the vortex of the plot-lines. Simplice had become the sole topic of Claira's conversation. To halt her was not a feasible proposition without recourse to a sledge-hammer. Madame Sarnot, demurely seated amid the books, might well have been dreaming of one.

Three weeks later, the larger de Meunier portrait from the Musée Miramelle hung in Claira Von Oeau's salon, above a small table of the period, draped like an altar and set like one with two candles, flowers, and a pair of mildewed gloves which, only possibly, may have been the property of Simplice.

'And have you *seen* Claira?' cried one of Madame Sarnot's own private friends. 'My God, Sophie. She will be committed. Or arrested. Or both.'

'It's true then? She's taken to dressing in male costume?'

'Of the eighteenth century.'

'I see.'

'You don't see, Sophie. But *I* have. Would you credit, she has had the finest tailors working on the cut of frock coats suitable for the female figure – if such a thing were possible – and her cravats have been ordered from –'

'Yes. I think I did catch a glimpse of those.'

'One ear has been pierced, as with this miller person, and has a gold earring. Her hair was cut and arranged by a leading coiffeur to resemble *his* – loose fair curls to the shoulders.'

'Fortuitously, he isn't depicted with moustache or beard.'

'But allied to this – ' screamed the private friend – 'Sophie, are you listening? – she has been making advances to half the women she meets. Apparently, the poet had a preference for small dark women –'

'Odd. An exact description of the pre-Meunier Claira.'

' – And Claira now flirts with anyone of that type who is silly enough to let her get within arm's reach. And of course she has nothing to back up her outrageous behaviour. Claira is not, and has never been, *une femme aux gauches*. I believe one of the poor little creatures, who is, has actually fallen in love with the bitch, and taken to lying across the door of the building, pining, with her black hair pouring down the steps.'

'Ah,' said Madame Sarnot, 'yes. Horace saw something there when he drove past yesterday. He thought it was a small black spaniel asleep on some washing . . .'

'I don't believe,' ranted the friend, 'you are taking this seriously.'

'I am. I'm most relieved about the spaniel.'

Perhaps two months after the start of the business, something strange occurred. It may, of course, be considered immoderate to refer to anything as *particularly* strange in such uncommon circumstances. However, readers must judge for themselves.

In all, Claira had now a collection of some twenty-four intact (or otherwise) works on the period of study, supplemented by sixteen or seventeen biographies of more important persons which, *en passant*, carried references to the drunken, opium-smoking poet. She had learned, in this piecemeal way, quite an amount about her second self. Of his date and place of birth, his latterly more famous companions, his various failures and his limited *fêtes*. She had learned also of the amorous adventures, and of how one abandoned damsel had drowned herself in the river. A verdict of madness, and some bribery, had ensured the girl a grave in sanctified ground. Thereafter, the lady's cousin, Simplice's best (and by then only) friend, had lured him to the graveyard, stunned and flung him over the appropriate headstone, then decapitating him with one stroke of a well-honed sword.

Scattered information, though, was not sufficient for Claira. And when it had come to her attention that a biography did indeed exist concerned solely with de Meunier, she hurried eagerly to the fount.

This was a loathsome shop on the rue de Clèche. Forcing open a door hardly wider than a pencil, Claira advanced between tottering staircases of black tomes, on the tops of which an occasional dining rat was seated. The clanking of the shop's bell brought from some recess another type of beast, yellowish, in carpet-slippers and a dressing-gown brocaded by a quantity of careless snacks.

'Yes, m'lord?' inquired the beast of Claira. He was maybe as ancient as his emporium, and in his younger days Claira's attire may well have been the norm – for men. Though he recognised her infallibly as a female, he was not adverse to flattering an effect.

'You have here,' said Claira, and named the book.

The beast laughed.

'Why, m'lord. *Had* here. I *had*.'

'Had? What have you done with it?'

'Sold, sir. Sold but yesterday.'

Claira was flabbergasted. She stood with her mouth open on a soundless cry. At length, 'To whom?' she demanded.

'Why, m'lord. With great respect – what affair is that of yours?'

For once, Claira did not tell him. That he did not recognise her alter-ego in herself was insultingly apparent. That he had sold her book – *hers* – to another, was distressing. What actually, however, so startled her, was that – and she must admit it even to herself – someone else seemed to be aware of, interested in and in pursuit, as she was, of Simplice de Meunier.

What she felt was not gratification, not even true irritation at the loss of her rightful property. What Claira experienced was a darkly definite pang of jealousy.

'Monsieur,' said Claira at last, 'the volume is of vital importance to me. You must get it back at once.'

'Oh, m'lord. Impossible.'

'Then tell me who has bought it.'

'I am the priest of my profession. My lips are sealed.'

'Then write it down with your hands,' said Claira, and handed him a bank note.

Having consulted this, the beast, unspeaking, went away for a while. When he returned, he had removed the dressing-gown and put on something very like it but which was, apparently, street-wear.

'If you would be so kind as to step out with me to the corner?'

Claira, mystified and furious, and throbbing with anxiety, agreed. A very notable pair they made, the slender principal boy with her blue frock coat, breeches, blonde curls, earring, walking stick, the beast from the bookshop clad as if for a wedding in hell.

Shortly they reached the corner of two sinister streets. Here a number of posters trailed in the wind.

'Peruse, if you will, sir, these. Run your eye over them. I think you will, by and by, get an idea as to whom the purchaser of the book might be. And I assure you, m'lord, you would not be wrong.'

With those words, the beast left Claira, and slunk away along the adjacent boulevard, towards some den of vice too original to imagine.

Infuriated, Claira could only do as suggested. Presently her eye was caught by a bill advertising the current production at the Théâtre D–. The play in question, which was itself quite famous though seldom now performed, contained in its title the name of a well-known rhetorician, which gave one to believe the work might be concerned with him. It so happened that this rhetorician had also been the brother of the best friend who, in the English cemetery of Notre-Dame du Nord, beheaded Simplice. Claira had heard of the drama, but did not know it. Nevertheless, logic was giving birth to a terrible suspicion.

Turning on the heel of her boot, she rushed back to the carriage.

That evening, Claira Von Oeau attended the theatre. She went in disguise; that is, she went in female attire. Recognised by some of the audience (the city had rather lost track of her recently), she was enthusiastically applauded. She received this accolade with unusual vagueness. Behind the lace visor of her hat, the fruits and foliage of which would have rendered another woman prostrate with migraine, she peered down at the closed curtains of the stage. 'I think you will, by and by, get an idea –' It did not take genius, even Claira's, to reason that a play dealing with the brother of Simplice's murderer might also deal with the murderer himself, and so, unavoidably, with Simplice.

In fact, the play dealt very generously with all three. Before the second scene of the first act was concluded, Simplice de Meunier had walked on to the stage. That is to say, an actor *representing* him had walked on to it. Fatefully, he had been chosen for the part due to a distinct resemblance to the painting of Simplice until recently on show in the Musée Miramelle.

To portray in turn Claira's agitation is unnecessary. Suffice it to say her breath grew short, her looks became daggers, and her black-gloved hands gripped the rail of her box like talons. What is so uniquely one's own, can be no other's.

And there, only feet below, a tall slim young man with fair curls and an earring disported himself in the way only one man can when awarded the character of another: entirely adequately. In fact, it was an exceptionally fine performance. The actor in question had obviously made something of a study of Simplice. He knew things about him that the play alone did not reveal. He had the same habit of twisting his gloves Simplice had had, of running one hand through his hair, of sometimes coughing when nervous. He had the same devilish quality, the teasing look. He went through it all, even to the seduction, some part of which was carried out on stage, of a petite dark actress with red ribbons.

Claira leaned over them, an unseen harpy which, if it had been granted wings, would have flown straight at him, shrieking. She was beside herself. Almost literally. There she was – *he* was – her own self on the boards, in the charge of another. A very clever and talented other. Who was so much more Simplice than she could ever be, now.

An admiring reader sent champagne to her box in the interval. Claira drank it like medicine. She glared at the programme and the name of her enemy, her rival – for what else could he be? – burned itself into her brain. She fidgeted through the next scenes of the play from which Simplice was absent. She sat like stone as he met hideous death in the graveyard, her hands pressed to her own throat in empathy, but her mind elsewhere. As the scandal of the murder enveloped the leading players, in the midst of the drama's climax, rather unquietly Claira left the theatre.

Having driven home, however, in gruesome silence, stumbled unnoticing over the prone brunette would-be lover on the steps, and reached her bed, Claira lay rigid all night. Each stroke of the distant clocks of the city seemed to proclaim a hated name.

It was *he*, of course, who had procured the biography of Simplice de Meunier, *he* who had cheated her of it. And of so much more. Of the indescribable things for which she hankered.

But she had not yet passed sentence.

The morning produced an innocently phrased, adulatory note, which was forthwith dispatched to the Théâtre D–, addressed to the actor Antoine Valère. She begged to know how he had achieved such understanding of the role of Simplice, that he handled it so adroitly. She signed herself with a flourish, not for one moment suspecting Monsieur Valère would never have heard of her, and would consequently omit to reply.

There followed a passage of some days and nights during which this omission was elaborated upon by others, and during which Claira commenced a veritable bombardment of notes, all offering equivalently the same honeyed phrases, each couched a little more threateningly than the last.

She did not see or hear Monsieur Valère, on receipt of the thirty-second note, inquire of someone: 'Who is this madwoman?' She did eventually receive his answer.

My dear mademoiselle,
I am most gratified by your praise. But I am haunted by the thought of the agony of penman's cramp you must be suffering. Do, I beg you, for both our sakes, stop writing to me.

Claira's response to this may again be pictured.

Also, her reaction to an interview with Valère that, subsequent to his great success in the part of de Meunier, appeared later in the week in the pages of the *Journal de la Cité*.

Valère had not been quite sober when the interview was given, and had not only basked and boasted, but revealed one wildly all-too-salient facet of his handle on Simplice. It transpired that the insights he received, while rehearsing the character, had become so astonishingly, even unnervingly apposite (both to himself and colleagues) that, half jokingly he had been driven to consult a medium. An eminent name was then mentioned which was not that of Madame Q–. 'I laugh at it myself,' continued Valère, 'and also, I admit, I am made somewhat afraid by it.' According to the consulted medium, Monsieur Valère was none other than a reincarnation of Monsieur de Meunier. Everything pointed to it. Similarity of physique, features, even of colouring, and of mannerisms; added to these an uncanny depth of comprehension and familiarity. 'He advised me,' the actor confided, 'to learn as much about Simplice as I could, in order to try to "recall", in a conscious and controlled manner. But very oddly,' he went on, in an offended way, 'someone seems always to have been there ahead of me. No sooner did I discover a book or paper which referred to him, than the only copies extant had been bought, in some cases only half an hour before I arrived at the venue.'

Claira saw no humour in this.

She had at no time asked herself why her present life had, in some curious way, so dismally let her down that she preferred to reach backwards to a previous one. Nor did she interrogate her motives now. She was aware only that the city was no longer large enough to shelter both herself and Antoine Valère.

It happened – such silly things do happen – that the door-keeper at the Théâtre D– was an avid reader of the novels of Mademoiselle Von Oeau. There in his cubby he had swallowed each lurid fantasy and epic as it was sprung from the presses. Hence, on her entry to his world, he was prepared to do anything in his power to assist her. This included being persuaded, on the flimsiest of evidence, that the actor Valère was expecting her after the performance. Valère, who was actually expecting a steak sandwich from the Café D– across the boulevard, invited her in at once.

Turning from the mirror, he then found himself confronted by a creature all in beetle black, with a gigantic black lid of a hat from which scarlet ostrich feathers erupted, like wired blood. She had come in disguise, again.

'Good God,' said Valère. He did not say he had mistaken her for a sandwich.

'I have been writing to you,' said Claira.

'Ah . . . yes,' said Valère, cautiously.

'I have also,' said Claira, 'read the interview in the *Journal*. I conclude that I am the person who has deprived you of all the material you wished to gather on de Meunier.' (It was second-name terms with the enemy.) 'While you –' she pointed a long black finger at the only book on a side table, 'have managed to get hold of *that*. The very volume I set my heart on reading.'

'That,' said Valère, indicating the book, 'is a railway timetable. Are you very interested in trains?'

Claira ignored this sally. 'I refer to the de Meunier biography.'

'Do I have that?'

'I am led to believe so.'

As if to insult her, he removed the gold earring, which was false, and shook out the fair curls, which were not.

'It seems to me,' said Claira, 'that a compromise might be effected. I could let you make selection from the volumes I have acquired, in exchange for the loan of the biography.'

Valère considered this. Obviously, he was as interested, in his own way, in the subject of Simplice as Claira was. Nor was he quite immune to the spectacle of opulence she presented. There is something stabilising in money.

'It seems,' said Valère, rather grudgingly, 'a straightforward offer.'

'It would be an honour to help you,' said Claira. 'I am your devoted adherent. Being slightly acquainted myself with the occult, I also sympathise with your view of reincarnation –'

'Yes, *that*,' said Valère, colouring, and evading her look. 'Partly a joke, at the expense of the *Journal*.'

Claira narrowed her eyes with hatred. It was bad enough to be usurped, but to be mocked in the process was beyond forgiveness. Not that she had any intention of forgiving him anything.

At this instant the genuine sandwich arrived.

'You can't eat that,' said Claira. 'Brilliance deserves its reward. Come with me. We shall dine at l'Auguste.'

Valère, who had no defensive weapons save a cruel tongue and an ability sometimes to be reticent, found himself being swept out into the street by Claira, the awful hat, and a creeping subcutaneous reverence for riches. So to the carriage, so to the palatial restaurant where, under the chandeliers, Claira peeled back her gloves in the reverse mode of the assassin, while champagne corks flew.

Dinner was not marked by anything untoward. Encouraged by good food and wine, Valère was quite prepared to divulge all he had learned and could remember of Simplice. Claira, who was determined to bleed him dry, sat as avidly as a praying mantis, hanging on every word with the fascination of the lover. When at last exhaustion caused his monologue to peter out, the social occasion was concluded. The waiters at l'Auguste knew better than to bat an eyelid when a lady paid the bill.

'And this last bottle of champagne,' said Claira, 'you may open it.'

The cork shot forth as three o'clock was struck throughout the city.

'We can take it with us, for you to drink in the carriage. Of course, my driver will convey you to your door.'

Valère, however, declined. He would prefer to stroll awhile by the river, to walk off the wine. (This was also an excellent ruse whereby to avoid Claira's learning his address.)

He had anticipated possible argument. None came. They had made no arrangements about the books, which Valère thought odd, but he had no intention of taking up the matter now. The supper had been good, there seemed no problem attached to it, this was the time to escape. Yet it was Claira who rose. 'I shall leave you, then. But drink the champagne.' She advanced the newly opened bottle across the table, filling his glass. 'A last toast to the one –' she paused and smiled at him, a wolfish smile that displayed a great many teeth –' the one you *were*, Monsieur Antoine.'

With that she departed, her plumage knocking a stuffed parrot from its swing near the door. She did not look back. Like a black bat, she was closed into the outer night.

Valère was tempted to drink one further glass of the perfect champagne. But he was not the drunkard de Meunier had been and a warning of dizziness in the end stopped him. Bidding a cheerful adieu to the waiters, he too made his way out into the darkness.

It is the custom that the wine the guests do not drink becomes a libation to commerce. The chef took most of the bottle, as was his wont. The waiters appropriated the dregs. One, craftier than the rest, downed behind a door Valère's full glass. He did not, thereby, do himself the favour he had thought. Imbibed with the wine was the dissolved pellet of arsenic and opium Mademoiselle Von Oeau had crumbled in the goblet.

'How curious,' said Horace Sarnot to his wife, over the croissants. 'I heard Claira was dining at l'Auguste last night, with some actor. Just one hour after, a waiter was found poisoned.' Madame Sarnot glanced up quizzically. 'It seems,' said Horace, 'this waiter had often threatened suicide. Something must have driven him over the edge.'

'Waiting on Claira, perhaps?'

'In any event, the doctors saved his life. First of all, he denied taking any poison and accused the chef. But it then seems the chef sent round his seconds and the charge is withdrawn, the suicide bid confessed.'

With such a gentle ripple as this, the initial attempt at homicide was destined to pass.

The arsenic ingredient had come from a tin of rat poison. The de Meunieresque opium Claira had long since installed, as a matter of course, on the sideboard with the sherry and oranges. She had not herself ever smoked it, just as she seldom drank alcohol. A natural hysteric, she generally did not require artificial aids.

But, as the first means had come fairly easily to hand, the second was, on the contrary, difficult.

'Sophie,' said Madame Sarnot's private friend, 'Claira has taken up shooting.'

'At whom?' asked Madame Sarnot, more prophetically than she could know.

'I mean, she is paying to be instructed in the use of a small hand-weapon.'

'But Simplice de Meunier never shot, did he?'

'Well, Sophie, I think that craze is dying out. Really I do. The little *femme gauche* has disappeared from the doorstep. And Claira has been seen about quite frequently in female clothes and those interesting hats of hers. Probably she'll write a book about him.'

'*Simplice: A Double Life . . .*' mused Madame Sarnot experimentally.

Meanwhile, on the rue Swanhilde, having shattered an image of herself in a mirror at ten paces, and while neighbours banged screeching on the doors, Claira wrote hurriedly in her diary, *I am not afraid to destroy myself in the battle, providing I do not pass the mortal gate alone.*

This was untrue. As with the inept attempt at poisoning, Claira had no actual conviction she would be caught in the act, or taken afterwards. Obliquely, she did have some understanding of human obtuseness. To the average mind, she had no motive in the world for slaughtering Antoine Valère, while actors were constantly the target of lunatics (lunatic being a category distinctly separate from her own).

A handful of nights later, three actors of the Théâtre D– Company, one of whom was Valère, were idling near midnight among the cafés on the Boule.

'It's very strange,' said one, who had the luck to play the part of an army officer, 'but I would swear something has been following us for the past half hour.'

'Something? What?' asked the second, none other than Simplice's proxy murderer.

'A shadow in a cloak.'

'What can it be? A thief? A ghost?'

'A prostitute?'

Later yet, as they went along by the river, pausing under a lamp to light their cigarettes, the army officer was heard to exclaim: 'Look! What did I say? Over *there*.'

Three lamp-yellowed faces were turned inquiringly, above the embers of three cigarettes and a dying match. Ironically, the proxy murderer was the only one of them who caught the impression of an arc of swaying feathers, like the crest of some huge bird, and of the straightening arm. Then the dreadful explosion of a shot rang out across the night.

The actors scattered with curses as the fragments of the broken lantern rained on their heads. (To hit a well-lit mirror at ten paces does not compare to trying to hit the heart of a man at thirty.)

Having blown out all illumination, the assassin's chances were further reduced, but gamely she tried again. Unbeknownst to any of them, this time she shot a surfacing fish in the river, the corpse of which, captured next day in a net, would prove the cause of wonder at a local dinner-table.

The actors had meanwhile taken to their heels, yelling for police. Claira was left alone in the blackness with the emptied pistol and a sense of injustice.

To say that Madame Sarnot approached Claira's apartment cautiously, or to say that she opened the ensuing conversation with finesse, subtlety, or any apparent regard for personal safety, would be untrue.

'My dear Claira,' said Madame Sarnot, as the door was closed on them, 'you really must stop trying to kill Antoine Valère.'

Claira poised aloofly by the fire, toying with the poker. She was dressed today au Monsieur de Meunier, to the last earring. (It is perhaps interesting, or informative, to note that while doing so, she had never omitted powder or mascara.)

'Whatever,' said Claira, 'do you mean?'

'What I say. I was so sorry for the poor waiter. He has a mistress to support, and six children. Not to mention a seventh child waiting, as it were, in the wings.'

'In that case,' said Claira, 'his mistress is probably sorry – someone – was not more efficient.'

'Now, now, Claira. You are not a benefactress. You are a poisoner.

And also a person who fires off pistols and indiscriminately shatters harmless lanterns.'

'You have lost me.'

'No, I have not lost you. The papers were full of the attempted assassination. Somehow they seem to have got the idea the intended victim was Monsieur Brun, who plays the rhetorician so . . . rhetorically. It transpires he is involved with somebody's wife, and threats have been made. Good gracious, Claira. The innocent husband has fallen under immediate suspicion and had to fly the police. Are you not ashamed?'

Claira patently was not. She stood, the poker shining in her hand bright as a sword, her beautiful brows slightly raised, like two bows about to let loose arrows. She was magnetic in her ghastliness.

'And what next, then?' said Madame Sarnot. 'May I suggest setting fire to the theatre? Or have you already done it? I passed a fire-wagon on the street; perhaps it was hastening there.' Claira said nothing. Madame Sarnot asked herself if she did not detect the quickening of inspiration in the arrow-head eyes. 'That last was a joke,' said Madame Sarnot firmly. 'But what I shall say next is not. If anything further happens, I shall be forced to seek the authorities.'

A response: 'Sophie!'

'Much as it may grieve me to do it.'

Another response, somewhat similar: 'Sophie –'

'And I shall tell them all I know. All I guess. They will probably be suspicious of me at first, but Horace occupies a high position, as you know, and is able to pull strings – witness your portrait from the Miramelle. Something will get done, eventually. Prison is not your ideal habitat. Consider it.'

'*Sophie –*'

'No. Accoladism and friendship aside, I won't be party to a murder. It is ridiculous. It is messy. That is all I have to say.'

'Judas,' said Claira, merely altering the name.

Madame Sarnot paused at the doors. Grimly, she said, 'Without Judas, where would Christianity be today?'

This, unfortunately, was perhaps not the best retort. It may have induced further notions of betrayed grandeur, undying reputation.

Two days after this interview had taken place, a fire broke out at the Théâtre D–, in the dressing-room of Antoine Valère. It was thought generally to have been the result of an accident – the entire company of actors' habit of smoking being to blame. The door-keeper privately supposed he had received a supernatural warning. Called outside by wild cries for help, he found no one, but had afterwards the weird recollection of a hooded shadow slipping by him, which he put down to a manifestation of the theatre ghost. When the commotion subsequently burst forth, he missed the second advent of the hooded shadow, slipping by him yet again, on its way out.

The fire was extinguished before much damage had been done. Antoine Valère, arriving rather late, missed all the excitement, but was forced to act that night in borrowed robes. His own costume (left strewn over the dressing-room sofa cushions, along with a curly blond sheepskin hat, the collection definitely resembling a sleeping Monsieur Valère to the hasty eye) had been burnt to a frazzle.

'There is a lady to see you,' announced the door-keeper to Valère the following evening.

'Ah. I think I have already left.'

The door-keeper ignored this.

'It's the wife of Monsieur Horace Sarnot, the minister of –.'

Surprised, an intuitive name-dropper in need of names to be dropped, Valère conceded he might after all still be in the theatre. Presently Madame Sarnot was ushered through.

'Good evening, I am here in a private capacity, if on a very serious mission.'

The city, or that portion of the city which kept itself *au courant* with the dramatic calendar, was presently intrigued and – in the case of those who had not yet seen the show – outraged, by the abrupt departure of Monsieur Antoine Valère for the provinces. It seemed an elderly relation – rich – had fallen ill. Valère had been summoned to the bedside, and modern medicine being what it was, it could only be expected he would be delayed there quite some time. The management of the Théâtre D– seemed curiously resigned. The new actor who took on the part of Simplice de Meunier was, according to the general consensus, '*palôt*'.

By mid-afternoon Claira had her bags packed, her blonde curls constrained beneath a, for Claira, nondescript hat, and the carriage was almost at the door. A number of the papers had ingenuously mentioned Monsieur Valère's destination as a mansion on the outskirts of the little town of Guisenne. This had accordingly also become Claira's destination. One fears one must imagine her two valises filled by a few garments and several means of sudden death.

A timid knock on the apartment door sent Claira springing to open it. It was not, however, the maid or the coachman, it was a small black-haired girl with ribbons, none other than Horace Sarnot's spaniel-and-washing of the door-step pining variety.

But, 'Who are you?' demanded Claira, who tended to forget very quickly those who no longer interested her.

The eyes of the once hopeful young lady filled with tears.

'Oh, Claira. How cruel you are.'

'Then I am cruel and in a hurry.'

'So I see. Well,' said the brunette, brushing tears from her lashes with a lace handkerchief, 'I see I'm not wanted, shall never be wanted. But I brought you this. Here, take it. A gift carries no obligations. *Oh*!'

And, in this palpitating way, in a mist of lilac scent, the lovely door-stop rushed away, having deposited in Claira's hands – which tended to grasp things automatically, as a hawk grasps prey – a brown paper parcel.

This, still wrapped and tied, was shortly taken out to the carriage with the valises of silk blouses and possible cheese-wire and gunpowder. In the thickening gold of late afternoon light, the carriage stormed westward, leaving the walled heights and embankments of the city, as if for ever.

The road to Guisenne was bumpy and long. The coachman, used to Claira, had not quibbled at the instruction to drive all night.

Claira though, caged, her active, grasshopper mind perhaps bored by unmitigated dreams of revenge, presently tore the wrapper off the parcel.

Within was a book. *The* book. Or at least, another copy of *the* book, for this one was neither a train timetable nor mildewed and falling apart. A biography, none the less, of Simplice de Meunier, its pages delicately brown as if lightly toasted. A small pink note proclaimed the obvious. The brunette had scoured the city in hopes of finding a token her beloved might appreciate. And lo! She had come across this volume, and also the pamphlet, which last item she had placed between the final page and the cover. At this point, the pamphlet fell out on the carriage seat.

It was a fragile thing, the pamphlet, pale and powdery, ostentatiously old. The title caught Claira's eye instantly, and with good reason. For some while she sat on the jouncing springs, staring.

The moon had begun to rise and they were half-way to Guisenne

when the coachman received an order to turn round, and hurry back
to the city.

'Someone,' said Madame Sarnot's private friend, 'seems to have died
and left Valère a small fortune. Or at least,' she added with a very
sharp glance, 'he has got a lot of money from somewhere.' Madame
Sarnot smiled, blankly. 'Which hasn't prevented his returning to
enormous success at the theatre. I gather one of the leading play-
wright managers has told the journals he will be writing a drama
solely on the subject of this miller poet, and will be approaching
Valère about the part.' Madame Sarnot smiled, less blankly. 'Then
again, somebody else has struck gold. Do you remember the *femme
gauche* who enhanced Claira's doorway for so long? She now owns a
house on the rue Lucette. I wouldn't be surprised if Claira hadn't paid
her off.'

Madame Sarnot continued to smile. She said, 'Yes, Claira has quite
altered in the past month. I like that seventeenth-century style. Rather
charming, don't you think?'

'The coiffeur who re-darkened her hair said that he was called from
his bed at six in the morning to do it.'

'Obviously a sudden decision.'

'The dressmakers were herded in on the same day, and only a few
hours after.'

'More interesting, perhaps, than all this, is the new novel.'

'It's true, then?'

'Well,' said Madame Sarnot, 'pages of manuscript seem to be
strewn about the apartment.'

'A Persian romance, I gather? Or is it Indian?'

'Or a mingling of both?'

Madame Sarnot reviewed in her mind a fragment she had been
lucky enough to gaze upon, in which a maiden sat playing a *sitar* at the
confluence of the rivers Tigris and Ganges. Claria's worlds were
normally exquisitely interconnected. She had spoken, too, for half an
hour on the subject of her hero. His hair was black, his rings upon his
fingers. He was not Simplice.

Not that the de Meunier portrait, procured from the Miramelle by
political strategy and the arm-twisting of Horace, was no longer on
display. No indeed, there it hung in all magnificence, the altar still laid
beneath with fresh flowers and candles, and aged gloves. A large
bookcase had been installed nearby, in which reposed the relevant

literature Claira had gathered. There was also a small glass case inside which lay a grey pamphlet, dainty as the proverbial moth's wing.

'Why, how tantalising,' said Madame Sarnot, peering in at it, seemingly striving to read the caption, which was obscured by a single white rose.

Claira exchanged a *look* with de Meunier, intimate and knowing in the extreme. 'Oh, yes.'

Her dark hair was now rather longer, and worn in a fashion appropriate to her current time continuum (1690?). She drifted into the salon. There was a femininity and languidness to Mademoiselle Von Oeau that had not been noticeable before. It was not that Claira had become restful, this was far from being one of her social talents. But *rested*, maybe. The tension of the wires of the lute had slackened, the bow-string was unarmed.

'And how is the novel?' asked Madame Sarnot.

Claira told her, which took three hours. Claira also revealed her intention of going to press in a slightly altered persona. 'My publishers, of course, object. I have told them, I shall take the manuscript elsewhere if they fail to agree.' The alteration was, apparently, only to the forename. Claira was to become 'Clarissa'. Claira did not explain why this was to be. There was about her, also, a secretiveness that was unusual. It seemed always on the verge of flowering into revelation, yet never did so. A cat, however, its closed mouth full of canary, could not have looked more pleased by the containment.

A month then elapsed. Another month. There came an evening when, at a reception of some importance, Horace Sarnot drew his wife to one side and whispered urgently, 'Claira is here, is she not?' 'Why, yes.' 'Valère has just walked through the door.' Madame Sarnot looked in the applicable direction, and beheld a goodlooking young man with blond curls and very correct evening-dress. Monsieur Sarnot who, as his wife had once pointed out, could get so many and curious things seen to, now stood powerlessly and nervously, tugging at his whiskers. But, 'Don't be alarmed,' said Madame Sarnot. 'I think it will hardly matter.'

At this very instant, their illustrious hostess had, ducking Claira's statuesque *perruque*, taken her arm. 'As one of our leading authoresses, you really should be introduced to one of the city's leading actors.' Claira allowed herself to be led. 'You see? That perfectly beautiful young man.' Claira saw. She saw with vague recognition, *dis*interested, *un*interested recognition, as one observes the landscape of another country one has never visited, and has no plans for visiting.

'*Mon Dieu*,' said Horace. 'They're meeting.'

'Calmly. You see? Meeting, smiling, parting. Valère has already forgotten Claira, who does, to be fair to him, look somewhat different.'

'And Claira . . .'

'Claira moves in another universe, Horace, than most of us. If Valère stepped inside the boundaries at any time, he has now retreated.'

'Oh dear,' the hostess was saying. Claira had congratulated an actor, famed everywhere for his portrayal of an eighteenth-century poet called Simplice, with the words: 'Of course, you must find *Hamlet* a most demanding role.' 'Mademoiselle Von Oeau, that was *Antoine Valère*.'

Claira regarded her hostess across the mists of two hundred years. 'Who?' she asked.

Returning shortly before one o'clock to her apartment on the rue Swanhilde, Claira lit the candles on the de Meunier altar, and took from its place the moth-wing pamphlet. For something so antique and so fragile, it must be remarked, the pamphlet bore up very well under its constant handling.

Claira inspected it often. Since the moment in the carriage when it had first fallen into her life, a day had not gone by without her attentions to it being renewed.

What then was this miraculous item, which had scattered arsenic and cheese-wire, bullets and gunpowder, not to mention opium, blondness, male attire and one earring, to the four winds of heaven?

The title and caption on the front of the pamphlet read as follows: *The de Meunier 'Phantom'. The bizarre and tragic case of a poet's obsession with the mysterious dark lady of whom he believed himself to be a reincarnation.*

Exclamations are, perhaps, at this point superfluous. Even explanations will be minimal.

The essay itself was short and comparatively succinct. It described how its conclusions had been evolved via the unearthing of particular pieces of correspondence between Simplice de Meunier and his agents, his elderly father, and so on. It was illustrated by extracts from these letters, in Simplice's unmistakable and sprawling hand which, as the opium intake increased, appeared to grow familiar with Chinese. Other illustrations were in the form of quoted portions of poetry.

There was also a reproduction of a pencil sketch, allegedly by de Meunier himself – when under the influence, and looking it.

The substance of the essay was simply this: from early manhood, the poet had been fixated on the mental image of a small, slight, dark-haired woman with very fine eyes. Initially, he wrote poems to her, and attempted, in his amorous career, to discover her in the arms of numerous female conquests. His faithlessness and callousness, the pamphlet revealed (as did the quoted letters, where at all readable), sprang from the dissimilarity between each woman Simplice seduced and the intellectual fixation. Eventually, a Monsieur Y–, a well-known medium of the era, meeting de Meunier by chance, revealed that the female *idée fixe* was none other than a recollected image of Simplice's last past life. This turned out to be a young woman, like himself a writer, although of scholarly classical romances. Her hair was black, her eyes fine, her figure small and slender. She had dwelled in the late sixteen hundreds, and was called – the medium regretted her obscurity (she had penned her epics in secret), would only give up a first name – Clarissa.

De Meunier continued obsessed by his Dark Lady, this Clarissa, with most unfortunate consequences. The opium he had, until then, only occasionally taken, became a daily and nightly recourse in his wild attempts to recall the prior life. Meanwhile, his frantic search to discover a look-alike in the female population of the city, rather than being sensibly abandoned as impossible, was resumed with all the heady contempt of failure's foregone conclusion. Thus eventually the cousin of the rhetorician's brother was caught up, cast off – left to drown herself. And hence the fatal fracas in the English cemetery of Notre-Dame du Nord, and a headless corpse draped across a grave.

Aside from the sections of poems the pamphlet included which feverishly mentioned the Dark Lady, there were also the other poems, which anyone who had researched de Meunier would already have read, and which also extolled her *ad nauseam*. As for the pencil sketch, labelled in de Meunier's unsteady hand: *Clarissa*, it was quite well-drawn, in a drunken way. In it, details of seventeenth-century dress were nicely apparent. It was also apparent that it very greatly resembled Claira Von Oeau.

It was a man's world . . . And though one had been a man, now one was a woman. There were, try as one would, certain areas . . . And then there was, too, Antoine Valère, a man so properly and damningly acting a man . . .

But the dove arrives in the nick of time, putting out the fuse with its dewy olive-branch. To be one's own beloved. What else does the personality require, after all? What else, after all, are we?

As Simplice, she had adored herself, even to *extremis*, as now she was. And as herself, she had no rivals, she was nonpareil. So Claira became herself once more, in the style of Clarissa, to please him – to please herself. And it did please her.

Indeed, everyone was pleased.

While the latest lurid, glorious epic, with its potato-eating rajas and its muezzins' dawn cry to worship Kali Ma, was a most spectacular success.

Antoine Valère, as demonstrated, was forgotten. It no longer mattered what he did or thought. Claira had overtaken him and was one jump ahead, perpetually.

One swallow does not, of course, always make a summer. But then, it rather depends on *what* one has swallowed.

Little remains otherwise to be said. Possibly it would be better to say nothing further. However. The recounting of the above incidents cannot properly be closed without this slight, tiresome addendum. The reader is asked only to note these few facts. That plainly Antoine Valère was paid temporarily to fly the scene, and secured during flight against professional injury; that the dark-haired young woman of the door-stop variety, who delivered biography and pamphlet, was next set up in a pleasant house; that Madame Sarnot was an honourable woman who abhorred murder as 'messy', understood the foolishness of most scruples, and had for a husband one wise in the matter of pulling strings. Lastly, that the pamphlet and its subject matter, which perhaps saved Valère's life, and undoubtedly Claira's neck, go unrecognised in the few extant works concerning Simplice. Nowhere else is there a reference to his having any interest in reincarnation. And though he surely preferred brunettes, some gentlemen do.

No more, then. Conclusions may be drawn or left strictly alone. Most events are open to conjecture. As for the behaviour of the cast of this drama, it behoves us, perhaps, to be lenient. Conceivably, as Hamlet (though never in the person of Antoine Valère) informs us, there is a divinity that shapes our ends, rough hew them how we will. But who, after all, would be brutish enough to deny any one of us use of a mallet and chisel?

The Truce

Dawn was already scarlet in the sky when Issla rose from the Prayer-Place. Issla had been there most of the night, not really praying, but finding some comfort from the unseen communion of the spirits of dead Ullakin. Today was the important and terrible day. So much rested upon the events of today that it was almost unbearable to think about it. Drael stood in the mouth of the Prayer-Place, spear in hand. Issla pressed herself to the known, loved body, seeking comfort, and at last the miserable and frightened tears welled out.

'Hush, darling,' Drael said, 'don't be afraid.'

'I am, I am,' Issla wept. 'How can I not be afraid? I am carrying the burden of life on me today, and even you, who love me, will let me go to the Truce Place and suffer there.'

'There'll be no suffering,' Drael said sternly. 'No one will hurt you. They must not break the Truce, even if they are beasts. I'll wait beside the cave mouth with my spear, and if you call out, I will kill the beast with you. Trust me.' Issla's weeping grew less. 'Come now,' Drael said, 'the Chief wants to bless you for the task.'

They went up the slope, Drael's arm about Issla's shoulders. The way was steep, old grey rock, a few thorn trees thrust out here and there. The fortress of the Ullakin was built into this rock, safe from their enemies, but bleak and comfortless nevertheless.

The Chief stood outside the Big Cave, the Ullakin warriors spread around, spears in hand, waiting. Issla came with bowed head and was solemnly blessed. Then the Chief pointed away from the rock to the scarred defile below, where once an ancient river had dried itself out. And they were coming already, the dark and terrible Ullaks, the eternal enemy of the Ullakin, passing unharmed between the watching sentries perched on the rock walls, because today was the day of Truce. Issla whimpered.

'Courage,' the Chief said, 'Drael is pledged to protect you, as we all are. Only be brave, and you may save our race – and theirs, though our ancestors know that is a bad price to pay.'

Issla stared at the approaching tribe and saw, after a while, that they were not as terrible as expected. Issla, who had never fought with the warriors, had never seen an Ullak close to, but they did not seem so very different from the Ullakin in fact, at least, not as different as the stories said. They were climbing the rough-hewn steps of the fortress now and arranging themselves on the plateau outside the sacred cave.

'Come,' the Chief commanded, and the Ullakin went towards the plateau also, in the first heat of the day.

'I am not so afraid now,' Issla said.

'That's good,' said Drael. 'Only remember, be on your guard. They're beasts, dirty sometimes in their ways of love.' With a sudden weird jealous spite, Drael spat.

The sacred cave, the cave which was to be so important today, was set roughly in the centre of the rock wall leaning over the plateau. A whitish woven cloth, painted with the ritualistic signs of the Ullakin, rippled at the entrance, hiding the interior. To the right of it the enemy chief stood, in front of the Ullak warriors. The skins they wore were badly cured and, coming this close to them, Issla became aware of their stink, a smell not only of the skins, but of their alien bodies and alien sweat.

I hate my enemy, Issla thought suddenly, the old traditional war vow, *but I must not hate. Not today.*

The two Chiefs went forward and confronted each other silently. The Ullak was bigger, grinning, leaning on a spear, deliberately ignoring the occasion's sanctity.

'You are my foe, but today I honour you,' the Ullakin Chief said.

The Ullak repeated the Truce promise. They stood looking at each other.

Ralka, the Ullakin's Pronouncer, came forward, and began to recite the already known reason for the coming together. And, although known, a great quiet hung on the plateau as every ear listened.

'We are met here, forgetting our enmity, to save ourselves. It is told us that in the old times, young could be made by love, carried in the body and brought forth whole. Now, neither of our races can produce young by this means, and we have relied on the breeding machines and hatcheries left us by our ancestors, praised be they. Now the machines have ceased to function. The birth-eggs crack and the young die. It is the same for both of us. It is told us that once the Ullak and the Ullakin were one people. Therefore, in answer to our prayers, our Oracle has told us to make Truce with you, and bring together one of our number and one of yours, hoping that a sign may be shown them, and that they may find some way of cross-breeding that will produce offspring. You have agreed to this.' Ralka beckoned and Issla, trembling, went forward. 'This is our Chosen One. Who is yours?' One of the Ullaks came shambling up. The large face Issla saw looming across the raw sunlight of the plateau seemed uneasy. Issla felt a sudden sympathy for this beast and fear diminished.

The Ullakin Chief said sternly:

'Let neither harm the other. You may kill our Chosen if harm comes to yours, and we claim the right to do likewise. Go, now, into the cave.'

Panicking, Issla stared back, and saw Drael's carved pale face and angry clenched hand on the spear. Drael's lips shaped the words, *Only call, and I will kill it.*

Then Issla was at the curtain, the Ullak was at the curtain, the woven stuff lifted, the gloom reached out, and they were inside together, alone in the dark and terrible cave.

Dried grasses lay over the floor. It was cool and dank. Little needles of muted light sewed through the tiny chinks in the rock's armour. Issla drew back against the cave wall and watched the Ullak draw back against another. After a minute, the Ullak spoke:

'I am called Kloll. How are you called?'

The voice was rough and different, but the words formed were familiar.

'I am Issla.'

'Let's sit down, `Kloll said. 'No, don't be afraid. You sit there and I'll stay here. What a way for our ancestors to pay us out, isn't it?'

Issla gasped and made a quick sign to avert sacred anger. The Ullak laughed.

'You Ullakin,' Kloll went on. 'You think you were the cream of the lost race, don't you? And the Ullaks were the degenerates, the morons, the deformed things, made out of spit and excrement?'

Issla sat wide-eyed, heart thudding.

'I'm sorry,' Kloll said, 'this isn't the way to go about it. Sacred Dark! What do they want us to do?'

'They hope our ancestors will grant us a sign,' Issla whispered.
And the Ullak laughed.

They sat for a long while in silence.

Outside, on the plateau, the magic drums beat, and religious smokes went up. The Chiefs would probably share an awkward meal at midday.

'Well,' said Kloll eventually, 'we'd better talk, perhaps. Tell me about yourself, Issla Ullakin.'

Issla sat still, not knowing what to say.

'Well,' Kloll said, 'don't you have a lover you want to praise to me?'

'Drael is my lover,' Issla said, 'one of the warriors. And you?'

'Oh, we're not so permanent as you. We chop and change. We have sacred orgies, too; I expect you've heard about them.'

'Yes,' Issla said, and repressed a shudder.

You must be strong, Issla's brain instructed.

Issla got up and moved closer to the Ullak, closer to the strangeness and alien smell, which now did not seem so repulsive. Presumably the Ullak must find the Ullakin odour equally obnoxious. Another silence fell, and then, after a while, the Ullak's great paw came out and touched Issla's hair. Issla trembled and found that the Ullak was trembling too.

'Don't be afraid,' Kloll whispered, and the whisper was suddenly like Drael's whisper in the cup of the night, gentle, anxious and intimate. Issla moved closer to Kloll until their bodies touched. And in this closeness they waited for their ancestors to speak to them.

Day grew gold, and darker gold, passing on into the swift savagery of sunset. Firelight mounted on the plateau, and stars burst their shells overhead. Drael waited near the cave mouth, eyes fixed. Root wine had gone round and the two enemy tribes were friendlier now, soaking their worry in the drink. But when the cup came to Drael, Drael pushed it away.

And in the cave –

'I know you now,' Kloll said suddenly.

'Yes,' Issla said.

They had not spoken for hours, simply sat close, waiting; out of the trance that they had woven between them, the answer seemed now to be coming.

'I am no longer afraid,' said Issla. 'Why have we been enemies all this while when, after all, we are so alike?'

'Listen,' Kloll said, 'they tell us, long ago, the young were made from love. Shall we pretend that we're lovers? Perhaps this is what our ancestors want.'

But Issla had stiffened.

'Your ways of love are different from ours,' Issla said.

'Perhaps that's what's needed.' And the Ullak touched Issla softly, as Drael would have done, in the long night.

'This is right,' Kloll whispered soon, 'I feel this is right.'

And Issla, washed away like a swimmer on the unexpected sea of the Ullak's hands, stirred, and seemed to know the strange lost hunger that possessed Kloll.

'Yes, this is right,' Issla moaned, 'yes, yes . . .'

And then, in the blackness, a wrongness, a pain.

'No,' Issla hissed, 'you're hurting me. No.'

'Wait,' Kloll pleaded. 'This is as it must be. I feel it. I know.'

But the Ullak had become again an enemy, and, after a moment of agonised terror, Issla screamed for Drael.

And Drael heard.

Drael's hands ripped aside the woven curtain, profaning the painted symbols. Drael paused one moment only, to ascertain which of the moving shadows was Issla and which the beast, and then the sharpened spear was thrust deep in the Ullak's back. With a small noise like despair, Kloll rolled over and died.

Drael lifted Issla.

'It's all right,' Drael said, 'I killed it as I said I would. Did it hurt you?'

'Yes,' Issla wept.

Drael pulled the Ullak by the embedded spear, and dragged the corpse out on to the plateau. A cry went up, shock and rage. Several of the Ullaks bounded forward. Drael ripped out the spear and threatened them with it.

'Wait, you defiled things,' Drael cried, 'your Chosen broke the Truce. Your Chosen wounded Issla.'

Issla came out of the cave, and there were red spots on the front of the Ullakin tunic from the wound Kloll had made. The Ullaks quietened, mumbled together.

Drael gazed at Issla a moment, then flung round to the Ullakin's Chief.

'Let's kill them, these beasts, now, while we have them in the stronghold!'

The growling of anger and fear broke out again, but the Chief stepped forward and slapped Drael across the face.

'Fool,' the Chief said, 'our ancestors will always remember how you sought to dishonour us.'

Drael fell back and turned away.

'Now,' the Chief said, 'Tribe of Ullak, go from us. Your Chosen has hurt our Chosen and, as it was agreed, we have killed. You cannot say we have not abided by our word. You Ullaks are the ones who broke the Truce.'

The Ullak Chief stood glowering in the firelight. Then the glowering turned to a great sorrow, a great regret.

'I know it to be true,' the Ullak said. 'It is sadness to me, as it is to you, that we can never now find peace together. Our ancestors have proved to us cruelly that new life can never spring from the joining of our two races.'

The Ullak Chief gestured to the Ullak warriors.

'We leave you now,' the Chief said, 'only give us Kloll's body so that we can bury it.'

'Take it,' the Ullakin Chief said, 'go, like the ancient river, to die out from the face of the earth, as we too must die, now there is no hope.'

So the tribe of men turned away into the darkness, carrying their dead one, leaving the fortress of women alone on their rock.

And Drael, her arms round the girl Issla, spat after them into the quiet night, 'I hate my enemy,' and pressed her mouth to Issla's hair.

The Squire's Tale

We came to a place, a barren place on the rim of the Dead Lands, where a yellowish dusk swam between the trees. The branches were black against the evening; nothing moved in the fern among the tree roots. No birds sang in the red rags of withering leaves.

My lord lifted up his helm and looked about him. All the time the horses shifted beneath us, ill at ease, stirring the earth with their feet.

'There is a smell here,' said my lord, 'the smell of a place which has been dirtied and misused. A blight has come down with the dew, and the sun drinks it up from the ground, and the stars spit it back at night.' A big white moon was rising. My lord looked at it and said: 'When the moon passes over this place, God knows what rises up. Come!' And quickly we spurred our mounts away, and they trembled with fear between our limbs.

As the pale eye of the moon came nearer, the evil lifted from the earth. It came mistily and like smoke, and through the trees strange shapes like fish and serpents seemed to slide. It was a wicked place. Beyond the wood was a stake such as men use to burn a witch upon, and the embers yet smouldered on a black corpse there. There was a stench that struck the air like fists.

My lord stretched out his hand and made the holy sign as he passed. But my hands were busy with my horse who rippled and shied beneath me. I felt a pain in my loins then, a quick agony that was gone before I had even space to cry aloud. But it was hot and wounding as a sword thrust. My sister had told me there was such a pain when my lord's brother took her; but it is a maid's pain and came for no reason at a part of me I had not, being a man.

Above the place there is the road to the town, and some way on, an inn. Smoke came out of its black nostril, and the yew branch was half-dipped to show the house was almost full. But for my lord any inn will be pleased to make room, and here, we were told, the beds were without fleas, and a magic stone was hung under the lintel to ward off ill.

The landlord gave us food in a small chamber, just beyond the crowd and noise of the tavern hall, with no company save a red cat coiled before the fire. As I tended him, my lord looked up from his meat and touched the landlord on the arm.

'There was a burning, was there not, farther back along the road?'

The landlord paled and made the holy sign. 'Truth,' he answered. 'Today.'

'A man, was it?' asked my lord.

'A woman,' said the landlord, 'and her body is not altogether burned. The flames held off a long while, so they say, and a devil danced by her.'

A pain ran round my chest like a great band then, and my lord put out his hand to steady me. They sat me in a chair, and as soon as the agony had passed, I blushed hot with shame, for this is not how a squire should conduct himself before his lord and strangers.

The landlord held the cup against my mouth, but my teeth were clenched and I could not swallow. The metal jarred on my lip.

'He will be well enough,' said my lord, 'when he has slept. He is too young perhaps for such long travelling.'

He was always gentle with me and compassionate, and he had defended the honour of my house, even against his own brother, but these words made me more ashamed than ever. For was I not a man? They had told me I should not be a man till I had lain with a woman, but the village girls would not, and the women that I had seen in the dark doors of the town were often foul with disease and they made me afraid.

The inn quietened about midnight, and my lord went to his bed where I drew off the mail coat from him and set to polishing his sword, such as my duty was. In the cold iron of the sword I saw his brown body burn like copper, and his hair white flaxen. As he lay on the bed, he folded his arms behind his head, and watched the last reflection of torchlight die on the vaulted roof beyond the tiny window.

'Their remarkable stone on the door will keep us safe tonight,' he said, laughing deep and soft. And after that he slept.

My own sleep came on me like death. I felt my heart rise beneath the flesh and knock as one mad to be free from prison. And then it grew slower and, before I slept, I felt it stop.

It was an ill sleep, dark and close, clutching with the claws of eagles. Such sleeps, men say, have no awakening. A year in a tomb I lay that night above the tavern hall, and once a white face shone in on me like a moon. Pale as thin milk it was, with great black eyes. And behind, a flame burning.

An hour before I woke, I heard the red cat singing in the tavern yard.

My lord shook me awake, gentle and rough, and went to bathe in the water they had brought up in seven ewers to our chamber. As I stripped away my shirt for fresh, for we had ridden long, fear came like an adder from the crevice of my thoughts and stung me, for my right side and my left above my rib bones had begun to swell. It was a soft swelling, but the male nipples had turned pink as a maid's.

We stayed not long at the inn. There was a commotion about the porch, where the magic stone had fallen from the lintel in the night, and smashed to fragments on the cobbled yard. Beyond the tavern, the road was blown with leaves.

It is a day's ride into the town. Without pause we journeyed it. At ebb-day we were within gates before the watch had closed them, and above the dark loom of the houses the sky blazed rosy-brazen.

The house of my lord's lord, his uncle, is fine, of timber blood-kissed with the last sun, where we knocked and were made welcome. It was many years since I last came here, and then not as a squire but as a little page, a hand higher than the great dogs. I had forgotten all that lived within, save for memories. But the huge chase-hound was splashed with grey and blind, yet he knew me and the smell of me, and came to nose my hand. His muzzle was wet and round as a pebble from the stream thrust into my palm, and then he baulked suddenly from me, as from something ill, and his white-stone eyes flinched as if he saw with them. He followed my lord to the fire, and never came near me after, though sometimes I called to him.

There was a girl too I had forgotten. Had I recalled her, it must have been as small and fey and thin, running and laughing and in favour with my lord's lord, though only the daughter of one of his wife's women.

And now I saw her beckon me, and remembered – though she had changed utterly and was a woman, with the face of a flower that smiled. It was her eyes made me unquiet, for there is a look a woman will get when another thing is gone. She laughed at me and took my hand.

'See how red my lord's squire is grown at the sight of me. But he is a fine man, and I am the one should blush.' She led me away along the stairs, my lord left below before the fire with his family. 'But I have ceased blushing,' said she, 'and there is the cause of it.' She pointed her finger at my lord's uncle, deep in talk and unknowing. 'It is a danger to be fair, is it not? There, the red sea is at high tide again.' And she drew me in at the shadowy bend of the stair above the hall, where none could see, and gave me her mouth to kiss. But such a kiss as she gave me had never been mine before, and when it was done she laughed again and was gone.

Faithful my heart, but I should have been mad afire for her, finding her so willing. But I was not. Rather, I was afraid of her and, as she sat that night at dinner, kept my eyes from those of hers, so fair and knowing woman's eyes they were. I was in discomfort too, for my clothes seemed all awry and would not fit me. I thought my sweat and the rain and the dry days had shrunk them.

When the house had gone to bed, I heard her, my lord's uncle's mistress; she came scratching at the door like a cat. I had just set down the candle, and I was alone. She scratched at the door until I opened it.

'Love,' she said, 'I hear you sing to my lord sweetly. Sing sweetly to me.'

'You will have me wake the whole house,' I answered her, but she had come into the room with me, and the door swung softly to.

'Your clothes are all misshapen on you,' said she. 'Shame to my lord that they are.'

And she thrust her hand within the lip of my doublet, as if to see how fast my heart might beat for her, which had grown dead and still.

Then the smile was gone from her face, the speech from her mouth, her hand leaped away from me as though there were poison on my flesh.

She said nothing. But something spoke in her throat, saying nothing. Her eyes were wide. Turning her head, she spat and fled from the chamber.

A shield hung on the wall. I looked in it, and now I saw the pale girl's face, the white smooth throat, and there, below the open neck of cloth, the milky roundness, and I tore wide my doublet with my hands.

The breath of life had gone from me, and still I lived, and there she lived, in the shield before me on the wall. A woman with her hair lopped short as a boy's, and the three white moons of breasts and face gleaming in the candle-shade.

My lord was gone to mass that dawn, and left me sleeping, out of kindness, that should have been beside him.

From the great stair I saw the hall, and the women at breakfast. And there the girl sat, who was my lord's uncle's harlot, wan and silent, the other maids laughing and trying to tempt her with a bowl of honey and milk. She would not eat and, as her eyes lifted, she saw me, and she shrank away. Beneath the board, I saw her hand move in the holy sign.

Like a leaf blowing, the thought came and led me, and I turned my back on them and went from the house. The streets were bright with frost.

My cloak was about me. I hid in its muffle from the crowds. I came to the market-place, and a gypsy called to me.

'Here, see, fair one – these will win your lord's favour.'

She was a huge woman, rust red, dangling two golden coils such as maids wear in their ears. I would have pulled back, but she gripped my arm.

'Lovesick, you are. I see it in your face. Give me a coin for the earrings and I will tell you how it will go for you.'

I struggled, but she had me fast as fate. She pushed back the hood from my head and round my cheeks I felt the hair fall, long and soft, a woman's hair, never shorn.

'Fine hair,' she said, 'summer hair. These earrings will love such hair.'

After a minute her face grew darker, a cloud on fire. 'Listen, young mistress, there are some will ask why a maid has on man's clothes.'

Her fingers bit my arm, and they taught me how it should be, for I sunk my teeth in her hand and she let me go, cursing. But there was blood in my mouth before she did.

Then I ran. Houses loomed and faded like ghosts in a nightmare, and once there was a bridge over green water where a white-faced girl looked up at me. Now the true terror came. A doorway and the spice of incense. I stood at the porch of a church, and saw far off the soft light of candles and lovely windows with the cold sky behind. How I longed then to run into that echoing gentle womb, and fall down before the altar, and call out loud to the angels and the Saviour to give me peace. But the sweet good smell drove me back, and I slunk away and vomited like a dog at the guttering.

Night fell soon after. There was no time in that place. Lamps were lit behind the shutters of windows as I passed. A lean dog howled dismally from some hidden yard.

As I walked, I heard the ash wind rustle at my feet and smelled the almond smell of burning. All around, from shapeless walls, faces of imagination peered at me. I sensed the beat of a great heart thundering through the town, which only I could hear, and through the doors and solid timbered houses I saw with a third eye. Families at a meal, children and dogs sprawling in firelight, a cream jug overturned, an old man dying, and once, two lovers moaning on a bed.

On the ground too I saw, and above my head, small things, little creatures moving and living, specks fluttering between the rooftops and the stars. I was both man and woman as I walked. Man below the scar of birth, hard and stirring, and woman above, milk-white and swan-soft, and, at the join, the ripple of snake's skin, fish's scale. My fear had been vomited forth. A new sensation had come on me, jealous of its place, denying all others.

It was the mid of night that I came to the door of my lord's uncle's house. The bolt was drawn and the porter asleep, but within I heard the old blind hound stir in his ease and whine. I tapped with my fingers lightly on the shutters and they flew wide, and softly I called in to them that my lord's squire was returned, and I smiled at my words. A wretched servant in bedclothes came then to let me in, my hood pulled close about my head, and shivered as I passed for the cold wind came in at my back from the street.

I was deaf to her scolding and made my way above stairs. Soon I came to the harlot's door, and through it I saw her lying in her white sleep. I lifted the door latch then, and went in and, as I came near her, she tossed and whimpered without waking. I drew back the covers to look at her, a thing carved out of marble, like myself, but she had the loins of a woman.

She woke when the air struck cold on her body, and she lay before me dumb with fear, her eyes wide and fixed as glass. And then she shut her eyes and began to pray, and so I left her.

I crept to the door of my chamber, looking for the dark. But in the grate a fire blazed, and before the fire stood my lord. As I entered, he lifted his head and, seeing only a shadow, called to me as his squire.

Then the fire caught me, and he stilled. All the woman's hair was about my face, and in the shield I saw for a moment how womanly the face had grown, dark eyed and small jawed. The man and the snake and the fish were hidden.

'Who are you?' he said, quiet almost as silence.

I made him no answer but pointed to the fire. And when he looked, his face grew white and he seized me and, dragging the silver cross from within his shirt, he pressed it on my throat. Such a fear came on me then as I had never known. The silver burned like ice and from its four arms a numbing chill rushed into my body. But, with the four strengths in me, I beat it away, and heard it fall, and turning, fled from the house through the closed door into the night.

The dawn came pale, with the dripping of the dew, and the watch made haste to open the gates for me, for I made my voice deep, and the badge of my lord's house was yet on my doublet.

It is a steep climb at first, and a day's journey for a mounted man, so I thought it would take me far longer. But about afternoon, a dull yellow light came down from the sky, and I heard the creaking of the twisted trees as they swung in the wind. The inn was locked against the dim dusk, but from an upper window I thought I saw a white face look out and vanish at a glimpse of me.

The black trees stretched away, bare and leaden, their sodden leaves rotting underfoot. A small ragged child came wandering by, with an armful of brittle twigs. I called to him, for he did not seem to see me, and he looked up with an idiot's face. The wind blew back my hood then, and washed through my hair. The child opened his mouth and gave a thin high scream and, dropping all the wood he had so carefully gathered, tumbled away.

Beyond the wood was a stake such as men use to burn a witch upon, but no proof of that burning remained now, no dead flesh or black bone.

It is hard to be rid of me, good people.

Discovered Country

1

At fifteen, Eunicea Cantel had seduced a space-sailor in the West Conclave of Portomars. The result of this seduction now stepped from the celerator of the Earthnorth Cantel Building.

Thirty-two solar revolutions had elapsed between these two events and the result was just thirty-one years of age, one and three-quarter metres in height, and weighed approximately sixty-seven kilograms. He was dressed in dark green velvet in a mode somewhere between the Renascence Italian and the Rationalist European of the final decade of the twentieth century. He had black hair, eyes whose irises were almost as black as the pupils, and the clear waxen skin of someone who has spent their recent vacation in a grave. He had also, in a world of equal opportunity and androgynous inclination, a face capable of launching ships.

Leaning on the wall to recover from the celerator, Eunicea's son glanced down the corridor. A couple of optic-responsive doors slid open to reveal a white cavern beyond, and a tall plump male in a white suit. The male clasped his hands, stared at the arrival in green velvet and executed a half bow.

'I'm Doebatt.'

'I know,' said the son of Eunicea Cantel. He sounded like a Shakespearian actor.

Doebatt was not surprised. He had been acquainted with Eunicea, and had therefore been prepared for anything.

'Would you like to come in?' Doebatt inquired, delicately, as a man might test the surface tension of ice, before stepping on it.

'You tell me. Would I?'

'I don't know. Although I *do* know quite a lot else about you – the monitor has been investigating ever since you came through the ground doors. By the time you reached the ninety-eighth floor *it* was perfectly certain of everything about you. Height, weight, racial admixture, the exact composition of your body structure, and the picturesque scar across your upper left pectoral.'

'Where my mother once stabbed me.'

'No doubt.'

Blandly, Doebatt gazed at Eunicea's son. He bore the Cantel name by law, which theoretically had entitled him, on Eunicea's death, to huge system-wide estates and a fortune in plutonium, electro-irradium and old-fashioned gold. So far he had been able to touch nothing. His name was Martian. Eunicea, a very devious woman, had always had a playful weakness for the unsubtle.

'Inside,' Doebatt murmured, 'there's some very fine Vertu champagne.'

'There would be,' said Martian Cantel.

It was hard to tell if his pallor were due to the celerator, illness, apprehension, or a morbid lifestyle. Probably it was just make-up. His eyes were alert and crystal clear, however, and Doebatt realised that long practice with Eunicea had paid off with her child. The resemblance of course was marked, and had perhaps helped Doebatt intuitively to strike the right series of notes. Martian Cantel had begun to stroll towards the open doors of the cavernous room.

The floor inside was laid with faked snow, which had piled up in a drift against one wall. Beyond this wall, something hummed. There were no windows, only light injections from the roof a further fifty storeys up. A blue pane of injected light lay tastefully behind the bottle of pale green champagne.

'Shall I turn on the snowstorm?'

'Oh please,' said Martian, apparently bored.

The snowstorm came on, warm insubstantial white flakes which dissolved in moistureless contact with flesh, clothing or wine. Martian drank the first glass rapidly and took the second Doebatt handed him. Glass in hand, he moved about the white room and through the panes of light. He paused by the humming wall amid the snowdrift.

'It's through here, presumably.'

'It?' Doebatt asked politely. With a Cantel it was always unwise to anticipate.

'Eunicea's . . . *thing.*'

'Quite so. Did you wish to see it at once?'

'That's why she wanted me here. Was the funeral nice, by the way?'

'Very colourful. I'm afraid there were some casualties when the asteroid exploded.'

Martian took no notice.

Eunicea had left orders that her body be cremated by nuclear explosion inside her estate on Demetria V1. The blast took the entire asteroid with it, an unpleasant surprise to some of the press shuttles which had been standing in too close.

Perhaps a questionable mistake, if no more questionable than Martian's absence from the black Cantel cruiser that overlooked the holocaust. But then, why ponder the ways of the Cantels?

Eunicea's will, buried in a vault on a little-known satellite of Pluto, had stipulated two things only. One, that her natural son Martian should receive no part of the vast Cantel fortune – unless he were to present himself at that section of the Earthnorth Cantel Building devoted to Eunicea's last project. The second portion of the will named Doebatt, Eunicea's erstwhile chief assistant and co-ordinator, as executor of certain instructions connected to the project, Martian, and several million Venus-standard credits dependent on obedience.

Doebatt handed Martian a third glass of Vertu.

'Let's go through then, shall we?'

A reactor in the floor, keyed to Doebatt's white leather shoes, opened the wall for them. Carrying the champagne, they passed through and the wall closed, leaving the snowstorm to rage among the blue panes of injected light.

Eunicea had died at the age of forty-seven. She had lived riotously, but cosmetic vitamins and various adjunctive preparations had kept most trace of ageing and all of riot from her face and body. She looked about thirty-one (the actual age of her son) the night she died. The fatal accident was reminiscent of Isadora Duncan's a couple of centuries before.

Her last project, the most mysterious but also the most extensive she had ever seriously mounted, had been apparently in its ultimate stages – or, according to some news sources, actually complete. The fresh will, drawn up one solar month before her demise, had made

Martian compulsory heir not only to her riches, but to the nameless experiment.

Martian Cantel stood in a second cavern room the other side of the cavern with the snow. A number of storeys had amalgamated in this second cavern, which was twenty-one metres high, and with a floor space eighty metres by forty. Three walls were a mosaic of uncountable neons, blink-lights, panels and wiring systems. All were active, apparently automatically, and were the cause of the gentle sonic humming. The 'Thing' itself was held upright against the fourth wall, in a golden bird-cage of tubing, leads and magnetic scaffolding. It was itself a golden oblong box, about three metres high by one and a half in diameter.

'Let me refill your glass,' said Doebatt.

'What now?' Martian said. Doebatt noticed Martian's hand was shaking, but not necessarily, of course, with fear.

'You enter, whenever you like.'

'Isn't there some sort of preliminary exercise?'

'No. The process is largely automatic and in a permanent state of readiness. The few keys that activate the sequence can be taken care of by one man, with the minimum of effort.'

'That sounds too easy.'

'Nothing can go wrong,' said Doebatt encouragingly.

'Something can always go wrong.'

'Truly not, in this case. It isn't at all dangerous. Only a sort of TV.'

'Yes?' said Martian. He extended an empty glass. 'But maybe you don't actually know any more about this than I do.'

'I'll admit, Eunicea kept most of us in the dark as far as was possible. At least in the preliminary stages. Not so difficult. One team worked on one aspect or facet of the experiment, other teams on others – and liaison between the teams was made utterly impossible. Those who tried to find out what went on were fired. And of course, the Cantel system of firing is fairly –'

'Terminal.'

Doebatt sighed. 'The press, naturally, invented or carried off a lot of stories. In the end, any information that was leaked was automatically distrusted. You'll have read some?'

'Let's not talk about me.'

'Yes, all right. In the month before Eunicea's death, she summoned me and told me what it was all about. Not the first experiment of its kind. But, she claimed, the first successful one.'

'Which kind?'

'Actually, one of those guessing news stories had the right idea. But nobody believed it by then.'

'Which right idea?'

'It's all rather a silly game, but I'm not supposed to say. You go over to the machine and get in, and it tells you.'

'And have you never,' said Martian, 'gone over to the machine and gotten in and been told? To make sure? Or did you always credit my mother implicitly?'

Doebatt laughed quietly, 'Whatever I credited – get into *Eunicea's* machine uninvited? I'm not that crazy. The display is meant for you. And now I think that's everything. Will you have a fifth glass of Vertu?'

Martian Cantel extended his empty glass.

His eyes were still clear, but slightly unfocused. He drank the fifth glass, and set it down. He began to walk slowly towards the golden sarcophagus sixty metres away.

Doebatt hastily caught him up. They walked side by side.

To his interest, presently Martian paused, turned and looked at him. 'I haven't really grasped why you're doing this at all,' Doebatt said, 'apart from the Cantel fortune –'

'Which doesn't matter to me,' said Martian.

'I supposed not. In the four years since you parted company with Eunicea, your life has been a most refreshing success story.'

'Hasn't it.'

Doebatt, recognising certain signs, was too intrigued to desist.

'First you wrote the *Jupitrix* novel – a sale of many billions. Then, Fire-Fencing Champion of the Venustra Tournament. Then the *Sun Concerto* based on the single fifth-note pun of Sol. The Air-Skating Award Delux. The seven-tier painting-optonal, the *Marriage of Moons*. It's an incredible list. You must have made, if you'll pardon the surmise, quite a profit.'

'And as you'll have noticed,' Martian said, 'I never do anything more than once.'

Martian turned again, and went on again. Doebatt rejoined him.

'Yes, I understand,' Doebatt said. 'And is this, then, perhaps, another of your one-time-only ventures?'

Martian Cantel failed to reply, as expected to fail. Now any communication would be met with silence, blankness. Doebatt stopped walking.

Martian Cantel approached the scaffolding alone, stepped on the auto-ladder, rose up and disappeared through the hatch of the golden box, which then seeped shut.

2

Outside the booth was gold. Inside, it was lined with a deep emerald green, a transparent glassic material. There was one button, a solitary pearl drop located on the greenness.

Otherwise, the interior was featureless, save for a small scratched sentence on the wall just over the chair. *Discovered country*, it said.

He thought about Eunicea. That is, he thought about himself, as a woman. For, aside from gender, he and she were very nearly identical: same black hair, same skin-tone of subterranean vampires, same features, same curious mental convolutions.

At fifteen, Eunicea had conceived. She had eluded her guardians, and bribed a madam to introduce her, as a virgin whore, to the man she fancied. She had looked like Juliet, and her desire was as intense and as brief. She had not wanted a baby, but even then some bizarre egomania had prevented her destroying anything that was partly hers. On her sixteenth birthday, she bore Martian, amidst beneficial technology, without pain or great inconvenience. Martian had imagined her, this pale and sombre Juliet-girl, crushed like a willing flower in the arms of his handsome momentary father, now pointing at the new-born with the words: 'Take care of it, because it's mine. Rear it, educate it. Give it the best. But don't trouble me with it. And now. Remove it from my sight.' The imagined words were not far from the mark, and Martian knew it. His sixteen-year-old mother sailed away on a silver Cantel launch, away and away into the solar night between the planets.

Her other instructions were also obeyed to the letter. Her child was raised in her absence on the Cantel's large Martian estate in the Cannalinda, five kilometres from Portomars. In an era of supreme education, Martian received the *crème de la suprême*. His relaxations were also superb. The estate-bred horses, the thin tall Martian 'flyers' that could never race in the denser gravity of Earth. Martian would ride over the pale brown sand-gardens, under clear-weather purple skies, or the pink storm haze of the Martian summer. Sometimes, his guardians took him to the Night-House on Deimos. One day, when he was seven, he was promised a special treat. He was going on a Cantel shuttle to the Vulcan Asteroid, to meet his mother.

He was small for his age, and insultingly beautiful. He was not afraid, but he was bewildered, and the bewilderment, by the time he reached the Vulcan Asteroid, had reduced him to a deadly apathy. The idea of a mother meant nothing to him, and his guardians' admonitions had not enlightened him as to her role in his life except, in some vague sense, as that of an important enemy he must impress.

Evidently, Eunicea had grown inquisitive about her son. She met him at the shuttle-dock, She wore white-green, and a long necklace of faceted, scarcely-flawed emeralds. She was twenty-three, and she blazed like an incandescence against the backdrop of the Vulcan Asteroid on and of which everything was black.

Boxes of games, intellectual toys and confectionery had been piled up for Martian in the centre room of the mansion. They were a contemptuous gesture on Eunicea's part, her sneering accolade to his age. Martian only glanced at them. At Eunicea, he stared. They stared at each other. There was a moment of shocked recognition, followed, in each of them, by a conscious denial.

'Sit,' said Eunicea. 'Do you know who I am?'

'No,' Martian answered. It was perfectly true. He did not know, beyond the maternal title, who she was at all.

'Surely they told you?'

'They said you were my mother.'

'Then you do know who I am.'

'No.'

Eunicea responded. She had deserted a small squalling animal. Now she confronted an intelligence.

'You're going to find out,' said Eunicea.

There commenced twelve impassioned, exciting, angry months, during which Eunicea dragged her son from world to world, from asteroid to planetoid. Martian was shown the splendours of the moons of Jupiter, the volcanoes of the Solstice Debris. He witnessed sea-planting drives on Venus, and followed the Great Methane-Sail Race from Uranus to Titania. *En route*, there were stopovers at Cantel estates on Pluto, Triton, Nineve and Demetria V1. Martian lived under apricot skies and bronze skies, and in the enveloping starry night of space, and at his side was a woman, glowing like a green flame.

Their mutual antagonism stimulated both of them, and though they did not find ease thereby, they became necessary to one another, an infinitely exhilarating drug. They would each try to surprise vulnerable exhibitions of pleasure or honesty in the other.

Then abruptly the war-like idyll ended. Eunicea chose for herself another lover. As the sun had shrunk to a great pale star over the wastes of Pluto, so the child shrank and dimmed in Eunicea's thoughts.

'It's time you went back to the Cannalinda,' she said to him.

'Why?'

'Because I'm bored with you. Later; maybe I'll see you again later.'

'I might die,' he said. It was the first, most sound intimation that she had become essential to him, but it fell on barren soil. 'Perhaps you'll never see me any more.'

'Never mind,' she said, thrusting home the needle of her inattention. She kissed him coldly on the lips. His dreadful beauty offended her. 'Go away now,' she said, 'I'm about to be busy.'

He went away, and two weeks later he was back on Mars, under the hazy skies, with a green pain and a clear green hatred, and five thousand toy gadgets Eunicea had sent with him, which systematically he destroyed.

When he was eleven, he saw her again for one whole Martian night. She threw a party at the Cannalinda Estate, and for weeks before, caterers came and went, and luminators, and artisans of various and extraordinary description. Under the fiery stars, in the radiance of invisible lamps, Eunicea walked with long white nails. Two men walked with her. They were a little younger than she, good-looking, and hanging on her words and her body helplessly. 'This is my son,' she said. They touched hands patronisingly with the boy. Presently, she took Martian aside. 'I've heard you're doing very well,' she said. He was not sure what she meant, but he was briefly, bitterly glad she had asked for reports on him. 'What do you want to do with your life?'

'Do I have to do anything with it?' he inquired.

'I have the idea of a project,' she said. 'Prince –' Prince was one of the two young men ' – has been telling me about some odd Eartheast experiments last year. A failure, of course. One of my companies could do much better.'

'You do everything better than everyone, Mother,' he said.

'Don't sulk and don't call me mother.'

A while before dawn, when she was rather drunk on the green champagne, Eunicea had come to his bedroom, woken him and begun to converse with him, a curious conversation which had hinged upon beauty and youth and the essential transience of life. ('What do you want to do with it? Why, *live* it. *Live*.')

And as she spoke she played with the necklace of seventy-eight emeralds. It was almost a metre in length, the necklace, each gem mounted on a hair-fine chain of irradium steel.

It was this necklace which, twenty years after, had caught in the whirling automatic wheel of the Eternal Clock at Lunarnet. As incapable of spontaneous breakage as the wheel was of reversal or terminus, the cheese-wire chain, pulled taut, had sliced through Eunicea's neck in seconds, crushing the emeralds in her blood, and severing the head from her body.

'Can you hear me?' Doebatt said from the air inside the sarcophagus booth. 'The intercom is functional. Just give me a "yes" if you would.'

'Yes,' Martian said.

'Good, very good. Thank you. Are you quite comfortable?'

'Yes.'

'Good. I've set up the relay. You have only to press the button in there, to start the projection.'

'Yes,' Martian said.

'Do you have any questions?' There was no answer. Doebatt realised that perversely, according to the prior request, Martian Cantel was only prepared to use the word 'yes'. 'No questions then. Why not press the button? I'm obliged to witness this.'

But Martian Cantel did not say 'yes' again.

Beyond the several million Venus-standard credits Doebatt stood to lose or gain on condition of Martian's and his own participation, Doebatt had other, less tangible worries. The credits, actually, did not really bother him. It was the experiment which concerned him, and his worries sprang from the experiment.

He could not ignore the unpleasing aptness of Eunicea's death, or the incongruity of her will; that Martian must follow her work in ignorance. But Doebatt was hopelessly concerned to propitiate Eunicea even after she was dead. Worse, he was irritatingly aware that here, at this juncture of man's achievements, there had interfered the effete, the uncommitted, the *unknown* quantity.

'You can always withdraw from the booth,' Doebatt said to the intercom. ('Yes'?) There was silence.

In embryonic rage, Doebatt nibbled his plump fingers.

* * *

The booth was comfortable, the chair cushoform. It held him like an accommodating, loving slave, the way he had most often been held.

Martian sat and watched the button, his eyes half-closed. He saw, through the button and the wall, Eunicea as she had been that night on Mars. How, before the brief firework of the Martian dawn, seated on his eleven-year-old bed, she had talked on and on to him about the transience of life, playing all the while with the necklace that twenty years later would cut off her head.

In the end, now, he reached out and pressed the button. The wall changed into a TV screen. There began to occur a long lecture, illustrated by shots of Cantel laboratories, industriously labouring persons, the use of experimental animals that everywhere else in the system had been banned for years, and was now illegal and unnecessary since the advent of 'mimic' tissue. The droning voice told him nothing. Neither did the screen tell him much. This too was her joke. Dead, she continued to annoy him. If 'annoy' was the word.

Finally he was shown a row of corpses extruding glowing elongated wires, like festival lights. New images were flung across the screen in the bold gaudy colours of dissection. Martian retched. Then stood up. He clapped and applauded in the booth, then pushed open the door. At once the screen and the sound went dead.

3

'Weep if you want to,' Martian said magnanimously. He sat on the floor, the bottle of Vertu at his side. Sometimes he drank from the bottle. He gazed at nothing intently. 'Don't mind me.'

'Please,' said Doebatt. 'You're making no sense. I don't really expect you to. But at the moment it's rather trying. You didn't stay till the end.'

'Sudden nausea.'

'Yes,' Doebatt said. He too sat slowly on the floor.

There were light beige hollows under Martian Cantel's eyes. 'Inside that box,' he said, 'my mother has inscribed the words *discovered country*. Now what can that mean?' Doebatt did not react. Martian drank from the bottle. Minutes passed. Doebatt looked up from his daze to register that questions and communication had again ceased.

'Are you,' said Doebatt, 'prepared to go in and see the rest?'

Martian smiled, He tilted the bottle.

'Are you?' Doebatt said.

Martian drank.

How childish the clever nearly always were. Something broke apart in Doebatt's suave soul. He jumped up and forwards, knocking away the bottle, grabbing Martian by the throat even as he landed on him. Whether he anticipated retaliation Doebatt did not pause to consider; maybe not, since Martian seemed to have drifted into the region of sublime incapacity. Then Martian's hand thudded into his liver, a paralysing wedge of pain. Doebatt tumbled over. Now he reclined, his head laved by a spreading lake of champagne, Martian crouched like a drunken lover over his body, faintly bewildered yet operationally homicidal.

Once more, intuition. 'You think Eunicea is only messing about?' Doebatt said. Martian's blank eyes wavered over his face. 'Very well,' Doebatt said. 'I myself will have to go in there and look and listen. Success . . . failure. I need, you see, to know. It may be rigged, the booth. It may kill me. Interested?'

'Doebatt, you're a christawful fool. Did Eunicea train you to a particular routine when dealing with Cantels? Get up.'

Doebatt got up.

He was eighteen when he saw her again.

He had assumed his majority at sixteen, an early age when, by the Gracemeyer Code of assessment, most majorities were not granted until the age of twenty-four or -five. Partly, as with Eunicea's own majority, the Cantel fortune had greased the wheels; though Martian's intelligence and ability were rated high, his ethic and social disciplines were not.

He had spent fifteen of his sixteen years on Mars and its adjacent satellites. Majority achieved and the bottomless coffers of Eunicea's wealth to back him, he began to investigate for himself the places of the Solar System, the summits and the sinks, the venues public and occult.

He possessed the two most useful – and dangerous – commodities of life – looks and cash. He had, too, the third requisite, probably the most lethal of all three, a fully functioning brain. The result was a continuous flaring up of excitement, the raging ecstasy of the explorer nearing the mountain's peak, and the bored despair of achievement's aftermath, the frantic search to find another mountain, preferably unscalable. While he was learning this about himself, he spent freely, dallied with various psychosms, phantasies and drugs, came to know many of the sexual and artistic permutations that pervaded mankind's cluster of humanised worlds. All this in two years. All these mountains and all these despairing aftermaths, and no anchorage. The evening of his eighteenth birthday, he stood on one of the bubble-domed balconies of the Solmer Building, staring through dark red clouds far below at the even farther pallid vistas of the Atlantic Ocean.

Solmer was itself a mountain. Located Earthsouth, in the Tropic of Capricorn, its foundations fused to the bedrock beneath the sea, its toweresque bulk rising fifteen kilometres from the ocean surface to establish topmost tiers in the stratosphere, it was the most ludicrous construction ever built. Stabilised as it was in every conceivable manner, shock-proofed, braced and chained, nevertheless, calamity must only be a matter of time. *Defy Nature*, the staff recruitment posters had read. *Do you dare employment in exotic Solmer, the System's greatest potential Death Trap?* Wages and benefits were proportionally fantastic. Later advertising blazoned forth with the words: *No luxury or thrill cannot be supplied to you at Solmer, including the terror-excitement of the ever-present risk of death! Will you be remembered forever as one of the thousands of victims of the world's most terrible recorded disaster? Will Solmer fall the night YOU are there?* An indication of Earth's mood, the waiting-list for a Solmer night was extensive, though nobody might enter without copy-documents of insurance and a disclaimer.

If the threat of death stimulated Martian, he did not analyse. The burgundy sunset below was blooming into cyanide, and above enormous stars, and the silver pseudo-stars of circling satellites, were evolving in a thick patina on the dusk. Martian was alone, for he tended to discard people absent-mindedly, like empty glasses. But, glancing along the length of the balcony, he had the uncanny sensation that, not only was he no longer alone, but he had split in two segments, the second of which now leaned against the balcony rail, fifty metres away. Then he noticed the near metre-long rope of emeralds.

Eunicea was thirty-four. She looked twenty-four. She was in the company of the piano-celanist, Lisalba. Martian knew later that she had, for some while, been conscious of his adventures through the planetary system and of the colossal demands his tastes had made on the bottomless Cantel coffers. She might have blocked these demands, but had not. Conversely she had grown curious. Enervated as was her son, she had at length pursued him. Her presence at Solmer was no coincidence. She had been observing Martian for an hour, from a fascinated distance.

Now she turned, smiled at him and, leaving Lisalba at the rail, walked over.

'Well,' she said, 'I don't believe you recollect me.' It was too arch. She knew he did.

'You're my mother,' Martian said. With a strange elation and some embarrassment, he realised that he felt faint.

'I'm your mother,' she acquiesced. 'But don't mention it again. My name is still Eunicea. Have you altered yours?'

'No.'

'Conservative boy. Though you're really quite enterprising, aren't you? Quite brilliantly innovating.'

He said nothing, and she stopped talking to him. They stared instead, as at their first true meeting on the Vulcan Asteroid. After three or four minutes, she remarked: 'You look as if you're about to die, Martian, or at least pass out. You'd better come and have a drink.'

She turned once more, started to walk off the balcony, and he followed her. When Lisalba joined them, Eunicea said quietly to him: 'You're a genius. What else do you need but your genius?'

'You want me to leave you,' Lisalba said placidly.

'This minute,' Eunicea said to one of the finest musicians of the century. Her dismissal signed his death warrant, but none of them knew that at the time.

Indeed, Martian noted bewilderedly that Lisalba was smiling with inscrutable genuine amusement as he went away. But Lisalba was, of course, himself unique.

Eunicea led Martian into the Damocles Bar. Here the notorious steel sword hung overhead by its glinting irradium hair. The walls behind the flasks and bottles were painted with scenes of crashing flaming towers and seething tidal waves.

Eunicea ordered a small tumbler of white brandy, and handed it to him like medicine. He drank and she said: 'Did you ever hear of Freud, Martian?'

'Yes.'

'Oedipus, too, perhaps.'

He continued the brandy and shut his eyes. 'I've heard of Oedipus. What do you want me to do about it? Kill your current lover, and then fuck you?'

'Oh, no,' she said. 'I don't need you to do that.'

'We don't need each other at all.'

'Open your eyes,' she said. He obeyed. He could smell one of the score of perfumes she wore, and now he realised that, though he had sometimes detected these scents on other rich women, the fragance had always smelled slightly wrong. And that was because he had been remembering how they had smelled on her. It seemed that during that year of his earliest childhood, she had established herself as a prototype in his mind, or rather, an archetype. 'I've missed a lot,' she said. 'I see now I was very stupid to avoid watching you grow up. I don't think it would have bored me at all.'

'Oh, it would have,' he said. He had the urge to pour the last of the brandy into the bosom of her dress. He had done such things with others, and much, much worse. But somehow he didn't want to spoil her marvellous symmetry. Was not even sure he could.

'You seem better,' she said. 'Pale as death, but no paler. Your pallor is my legacy to you. It comes of my living so much of my childhood on sun-distant planets, and scorning the solariums that made everyone else so brown and healthy and indistinguishable from well-done steak.'

He was about to say something to her – afterwards he could never recall what, only that his lips had parted and he had drawn breath to speak – when a wild rending shudder went over the bar; floor, ceiling and walls.

There was an instant total silence, broken only momentarily by a couple of dropped glasses ringing on the surface underfoot. Then the shuddering was repeated and a terrible mass screaming and direction-less shoving broke out, which he could imagine duplicated down the whole interminable fifteen-kilometre length of the building.

Eunicea did not move. She was probably the only person in the bar not to respond, possibly in all the tiers of Solmer.

'It's faked,' she said to him. 'I've heard they do it every few nights, a controlled de-stabilisation for a minute or two, to give the patrons an extra thrill.'

Then the shuddering came again, and up the painted skin of one of the walls an incredible crack ascended, from which showered out powders, cements, reinforcers and a fluid like grey sea water. Briefly, the wall continued to disgorge its linings in this fashion, till, with a dull crunching sound, it split and crumbled. The noise became a thunder that overwhelmed even the screaming, and was jabbed spasmodically with intermezzos of crashing – the 'delicacy' glass along the bar platform beneath. The large room fogged with pinkish dusts.

Even in the midst of this chaos of the collapsing wall, another shock burst through the tower. The floor tilted, and Martian beheld men and women trying to claw their way towards an exit point over each other's struggling bodies, and through a torture park of smashed glass. He himself had remained quite still. Perhaps it was the sort of panic-petrification that happens to rabbits. Perhaps the mirror effect of Eunicea's immobility. And, by a stroke of fate, their section of the room had shifted the least.

Softly, she said, her voice pitched under the tumult: 'Do you know, I think it must be real, after all.'

'Yes,' he said, 'I think it is.'

A herd of people pushed by them, and they slid together almost mechanically. Overhead, the only stable factor, the sword went on hanging by its glinting hair.

'How long do you suppose we've got?' he said.

'I've heard they have stratospheric life-rafts, contrary to the publicity. Are you afraid?'

'I think I'm terrified,' he said, 'but I don't really know.'

'This is such a shame,' she said, 'you're only seventeen.'

'Eighteen,' he corrected her automatically. 'And that doesn't matter.'

'Oh, darling,' she said, and they put their arms around each other, very gently, and remained like that, with their faces buried in each other's black hair.

They were the only sane people left in the whole of the Solmer Building, and having found sanity, they retained it, until gradually the shrieking melted away into groans and curses and the biscuity crunching of the last glass trodden underfoot. Presently a steward tapped Martian on the shoulder. The shocks, caused by some seismic disturbance of the bed-rock, were now over. The building was being evacuated by stratospheric raft.

Upwards of a hundred people had been killed, many more hurt. The inscrutably smiling Lisalba was among the dead. That the tower had not fallen, or the upper oxygenated outer casings blown, was one of the several absurd miracles of the age. The advertising was accordingly altered: *Next year, or tomorrow, Solmer may fall. But who can ever forget the night when Solmer shook, and yet remained standing? Do you dare to visit the Tower of Towers that rests in the hand of the gods?*

For Eunicea and Martian, their fragment of recondite tenderness was over. But it had provided the traumatic manacles which would hold them together, thereafter, for nine years.

4

If she had already begun to work on her ultimate unnamed project, it had been shelved by the night Solmer shook Martian and Eunicea together again. In the year of her third meeting with her son, Eunicea's attention was quite publicly directed to the Parkland Project at Lunarnet, on the darkside of the Earthmoon.

The vast dome with its green plantings sprouting beneath, the scalding springs dredged from the partially revitalised hot core, and the white volcanoes, like lovely wind-scoured bones, became the backdrop to their first mesmerised adherings and their first screaming-matches. They played together, a ferocious duo, they were disturbing rivals in the fencing arenas and slide-car races, and on the raw skop-ski slopes of the volcanoes. They drank each other blind at the bars. They laughed and taunted and praised each other, stared at each other across tables and filled rooms. When they fought verbally, the sparks made their vicinity intolerable for anyone else. They were truly horrible and truly fabulous. The glamorous, rather unsavoury legends each had already made as an individual, fastened together to create a *gestalt* of alarming velocity and brilliance. In their double presence, others felt superfluous, or used.

Their relationship was not sexual, save at its most obscure and ambiguous levels. Each took lovers, and shredded the lovers in private with the other one.

Later, they journeyed as formerly, in Cantel shuttles, liners and cruisers, to wastelands, yellow oceans, casinos, paradises and deep holes in the metaphorical slime. Their relationship did not change. It merely intensified. They slid away and rolled back together. They were never absent from each other's proximity for more than five days at a stretch. They were the cause of some awesome and some wicked things. They survived a shuttle crash ten kilometres outside Fells City in the sub-arctic of the Candice planetoid. A girl thrust herself unsuited from Martian's pressure window in the Night-House on Juno, and floated, caught by her sash, blue-faced and pop-eyed, with her depressurised ribs caved in. The X derivative of irradium was separated by the Cantel Group, under Eunicea's guidance. Martian won the Great Methane-Sail Race from Uranus to Titania. One of Eunicea's lovers, trying to shoot Martian, or possibly Eunicea, during the Flyer race at Portomars, slaughtered instead twelve bystanders when the volt-gun, presumably tampered with, mis-fired.

If they were happy, the mother and her son, was not clear.

They would videophone each other in the depths of night, from foreign beds, lying beside listening humiliated bodies, to discuss mathematical calculi, the principles of Semantic Theory, or dreams.

'Discovered country,' Martian repeated to Doebatt, who was still repetitively seated on the floor, biting his fingers.

'What?'

'You heard.'

'Yes. Your voice has a nice pitch.'

'Oh, good. I'm so glad. But I want to know how that phrase my mother has written up connects to her project, her plans for me.'

'Go back. Find out.'

'She carefully put into the TV visual a sequence of dissection guaranteed to make me spew up on the floor. Which I almost did. Who clears up? You?'

'After some of the things you've done,' Doebatt remarked pleasantly, 'I'm surprised you have a weak stomach.'

'Death affects me that way.' (Doebatt grunted.) 'And death, of course,' said Martian coldly, 'is what all this is about, isn't it?'

'Really?' said Doebatt.

'Such a little revenge, why bother? You know, I know. Like any vitally thinking thing, vitally alive, she was scared shitless and witless by the notion of dying. All that *ego* to go out in one dull camera fade.'

Doebatt bridled. 'You're arguing logically now, which I resent, after the earlier performance.'

'Try this, then. The dread of something after death, the undis-covered country from whose bourn no traveller returns –'

'Oh,' said Doebatt.

'Shakespeare, the glorious syphilitic scholar with the feather pen. The undiscovered country. But Eunicea excluded the "un". She wrote –'

'I'm afraid you must go back in the box,' said Doebatt. His eyelids and his knees twitched.

But Martian said quietly, 'And I'm afraid I must.'

5

On the day of his twenty-seventh birthday (the day of Eunicea's forty-third birthday), Martian had suddenly grasped, or thought he had grasped, a fearful knowledge. That his mother was eating him alive.

Later he could never recall what had brought about this dreadful revelation. Maybe the chance spite of an acquaintance, or a chance comparison of his mode of existence with that of another. Maybe a catalyst was not important.

Having concluded she was destroying him, he decided, not on immediate escape, but rather to prove her guilt in open session. He was not, in fact, frightened. He felt a quite comforting hatred for her. Actually, it was the same hate he had always felt, just as the devouring had always been the same, and to a certain extent mutual. If she had damaged him psychologically or emotionally was a moot point. Probably no more than she had merely by giving birth to him from her body, enriched with her genetic Cantel heritage, and the deadly nightshade of good looks and wealth. However.

The prosecution was fairly straightforward and not wonderfully original. He had been aware all through their nine years together that Eunicea was jealous of none of his lovers – unless he himself took more than a brief interest in them. Twenty-four hours to a week was acceptable. Providing he referred to the meetings with scorn and to the participants with indifference. Once or twice, a flicker of involvement had brought vitriol. 'He's amusing and makes me laugh,' Martian had once said. He had been twenty then, and the new companion was male, a rarity, the comment pure euphemistic sarcasm. But Eunicea had smiled, 'I think he's funny, too, darling. Particularly his ghastly Venus-side accent.' Another time, Martian had spent four days with a girl, and become infatuated by her colouring, which was black skin and saffron eyes. In a call to Eunicea, he had unguardedly revealed the nature of the obsession. On the fifth day, the girl became feverish and her skin turned a muddy beige. Eunicea had arranged to have an anti-melanine drug introduced into her food.

Now, with a tingling of nervous excitement, Martian set about devising a stagey concoction, which was to be the True Love of his Life, for the benefit of his mother.

They were in the artificial gravitised Domewald on Triton, and it was artificial gravitised summer. For two months, Martian toured the boulevards and tunnels, in mobiles and in dragonflies, searching. At length he saw her. She was precisely what he had had in mind. She was seated at a pavement table in the Thetis Conclave, eating a kind of white candy floss from a jar with a long spoon. Her hair was identical to the candy floss, her skin was golden, her eyes vacuous, large and intransigently blue.

'Hallo,' Martian said to her.

She glanced at the gleaming shark-like car, at Martian. She lowered her spoon into the jar. "Lo.'

'Don't be shy,' he said.

'I amn't,' she said, in the weird polyglot of the native Domewalder.

'Let me drive you somewhere.'

'Oure?'

'To my place.'

'No.'

'I'll pay three thousand domgelts into your account.'

'Poure?'

'Because I've fallen in love with you.'

'Gek maken,' she said.

'Not crazy. Don't you believe in love, little girl?'

'Yes, I 'lieve in love.'

He came and sat at her table, stroked her fluffy blanched hair and bought her three white drinks which tasted of aniseed. In the end, she leaned on his shoulder. They loved each other. It was settled.

He called Eunicea the second night.

'I've met this idiotic girl. She has the brain of a particularly tiny flea. But she's wonderful.'

'I'm sure she isn't, darling,' said Eunicea.

After that, he took his lover off-moon, on a trip to asteroids and debris belts. They were gone ten days. Then he took her home, to the Cantel mansion in the Domewald.

'Mother,' he said, 'this is Virgine. I wanted you to meet her very much.'

"Lo.' Virgine said. Her tanned blondness made Eunicea's vampire skin and coal hair into an ancient photographic negative.

'What am I supposed to do,' Eunicea inquired, 'with this,' she over-emphasised the pronunciation, '*Veersheen*?'

'Welcome her, Mother,'

'Is she staying here?'

'I thought so.'

'For how long?'

'A long time, Mother.'

Eunicea's ice cracked. 'Why are you calling me by that obsolete and ridiculous misnomer?'

Virgine, not having properly followed the conversation, had begun to delve in a box of sweets Martian had bought her at the port.

'Does she always eat sugar this rapaciously?' Eunicea asked. 'Presumably her teeth are implants. Don't let her touch anything with her sticky little paws.'

Martian put his arm about Virgine and kissed her intently on the cheek. Virgine closed her eyes. She seemed to swallow the taste of the confectionery and the sensuality of the kiss as one.

'This is disgusting,' Eunicea said. 'If you must keep her here, please keep her also out of my sight.'

'I'm sorry you don't like her, Mother.'

Virgine, whose hair and mind both resembled candy floss, smiled at Eunicea and offered her the box of sweets.

Then, and for the first time in his life, Martian beheld his mother in retreat. He found the moment terrifyingly and painfully exhilarating, like falling, through the ether of some world, in the instant of doubt before the parachute opened.

'Goddam the pair of you,' Eunicea opined.

As the slide doors swept to in her wake, Martian heard the radiant-silk para tear overhead, and knew the fall was for real, at last.

That he put the girl at risk was obvious to him and unimportant. The stage had only its two embattled actors, everyone else being a walk-on.

To preserve the illusion intact, though not Virgine, he had her food analysed, her bath water, even her garments before she put them on. Rather to his added excitement, Eunicea attempted nothing in that line. He guessed then at the pit of her insecurity.

He spent almost every hour with Virgine. This was a trial of endurance. All through the crisp, false, ultra-violet summer days, they rode together, drove together, ate and drank together. He bought her an endless succession of gifts. (While she was in the fitting cubicle, he had a few minutes' relief from her presence.) They flew together, went to races and theatres, parks and arenas, into the dark and into the gaudy light, around a couple of worlds and back again. Virgine's glassy eyes gazed vaguely at some of the most ravishing and least wholesome sights that end of the System. Sometimes she blinked and sometimes yawned. She nibbled through boxes of crystallised fruits, flowers and nuts. She fell asleep at the Neptunia Concert, when the whole spectrum was painted and repainted on the dome sky by the wild strokes of the music, and two million people wept, shrieked and fainted throughout the great auditorium.

At various hours and through the nights, they shared sex and silence. Insomniac, Martian would stare at her somnolent form, repressing an urge to fling her from the nearest window (Juno?) or abscond himself. 'Do you love me?' he said to her as they walked through the mauve grass of the estate: Eunicea might be watching, listening. 'Love you,' said Virgine. It was true, the thin waters of her heart were all of love for him. Quite enough love to fill a thimble. He felt an awful pity for her and a sickening disgust. The infection spread. He started to hate himself, and the joy of hating Eunicea became a raw scab. He writhed, longing for the storm to break and for it all to be over in a vast explosion of fire and ichor.

Then Eunicea gave a party. It was one of those vast Cantel affairs, air dripping soft neons, a torch-lit maze, odd foods and obscure liquor. Martian had not communicated with Eunicea for twenty days. A troubling notion had come to him that perhaps she had divined his game and resolved not to play. But the party reassured him. It gave evidence of counter-activity. Quantities of the most beautiful women in the System mingled delicately, like fastidious butterflies, with Eunicea's guests, some of the most beautiful men posed like Greek charioteers. All the modulations of the genders, the various ages of desire, the dark, the fair, the languid, the vivacious, the serene. Someone – never Eunicea – came and introduced each of them to him. Eunicea herself moved far off, a dimly glimpsed pale flame.

Virgine wore scarlet and a shoulder-length wig of plaited rubies.

Martian loathed her so much now he could hardly stand to touch her. Every time he took her hand, or slid his arm about her, bright nauseating barbs shot through his skin at the area of contact, like the pain-warnings of a broken tooth. His nerves were so bad that his wrists shook and his vision was occasionally flecked with small diamonds. He continually felt the urge to burst into tears. More than anything, he wanted to sleep – alone, and in a jet-black room.

Then suddenly he was confronting Eunicea across a couple of metres of grass, at the edge of the torch-lit maze.

The usual coterie of men were present. Eunicea glowed in their midst. She looked ten years less than her age, probably more, since, as she grew older, her rejuvenating preparations grew stronger, and she appeared younger.

'Having fun?' she inquired of Martian.

'Wonderful!'

'And Veersheen?' Eunicea asked.

'She's loving it,' he blurted.

He wanted to go and sit down on the grass beside Eunicea's chair. He wanted to lean against the cool fabric of her dress. She was so much himself that he need do nothing, she would do all of it for him, all the living that was required of him; and he could rest. But instead he turned to Virgine and kissed her, the barbs spearing through his lips.

'How blue your eyes are,' he said to Virgine. He smiled at Eunicea. 'I never saw anyone with such blue eyes.'

To himself, it lacked conviction utterly. But, of course, the drama had gone so far by now, it was capable of spontaneous motion, like a vehicle running downhill.

'I've always thought, in the instance of Veersheen,' Eunicea said lightly, 'that the blueness of her eyes is caused by the same thing that would cause blueness of the lips in anyone else: cyanosis; failure of the blood to reach the brain.'

Falling free, with a world's surface waiting and the parachute torn, Martian laughed. It was not a melodramatic laugh, merely an extension of, or substitute for, his neurasthenia.

'My mother's a bitch, Virgine,' he managed to say.

'J'ai faim,' said Virgine. 'Willn't you find me some chocolate?'

He took her away.

Virgine ate chocolate, and he watched her. He had never seen Virgine eat anything but confectionery. Yet she remained healthy, slender and unblemished. Perhaps she was entirely composed of internal sugars, white candy bones, gingerbread flesh . . . He drank the Vertu champagne Eunicea's parties invariably supplied. Perhaps his blood would become champagne before he struck the world surface, trailing the rent parachute.

In the dark before Domewald dawn-up, he woke to Virgine crawling over him, soft as a clawless cat.

'Make love,' she said.

Too exhausted even to feel the barbs of contact, he lay and let her work upon him. His pulses ran up the scale like shouts heard in the distance and, over Virgine's agitated shoulder, he saw Eunicea, poised in the room, looking at them. She did not seem to respond to their actions in any way. Her face was in shadow.

When Virgine gave a series of miniature squeaks, and rolled aside, Martian lay still, waiting, and Eunicea moved forward.

'True love,' said Eunicea, 'is very touching to observe.' She glanced over his nakedness without specified curiosity or interest. 'I think the best thing would be,' she said, 'if you removed Veersheen from my house. I don't want her here any more, but I don't wish to stand in your way. I intend to settle a million safe-standard credits on her. With investment, you can go far on that. Not as far as you're used to, of course. You, I intend to dispossess.'

He grinned. It was The Moment at last, and he scarcely felt it, for he had imagined it too often and so robbed it of its power.

'I'm dispossessed, then,' he said. 'Stripped of the Cantel funds.'

'No. Providing you cleave to Virgine, you can share her million.'

'Then I shall be in clover, shan't I?'

'You will plant the clover, I hope, somewhere away from me.'

'A long, long way,' he said. 'I promise. Really I do.'

Then her face contorted, and a spasm of horrified delight wrenched through him after all. She leaned forward and struck him hard, high on the left side of the chest. It was not until her hand sprang up and he saw the blood, that he realised she had stabbed him. His heart jumped, and a huge blurring numbness covered him. The shock was considerable and he wondered if she had actually pierced the vital organ.

'It would have been easy to kill you,' she said, 'and it wouldn't solve anything. To kill you now.'

He was conscious of Virgine creeping off the couch, and away from both of them. It was probably instinct, she did not look afraid.

When he opened his eyes again, the room was empty apart from himself. He supposed he would bleed to death, but was too confused to know if he were relieved. Then somebody came in. There was a medical sealing job effected, some bandaging, and next a smudgy dragonfly ride through darkness.

He came fully aware again in a public hospital in the southern section of the Domewald. He had no money, no clothes and no word of Eunicea, beyond a news-view that mentioned her departure off-moon. So he lay on his back and cried a little and pondered what life would be like now he was free and had been split in half once more.

6

The apartment was on the west side of the Cantel Building, subtly decorated, lit by low-key injections of stored moonlight, amplified and warmly tinted. The wide window displayed the electro-irradium sparkle of benighted Greenland City three hundred and sixty-two metres below.

'Repeat it to me,' said Doebatt. 'Convince me. Don't ask me why you should.'

'Life after death,' Martian said, just as he had said it, emerging from the golden sarcophagus, his black hair running with sweat, grinning. Now he lay on a pale black couch, staring remorselessly at the pastel sand-painting on the ceiling. He added something. 'Makes you glad?'

Doebatt miserably picked at a synthetic chicken-leg. It was good, but he could not taste it. Martian had not eaten anything, but Martian seldom ate food these days, going on general report.

'I want to know,' Doebatt said, 'what the film showed, and vocalised. I know the booth is booby-trapped for me – anyone but you. I can't go near it. She told me.'

'Sweet-natured to the last.'

Martian swung his legs off the couch and sat up. He put his hand inside the lapel of his Rationalist jacket, and brought out a long hair-fine chain.

'The one unconditional property Eunicea left me on her demise,' Martian said. 'The instrument of her execution. Minus the emeralds of her red and green death.'

Martian thought how the scene had been described to him, and how he had first viewed it depicted in a news-view 'live' re-enactment: the model, dressed and facially prepared to resemble Eunicea closely, laughing, admiring the workings of the huge Clock, its ticking, whirring synchrony all about her; the cluster of men and hangers-on; the gigantic wheels spinning. And then, the casual toss of the emerald rope behind her. The chain catching on the spoke of one of the inexhaustible, unstoppable wheels, the chain shooting taut, the head of the Eunicea-model wrenched backwards, the faked strangled death-mask of her face, the faked severing, the blood, the frozen tableau left stranded amid the fluorescent light.

'*I might die,*' the child said. '*Perhaps you'll never see me any more.*'

'She committed suicide,' Martian said. 'You understand that?'

'I – *wondered.*'

'Which leads you to believe that what her computers proved exists beyond physical extinction was so tremendously good, exciting and improved, she just couldn't wait to get over there.'

'Logically.'

'Don't confuse logic with my mother. Some of the most brilliant mathematics evolve from the elimination of logic, the application of apparently random chance.'

'But it's there.'

'What is where?'

'In the record – the proof – the means to follow it up – she said –'

'What she said, and what she did. These may be misleading.'

'Don't,' said Doebatt, very quietly. 'You came out of the booth and you told me she had left you a record which –'

'Proved life is eternal. Did I?'

'You know that you –'

'Or, did *she*? What I'm trying to break to you, Doebatt, is that we only have Eunicea's word for it, and she was wise enough to be able to falsify her records, and shocking enough, dear Doebatt, to lie.'

'Oh, my God.'

'Or not, as the case may be.'

Martian went to the wide window and looked out across the glittering city, the fields of sharp stars.

Yes. It had all been there. The proofs. A sub, ultra, alter world, an electric world cheek by cheek with the world of life, whose being had been isolated, traced. And a thing like a soul, a life-signal persistent beyond physical death, reeling away into that otherness – that newly discovered country, invisible as certain rays, now made visible, inaudible as certain frequencies, now to be heard, measured. Believable. True.

And the best proof of all, the unscientific proof. A severed head.

Life was not to be put up with. He supposed he had been saying that, and demonstrating that, since he was sixteen years old. He, and she, the same. The same statement, the same bored terror. And so the endless flirtation with death, which was all that made life bearable to them. And here was the proof that something offered, better than a mountain, or another mountain. One could make the leap – the terrible fall through air into the abyss, the crash of the tower – and still *go on*. One tried to kill oneself in little ways, alcohol, drugs, riot, quiescence, because one must leave the option for life. But now life was there, always there, endless, why not fling the jewelled noose over the shoulder, garotte oneself on a clock, an *eternal unstoppable* clock. Oh yes, one could slash one's wrists over a hangnail, now.

And she had done it. And from the other country, she cried back to him, so merrily, come after! Join me in the greatest adventure of your *life*. Perhaps, as she swung the chain towards the wheel she even pictured it, her son hanged by the neck until dead in the golden box.

They might have died together at Solmer. She had never forgotten that. And he had never forgotten her calm – *their* calm – because they would have gone together.

It was conceivable her records were true. But there was always this other chance. They needed each other, they hated each other. It might have been worth it to her, to rush into oblivion if she could drag him after. Together, but – since there was nothing – not together at all. The problem solved. For ever. All the proofs in the machine might be lies to this end. She was capable of perverting the last desperate dream of humanity into a snare to catch one man.

'Where are you going?' Doebatt said.

'I wonder.'

'When do I expect you back? I mean to re-open the project, naturally. Though not to the public or the media.'

'You're forgetting how to manipulate a Cantel,' said Martian. 'She knew. But then she *was* a Cantel. But then, also, so am I.'

The door whispered, opening to let him by into a corridor like cold black ice.

'You're not going to take part in the project,' said Doebatt.

'You don't seem to realise, we're *all* part of the damn project, whether we want to be or not. I'm sorry you won't get your credits. Or maybe you can corrupt someone.'

'I don't care about the bloody credits. You don't believe the record.'

'Why worry? The Cantel innings, left to itself, is usually pushing two hundred.'

'You're still fighting her,' Doebatt accused him, red-eyed, clutching the leg of a chicken which had never lived.

'Perhaps. But it doesn't really matter.' Martian stepped through into the corridor. His body was tempered by vague generalised symptoms of slight illness, fatigue, sickness. But she had not left poison for him. He was meant to go voluntarily. Otherwise it was no fun at all. The door began to close, and the corridor lights came up like sun on a glacier. He said to Doebatt, 'After all, I may never see her again.'

Winter White

     Crovak the warrior came home in the snow with eighty men, and with one other, so they say. This is how it was:

There had been a war, near summer's end, in the High Country. Ten of the clans were in it, and Crovak had gone from his hold with the rest, to fight and kill and take spoil, man's work for which he was well fitted, being very much a man. Over six feet in height he was, broad in the shoulder, and as strong as he needed to be with strength to spare. His hair and his eyes were brown, but his beard was black and the hair on his body black, and he could get up a black temper too, when he had a mind to it. But his teeth were white as salt and he got his name from them, Crovak White-Tooth, though later he had other names. He was vain of his teeth, and vain all through if truth be told, not of his looks but of his battle skills, his chiefdom, vain of his manhood and of the fact he was a man. Being a man had been lucky for him. It was his boast that none could out-fight him, out-drink him or out-ride him in the horizontal act. He had sired only sons. 'A man makes men,' he would say. He had lost two wives that way, getting sons out of them. But the third wife, she was healthy, a red-haired vixen.

After the war was done, Crovak and his eighty warriors were going homewards with their spoil, but half-way to Drom-Crovak the winter woke early. Snow began to come down, and night closed in, and the warriors lost their road. They were in a wild unfamiliar place, on rocky hills with a pelt of thin forest, land where the wolf-folk live more often than men.

They cursed the snow, the warriors, but the snow paid no heed.

Then, riding blind down through the tree-line in the storm, they came on a narrow valley, and in the valley was an old Drom-hall. Not one of them knew the spot, neither of the hall, which plainly was long empty, though curiously not derelict. Still, they took it for shelter and fortune, and they rode their red horses straight in at the gate and through the doors into the house.

A great house it was too, or had been. The pointed roof went up a good forty feet or more, and the cross beams, jet black with ancient smokes, were intricately carved in a fashion not instantly recognisable. The central hearth was years cold, yet by the hearth lay a huge bundle of wood, as if in readiness for them. One or two of the warriors discussed this uneasily, but Crovak gave them the edge of his anger and they shut their mouths. Certainly, when the wood was lit on the hearth and the sparking reek going up, they were glad enough of it. Outside the snow went on falling and piled against the doors and the ledges of the windows, but the fire burned within, and the men ate the dry meat they had saved over and drank their beer. They made a racket, eating, drinking, crowing over victories in the war, over loot, over women, and over each other's women in Drom-Crovak, and how glad they would be to have their men back after so many nights alone. Only they kept quiet on the matter of Crovak's wife, for none but he might make a story of her, how hot she was and how willing. But Crovak was not apparently in the mood for talking of women, and soon he got up, dipped a brand from the hearth, went about the Drom, through the hall, and at length up the inner stairway to the one big upper room which was the Chief's place, or would have been if any chief had remained. Everyone knew what was in Crovak's mind then, he was on the look-out for fresh spoil, as if he scented it here as a hound scents his home-hearth. None followed, for Crovak had summoned none to follow him. Whatever he found he would most probably keep, it was his by chief's right, and if he was greedy nobody cared to cross him.

Crovak was indeed very restless. He liked to be up and doing, warring or hunting; if at rest, then with a girl or getting drunk, and they had no girls, and not enough beer with them to get drunk on. So he paced about, peering into the shadows of the Drom. He hardly expected to come on any riches left behind, and when he discovered the tall black chests standing in the upper room, he put his foot through their doors without much hope of reward, and truly there was none, for they were bare. The frame of an enormous antique bed stood against the far wall, and here spiders had got to work as they had in the corners of the room below. Crovak, what with the shadows and the webs of these spinner-people, nearly missed what rested on the sinister post of the bed. But just as he was going out with an oath, the brand he held caught a red glint in the dark, and Crovak returned to see.

What he saw was a thing all bound over with grey spider flax, with its one red eye shining out at him. So he pulled the thing loose and picked off the webs, and presently he beheld a slender small hollow pipe of ivory, with three black holes in it and a scarlet gem set where the fourth hole was not. Now Crovak was not a man given to superstition or to fancies of any kind, but it seemed to him, suddenly, that everything in the upper room had grown very still. Even the brand had stopped flickering in his grasp, even the spiders had paused upon their threads. But this was only for a moment. Crovak shook the pipe, and the flame on the brand jumped again, and the webs swayed and the shadows lurched. Then Crovak put his mouth to the pipe to blow the dust from it. The pipe made a sound when he did this, a thin high squeal, and for some reason the sound reminded Crovak instantly of the noise a woman might make when a man struck her, or raped her. This amused him, and he put the pipe to his lips a second time and blew it, but now no sound came out, and try as he would, no sound could he make to come from it. Still, for the ruby at its other end, it was not valueless.

Crovak left the room and swaggered down the stair. He toyed with the pipe, artfully not speaking, till the warriors asked where he had got it. He told then, and later he spoke of his wife and how she would run to him and hang on him when they got home. When the men slept, Crovak lay awake some while, considering that.

In the morning the snow was all down, but hard with frost, and a chill bright sun stood over it. They found their road again easily, Crovak and his eighty men, and by noon they were far from the old Drom where it lay empty and hearth-cold once more under the whiteness.

There were three more days of riding before they should reach Drom-Crovak.

All the first day, Crovak's horse acted oddly, swerving at nothing, trembling at nothing. Crovak cursed it, beat it and finally gifted it to another man and took that man's horse in exchange. After which Crovak's own horse became steady and the new horse under him began shying and stalling. That night they made their camp in the wretched open. Wolves howled on the hollow hills behind them, and the stars had a look of that same hungry howling, so swollen and brilliant they were in the sky. Yet the men had taken a deer and eaten fresh meat that night. Crovak slept under his cloak and dreamed he had his woman with him. A very real dream it was, yet she was not as she had been, her body stony in his grip. He woke in the dawn and took out the ivory pipe and set it grinning to his mouth, attempting to evoke again that female squeal of pain or fear, but no sound came.

The second day, there was the same trouble with the horse. The warriors came into the lowlands and passed by a frozen river. Somewhere here, Crovak began to feel a certain strangeness at his back, as if something pressed against him, and not long after, the horse reared up and fell, throwing him. Then Crovak, in his fury, took a boulder and brained the horse as it struggled to rise.

The man whose horse it had been was angry. Altercation broke out, and Crovak struck him down with a blow that near broke his jaw. Crovak took back his own mount, and the horseless warrior must ride behind another. Crovak's horse shied at nothing, and trembled, but knew better than to throw him.

Just before the sun left the white plain, they passed a stretch of the river where the ice was broken and, glancing aside, Crovak saw his own reflection there astride the red horse, and something up behind him, riding pillion as the horseless warrior rode behind another.

Crovak drew rein, and turned about to see, and saw nothing, only the dying ruddy light, and his men at his back.

Some would dwell on an occurrence of this sort, but Crovak's mind was not constructed to dwell on shadows or on dreams. Yet, when they made their camp, he drew out the ivory pipe, and offered it to one of the men.

'It has a pleasing note,' said he, 'but it is a stubborn object.'

The man took the pipe and rolled it between his fingers.

'I never met such a thing before, Crovak-lord,' said he. 'But I will not offer to sound it.'

'Come, if I say sound it, you shall,' said Crovak.

'I say I will not, Crovak-lord.'

'What are you afraid of? Is it a woman's cringing heart you have? Perhaps I should wed you to one of my ten-year-old sons, and see if he can get you with child.'

The other warriors joined his jeering. One said he would try the pipe, but when he was about to put it to his mouth he sneezed, and each time he raised the pipe he sneezed, a curious happening. And another man who snatched the pipe was taken with a fit of choking, while a third had the pipe at his lip, but the fire spat and a piece of flaming tinder flew up and lodged in his cloak, and he dropped the pipe to beat out the burning. Then Crovak retrieved the pipe with a snarl of laughter.

'The wench is wed to me,' he said, and put the ivory away in his belt, and laughed again.

The next day's riding was hard, but they were getting near Drom-Crovak; the curve of the land, the trees, the tracks, all took on the look of home things, even beneath the snow. Here and there they passed by a small steading, the outlying holds of the Drom, which owed Crovak tythe. Generally when the Drom warriors went riding, the out-women kept from sight, but a few miles from the Drom there was a girl child, not more than four or five, playing on the track. It was ill-luck, and worse, unlawful among the clans, to kill a child, even a peasant's or a slave's brat. The warriors reined aside, and then a dour skinny woman ran from the huddle of huts nearby to scoop the child up. Not looking at Crovak, she mumbled for his pardon and received instead a gob of his spit. As the men moved off, the girl child's voice rose thin and clear above the crunch of hoofs in the snow: 'White woman! See.'

Crovak heard, and something caught him in the cry, he could not have said what, but it inflamed his temper. He swung round and rode back.

'Speak, sow. What does your filthy bairn mean?'

'I do not know, Crovak-lord.'

'White woman,' said the child again, 'on big man's dog.'

'What?' shouted Crovak.

'Pardon, Crovak-lord. She thinks a horse a dog. She means on your horse, Crovak-lord. But no one is there.'

'White woman,' said the child, the third time.

'Get from my sight!' Crovak shouted. He struck the woman a blow with his whip across her thighs, before she could run. But somehow she ran after the blow, hauling the child with her, silent, into the nearest hut.

Crovak was not frightened, did not think to be. But he was angry, with a mad unmotivated rage. He slashed his horse about the neck, and it plunged forward snorting. The warriors tore after. Yet, even riding so swift, Crovak felt a constriction at his chest and, glancing down, he saw an odd thing. Two white arms, white as the snow, were round his ribs and held him fast, and two white hands, their fingers knotted among his furs.

Then the anger, not the fear, overwhelmed Crovak, and with a bellow he strove to thrust and tear the fragile clinging white arms from him, and he must indeed have had his will, for they were suddenly gone. And when he looked before him again, and shook the freezing sweat from his scowling face, he perceived the track winding down between the shallow hills of the Low Country, leading to his Drom.

Crovak the warrior came home in the snow with his eighty men just at fall of night, and he saw the long stockade and the terraced earth-mound behind with the Drom huts circling up on it, and the great hall at its summit. The torches were red on the stockade gates; between them, the men Crovak had left here, when he went to war, were patrolling with their spears, looking out for enemies. Above, other torches blazed from the cross-alleys between the dwellings, and brazen from the doors of the hall. It was a good thing to return and see, the Drom so sturdy, so safe and so fine with its lights, as if the night had no power over it.

Crovak had no sense of foreboding, or at least he would not have confessed one. But he said to his men: 'Make camp here an hour, for I am going back alone. I would see how well my laws are kept when I am from the hearth.'

The men laughed, and one dared to say that Crovak's wife would be weeping, with her loom set by and her face in the ashes. Crovak grinned and, leaving his horse, he stole down on his own hold like the thief.

He got over the stockade like a thief, too. No other but the master could have done it, for the watch-hounds knew his scent, and kept quiet when he bade them – one man who came to apprehend him, Crovak crowned with his fist. He was taking no chances. He stole up through the cross-alleys, muffled in his furs, and reached the hall door and went by it. Not only an inner but an outer stair led to the upper chamber, this outer stair infrequently used, but now Crovak used it. It was not yet the time for dinner, besides, the chief's wife did not sit in hall when he was absent, at least, not the wife of Crovak.

He knew she was in the chamber as soon as he reached the outer door, for he could scent her, the hot russet smell of her hair and the ripeness of her flesh. When he pushed open the door, he knew also why the perfume of her was so strong. She did not hear him enter, she was too preoccupied. Neither did the man hear.

They lay on Crovak's bed, intent on their journey.

Crovak, whose reaction to fury was usually one of clamour, made no noise at all as he crept about and took down from the wall one of his boar spears. He stood a moment, the spear resting in his hands, watching his wife and the man who rode her. Crovak did not feel surprise or hurt. But when he leaped forward and plunged the spear down through both their bodies, with his massive strength, through the two of them and through the bed itself into a crevice of the stone floor beneath, he felt a boiling spasm of pleasure at their deaths. He stood and watched them die. The eyes of his vixen wife pleaded with him; even dying, she pleaded dumbly for mercy, till the soul left her.

Crovak took out the ivory pipe. He looked at it with hatred and fondness.

'Cunning, you warn me,' he said.

Then he went out to call his warriors in, and rouse the Drom to his arrival.

Of course, he did not mourn her. The man, Crovak gave to his kin to bury, that was their business. But she, his woman, Crovak had thrown a little distance outside the gates of the Drom, for beasts to feed on. The night meal was served late that night, but served it was, and Crovak sat down in his hall to it, sat in his carved chair, as if no untoward thing had hapened. His rage was gone to a sort of grizzly playfulness. Not a man there but knew he must be wary for his skin's sake. Particularly that night, they only laughed when Crovak did, and when he said no word, no man spoke, and the quiet hung from the rafters with the smoke. And the warrior who had jested of Crovak's wife's weeping, he stayed away.

Finally Crovak called for his drinking cup, the cup which usually he kept for a feast. It was made from the skull of one of Crovak's enemies, slain in an earlier war, the eyes, the nostrils and the mouth closed with red gold, and the brink rimmed with gold. This goblet was filled for Crovak with beer, and he drank it to the last drop and banged his bone cup down on the board.

Just at that instant, there was another banging, much lighter – yet he heard it – on the doors of the hall. And, at the rapping, the doors opened.

Crovak sat staring, and his mouth set in its grin, showing his flawless and glistening teeth. Through the doors came neither warrior nor slave nor servant; not a traveller, not an itinerant musician with his harp on his back. No, none of these. Through the doors came a woman, and she was white as the winter snow.

Crovak recognised her at once. He shouted at her:

'So you have come to claim payment for your warning, have you?'

It seemed she had. Up the silent hall, more silent than ever after Crovak's shout, she moved. She had no look of anything real, more like something painted or enamelled than a living thing. Her gown was white, and not of the fashion of the time, and it left bare her shoulders, though she had been walking in the snow. Her gown was white, and as white as the gown was her flesh, as if there were no blood in it, and her flaxen hair was nearly as white. There was no colour in her face, even her mouth was bloodless, but her brows were black and her eyes were black, and the nails of her hands were red as rubies, as if they, out of all her bloodlessness, had been dipped in blood. And indeed, her hands were so pale on the pale gown that it was hard to make them out, but for those nails like ten drops of blood splashed there.

'What will you have, woman?' Crovak roared. 'Ask your price.'

The woman kept walking towards him, but she did not speak. Alongside, the warriors glanced this way and that, at Crovak, then where he stared, at her. It seemed to the warriors that Crovak was afraid. Sweat stood on his forehead and in his black beard, though he grinned. But Crovak did not feel himself afraid. Not even when the woman reached him, and halted, facing him across the board. Her face was blank, and her mouth so pale he could not tell if it smiled or grimaced at him.

'Well, she-wolf,' said Crovak, 'I never believed in your like before, but here you are. Will you sit with me? You will be the first of your sex to sit at my table, but then you are fey, so perhaps you have earned it.' Then he called for more beer to fill his skull-cup. The woman, however, did not sit, nor touch anything on the board. She only gazed at Crovak with her eyes as black as ravens. Crovak turned to his men. 'What do you think of her?'

A man near to him, a fool, said haltingly: 'Who are you seeing, Crovak-lord? Is it your dead woman?'

Crovak gave a cry of rage, and turning about, struck the man sprawling.

'Who does not see her?' Crovak shouted.

The men looked at each other, the slaves huddled by the hearth and hid their eyes. It was borne in on Crovak that none but he could perceive the woman. At that, he laughed again.

'Only for me, are you?' He drank deep, and drank. 'Only for me?'

When the fourth skull-full of beer was in his belly, he reached across the board and put his hand on her naked shoulder. She felt more real than she appeared, but her flesh was very smooth, as if there were not a pore in it, very smooth and cool. 'Now, lass, shall you tell me what you want, or is it only to feast your glance on Crovak White-Tooth? Feast then.'

Crovak called for more beer. He drank till the skin was empty, till he was drunken and the hall blurred and the sensations of his body blurred. Yet still her he could see very clearly, her with her black eyes. At length he rose, staggering and merry. He turned his back on her, and slurred over his shoulder at her: 'Bid you good night, white sow,' and he rolled through the silent hall and up the stair, through the hanging into the upper room where seven hours before he had ended his marriage to his red-headed wife. The blood had been cleaned away and the bedding changed, but the frame of the bed and the floor would always hold the mark of the spear's passage, which would be a grand thing to show the next wife he lay down here with.

Crovak stripped his boots and belt, went to the outer door and urinated out upon the stair. Turning back into the room, he beheld the white woman standing at the bed's foot.

Crovak shouted, wordlessly now. Just for one second, he went cold in his belly. Then he showed his teeth to her again and he said: 'You would be wife to me, would you?' And he strode to her, rocking somewhat in his gait, and seized her in his two strong hands.

She made no resistance and no remonstrance as he half lifted her to the bed and slung her down there. He was ready for a woman, and pushed up her skirts. Even that part of her was pallid, but it did not deter him, nor the white points of her breasts which should have had some colour in them, when he dragged down the neck of her bodice to see. He had her, but the drink made him slow. Slow enough he could notice how she watched him, kept on watching as he worked inside her. She did not catch her breath, she did not make a sound, and her eyes were wide. Her eyes bored into him, cold for his heat. And when he shuddered and grunted and fell down upon her, even then her eyes were somehow watching him, observing his fit with a pitiless and detached interest.

No sooner was the paroxysm over than a vile sickness took him, and lurching up and to the door, he vomited forth the beer.

She watched that too.

And when again he lay groaning on the bed, still she watched. And when he summoned his strength and struck her from the bed, next moment she was there again beside him, her face turned to him, unbruised, her eyes watching.

He grew faint, or else he dozed. When he woke, darkness filled the Drom, and dimly through the outer door he scented the stench of his own sickness, and there she lay beside him yet.

'How now, bitch? Fey or not, you have outstayed my leave.'

Rising then, he raised her too, and she was light to carry. He went through the hanging to the inner stair, and he tossed her down it with no trouble. He saw her motionless at the stair's foot, against the dim glow of a single torch left burning in the hall.

Crovak chuckled. He feared her not at all.

He went to his bed and slept heavily. But when he roused in the hour before sunrise, she was beside him again, her eyes mere inches from his own, polished, frigid and terrible as the eyes of a serpent.

At that Crovak beat her. He gave her a beating no woman could take and live, and few men. She did not attempt to defend herself, neither did she cower away. She must be mute for she made no outcry even now, yet once he thought he glimpsed her tongue – pointed and pale – he thought he noted blood too, and when she tumbled on the ground, he applied his feet, kicking her in the shank and stomach. All this while he was bellowing like the bull, till his men came running up the stair and burst into the room, blear-eyed with swords in their hands.

'What is amiss, Crovak-lord?'

'Nothing!' he ranted, kicking at her, knowing they would not see, that she was his alone, snarling his hate while the sweat flew from his congested face. 'Get to your kennels, and leave me to my own deeds.'

Later, when they had gone, Crovak took the white woman down the outer stair and threw her over a horse, and calling two slaves from the straw where they slept, he sent them off with the horse in the chill grey dawn. 'Ride him fast, and leave him when he is done.'

The slaves' eyes were huge. Wolves came near the Drom in winter. Wolves would have the horse and possibly themselves also. But Crovak had gone mad, gone mad when he caught his wife at her game, gone mad even before, on the way home, some said . . . The slaves, not daring to disobey, raced the horse out of the stockade gate. Crovak watched them go with the horse and the white woman on its back. He grinned, but the cold day struck into his jaw and made it ache, though his jaw had never ached till then.

The warriors were muttering in the hold, but when Crovak came close, they were dumb.

Crovak carved for himself a piece of last night's roast, and turning about, with his knife in his grip, beheld the woman at his elbow.

Crovak screamed. He thrust the knife into her breast and snatched it out. She stood unharmed, unbloody, watching him. Crovak laughed. He laughed and crashed his fist upon the wall, laughed till the warriors slunk from his hall and the slaves hid themselves beneath the benches.

'Am I not to be rid of you? Be damned then, companion me!'

'How long have we to brook this?' the men asked each other. 'Our lord by right, well, so he is. And if he was high-handed in the past, we bore with him, for he was a man, a warrior. We did well enough. But this winter –'

'He is mad this winter,' others said. 'Some new lord should master the Drom. Must we vow our swords to a madman?'

But still they feared Crovak too much to rebel openly against him. He had taught them that fear ten years, though now they had had a taste of his lunacy for two months. They had seen him strike out and mutter and shout at nothing, they had seen him sneer over his shoulder at nothing. They had seen him linger in the hall till sun-up and not go to his bed, as if he feared to go, nor did he ever take a woman. If any offered, he would knock them down. 'I *have* a woman!'

The men did not see this: how Crovak, when exhaustedly he had sought his bed, would try to hold himself awake, knowing that as he slept two polished, greasy-shining black stones would stare at him. Nor did the men see how once or twice he had lain down on this woman of his, and how Lusty Crovak could not take his pleasure with her, his fire put out by her cold water. Even her loins were cold, winter cold, and winter white as the rest of her. He gripped her feverishly and struggled to be a man with her, but she was stone and he was dead. And even the huzzies of the hall could not stir him, for he was aware that she would be by, watching, watching.

He grew morose. Always he spoke to her. He spoke because she did not and he must speak for both.

'What are you wanting? Tell me. You shall have it. Is it the pipe, the pipe with the ruby which called you? Eh? Will I give it you back? Here, take it.' But her red-tipped hands stayed at her sides, blood drops on the white gown. He put the pipe under his heel, but it would not break. He tossed it away from him, but it reappeared in his belt, as always she reappeared at his side.

Certain of the warriors of Drom-Crovak began to steal out, generally by night, in bands of five or six, ten or fourteen. They went to seek other Droms, other lords. Some, whose kin were in Drom-Crovak, and whose roots ran deeper there, began small plots, but discarded them. Clan law was stringent, and they could not quite forget it. Nor the strength of Crovak's arm. Once in the dusk, as Crovak made water up against a wall, a man came by with a knife, but Crovak, with the white woman at his side watching even this, was aware of the man creeping near, and slew him. Truly, Crovak was swift and powerful.

But was he as powerful as he had been? At drink, and he was often drunken now, his hands shook. Sometimes he sat holding his jaw, for his teeth ached. In the second month, this trouble in his jaw became so bad his face was swollen, and he called the smith to pull out one of his front teeth. He howled with the pain, and started up as if he would kill the smith. No longer would they call Crovak 'White-Tooth', with the black gap there. He lost another tooth later; it turned brown and cracked in his mouth. It was a strange thing, but it showed how his strength was leaving him.

The winter thickened on the Low Country. The snows descended, turning the black nights grey. The wolves showed themselves even at the gates of the stockade, and the men of Drom-Crovak went hunting them, and as Crovak rode, he turned often to the air behind him and jeered and spat at this air: 'Are you comfortable, sow? Is it good to ride with Crovak?' And when he cast his spears, they missed their aim.

Then came an evening when Crovak jumped up from the board and began to roar and rant without ceasing. It was the third month, and he brought more fear on his depleted hall than ever before. He was berserk and it seemed he would never be calm again. He over-set the

benches in his raving. He picked up a slave boy and flung him the
breadth of the room. They did not know what particular thing had
caused this outburst, nor why he screamed at them his old boast: 'A
man makes men!'

But abruptly he blundered out into the torchlit darkness, and flung
himself on a horse and plunged from the Drom, all the while yet
screaming. And his noise died away on the night silence as a man's cry
dies away down the length of a precipice from which he has fallen.

The woman shuddered with horror as she listened at the bolted door of
the hut.

'Who is there?'

'I, bitch,' the huge hoarse mad voice thundered. 'Crovak. Now
open, or I kick in the door.'

The woman backed away, and the next moment the door was
indeed broken in shivers, and Crovak strode in. The woman
ascertained a great change in him, his ruined teeth, the grey in his
black beard, the red veins in his eyes and his shaking demented body.
This woman's man was dead, wolves had had him not a month ago.
Now she was hard put to it to fend for herself. She stared at the Drom
chieftain with miserable terror and no surprise, for who did not
understand her life would be bitter and brief.

'Where is your bratling?' Crovak demanded.

Fresh horror – what would he do to her child?

'Come,' he snapped, 'your bairn is fey, is it not? It sees what others
are blind to.'

'It is sometimes thus with the very young, or the old ones, Crovak-
lord – they are nearer life's edge –'

'Get your piglet!' he screamed at her.

The woman turned and lifted the child up from the hearth. The din
had not woken it, but now it woke, and looked at Crovak.

Crovak sighed. He glared dully at the woman. 'Tell me first, sow, if
I am alone.'

The woman nodded, holding tight to her infant.

'Now you,' Crovak said to the child, 'you tell me.'

The child giggled. The woman, in alarm, coaxed it: 'Tell the lord
what you see. If any are with him.'

'White woman,' said the child.

'Where?' rasped Crovak, his eyes ablaze.

'By your left shoulder.'

'Yes, you snake. My left shoulder. So. Now say how she is.'

The child lowered its eyes and crooned, playing with the mother's hair. The mother became distrait, coaxing, coaxing: 'Tell the lord, tell him –'

'All white,' said the child, 'but soot on her eyes and red on her fingers.'

Crovak panted, showing his discoloured teeth. He muttered.

'And she is thicker at the waist than she was, plumper, is she not? Three months since I lay with her . . .'

The child's mother put her free hand to her mouth. The girl child simpered. It had suddenly a sly and canny look.

Crovak rode home, and he entered the gate and saw all about him the concealed glances of wary dislike, mistrust and underlying scorn. Crovak announced a feast in his hall. He ordered three cows slaughtered, five sheep, ten beer barrels broached, though there were less men now in Drom-Crovak than there had ever been. Fewer slaves, too, for many had fled. Even fewer women, for five of those Crovak had struck down in his fierce moods had died.

'This feast,' Crovak told the Drom folk, spit running from his mouth, 'is to celebrate the coming of another son to me. My demon wife is with child. Behold her belly – no, but you cannot. Little matter. She carries. She will give me a boy.'

The feast was a grim and a weird one. Crovak went on drinking three nights and the days between. Sometimes he would go out and throw up what he had taken, then come back to eat and drink again. He dragged the women on to the board before him, and pawed them and straddled them, but he did not have them. 'Note how faithful I am, my wife,' he said.

Eventually Crovak crashed forward in a stupor, and when he recovered himself he found he lay on the floor of his hall, bound and helpless and his mouth stopped with a rag. And all about his warriors stood with their swords.

They had not killed him. As with the slaughter of a child, it was bad luck and unlawful to slay a sleeping man, let alone the chief. But they had spoken long, the warriors of Drom-Crovak. How their women were not safe, how the Drom was cursed, how priests were needed there, and the jurisdiction of the Clan elders. Even the legal sons of Crovak sanctioned what was to be done. No one but did not fear the bane which had fallen on their chieftain and hence upon his hold.

Sluggish and stupid, Crovak writhed in his bonds. The men informed him of what was to be done, informed him courteously. They could afford to be courteous, seeing they had the upper hand at last.

He was put over a horse and carried to a deserted steading about two miles from the Drom. Here was a hut made of stone and weather-proofed to some extent. In the floor was a stone post and a length of iron fetter attached to it – hostages taken in war had been brought to this place now and then, and kept for ransom. It served very well for mad Crovak. Though he was yet strong, they said, he could not rip his way free from iron chains.

Nor did he. Four months he rotted there.

Rotted there, and sat or lay on the straw mattress, or paced about on his short leash, like a restless dog. He had warmth, for his men left him pelts and furs to wrap himself in, bundles of wood to feed the fire, and every five days someone would come and leave more wood, and food, and drink besides, and while this one saw to that, three others would keep watch on Crovak. One other kept her watch, too.

They swore to him that when the snow broke, they would send word to the elders of the Clan and ask for the Council to be held, and there decide his fate.

But each time they visited him, Crovak was a fraction more sullen, or else louder; he lunged at them or he whimpered. It seemed he became madder and more mad. And he would frequently turn to his invisible demon and tell her things. If any warrior recalled the ivory pipe taken from the empty Drom that night the snow came, none spoke of it. For a superstitious folk, they had given small specific heed to Crovak's demon, and maybe they were wise.

She sat facing him, across his fire. She never ceased to fix her look on him. At night she lay by him, but he had no warmth from her. Her eyes never closed, she never blinked. Her belly swelled.

One night, in the fourth month, he woke and, in the dull shine of the fire's embers, he seized her throat and tried to throttle her, although he knew there was no use in it. He ground his decaying teeth and squeezed with all his might, and her black eyes went on staring into his, and the swollen belly pressed into his groin which had made it and now could make nothing.

'Will you kill me then?' he crowed at her. 'Will you take my soul too?'

When he let go her throat, there was no bruise on it. His arms ached like his teeth now, from straining to murder her.

As he lay there, whining softly at his pains, his mind ran back to the Drom where he had found the pipe. He thought of the wood on the floor laid ready, and the emptiness without dereliction, and he wondered if some other man had been enslaved there in the same way that he now was, enslaved there till he died. Crovak thought of the spiders scampering on their threads. He thought of the pipe, and how he had blown it and it had squealed like a woman in terror or hurt, and then he took the pipe out and rolled it in his fingers.

He had blown her into the world, if only he might blow her out, reverse the bane, be rid of her.

In a dreadful manner, he had almost grown accustomed to her stare, and turning from her, idly, he began to pick at the ruby that was set in where the fourth hole of the pipe was not. And then, growing weary of this, Crovak set the pipe to his lips and tapped it there.

It seemed to him, abruptly, that in her white face which watched him, there was the slightest and most subtle alteration. Crovak was undeniably insane by this season, but not with a blind insanity. Through the wreckage of his wits a strange idea came to him, and he slowly turned the pipe about in his hand, so its other end was to his mouth, and, holding it in this fashion, he blew it.

It made a sound. Not as at the previous hour, not a squeal of distress. This time, shrill and thin, it *laughed*.

The woman did two things, two things she had not done before. She opened her mouth very wide, and this was how he saw her teeth were gleaming and coal black as her eyes – which all at once she shut. Then she did a third new thing. She fell backwards on the stone floor and she vanished.

Crovak could hardly credit what he beheld this plainly. He grunted, and he shuffled in his chains, and he waited, his tongue lolling, for her to reappear. And this she did not do.

When day came, still he looked for her, and still she was absent.

Four whole days he waited; four whole days she did not come back. The fourth night he poked out a hole between the stones of the floor and thrust the pipe down into it, and covered it, smiling. The fifth day, Crovak went on smiling to himself, hugging himself, rattling the chain. He built up the fire. When the warriors came to feed him, he spoke to them. He told them all was well, he had outwitted the demon, but he slavered as he spoke, and they paid no heed. Yet he had a strange cunning by then, and he stole a knife from one, and when the men were gone he hacked off his thumb, which made his hand slight enough to slip from the fetter.

He felt the agony only as a distant nudging, and packed snow on the wound, which numbed it. He followed the hoof-pocks in the whiteness the two miles back to Drom-Crovak. It was dusk and the torches burned on the gates. He came on a man there, patrolling the wall, and killed him with the knife and took his sword. After that, Crovak ran into his hold, and he laid about him with the stolen sword, and very many he butchered till he grew weary of the sport. He got a horse then, and rode away into the winter land, red with blood, and his mad eyes red, singing.

What else then do they say of Crovak? They say this:

He wandered the winter two months more. He lived like a beast, preying on the steadings thereabouts which once had paid him tythe. They had been in fear of him before, but now they had a better cause to fear him. Whole families he cut down, only for a loaf or a bit of meat. They say he drank men's blood. How he lived or where, is not certain, in some ruined hut perhaps. His madness kept him alive. Bands of men from the Drom rode out to catch and kill him, but they never found him out.

It had been a harsh unnatural winter, eager to arrive, reluctant to take its leave, but in the end the snow had gone, the ways were brown and muddy, the rivers running bright.

Crovak strode from the forest land which was putting on its green. His horse was dead by then, and he a fearsome sight, ragged, filthy, and his rotten teeth showing in that beard half grey and knotted with the debris of the woods.

He had forgotten much, and no longer did he reason in any form as a man does. Yet enough he remembered, and he took a perverse pleasure in his survival.

When he came to the field he did not quite recall it. The ground was raw with earth and rank grass, but a stand of trees was at its centre, and nearby a group of huts, and beyond them a track. The track he knew, it led to the Drom, down over the curving shallow hills. A girl child was playing in the field. He recollected the child.

Crovak moved towards the child. He had no positive intention, but a kind of malicious crazy urge to startle it. But the grasses rustled, not merely at his passage, but as if a tiny beast were rummaging there, and the child looked up and saw Crovak.

The wild man snarled down at her, but the child exhibited no nervousness. In fact, confronting the child again, it was Crovak who felt a sudden ice in his belly. He made a guttural noise at the child, for speech did not come fluently any more to him. After a try or two, he got his defiance out:

'What do you see? Is she there, eh? Is she? The white sow?'

The child shook its head.

'No.'

Crovak grinned.

'No. No winter woman. I have sent her back. Clever Crovak, Crovak White-Tooth.'

Just then the mother came from one of the huts and, catching sight of him, froze. This amused Crovak. He sucked his nine black nails. Behind him, in the rank grass, the creature rustled again, and the child gazed past Crovak, downward, and she giggled.

'What?' said Crovak. He laughed. 'Tell me, what? A fox? I have eaten foxes in the wood.'

'See,' said the child.

By the huts, the woman held her hands to Crovak imploringly.

'Shall I eat you then?' asked Crovak. 'Like the fox.'

'See,' said the child a second time. She was watching something just at Crovak's back and somewhat to his left, in stature a third of the distance up his calf.

'Will she play with me?' asked the child insistently.

Crovak did not turn.

'She is not there,' he said, 'the white woman.'

'No,' said the child.

Crovak would not turn. He would not think of the swollen belly which had pressed against him. He would not think of his boast of sons.

'She is small as me, she has no clothes,' said the child, 'but her fingers are red.'

Crovak shrieked. He flung about and ran. Behind him, faintly, came the rustling of some tiny thing, which yet managed to keep pace with him. Which kept pace with him, and kept pace with him, and never slackened.

No more is known, or said, of Crovak.

Written in Water

It was a still summer night, coloured through by darkness. A snow-white star fell out of the sky and into the black field half a mile from the house. Ten minutes later, Jaina had walked from the house, through the fenced garden patch, the creaking gate, towards the place where the star had fallen. Presently, she was standing over a young man, lying tangled in a silver web, on the burned lap of the Earth.

'Who are you?' said Jaina. 'What's happened to you? Can you talk? Can you tell me?'

The young man, who was very young, about twenty-two or -three, moved his slim young body, turning his face. He was wonderful to look at, so wonderful, Jaina needed to take a deep breath before she spoke to him again.

'I want to help you. Can you say anything?'

He opened a pair of eyes, like two windows opening on sunlight in the dark. His eyes were beautiful, and very golden. He said nothing, not even anything she could not understand. She looked at him, drinking in, intuitively, his beauty; knowing, also intuitively, that he had nothing to do either with her world, or her time.

'Where did you come from?' she said.

He looked back at her. He seemed to guess, and then to consider. Gravely, gracefully, he lifted one arm from the tangle of the web, and pointed at the sky.

He sat in her kitchen, at her table. She offered him medication, food, alcohol, and caffeine from a tall bronzed coffee pot. He shook his head, slowly. Semantically, some gestures were the same. Yet not the same. Even in the shaking of his head, she perceived he was alien. His hair was the colour of the coffee he refused. Coffee, with a few drops of milk in it, and a burnish like satin. His skin was pale. So pale, it too was barely humanly associable. She had an inspiration, and filled a glass with water. The water was pure, filtered through the faucet from the well in the courtyard, without chemicals or additives. Even so, it might poison him. He had not seemed hurt after all, merely stunned, shaken. He had walked to her house quietly, at her side, responding to her swift angular little gestures of beckoning and reception. Now she wanted to give him something.

She placed the glass before him. He looked at it, and took it up in two finely made, strong, articulate hands. They were the hands of a dancer, a musician. They had each only four fingers, one thumb, quite normal. He carried the glass to his mouth. She held her breath, wondering, waiting. He put the glass down carefully, and moved it, as carefully, away from him. He laid his arms across the table and his head upon his arms, and he wept.

Jaina stood staring at him. A single strand of silver, left adhering when he stripped himself of the web, lay across his arm, glittering as his shoulders shook. She listened to him crying, a young man's sobs, painful, tearing him. She approached him, and muttered: 'What is it? What is it?' helplessly.

Of course, it was only grief. She put her hand on his shoulder, anxious, for he might flinch from her touch, or some inimical thing in their separate chemistries might damage both of them. But he did not flinch, and no flame burst out between her palm and the dark, apparently seamless clothing which he wore.

'Don't cry,' she said. But she did not mean it. His distress afforded her an exquisite agony of empathic pain. She had not felt anything for a very long time. She stroked his hair gently. Perhaps some subtle radiation clung to him, some killer dust from a far-away star. She did not care. 'Oh, don't cry, don't cry,' she murmured, swimming in his tears.

She drove into the morning town in her ramshackle car, as usual not paying much attention to anything about her. Nor was her programme much changed. First, petrol from the self-service station, then a tour of the shops, going in and out of their uninviting façades: a tour of duty. In the large hypermarket at the edge of town, she made her way through the plastic and the cans, vaguely irritated, as always, by the soft mush of music, which came and went on a time switch, regardless of who wanted it, or no longer did. Once, she had seen a rat scuttle over the floor behind the frozen-meat section. Jaina had done her best to ignore such evidence of neglect. She had walked out of the shop stiffly.

She had never liked people very much. They had always hurt her, or degraded her, always imposed on her in some way. Finally, she had retreated into the old house, wanting to be alone, a hermitess. Her ultimate loneliness, deeper than any state she had actually imagined for herself, was almost like a judgement. She was thirty-five and, to herself, resembled a burned-out lamp. The dry leaf-brownness of her skin, the tindery quality of her hair, gave her but further evidence of this consuming. Alone, alone. She had been alone so long. And burned, a charred stick, incapable of moistures, fluidities. And yet, streams and oceans had moved in her when the young man from outer space had sobbed with his arms on her table.

She supposed, wryly, that the normal human reaction to what had happened would be a desire to contact someone, inform someone of her miraculous find, her 'Encounter'. She only played with this idea, comparing it to her present circumstances. She felt, of course, no onus on her to act in a rational way. Besides, whom should she approach with her story, who would be likely to credit her? While she herself had no doubts.

But as she was turning on to the dirt road that led to the house, she became the prey of sudden insecurities. Perhaps the ultimate loneliness had told, she had gone insane, fantasising the falling star of the parachute, imagining the young man with eyes like golden sovereigns. Or, if it were true . . . Possibly, virulent Terran germs, carried by herself, her touch, had already killed him. She pictured, irresistibly, Wells' Martians lying dead and decaying in their great machines, slain by the microbes of Earth.

Last night, when he had grown calm, or only tired, she had led him to her bedroom and shown her her bed. It was a narrow bed, what else, fit only for one. Past lovers had taught her that the single bed was to be hers, in spite of them, forever. But he had lain down there without a word. She had slept in the room below, in a straight-backed chair between the bureau and the TV set which did not work any more. Waking at sunrise, with a shamed awareness of a new feeling, which was that of a child on Christmas morning, she had slunk to look at him asleep. And she was reminded of some poem she had read, long, long ago:

How beautiful you look when sleeping; so beautiful
It seems that you have gone away . . .

She had left him there, afraid to disturb such completion, afraid to stand and feed parasitically on him. She had driven instead into town for extra supplies. She wanted to bring him things; food he might not eat, drink he might not drink. Even music, even books he could not assimilate.

But now – he might be gone, never have existed. Or he might be dead.

She spun the car to a complaining halt in the summer dust. She ran between the tall carboniferous trees, around the fence. Her heart was in her throat, congesting and blinding her.

The whole day lay out over the country in a white-hot film. She turned her head, trying to see through this film, as if underwater. The house looked silent, mummified. Empty. The land was the same, an erased tape. She glanced at the blackened field.

As she stumbled towards the house, her breathing harsh, he came out through the open door.

He carried the spade which she had used to turn the pitiful garden. He had been cleaning the spade; it looked bright and shiny. He leaned it on the porch and walked towards her. As she stared at him, taking oxygen in great gulps, he went by her, and began to lift things out of the car and carry them to the house.

'I thought you were dead,' she said stupidly. She stood stupidly, her head stupidly hanging, feeling suddenly very sick and drained.

After a while she too walked slowly into the house. While he continued to fetch the boxes and tins into her kitchen like an errand boy, she sat at the table, where he had sat the night before. It occurred to her that she could have brought him fresh clothing from the stores in the town, but it would have embarrassed her slightly to choose things for him, even randomly off the peg in the hypermarket.

His intention had presumably been to work on her garden, some sort of repayment for her haphazard, inadequate hospitality. And for this work he had stripped bare to the waist. She was afraid to look at him. The torso, what was revealed of it, was also like a dancer's – supple, the musculature developed and flawless. She debated, in a dim terror of herself, if his human maleness extended to all regions of his body.

After a long time, he stopped bringing in the supplies, and took up the spade once more.

'Are you hungry?' she said to him. She showed him one of the cans. As previously, slow and quiet, he shook his head.

Perhaps he did not need to eat. Perhaps he would drink her blood. Her veins filled with fire, and she left the table, and went quickly upstairs. She should tell someone about him. If only she were able to. But she could not.

He was hers.

She lay in the bath, in the cool water, letting her washed wet hair float around her. She was Ophelia. Not swimming; drowning. A slender glass of greenish gin on five rocks of milky ice pulsed in her fingers to the rhythm of her heart.

Below, she heard the spade ring tirelessly on stone. She had struggled with the plot, raising a few beans, tomatoes, potatoes which blackened and a vine which died. But he would make her garden grow. Oh, yes.

She rested her head on the bath's porcelain rim, and laughed, trembling, the tips of her breasts breaking the water like buds.

She visualised a silver bud in the sky, blossoming into a huge and fiery ship. The ship came down on the black field. It had come for him, come to take him home. She held his hand and pleaded, in a language he did not comprehend, and a voice spoke to him out of the ship, in a language which he knew well. She clung to his ankle, and he pulled her through the scorched grass, not noticing her, as he ran towards the blazing port.

Why else had he wept? Somehow and somewhere, out beyond the moon, his inexplicable craft had foundered. Everything was lost to him. His vessel, his home, his world, his kind. Instead there was a bony house, a bony, dried-out hag, food he could not eat. A living death.

Jaina felt anger. She felt anger as she had not felt it for several months, hearing that spade ring on the indomitable rock under the soil. Still alone.

When the clock chimed six times that meant it was one-quarter past five, and Jaina came down the stairs of the house. She wore a dress like white tissue, and a marvellous scent out of a crystal bottle. She had seen herself in a mirror, brushing her face with delicate pastel dusts, and her eyes with cinnamon and charcoal.

She stood on the porch, feeling a butterfly lightness. She stretched up her hand to shield her eyes, the gesture of a heroine upon the veranda of a dream. He rested on the spade, watching her.

See how I am, she thought. *Please, please, see me, see me.*

She walked off the porch, across the garden. She went straight up to him. The sun in his eyes blinded her. She could not smile at him. She pointed to her breast.

'*Jaina*,' she said. 'I am *Jaina*.' She pointed to him. She did not touch him. 'You?'

She had seen it done so frequently. In films. She had read it in books. Now he himself would smile slightly, uneasily touch his own chest and say, in some foreign otherworld tongue: *I am* . . .

But he did not. He gazed at her, and once more he slowly shook his head. Suddenly, all the glorious pity and complementary grief she had felt through him before flooded back, overwhelming her. Could it be he did not know, could not remember, who he was? His name, his race, his planet? He had fallen out of the stars. He was amnesiac. Truly defenceless, then. Truly hers.

'Don't work anymore,' she said. She took the spade from his hand, and let it drop on the upturned soil.

Again, she led him back to the house, still not touching him.

In the kitchen, she said to him, 'You must try and tell me what food you need to eat. You really must.'

He continued to watch her, if he actually saw her at all. She imagined him biting off her arm, and shivered. Perhaps he did not eat – she had considered that before. Not eat, not sleep – the illusion of sleep only a suspended state, induced to please her, or pacify her. She did not think he had used the bathroom. He did not seem to sweat. How odd he should have been able to shed tears.

She dismissed the idea of eating for herself, too. She poured herself another deep swamp of ice and gin. She sat on the porch and he sat beside her.

His eyes looked out across the country. Looking for escape? She could smell the strange sweatless, poreless, yet indefinably masculine scent of him. His extraordinary skin had taken on a watercolour glaze of sunburn.

The day flickered along the varied tops of the reddening horizon. Birds swirled over like a flight of miniature planes. When the first star appeared, she knew she would catch her breath in fear.

The valves of the sky loosened, and blueness poured into it. The sun had gone. He could not understand her, so she said to him: 'I love you.'

'I love you,' she said. 'I'm the last woman on Earth, and you're not even local talent. And I love you. I'm lonely,' she said. And, unlike him, she cried quietly.

After a while, just as she would have wished him to if this had been a film, and she directing it, he put his arm about her, gently, gently. She lay against him, and he stroked her hair. She thought, with a strange ghostly sorrow: *he has learned such gestures from me.*

Of course, she did not love him, and of course she did. She was the last survivor, and he was also a survivor. Inevitably they must come together, find each other, love. She wished she was younger. She began to feel younger as his arm supported her, and his articulate fingers silked through and through her hair. In a low voice, although he could not understand, she began to tell him about the plague. How it had come, a whisper, the fall of a leaf far away. How it had swept over the world, its continents, its cities, like a sea. A sea of leaves, burning. A fire. They had not called it plague. The official name for it had been 'Pandemic'. At first, the radios had chattered with it, the glowing pools of the TVs had crackled with it. She had seen the hospitals packed like great antiseptic trays with racks of the dying. She had heard how silence came. At length, more than silence came. They burned the dead, or cremated them with burning chemicals. They evacuated the towns. Then 'they' too ceased to organise anything. It was a selective disease. It killed men and women and children. It could not destroy the animals, the insects, the birds. Or Jaina.

At first, the first falling of the leaf, she had not believed. It was hard to believe that such an unstoppable engine had been started. The radio and the television set spoke of decaying cylinders in the sea, or satellites which corroded, letting go their cargoes of viruses, mistimed, on the Earth. Governments denied responsibility, and died denying it.

Jaina heard the tread of death draw near, and nearer. From disbelief, she came to fear. She stocked her hermitage, as she had always done, and crouched in new terror behind her door. As the radio turned dumb, and the TV spluttered and choked to blindness, Jaina stared from her porch, looking for a huge black shadow to descend across the land.

They burned a pile of the dead on a giant bonfire in the field, half a mile from the house. The ashes blew across the sunset. The sky was burning its dead, too.

A day later, Jaina found little fiery mottles over her skin. Her head throbbed, just as the walls were doing. She lay down with her terror, afraid to die. Then she did not care if she died. She wanted to die. Then she did not die at all.

A month later, she drove into the town. She found the emptiness of the evacuation and, two miles away, the marks of another enormous bonfire. And a mile beyond that, dead people lying out in the sun, turning to pillars of salt and white sticks of candy, and the fearless birds, immune, dropping like black rain on the place.

Jaina drove home, and became the last woman on Earth.

Her life was not so very different, she had been quite solitary for many years before the plague came.

She had sometimes mused as to why she had lived, but only in the silly, falsely modest way of any survivor. Everyone knew they could not die, hang the rest, they alone must come through. They had all been wrong, all but Jaina.

And then, one night, a snow-white star, the silver web of the alien parachute, a young man more beautiful than truth.

She told him everything as she lay against his shoulder. He might still be capable of dying, a Martian, susceptible to the plague virus. Or he might go away.

It was dark now. She lifted her mouth to his in the darkness. As she kissed him, she was unsure what he would do. He did not seem to react in any way. Would he make love to her, or want to, or was he able to? She slid her hands over his skin, like warm smooth stone. She loved him. But perhaps he was only a robot.

After a little while, she drew away, and left him seated on the porch. She went into the kitchen and threw the melted ice in her glass into the sink.

She climbed the stairs; she lay down on the narrow bed. Alone. Alone. But somehow even then, she sensed the irony was incomplete. And when he came into the room, she was not surprised. He leaned over her, silently, and his eyes shone in the darkness, like the eyes of a cat. She attempted to be afraid of him.

'Go away,' she said.

But he stretched out beside her, very near, the bed so narrow . . . As if he had learned now the etiquette of human love-making, reading its symbols from her mind.

'You're a robot, an android,' she said. 'Leave me alone.'

He put his mouth over hers. She closed her eyes and saw a star, a nova. He was not a robot, he was a man, a beautiful man, and she loved him . . .

Twenty million miles away, the clock chimed eight times. It was one quarter past seven, on the first night of the world.

In the morning she baked bread, and brought him some, still warm. He held the bread cupped in his hands like a paralysed bird. She pointed to herself. 'Please. Call me by my name. *Jaina.*'

She was sure she could make him grasp the meaning. She knew he had a voice. She had heard his tears, and, during their love-making, heard him groan. She would teach him to eat and drink, too. She would teach him everything.

He tilled the garden; he had found seedlings in the leaning shed and was planting them, until she came to him and led him to the ramshackle car. She drove him into town, then took him into the clothing stores, directing him, diffidently. In accordance with her instructions, he loaded the car. She had never seen him smile. She pondered if she ever would. He carried piled jeans with the same eternally dispassionate disinterest: still the errand boy.

During the afternoon she watched him in the garden. Her pulses raced, and she could think of nothing else but the play of muscles under his swiftly and mellifluously tanning skin. He hypnotised her. She fell asleep and dreamed of him.

She roused at a sound of light blows on metal. Alarmed, she walked out into the last gasps of the day, to find him behind the courtyard, hammering dents out of the battered car. She perceived he had changed a tyre she had not bothered with, though it was worn. She relaxed against the wall, brooding on him. He was going to be almost ludicrously useful. For some reason, the archaic word *help-meet* stole into her mind.

Over it all hung the smoke of premonition. He would be going away. Stranded, marooned, shipwrecked, the great liner would move out of the firmament, cruel as God, to rescue him.

She woke somewhere in the centre of the night, her lips against his spine, with a dreadful knowledge.

For a long while she lay immobile, then lifted herself on to one elbow. She stayed that way, looking at him, his feigned sleep, or the real unconsciousness which appeared to have claimed him. *It seems that you have gone away.* No. He would not be going anywhere.

His hair gleamed, his lashes lay in long brushstrokes on his cheeks. He was quiescent, limpid, as if poured from a jar. She touched his flank, coldly.

After a minute, she rose and went to the window, and looked out and upward into the vault of the night sky. A low blaring of hatred and contempt ran through her. *Where are you*? she thought. *Do you see? Are you laughing?*

She walked down the stairs and into the room where the dead TV sat in the dark. She opened a drawer in the bureau and took out a revolver. She loaded it carefully from the clip. She held it pointed before her as she went back up into the bedroom.

He did not wake up – or whatever simulation he contrived that passed for waking – until the hour before the dawn. She had sat there all the time, waiting for him, wanting him to open his eyes and see her, seated facing him, her hand resting on her knee, the revolver in her hand. Pointing now at him.

There was a chance he might not know what the gun was. Yet weapons, like certain semantic signs, would surely be instantly, instinctively recognisable. So she thought. As his eyes opened and fixed on the gun, she believed he knew perfectly well what it was, and that she had brought it there to kill him with.

His eyes grew very wide, but he did not move. He did not appear afraid, yet she considered he must be afraid. As afraid of her as she might have been expected to be of him, and yet had never been: the natural fear of an alien, xenophobia. She thought he could, after all, understand her words, had understood her from the beginning, her language, her loneliness. It would have been part of his instruction. Along with the lessons which had taught him how to work the land, change a tyre, make love, pretend to sleep . . . About the same time, they must have inoculated him against the deadly plague virus, indeed all the viruses of Earth.

'Yes,' she said. 'I *am* going to kill you.'

He only looked at her. She remembered how he had wept, out of dread of her, loathing and despair. Because he had known there would be no rescue for him. Neither rescue from her planet nor from herself. He had not fallen from a burning spacecraft into the world. The craft had been whole, and he had been dropped neatly out of it, at a designated hour, at a calculated altitude, his parachute unfolding, a preprogrammed cloud. Not shipwrecked, but despatched. Air mail. A present.

The great silent ship would not come seeking him. It had already come, and gone.

Why did they care so much? She could not fathom that. An interfering streak – was this the prerogative of gods? Altruistic benefactors, or simply playing with toys. Or it might be an experiment of some sort. They had not been able to prevent the plague, or had not wanted to – recall the Flood, Gomorrah – but when the plague had drawn away down its tidal drain, washing humanity with it, they had looked and seen Jaina wandering alone on the Earth, mistress of it, the last of her kind. So they had made for her a helpmate and companion. Presumably not made him in *their* extraterrestrial image, whoever, whatever they omnipotently were, but in the image of a man.

She was uncertain what had triggered her final deduction. His acquiescence, the unlikely aptness of it all, the foolish coincidence of survivor flung down beside survivor, pat. Or was it the theatricality which had itself suggested puppet-masters to her subconscious: the last man and the last woman left to propagate continuance of a species. Or was it only her mistrust? All the wrongs she had, or imagined she had suffered, clamouring that this was no different from any other time. Someone still manipulated, still *imposed* on her.

'Well,' she said softly, looking at him, it appeared to her, through the eye of the gun, 'I seem to be missing a rib. Do I call you Adam? Or would it be *Eve*?' She clicked off the safety-catch. She trembled violently, though her voice was steady. 'What about contraception, Adameve? Did they think I'd never heard of it, or used it? Did they think I'd risk having babies, with no hospitals, not even a vet in sight? At thirty-five years of age? When I dressed up for you, I dressed thoroughly, *all* of me. Just in case. Seems I was wise. I don't think even your specially designed seed is so potent it can negate my precautions. In the tank where they grew you, or the machine-shop where they built you, did they think of *that*? I don't want you,' she whispered. 'You cried like a child because they condemned you to live on my world, with me. Do you think I can forgive you that? Do you think I want you after that, now I *know*?'

She raised the gun and fired. She watched the sun go out in the windows of his eyes. His blood was red, quite normal.

Jaina walked across the burn-scar of the field. She pictured a huge wheel hanging over her, beyond and above the sky, pictured it no longer watching, already drawing inexorably away and away. She dragged the spade along the ground, as she had dragged his body. Now the spade had turned potatoes, and beans, and alien flesh.

She stood in the the kitchen of the old house, and the darkness like space came and coloured the sky through. Jaina held her breath, held it and held it, as if the air had filled with water, closing over her head. For she knew. Long before it happened, she knew. She only let out her breath in a slow sigh, horribly flattered, as the second snow-white star fell out of the summer sky.

Mirage and Magia

During the Ninth Dynasty of the Jat Calendar, Taisia-Tua lived at the town of Qon Oshen, in a mansion of masks and mirrors.

At that time, being far inland, and unlinked by road or bridge to any of the great seaports of the Western Peninsula, Qon Oshen was an obscure and fulminating area. Its riches, born of itself and turned back like radiations upon itself, had made it both exotic and psychologically impenetrable to most of those foreigners who very occasionally entered it. Generally, it was come on by air, almost by accident, by riders of galvanic silver and crimson balloon-ships. Held in a clasp of pointed, platinum-coloured hills, in which one break only poured to the shore of an iridium lake, Qon Oshen presented latticed towers, phantasmal soaring bridgeways, a game board of square plazas and circular trafficuli. Sometimes, gauzelike clouds, attracted to the chemical and auric emanations of the town, would hang low over it, foaming the tower tops. In a similar manner, the reputation of Taisia-Tua hung over the streets, insubstantial, dreamlike, menacing.

She had come from the north, riding in a high white grasshopper carriage, which strode on fragile legs several feet in the air. The date of her coming varied depending on who recounted it. Seventeen years ago, ten, the year when Saturo, the demon-god, sent fire, and the cinnamon harvest was lost. Her purpose for arrival was equally elusive. She chose for her dwelling a mansion of rose-red tilework, spiralled about with thin stone balustrades on which squatted antimony toads and jade cats, and enclosed by gates of wrought iron, five yards high. Dark green deciduous, and pale-grey fan-shaped pines spread around the mansion, as if to shield it. After sunset, its windows of stained glass turned slotted eyes of purple, magenta, blue, emerald and gold upon the town. Within the masking trees and behind the masking windows, the Magia – for everyone had known at once she was an enchantress – paced out the dance moves of her strange and insular life.

One thing was always remembered. On the morning or noon or evening or midnight of her arrival, someone had snatched a glimpse inside the grasshopper carriage. This someone (a fool, for who but a fool would risk such a glimpse?) had told how there were no windows but that, opposite the seat of lush plum silk, the wall above the driver's keys was all one polished mirror. The only view Taisia-Tua had apparently had, all the way from the north to Qon Oshen, was that of her own self.

'Is she beautiful, then?'

'Most beautiful.'

'Not at all beautiful.'

'*Ugly.*'

'*Gorgeous.*'

'One cannot be sure. Whenever she passes through the town she is always partly masked or veiled. Nor has anyone ever seen her in the same gown twice, or the same wig (she is always wigged). Even her slippers and her jewellery are ephemeral.'

It was usually agreed this diversity might be due to such powers of illusion as an enchantress would possess. Or simply to enormous wealth and extravagance – each of which qualities the town was prepared to admire. Certainly, in whatever clothing or guise, Taisia-Tua Magia was never mistaken for another.

At Midsummer of her first year, whenever that was, at Qon Oshen, she perpetrated her first magic. There were scores of witnesses.

A round moon, yellow as wine, hung over the town, and all the towers and bridgeways seemed to reach and stretch to catch its light. The scent of a thousand peach trees, apricot gardens, lily pools and jasmin pergolas filled the darkness. Gently feverish with the drunkenness of summer, men and women stole from the inns and the temples – on such nights, even the demon-god might be worshipped – and wandered abroad everywhere. And into Seventh Plaza Taisia-Tua walked with slow measured steps, a moment or so behind the midnight bell. Her gown was black and sewn with peacocks' eyes. Her hair was deepest blue. Her face was white, rouged the softest, most transparent of vermilions at cheekbones and lips, and like violet smoulder along the eyelids. This face itself was like a mask, but an extra mask of stiff silver hid her forehead, brows, and the hollows under the painted eyes. Her nails were silver, too, and each of them four inches in length, which presumably indicated these also were unreal. Her feet were gloved in silk mounted on golden soles which went *chink-chink-chink* as she moved. She was unaccompanied, save by her supposed reputation. The crowd in the plaza fell back, muttered, and carefully observed. Instinctively, it seemed, they had always guessed this creature boded them no particular good. But her exoticism was so suitable to the mode, they had as yet no wish to censure.

For some while, the Magia walked about, very slowly, gazing this way and that. She took her time, glancing where she would, paying no apparent heed to any who gazed or glanced at her. She was, naturally, protected by her masks, and perhaps by the tiny looking-glass that hung on a chain from her belt, and which, now and then, she raised, gazing also at herself.

At length, she crossed the plaza to the spot where the three-tiered fountain played, turning now indigo, now orchid. Here a young man was standing, with his friends. He was of the Linla family, one of the highest, richest houses in the town, and his name was Iye. Not merely an aristocrat and rich, either, but exceedingly handsome and popular. To this person the enchantress proceeded, and he, caught in mid-sentence and mid-thought, paused, watching her wide-eyed. When she was some few feet from him, Taisia-Tua halted. She spoke, in a still, curious, lifeless little voice.

'*Follow* me.'

Iye Linla turned to his friends, laughing, looking for their support, but they did not laugh at all.

'Magia,' said Iye, after a moment, staring her out and faltering, for it was hard to stare out a mask and two masked unblinking eyes. 'Magia, I do not follow anyone without good reason. Excuse me, but I have business here.'

Taisia-Tua made a very slight gesture, which spread her wide sleeves like the wings of some macabre night butterfly. That was all. Then she turned, and her golden soles went *chink-chink-chink* as she walked away.

One of Iye's friends caught his shoulder. 'On no account go after her.'

'I? Go after that hag – more likely I would go with demoniac Saturo –'

But already he had taken a step in her direction. Shocked, Iye attempted to secure himself to the ground. Presently, finding he could not, he gripped the wrists and clothing of his companions. But an uncanny bodily motivation possessed him. Like one who is drowning, he slipped inexorably from their grasp. There was no longer any conversation. With expressions of dismay and horror, the friends of Iye Linla beheld him walk after the enchantress, at first reluctantly, soon with a steady, unrelenting stride. Like her dog, it seemed, he would pursue her all the way home. They broke abruptly from their stupor, and ran to summon Iye's father, the Linla kindred and guards. But by the time such forces had been marshalled and brought to the mansion of rose-red tile, the gates were shut, nor did any answer the shouts and knocking, the threats and imprecations, while on their pedestals, the ghostly toads and greenish cats grinned at the sinking moon.

Only one old uncle of the Linla house was heard to remark that a night in bed with a mage-lady might do young Iye no harm at all. He was shortly to repent these words, and half a year later the old man ritually stabbed himself before the family altar because of his ill-omened utterance. For the night passed, and the dawn began to surface like a great shoal of luminous fishes in the east. And a second or so after the sunrise bell, a slim carved door opened in the mansion, and then closed again behind the form of Iye Linla. A second more, and a pair of ironwork gates parted in their turn, but Iye Linla advanced no further than the courtyard. Soon, some of his kindred hastened into the court, others standing by the gates to keep them wide, and hurried the young man from the witch's yard.

On the street, they slapped his cheeks and hands, forced wine between his lips, implored him, cursed him. To no avail. His open eyes were opaque, seldom blinking, indicating blindness. They led him home, where the most eminent physicians and psychologists were called, but none of these made an iota of progress with him. Eventually, Iye's official courtesan stole in to visit him, prepared to try such remedies as her sensual arts had taught her. She had been in the chamber scarcely two minutes when her single piercing shriek brought half the household into the apartment, demanding what new thing was amiss.

Iye's courtesan stood in a rain of her own burnished hair, and of her own weeping, and she said, 'His eyes – his eyes – Oh, I looked into his eyes – Saturo has eaten his soul.'

226

'The woman is mad,' was the common consensus, but one of the physicians, ignoring this, went to Iye, and himself peered between the young man's lids. This physician then spoke in a hushed and awful manner that brought quiet and terror on the whole room.

'The courtesan is clever. Some strange spell has been worked here, and any may see it that will look. It is usual, when glancing into the eyes of another, to see pictured there, since these lenses are reflective, a minute image of oneself. But in the eyes of Iye Linla I perceive only this: the minute image of Iye Linla himself, and, what is more, I perceive him from the back.'

Fear was, in this event, mightier than speculation.

By noon, most of Qon Oshen knew of Iye's peculiar fate, and brooded on it. A re-emergence of the enchantress was expected with misgiving. However, Taisia-Tua did not walk in the town again for several weeks. In her stead, there began to be seen about, in the high skies of twilight or early morning, a mysterious silvery kite, across whose elongated tail were inscribed these words:

IS THERE A GREATER MAGICIAN THAN I?

In Qon Oshen, not one man asked another to whom this kite belonged.

It may be supposed, though such deeds were performed in secret, that the Linla family sent to the enchantress's house various embassies, pleas and warnings, not to mention coffers full of bribes. But the spell, such as it was, was not removed from Iye. He, the hope of his house, remained thereafter like an idiot, who must be tended and fed and laid down to sleep and roused up again, exercised like a beast, and nursed like a baby. Sallow death banners were hung from the Linla gates about the time the kite manifested in the sky. By the autumn's end, another two houses of Qon Oshen were mourning in similar fashion.

At the Chrysanthemum Festival, Taisia-Tua, in a gown like fire, hair like burning coals, wings of cinnabar concealing cheeks and chin, scratched with a turquoise nail-tip the sleeve of a young priest, an acolyte of the Ninth Temple. He was devout and handsome, an intellectual, moreover a son of the aristocratic house of Kli-Sra. Yet he went after the Magia just as Iye Linla had done. And came forth from her mansion after the sunrise bell also just as Iye Linla did, so that in his eyes men beheld the young priest's own image, reversed, and to be seen only from the back.

A month later (only a month), when the toasted leaves were falling and sailing on the oval ponds and inconsequently rushing along the narrow marble lanes of Qon Oshen, an artist of great fame and genius turned from his scroll, the gilded pen in his hand, and found the Magia behind him, her lower face hidden by a veil of ivory plaques, her clothes embroidered by praying mantises.

'Spare me,' the artist said to her, 'from whatever fate it is you put on those others you summoned. For the sake of the creative force which is in me, if not from pity because I am a human man.'

But – '*Follow* me,' she said, and moved away from him. This time the soles on her gloved feet were of wood, and they made a noise like fans snapping shut. The artist crushed the gilded pen in his hand. The nib pierced his palm and his blood fell on the scroll. The pattern it made, such was his talent, was as fair as the considered lines any other might have devised. Yet he had no choice but to obey the witch, and when the morning rose from the lake, he was like the others who had done so.

Sometimes the Magia's kite blew in the skies, sometimes not. Sometimes some swore they had seen it, while others denied it had been visible, but all knew the frightful challenge of its writing:

IS THERE A GREATER MAGICIAN THAN I?

Sometimes a man would vanish from his home, and they would say: '*She* has taken him.' This was not always the case. Yet she *did* take. In the pure blue days of winter, when all the town was a miracle of ice, each pinnacle like glass, and to step on the streets seemed likely to break every vista in a myriad pieces, then she would come and go, and men would follow her, and men would return – no longer sensible or living, though alive. And in the spring when the blossoms bubbled over and splashed and cascaded from every wall and walk, then, too, she would work her magic. And in the green, fermenting bottle of summer, in its simmering days and restless nights, and in autumn when the world of the town fell upward through a downfalling of purple and amber leaves – then. Randomly, persistently, seemingly without excuse. Unavoidably, despite war being made against her by the nobility of the place, despite intrigues and jurisdiction, despite the employment of other magicians, whose spells to hers were, as it turned out, like blades of grass standing before the curtain of the cyclone. Despite sorties and attacks of a physical nature. Despite the lunacy of firing a missile from a nearby hill in a reaction of fury and madness of the family Mhey, which had lost to her three of its sons. The rocket exploded by night against the roof of the rose-tile mansion with a clap like forty thunders, a rose itself of flame and smoke, to wake most of the town with screams and cries. But running to the spot there were discovered only huge hills of clinker and cooling cinders in the street. The mansion was unscathed, its metals and stones untwisted, its jewellery windows unsmashed, its beasts of antimony and jade leering now downward at those who had come to see.

'Her powers are alarming. Why does she work evil against us?'

'What are her reasons?'

'What is the method of the dreadful spell?'

Qon Oshen prayed for her destruction. They prayed for one to come who would destroy her.

But she preyed upon them like a leopard, and they did not know how, or why.

There was a thief in Qon Oshen who was named Locust. Locust was hideous, and very cunning, and partly insane with the insanity of the wise. He slipped in among a gathering of respected rich men, flung off his official-seeming cloak, and laughed at their surprise. Although he was a thief, and had stolen from each of them, and each surmised it, Locust fitted within the oblique ethics of the town, for he was a lord of his trade and admired for the artistry of his evil-doing. If he were ever caught at his work, he knew well they had vowed to condemn him to the Eight Agonising Deaths. But while he eluded justice, sourly they revelled in his theatrical deeds against their neighbours and bore perforce with those nearer home.

'I, Locust, knowing how well you love me, for a certain sum, will perform a useful task for you.'

The rich men turned to glance at each other. Their quick minds had already telepathically received the impression of his next words.

'Excellently deduced, your excellencies. I will pierce into the Magia's mansion, and presently come tell you what goes on there.'

Some hours after, when the bow of the moon was raising its eyebrow at him, Locust, lord of thieves, penetrated, by means of burglars' skills and certain sorceries he himself was adept in, the mansion of rose-red tiling. Penetrated and watched, played hide and seek with shades and with more than shades, and escaped to report his news. Though from that hour of revelation, he reckoned himself – in indefinable, subtle, sinister ways – altered. And when, years later, he faltered in his profession, was snatched by the law, and – humiliatingly – pardoned, he claimed he had contracted emanations of the witch's house like a virus, and the ailment had gradually eroded his confidence in himself.

'It was a trick of leaping to get over the gate – my secret. Entering then by a window too small to admit even a cat – for I can occasionally condense and twist my bones in a fashion unnormal, possibly uncivilised, I dealt with such uncanny safeguards as seemed extant by invoking my demon patron, Saturo; we are great friends. I then dropped down into a lobby.'

It was afterward remarked how curious it was that a thief might breach the defenses of the mansion which a fire missile could not destroy.

But Locust, then full of his cleverness, did not remark it. He went on to speak of the bewildering aspect the mansion had come, internally, to display. A bewilderment due mainly to the labyrinthine and accumulative and mirage-making and virtually hallucinatory effects that resulted from a multitude of mirrors, set everywhere and overlapping like scales. Mirrors, too, of all shapes, sizes, constructions and substances, from those of sheerest and most reflective glass, to those of polished copper and bronze, to those formed by sheets of water held bizarrely in stasis over underlying sheets of black onyx. A fearful confusion, even madness, might have overcome another, finding himself unguided in the midst of such phenomena. For of course the mirrors did not merely reflect, they reflected into each other. Image rebounded upon image like a hail of crystal bullets fired into infinity. Many times, Locust lost himself, fell to his knees, grew cold, grew heated, grew nauseous, passed near to fainting or screaming, but his own pragmatism saved him. From room to unconscionable room he wended, and with him went thousands of replicas of himself (but, accustomed to his own unbeauty, he did not pay these companions much heed). Here and there an article of science or aesthetics might arrest him, but mostly he was bemused, until hesitating to examine a long-stemmed rose of a singular purple-crimson, he was startled into a yell. Without warning, the flower commenced to spin, and as it spun to peel off glowing droplets, as if it wept fire. A moment more and the door of the mansion, far away through the forest of mirrors, opened with a mysterious sigh. Locust hastily withdrew behind a mirror resembling an enormous eye.

In twenty seconds the Magia came gliding in, lavender-haired and clad in a gown like a wave drawn down from the moon. And behind her stumbled the handsome fourth son of the house of Uqet.

And so Locust the thief came to be the only intimate witness to the spell the Magia wove about her victims.

Firstly she seated herself on a pillow of silk. Then she folded her hands upon her lap, and raised her face, which on that day was masked across eyes and forehead in the plumage of a bird of prey. It seemed she sat and gazed at her visitor as if to attract his attention, gazed with her plumaged eyes, her very porcelain skin, her strawberry mouth, even her long, long nails seemed to gaze at him. She was, Locust explained, an object to rivet the awareness, had it not been for the quantities of mirrors, which plainly distracted the young man, so he did not look at Taisia-Tua the enchantress, but around and around, now into this image of himself, now into that. And soon he began to fumble about the room, peering into his own face in crystal, in platinum, in water, jade and brass. For perhaps two hours this went on, or maybe it was longer, or less long. But the son of Uqet wavered from looking-glass to looking-glass, at each snagging upon his own reflection, adhering to it, and his countenance grew stranger and stranger and more wild and – oddly – more fixed, until at last all expression faded from it. And all the while, saying nothing, doing nothing, Taisia-Tua Magia sat at the room's centre on the pillow of silk.

Finally the son of Uqet came to stare down into the mirror paving under his feet, and there he ceased to move. Until, after several minutes, he fell abruptly to his knees, and so to his face. And there he lay, breathing mist against his own reflected mouth, and the witch came to her feet and stepped straight out of the chamber. But as she went by him, Locust heard her say aloud: 'You are all the same. All the same as he who was before you. Is there no answer?'

This puzzled Locust so much, he left it out of his report.

At the witch's exit, it did occur to the thief to attempt reviving the young man from his trance, but when a few pinches and shakings had failed to cause awakening, Locust abandoned Uqet and used his wits instead to gain departure before the enchantress should locate him.

This story, thereafter recited (or most of it), earned much low-voiced meditation from his listeners.

'But did she summon no demon?'

'Did she utter no malady?'

'Did she not employ wand or ring, or other device?'

'No.'

Uqet was found in the morning, lying in Taisia-Tua's yard: Locust's proof. Uqet's eyes were now a familiar sightless sight.

Immediately a whole tribe of fresh magicians was sent for. Their powers to hers were like wisps of foam blowing before the tidal wave. Not the strongest nor the shrewdest could destroy the horror of her enchantment, nor break a single mirror in her mansion. Houses of antique lineage removed themselves from the vicinity. Some remained, but refused to allow their heirs ever to walk abroad.

They prayed for her destruction. For one to come who would destroy her.

The kite inquired of heaven and earth:

IS THERE A GREATER MAGICIAN THAN I?'

In a confusion of datelessness, the years shrivelled and fell like the leaves . . .

But though the date of her arrival was uncertain, the date of his arrival was exactly remembered.

It was in the year of the Scorpion, on the day of the blooming of the ancient acacia tree in Thirty-Third Plaza, that only put forth flowers once in every twenty-sixth decade. As the sun began to shine over the towers and bridges, he appeared under the glistening branches of this acacia, seated cross-legged on the ground. The fretwork of light and shadow, and the mothlike blooms of the tree, made it hard to be sure of what he was, or even if he was substantially there. He was indeed discernible first by an unearthly metallic music that sewed a way out through the foliage and ran down the plaza like streams of water, till a crowd began to gather to discover the source.

The music came from a pipe of bone which was linked, as if by an umbilical cord of silver tubing, to a small tablet of lacquer keys. Having observed the reason for the pipe's curious tone, the crowd moved its attention to the piper. Nor was his tone at all usual. The colours of his garments were of blood and sky, the shades, conceivably, of pain and hope. Around his bowed face and over his pale hands as he played hung a cloud of hair dark red as mahogany, but to which the sun rendered its own edging of blood and sky-blue rainbows.

When the music ceased, the crowd would have thrown him cash, but at that moment he raised his head, and revealed he was masked, that a face of alabaster covered his own, a formless blank of face that conveyed only the most innocent wickedness. Although through the long slits of the eyes, something was just detectable, some flicker of life, like two blue ghosts dwelling behind a wall. Then, before the crowd had scarcely formed a thought, he set the instruments of music aside and came to his feet (which were bare), rose straight and tall and pliant as smoke rising from a fire. He held up one hand and a scarlet bird soared out of his palm. He opened the other hand and an azure bird soared out of that. The two birds dashed together, merged, fell apart in a shattering of gems, rubies, garnets, sapphires, aquamarines, that dewed the pavement for yards around. With involuntary cries of delight and avarice, men bent to pick them up and found peonies and hyacinths instead had rooted in the tiles.

'Then stars spun through the air, and he juggled them – ten stars or twenty.'

'Stars by day – day-stars? They were fires he juggled from hand to hand.'

'He seemed clothed in fire. All but the white face, like a bowl of white thoughts.'

'Then he walked on his hands and made the children laugh.'

'A vast throng of people had congregated when he removed several golden fish from the acacia tree. These spread their fins and flew away.'

'He turned three somersaults backwards, one after another with no pause.'

'The light changed where he was standing.'

'Where did he come from?'

'That is speculation. But to our chagrin, many of us saw where he proceeded.'

Into the crowd, like the probing of a narrow spear, the presence of the enchantress had pressed its way. They became aware of her as they would become aware of a sudden lowering of the temperature, and, not even looking to see what they had no need or wish to see, they slid from her like water from a blade. She wore violet sewn with beads the colour of green ice. All her face, save only the eyes, was caged in an openwork visor of fine thin curving horizontal bars of gold. Her hair today was the tint of tarnished orichalc.

She stood within the vortex the crowd had made for her, she stood and watched the magician-musician. She watched him produce silver rings from the air, fling them together to represent atoms or universes, and cast them into space in order to balance upside down on his head, catching the rings with his toes. Certainly, she had had some inkling of the array of mages who had been called to Qon Oshen against her. If it struck her that this was like some parody of their arts, some game played with the concept of witchcraft, she did not demonstrate. But that she considered him, contemplated him, was very evident. The crowd duly grew grim and silent, hanging on the edges of her almost tangible concentration as if from spikes. Then, with a hundred muffled exclamations, it beheld the Magia turn without a word and go away again, having approached no one, having failed to issue that foreboding commandment: *Follow* me.

But it seemed this once she had had no necessity to say the ritual aloud. For, taking up the pipe and the tablet of keys, leaving seven or eight phantasms to dissolve on the air, five or six realities – gilded apples, paper animals – to flutter into the hands of waiting children, the masked, red-headed man walked from under the acacia tree, and followed her *without* being requested.

A few cried out to him, warning or plea. Most hugged their silence, and as he passed them, the nerves tingled in their spines. While long after he had disappeared from view, they heard the dim, clear notes of the pipe start up along the delicate arteries of the town, like new blood running there in the body of Qon Oshen. It seemed he woke music for her as he pursued her and what must be his destruction.

Men lingered in Thirty-Third Plaza. At last, one of the Mhey household spoke out in a tone of fearful satisfaction: 'Whatever else, I think on this occasion she has summoned up a devil to go with her.'

'It is Saturo,' responded a priest in the crowd, 'the demon-god of darkness and fire. Her evil genius come to devour her.'

In alarm and excitement, the people gazed about them, wondering if the town would perish in such a confrontation.

She never once looked back, and never once, as those persons attested which saw him go by, did he falter, or the long sheaves and rills of notes falter, that issued from the pipe and the tablet of lacquer keys.

Taisia-Tua reached her mansion gates, and they swung shut behind her. Next, a carved door parted and she drew herself inside the house as a hand is drawn into a glove, and the door, too, shut itself firmly. In the space of half a minute the demon, if such he was, Saturo, if so he was called, had reached the iron gates. Whole families and their guards had been unable to breach these gates, just as the rocket had been unable to disunify the architecture. Locust the thief had wiggled in by tricks and incantations, but the law of Balance in magic may have decreed just such a ludicrous loophole should be woven in the fabric of the Magia's safeguards. Or she may have had some need for one at least to spy the sole enchantment she dealt inside her rose-red walls.

He who was supposed to be, and might have been, Saturo, the demon-god of flame and shade, poised then at one of the gates. Even through the blank white mask, any who were near could have heard his soft, unmistakable voice say to the gate: 'Why shut me out, when you wish me to come in?'

And at these words the gate opened itself and he went through it.

And at the carved door he said: 'Unless you unlock yourself, how am I to enter?'

The door swung the slender slice of itself inward, and the demon entered the mansion of the witch.

The mirrors hung and burned, and fleered and sheered all about him then, scaled over each other, winking, shifting, promising worlds that were not. Saturo paid no attention to any of them. He walked straight as a panther through the house, and the myriad straight and savage images of him, sky and snow, and the drowning redness of his hair, walked with him – but he never glanced at them.

So he arrived quickly in the room where the rose spun and threw off its fiery tears. And here the enchantress had already seated herself on the pillow of silk. Her face, in its golden cage, was raised to his. Her eyelids were rouged a soft, dull purple, the paint on her skin – a second skin – dazzled. Each of her terrible clawlike nails crossed over another. Her eyes, whose hue and character were obscured, stared. She looked merciless. Or simply devoid of anything, which must, therefore, include mercy.

Saturo the demon advanced to within two feet of her, and seated himself on the patterned floor in front of her. So they stared at each other, like two masked dolls, and neither moved for a very long while.

At length, after this very long while had dripped and melted from the chamber like wax, Taisia-Tua spoke to the demon.

'Can it be you alone are immune to my wonderful magery?'

There was no reply, only the stare of the mask continuing unalleviated, the suspicion of two eyes behind the mask, unblinking. Another season of time went by, and Taisia-Tua said: 'Will you not look about you? See, you are everywhere. Twenty to one hundred replicas of yourself are to be found on every wall, the floor, the ceiling. Why gaze at me, when you might gaze at yourself? Or can it be you are as hideous as that other who broke in here, and like him do not wish to be shown to your own eyes? Remove your mask, let me see to which family of the demons you belong.'

'Are you not afraid,' said Saturo, 'of what kind of face a demon keeps behind a mask?'

'A face of black shadow and formlessness, or of blazing fire. The prayers of the town to be delivered from me have obviously drawn you here. But I am not afraid.'

'Then, Taisia-Tua Magia, you yourself may pluck away the mask.'

Having said this, he leaned toward her, so close his dark red hair brushed her suddenly uplifted hands, which she had raised as if to ward him off. And as if she could not help herself then, the edges of her monstrous nails met the white mask's edges, and it fell, like half an eggshell, to the floor. It was no face of dark or flame which appeared. But pale and still, and barely human in its beauty, the face looked back at her and the sombre pallor of the eyes, that were indeed like two blue ghosts haunting it. It was a cruel face, and kind, compassionate and pitiless, and the antithesis of all masks. And the moment she saw it, never having seen it before, she recognised it, as she had recognised him under the acacia tree. But she said hastily and coldly, as if it were sensible and a protection to say such things to such a creature: 'You are more handsome than all the rest. Look into the mirrors. Look into the mirrors and see yourself.'

'I would rather,' said Saturo, who maybe was not Saturo, 'look at you.'

'Fool,' said the enchantress, in a voice smaller than the smallest bead on her gown. 'If you will not surrender to your vanity, how is my magic to work on you?'

'Your magic has worked. Not the magic of your spells. Your own magic.'

'Liar,' said the witch. 'But I see you are bemused, as no other was, by fashion.' At this, she pulled the gold cage from her face, and the orichalc wig from her hair – which flew up fine and electric about her head. 'See, I am less than you thought,' said Taisia-Tua. 'Surely you would rather look at yourself?' And she smeared the paint from her face and wiped it clean and pale as paper. 'Surely you would rather look at yourself?' And she threw off her jewels, and the nails, and the outer robe of violet, and sat there in the plain undergown. 'Surely you would rather look at yourself?' And uncoloured and unmasked she sat there and lowered her eyes, which was now the only way she could hide herself. 'Surely, surely,' she muttered, 'you would rather look at yourself.'

'Who,' said he, quieter than quietness, and much deeper than depth, 'hurt you so in the north that you came to this place to revenge yourself forever? Who wounded you so you must plunge knives into others, which certainly remained the same knife, plunged again and again into your own heart? Why did the heart break that now enables these mirrors not to break? Who loved himself so much more than you that you believed you also must learn to love only your own image, since no other could love you, or choose to gaze on you rather than on himself? True of most, which you have proven. Not true of all. What silly game have you been playing, with pain turned into sorcery and vanity turned into a spell? And have you never once laughed, young woman, not even at yourself?'

Her head still bowed, the enchantress whispered, 'How do you know these things?'

'Any would know it, that knew you. Perhaps I came in answer to praying, not theirs, but yours. Your prayers of glass and live-dead men.'

Then taking her hand he stood up and made her stand with him.

'Look,' he said, and now he leaned close enough she could gaze into the two mirrors of his eyes. And there she saw, not another man staring in forever at himself, but, for the first time, her own face gazing back at her – for this is what he saw. And finding this, Taisia-Tua, not the rose, wept, and as every one of her tears fell from her eyes, there was the sound of mirror-glass breaking somewhere in the house.

While, here and there about Qon Oshen, as the mirrors splintered, inverted images crumbled inside the eyes of young men, and were gone.

Iye Linla yawned and cursed, and called for food. The sons of Mhey came back to themselves and rolled in a riotous heap like inebriated puppies. A priest bellowed, an aristocrat frowned, at discovering themselves propped up like invalids, their relatives bobbing, sobbing, about the bed. Each returned and made vocal his return. In Twenty-First Plaza, an artist rushed from his house, shouting for the parchment with the bloodstain of his genius upon it.

By dusk, when the stars cast their own bright broken glass across the sky, the general opinion was that the witch was dead. And decidedly, none saw that wigged and masked nightmare lady again.

For her own hair was light and fine, and her skin paler yet, and her eyes were grey as the iridium lake. She was much less beautiful, and much more beautiful than all her masks. And in this disguise, her own self, she went away unknown from Qon Oshen, leaving all behind her, missing none of it, for he had said to her: '*Follow* me.'

A month of plots and uneasiness later, men burst in the doors of the vacant mansion, hurling themselves beneath the grinning toads and the frigid cats of greenish jade, as if afraid to be spat on. But inside they found only the webs of spiders and the shards of exploded mirrors. Not a gem remained, or had ever existed, to appease them. No treasure and no hoard of magery. Her power, by which she had pinned them so dreadfully, was plainly merely their own power, those energies of self-love and curiosity and fear turned back (ever mirror-fashion) on themselves. Like the reflection of a moon, she had waned, and the mirage sunk away, but not until a year was gone did they sigh with nostalgia for her empire of uncertainty and terror forever lost to them. 'When the Magia ruled us, and we trembled,' they would boastfully say. They even boasted of the mocking kite, until one evening a sightseer, roaming the witch's mansion – now a feature of great interest in Qon Oshen – came on a scrap of silk, and on the silk a line of writing.

Then Qon Oshen was briefly ashamed of Taisia-Tua Magia. For the writing read: LOVE, LOVE, LOVE THE MAGICIAN IS GREATER, FAR GREATER, THAN I.

The Thaw

Ladies first, they said.

That was okay. Then they put a histotrace on the lady in question, and called me.

'No thanks,' I said.

'Listen,' they said, 'you're a generative blood-line descendant of Carla Brice. Aren't you interested, for God's sakes? This is a unique moment, a unique experience. She's going to need support, understanding. A contact. Come on. Don't be frigid about it.'

'I guess Carla is more frigid than I'm ever likely to be.'

They laughed, to keep up the informalities. Then they mentioned the Institute grant I'd receive, just for hanging around and being supportive. To a quasi-unemployed artist, that was temptation and a half. They also reminded me that on this initial bout there wouldn't be much publicity, so later, if I wanted to capitalise as an eyewitness, and providing good old Carla was willing – I had a sudden vision of getting very rich, very quick, and with the minimum of effort, and I succumbed ungracefully.

Which accurately demonstrated my three strongest qualities: laziness, optimism, and blind stupidity. Which in turn sums up the whole story, more or less. And that's probably why I was told to write it down for the archives of the human race. I can't think of a better way to depress and wreck the hopes of frenzied, shackled, bleating humanity.

But to return to Carla. She was, I believe, my great-great-great-great-great-grandmother. Give or take a great. Absolute accuracy isn't one of my talents, either. The relevant part is, however, that at thirty-three, Carla had developed the rare heart complaint valu – val – well, she'd developed it. She had a few months, or less, and so she opted, along with seventy other people that year, to undergo Cryogenic Suspension till a cure could be found. Cry Sus had been getting progressively more popular, ever since the 1980s. Remember? It's the freezing method of holding a body in refrigerated stasis, indefinitely preserving thereby flesh, bones, organs and the rest, perfect and pristine, in a frosty crystal box. (Just stick a tray of water in the freezer and see for yourself.) It may not strike you as cosy any more, but that's hardly surprising. In 1993, ninety-one persons, of whom four-or-five-or-six-great-granny Carla was one, saw it as the only feasible alternative to death. In the following two hundred years, four thousand others copied their example. They froze their malignancies, their unreliable hearts and their corroding tissues, and as the light faded from their snowed-over eyes, they must have dreamed of waking up in the fabulous future.

Funny thing about the future. Each next second is the future. And now it's the present. And now it's the past.

Those all-together four thousand and ninety-one, who deposited their physiognomies in the cold-storage compartments of the world were looking forward to the future. And here it was. And we were it.

And smack in the middle of this future, which I naïvely called Now, was I, Tacey Brice, a rotten little unskilled artist, painting gimcrack flying saucers for the spacines. There was a big flying-saucer sighting boom that year of 2193. Either you recollect that, or you don't. Nearly as big as the historic boom between the 1930s and '90s. Psychologists had told us it was our human inadequacy, searching all over for a father-mother figure to replace God. Besides, we were getting desperate. We'd penetrated our solar system to a limited extent, but without meeting anybody on the way.

That's another weird thing. When you read the speculativia of the 1900s, you can see just how much they expected of us. It was going to be all, or nothing. Either the world would become a miracle of rare device with plastisteel igloos balanced on the stratosphere and metal giblets, or we'd have gone out in a blast of radiation. Neither of which had happened. We'd had problems, of course. Over two hundred years, problems occur. There had been the Fission Tragedy, and the World Flood of '14. There'd been the huge pollution clear-ups complete with the rationing that entailed, and one pretty nasty pandemic. They had set us back, that's obvious. But not halted us. So we reached 2193 mostly unscathed, with a whizz-bang technology not quite as whizz, or bang, as prophesied. A place where doors opened when they saw who you were, and with a colony on Mars, but where they hadn't solved the unemployment problem or the geriatric problem. Up in the ether there were about six hundred buzz-whuzzes headed out into nowhere, bleeping information about earth. But we hadn't landed on Alpha Centauri yet. And if the waste-disposal jammed, brother, it jammed. What I'm trying to say (superfluously, because you're ahead of me) is that their future, those four thousand and ninety-one, their future which was our present, wasn't as spectacular as they'd trusted or feared. Excepting the Salenic Vena-derivative drugs, which had rendered most of the diseases of the 1900s and the 2000s obsolete.

And suddenly, one day, someone had a notion.

'Hey, guys,' this someone suggested, 'you recall all those sealed frosty boxes the medic centres have? You know, with the on-ice carcinomas and valu-diddums in 'em? Well, don't you think it'd be grand to defrost the lot of them and pump 'em full of health?'

'Crazy,' said everybody else, and wet themselves with enthusiasm.

After that, they got the thing organised on a global scale. And first off, not wanting to chance any public mishaps, they intended to unfreeze a single frost box, in relative privacy. Perhaps they put all the names in a hat. Whatever, they picked Carla Brice, or Brr-Ice, if you liked that newsies' tablotape pun.

And since Carla Brr-Ice might feel a touch extra chilly, coming back to life two hundred years after she'd cryonised out of it, they dredged up a blood-line descendant to hold her cold old thirty-three-year hand. And that was Tacey Brr-Ice. Me.

The room below was pink, but the cold pink of strawberry ice cream. There were forty doctors of every gender prowling about in it and round the crystal slab. It put me in mind of a pack of wolves with a carcase they couldn't quite decide when to eat. But then, I was having a nervous attack, up in the spectator gallery where they'd sat me. The countdown had begun two days ago, and I'd been ushered in at noon today. For an hour now, the crystal had been clear. I could see a sort of blob in it, which gradually resolved into a naked woman. Straight off, even with her lying there stiff as a board and utterly defenceless, I could tell she was the sort of lady who scared me dizzy. She was large and well-shaped, with a mane of dark red hair. She was the type that goes outdoor swimmming at all seasons, skis, shoots rapids in a canoe, becomes the co-ordinator on a moon colony. The type that bites. Valu-diddums had got her, but nothing else could have done. Not child, beast, nor man. Certainly not another woman. Oh my. And this was my multiple-great-granny that I was about to offer the hand of reassurance.

Another hour, and some dial and click mechanisms down in the strawberry ice room started to dicker. The wolves flew in for the kill. A dead lioness, that was Carla. Then the box rattled and there was a yell. I couldn't see for scrabbling medics.

'What happened?'

The young medic detailed to sit in the spec gallery with me, sighed. 'I'd say she's opened her eyes.'

The young medic was black as space and beautiful as the stars therein. But he didn't give a damn about me. You could see he was in love with Carla the lioness. I was simply a pain he had to put up with for two or three hours, while he stared at the goddess beneath.

But now the medics had drawn off. I thought of the Sleeping Beauty story, and Snow White. Her eyes were open indeed. Coppery brown to tone with the mane. She didn't appear dazed. She appeared contemptuous. Precisely as I'd anticipated. Then the crystal box lid began to rise.

'Jesus,' I said.

'Strange you should say that,' said the black medic. His own wonderful eyes fixed on Carla, he'd waxed profound and enigmatic. 'The manner in which we all still use these outdated religious expletives: *God, Christ, Hell*, long after we've ceased to credit their religious basis as such. The successful completion of this experiment in life-suspense and restoration has a bearing on the same matter,' he murmured, his inch-long lashes brushing the plastase pane. 'You've read of the controversy regarding this process? It was seen at one era as an infringement of religious faith.'

'Oh, yes?'

I kept on staring at him. Infinitely preferable to Carla, with her open eyes, and the solitary bending medic with the supadermic.

'The idea of the soul,' said the medic in the gallery. 'The immortal part which survives death. But what befalls a soul trapped for years, centuries, in a living yet statically frozen body? In a physical limbo, a living death. You see the problem this would pose for the religious?'

'I – uh –'

'But, of course, today,' he spread his hands. 'There is no such barrier to lucid thought. The life force, we now know, resides purely in the brain, and thereafter in the motor nerves, the spinal cord, and attendant reflexive centres. There is no *soul*.'

Then he shut up and nearly swooned away, and I realised Carla had met his eye.

I looked, and she was sitting, part reclined against some medic's arm. The medic was telling her where she was and what year it was and how, by this evening, the valu-diddums would be no more than a bad dream, and then she could go out into the amazing new world with her loving descendant, who she could observe up there in the gallery.

She did spare a glance for me. It lasted about .09 of a mini-instant. I tried to unglue my mouth and flash her a warming welcoming grin, but before I could manage it, she was back to studying the black medic.

At that moment somebody came and whipped me away for celebratory alcohol, and two hours later, when I'd celebrated rather too much, they took me up a plushy corridor to meet Carla, skin to skin.

Actually, she was dressed on this occasion. She'd had a shower and a couple of post-defrosting tests and some shots and the anti-valu-diddums stuff. Her hair was smouldering like a fire in a forest. She wore the shiny smock medical centres insisted that you wore, but on her it was like a design original. She'd even had a tan frozen in with her, or maybe it was my dazzled eyes that made her seem all bronzed and glowing. Nobody could look that good, that *healthy*, after two hundred years on ice. And if they did, they shouldn't. Her room was crammed with flowers and bottles of scent and exotic light paintings, courtesy of the Institute. And then they trundled me in.

Not astoundingly, she gazed at me with bored amusement. Like she'd come to the dregs at the bottom of the wine.

'This is Tacey,' somebody said, making free with my forename.

Carla spoke, in a voice of maroon velvet. 'Hallo, er, Tacey.' Patently, my cognomen was a big mistake. Never mind, she'd overlook it for now. 'I gather we are related.'

I was drunk, but it wasn't helping. 'I'm your gr – yes, we are, but –' I intelligently blurted. The 'but' was going to be a prologue to some nauseating, placatory, crawler's drivel about her gorgeousness and youth. It wasn't necessary, not even to let her know how scared I was.

She could tell that easily, plus how I'd shrunk to a shadow in her voltage glare. Before I could complete my hiccuping sycophancy, anyway, the medic in charge said: 'Tacey is your link, Mz Brice, with civilisation as it currently is.'

Carla couldn't resist it. She raised one manicured eyebrow, frozen exquisite for two centuries. If Tacey was the link, civilisation could take a walk.

'My apartment,' I went on blurting, 'it's medium, but –'

What was I going to say now? About how all my grant from the Institute I would willingly spend on gowns and perfumes and skis and automatic rifles, or whatever Carla wanted. How I'd move out and she could have the apartment to herself. (She wouldn't like the spacine murals on the walls.)

'It's just a br – a bridge,' I managed. 'Till you get acclimatosed – atised.'

She watched me as I made a fool of myself, or rather, displayed my true foolishness. Finally I comprehended the message in her copper eyes: don't bother. That was all; don't bother. You're a failure, Carla's copper irises informed me, as if I didn't know. Don't make excuses. You can alter nothing. I expect nothing from you. I will stay while I must in your ineffectual vicinity, and you may fly round me and scorch your wings if you like. When I am ready, I shall leave immediately, searing over your sky like a meteor. You can offer no aid, no interest, no grain I cannot garner for myself.

'How kind of Tacey,' Carla's voice said. 'Come, darling, and let me kiss you.'

Somehow, I'd imagined her still as very cold from the frosty box, but she was blood heat. Ashamed, I let her brush my cheek with her meteoric lips. Perhaps I'd burn.

'I'd say this calls for a toast,' said the medic in charge. 'But just rose-juice for Mz Brice, I'm afraid, at present.'

Carla smiled at him, and I hallucinated a rose-bush, thorns too, eviscerated by her teeth. Lions drink blood, not roses.

I got home paralysed and floundered about trying to change things. In the middle of attempting to re-spray-paint over a wall, I sank on a pillow and slept. Next day I was angry, the way you can only be angry over something against which you are powerless. So damn it. Let her arrive and see space-shuttles, mother-ships and whirly bug-eyed monsters all across the plastase. And don't pull the ready-cook out of the alcove to clean the feed-pipes behind it that I hadn't seen for three years. Or dig the plant out of the cooled-water dispenser. Or buy any new garments, blinds, rugs, sheets. And don't conceal the Wage-Increment cheques when they skitter down the shute. Or prop up the better spacines I'd illustrated on the table where she won't miss them.

I visited her one more time during the month she stayed at the Institute. I didn't have the courage not to take her anything, although I knew that whatever I offered would be wrong. Actually, I had an impulse to blow my first grant cheque and my W–I together and buy her a little antique stiletto of Toledo steel. It was blatantly meant to commit murder with, and as I handed it to her I'd bow and say, 'For you, Carla. I just know you can find a use for it.' But naturally I didn't have the bravura. I bought her a flagon of expensive scent she didn't need and was rewarded by seeing her put it on a shelf with three other identically packaged flagons, each twice the size of mine. She was wearing a reclinerobe of amber silk, and I almost reached for sunglasses. We didn't say much. I tottered from her room, sunburned and peeling. And that night I painted another flying saucer on the wall.

The day she left the Institute, they sent a mobile for me. I was supposed to collect and ride to the apartment with Carla, to make her feel homey. I felt sick.

Before I met her, though, the medic in charge wafted me into his office. 'We're lucky,' he said. 'Mz Brice is a most independent lady. Her readjustment has been, in fact, remarkable. None of the traumas or rebuttals we've been anxious about. I doubt if most of the other subjects to be revived from cryogenesis will demonstrate the equivalent rate of success.'

'They're really reviving them, then?' I inquired lamely. I was glad to be in here, putting off my fourth congress with inadequacy.

'A month from today. Dependent on the ultimately positive results of our post-resuscitation analysis of Mz Brice. But, as I intimated, I hardly predict any hitch there.'

'And how long,' I swallowed, 'how long do you think Carla will want to stay with me?'

'Well, she seems to have formed quite an attachment for you, Tacey. It's a great compliment, you know, from a woman like that. A proud, volatile spirit. But she needs an anchor for a while. We all need our anchors. Probably, her proximity will benefit you, in return. Don't you agree?'

I didn't answer, and he concluded I was overwhelmed. He started to describe to me that glorious scheduled event, the global link-up, when every single cryogene was to be revived, as simultaneously with each other as they could arrange it. The process would be going out on five channels of the Spatials, visible to us all. Technology triumphant yet again, bringing us a minute or two of transcendental catharsis. I thought about the beautiful black medic and his words on religion. And this is how we replaced it, presumably (when we weren't saucer-sighting), shedding tears sentimentally over four thousand and ninety idiots fumbling out of the deep-freeze.

'One last, small warning,' the medic in charge added. 'You may notice – or you may not, I can't be positive – the occasional lapse in the behavioural patterns of Mz Brice.'

There was a fantasy for me. Carla, *lapsed*.

'In what way?' I asked, miserably enjoying the unlikelihood.

'Mere items. A mood, an aberration – a brief disorientation even. These are to be expected in a woman reclaimed by life after two hundred years, and in a world she is no longer familiar with. As I explained, I looked for much worse and far greater quantity. The odd personality slip is inevitable. You musn't be alarmed. At such moments the most steadying influence on Mz Brice will be a non-Institutional normalcy of surrounding. And the presence of yourself.'

I nearly laughed.

I would have, if the door hadn't opened, and if Carla, in mock red-lynx fur, hadn't stalked into the room.

I didn't even try to create chatter. Alone in the mobile, with the auto driving us along the cool concrete highways, there wasn't any requirement to pretend for the benefit of others. Carla reckoned I was a schmoil, and I duly schmoiled. Mind you, now and again, she put out a silk paw and gave me a playful tap. Like when she asked me where I got my hair *done*. But I just told her about the ready-set parlours and she quit. Then again, she asked a couple of less abstract questions. Did libraries still exist, that was one. The second one was if I slept well.

I went along with everything in a dank stupor. I think I was half kidding myself it was going to be over soon. Then the mobile drove into the auto-lift of my apartment block, the gates gaped and we got out. As my door recognised me and split wide, it abruptly hit me that Carla and I were going to be hand in glove for some while. A month at least, while the Institute completed its final tests. Maybe more, if Carla had my lazy streak somewhere in her bronze and permasteel frame.

She strode into my apartment and stood flaming among the flying saucers and the wine-ringed furniture. The fake-fur looked as if she'd shot it herself. She was a head taller than I was ever going to be. And then she startled me, about the only way she could right then.

'I'm tired, Tacey,' said Carla.

No wise-cracks, no vitriol, no stare from Olympus.

She glided to the bedroom. Okay. I'd allocated the bed as hers, the couch as mine. She paused, gold digit on the panel that I'd pre-set to respond to her finger.

'Will you forgive me?' she wondered.

Her voice was soporific. I yawned.

'Sure, Carla.'

She stayed behind the closed panels for hours. The day reddened over the city, colours as usual heightened by the weather control that operates a quarter of a mile up. I slumped here and there, unable to eat or rest or read or doodle. I was finding out what it was going to be like, having an apartment and knowing it wasn't mine any more. Even through a door, Carla dominated.

Around nineteen, I knocked. No reply.

Intimidated, I slunk off. I wouldn't play the septophones, even with the ear-pieces only, even with the volume way down. Might wake granny. You see, if you could wake her from two hundred years in the freezer, you could certainly wake her after eight hours on a dormadais.

At twenty-four midnight, she still hadn't come out.

Coward, I knocked again, and feebly called: 'Night, Carla. See you tomorrow.'

On the couch I had nightmares, or nightcarlas to be explicit. Some were very realistic, like the one where the trust bonds Carla's estate had left for her hadn't accumulated after all and she was destitute, and going to remain with me for ever and ever. Or there were the comic-strip ones where the fake red-lynx got under the cover and bit me. Or the surreal ones where Carla came floating towards me, clad only in her smouldering hair, and everything caught fire from it, and I kept saying, 'Please, Carla, don't set the rug alight. Please, Carla, don't set the couch alight.' In the end there was merely a dream where Carla bent over me, hissing something like an anaconda – if they do hiss. She wanted me to stay asleep, apparently, and for some reason I was fighting her, though I was almost comatose. The strange thing in this dream was that Carla's eyes had altered from copper to a brilliant topaz yellow, like the lynx's.

It must have been about four in the morning that I woke up. I think it was the washer unit that woke me. Or it could have been the septophones. Or the waste-disposal. Or the drier. Or any of the several gadgets a modern apartment was equipped with. Because they were all on. It sounded like a madhouse. Looked like one. All the lights were on, too. In the middle of chaos: Carla. She was quite naked, the way I'd seen her at the first, but she had the sort of nakedness that seems like clothes, clean-cut, firm and flawless. The sort that makes me want to hide inside a stone. She was reminiscent of a sorceress in the midst of her sorcery, the erupting mechanisms sprawling round her amid the fierce light. I had a silly thought: *Carla's going nova*. Then she turned and saw me. My mouth felt as if it had been security-sealed, but I got out, 'You okay, Carla?'

'I am, darling. Go back to sleep now.'

That's the last thing I remember till ten a.m. the next day.

I wondered initially if Carla and the gadgets had been an additional dream. But when I checked the energy-meter I discovered they hadn't. I was plodding to the ready-cook when Carla emerged from the bedroom in her amber reclinerobe.

She didn't say a word. She just relaxed at the counter and let me be her slave. I got the ready to prepare her the large breakfast she outlined. Then I ran her bath. When the water-meter shut off half through, Carla suggested I put in the extra tags to ensure the tub was filled right up.

As she bathed, I sat at the counter and had another nervous attack.

Of course, Carla was predictably curious. Back in 1993, many of our gadgets hadn't been invented, or at least not developed to their present standard. Why not get up in the night and turn everything on? Why did it have to seem sinister? Maybe my sleeping through it practically non-stop was the thing that troubled me. All right. So Carla was a hypnotist. Come to consider, should I run a histotrace myself, in an attempt to learn what Carla was – had been?

But let's face it, what really upset me was the low on the energy-meter, the water-meter taking a third of my week's water tags in one morning. And Carla luxuriously wallowing, leaving me to foot the bill.

Could I say anything? No. I knew she'd immobilise me before I'd begun.

When she came from the bathroom, I asked her did she want to go out. She said no, but I could visit the library, if I would, and pick up this book and tape list she'd called through to them. I checked the call-meter. That was down, too.

'I intend to act the hermit for a while, Tacey,' Carla murmured behind me as I guiltily flinched away from the meter. 'I don't want to get involved in a furore of publicity. I gather the news of my successful revival will have been leaked today. The tablotapes will be sporting it. But I understand, by the news publishing codes of the eighties, that unless I approach the Newsies voluntarily, they are not permitted to approach me.'

'Yes, that's right.' I gazed pleadingly into the air. 'I guess you wouldn't ever reconsider that, Carla? It could mean a lot of money. That is, not for you to contact the Newsies. But if you'd all-allow me to on your beh-half.'

She chuckled like a lioness with her throat full of gazelle. The hair rose on my neck as she slunk closer. When her big, warm, elegant hand curved over my skull, I shuddered.

'No, Tacey. I don't think I'd care for that. I don't need the cash. My estate investments, I hear, are flourishing.'

'I was thinking of m – I was thinking of me, Carla. I cou-could use the tags.'

The hand slid from my head and batted me lightly. Somehow, I was glad I hadn't given her the Toledo knife after all.

'No, I don't think so. I think it will do you much more good to continue as you are. Now, run along to the library, darling.'

I went mainly because I was glad to get away from her. To utter the spineless whining I had, had drained entirely my thin reserves of courage. I was shaking when I reached the auto-lift. I had a wild plan of leaving town, and leaving my apartment with Carla in it, and going to ground. It was more than just inadequacy now. Hunter and hunted. And as I crept through the long grass, her fiery breath was on my heels.

I collected the twenty books and the fifty tapes and paid for the loan. I took them back to the apartment and laid them before my astonishing amber granny. I was too scared even to hide. Much too scared to disobey.

I sat on the sun-patio, though it was the weather-control day for rain. Through the plastase panels I heard the tapes educating Carla on every aspect of contemporary life: social, political, economic, geographic and carnal.

When she summoned me, I fixed lunch. Later, drinks and supper.

Then I was nervous to go to sleep. I passed out in the bathroom, sitting in the shower cubicle. Had nightcarlas. Carla eating salad. Didn't wake up till ten a.m. Checked. All meters down again.

When I trod on smashed plastase I thought it was sugar. Then I saw the cooled-water dispenser was in ninety-five bits. Where the plant had been, there was only soil and condensation and trailing roots.

I looked, and everywhere beheld torn-off leaves and tiny clots of earth. There was a leaf by Carla's bedroom. I knocked and my heart knocked to keep my hand company.

But Carla wasn't interested in breakfast, wasn't hungry.

I knew why not. She'd eaten my plant.

You can take a bet I meant to call up the Institute right away. Somehow, I didn't. For one thing, I didn't want to call from the apartment and risk Carla catching me at it. For another, I didn't want to go out and leave her, in case she did something worse. Then again, I was terrified to linger in her vicinity. A *lapse*, the medic in charge had postulated. It was certainly that. Had she done anything like it at the Institute? Somehow I had the idea she hadn't. She'd saved it for me. Out of playful malice.

I dithered for an hour, till I panicked, pressed the call button and spoke the digits. I never heard the door open. She seemed to know exactly when to – *strike*; yes that *is* the word I want. I sensed her there. She didn't even touch me. I let go the call button.

'Who were you calling?' Carla asked.

'Just a guy I used to pair with,' I said, but it came out husky and gulped and quivering.

'Well, go ahead. Don't mind me.'

Her maroon voice, bored and amused and indifferent to anything I might do, held me like a steel claw. And I discovered I had to turn round and face her. I had to stare into her eyes.

The scorn in them was killing. I wanted to shrivel and roll under the rug, but I couldn't look away.

'But if you're not going to call anyone, run my bath, darling,' Carla said.

I ran her bath.

It was that easy. Of course.

She was magnetic. Irresistible.

I couldn't –

I could *not* –

Partly, it had all become incredible. I couldn't picture myself accusing Carla of house-plant-eating to the medics at the Institute. Who'd believe it? It was nuts. I mean, too nuts even for them. And presently, I left off quite believing it myself.

Nevertheless, somewhere in my brain I kept on replaying those sentences of the medic in charge: *the occasional lapse in the behavioural patterns . . . a mood, an aberration . . .* And against that, point counterpoint, there kept on playing that phrase the beautiful black medic reeled off enigmatically as a cultural jest: *but what befalls a soul trapped for years, centuries, in a living yet statically frozen body?*

Meanwhile, by sheer will, by the force of her persona, she'd stopped me calling. And that same thing stopped me talking about her to anybody on the street, sent me tongue-tied to fetch groceries, sent me grovelling to conjure meals. It was almost as if it also shoved me asleep when she wanted and brought me awake ditto.

Doesn't time fly when you're having fun?

Twenty days, each more or less resembling each, hurried by. Carla didn't do anything else particularly weird, at least not that I saw or detected. But then, I never woke up nights any more. And I had an insane theory that the meters had been fiddled, because they weren't low, but they felt as if they should be. I hadn't got any more plants. I missed some packaged paper lingerie but it turned up under Carla's bed, where I'd kicked it when the bed was mine. Twenty days, twenty-five. The month of Carla's post-resuscitation tests was nearly through. One morning, I was stumbling about like a zombie, cleaning the apartment because the dustease had jammed and Carla had spent five minutes in silent comment on the dust. I was moving in that combined sludge of terror, mindlessness and masochistic cringing she'd taught me, when the door signal went.

When I opened the door, there stood the black medic with a slim case of file-tapes. I felt transparent, and that was how he treated me. He gazed straight through me to the empty room where he had hoped my granny would be.

'I'm afraid your call doesn't seem to be working,' he said. (Why had I the notion Carla had done something to the call?) 'I'd be grateful to see Mz Brice, if she can spare me a few minutes. Just something we'd like to check for the files.'

That instant, splendid on her cue, Carla manifested from the bathroom. The medic had seen her naked in the frosty box, but not a naked that was vaguely and fluently sheathed in a damp towel. It had the predictable effect. As he paused transfixed, Carla bestowed her most gracious smile.

'Sit down,' she said. 'What check is this? Tacey, darling, why not arrange some fresh coffee?'

Tacey darling went to the coffee cone. Over its bubbling, I heard him say to her, 'It's simply that Doctor Something was a little worried by a possible amnesia. Certainly, none of the memory areas seem physically impaired. But you see, here and there on the tape –'

'Give me an example, please,' drawled Carla.

The black medic lowered his lashes as if to sweep the tablotape. 'Some confusion over places, and names. Your second husband, Francis, for instance, who you named as Frederick. And there, the red mark – Doctor Something-Else mentioned the satellite disaster of '91, and it seems you did not recoll –'

'You're referring to the malfunction of the Ixion 11, which broke up and crashed in the mid-west, taking three hundred lives,' said Carla. She sounded like a purring textbook. She leaned forward, and I could watch him tremble all across from the coffee cone. 'Doctor Something and Doctor Something-Else,' said Carla, 'will have to make allowances for my excitement at rebirth. Now, I can't have you driving out this way for nothing. How about you come to dinner, the night before the great day. Tacey doesn't see nearly enough people her own age. As for me, let's say you'll make a two-hundred-year-old lady very happy.'

The air between them was electric enough to form sparks. By the 'great day' she meant, patently, the five-channel spatial event when her four thousand and ninety confrères got liberated from the sub-zero. But he plainly didn't care so much about defrostings any more.

The coffee cone boiled over. I noticed with a shock I was crying. Nobody else did.

What I wanted to do was programme the ready-cook for the meal, get in some wine, and get the hell out of the apartment and leave the two of them alone. I'd pass the night at one of the all-night Populars, and creep in around ten a.m. the next morning. That's the state I frankly acknowledged she had reduced me to. I'd have been honestly grateful to have done that. But Carla wouldn't let me.

'Out?' she inquired. 'But this whole party is for you, darling.'

There was nobody about. She didn't have to pretend. She and I knew I was the slave. She and I knew her long-refrigerated soul, returning in fire, had scalded me into a melty on the ground. So it could only be cruelty, this. She seemed to be experimenting, even, as she had with the gadgets. The psychological dissection of an inferior inhabitant of the future.

What I had to do therefore, was to visit the ready-set hair parlour, and buy a dress with my bi-monthly second W–I cheque. Carla, though naturally she didn't go with me, somehow instigated and oversaw these ventures. Choosing the dress, she was oddly at my elbow. *That* one, her detached and omnipresent aura instructed me. It was expensive, and it was scarlet and gold. It would have looked wonderful on somebody else. But on me. That dress just sucked the little life I've got right out of me.

Come the big night (before the big day, for which the countdown must already have, in fact, begun), there I was, done up like a New Year parcel, and with my own problematical soul wizened within me. The door signal went, and the slave accordingly opened the door, and the dark angel entered, politely thanking me as he nearly walked straight through me.

He looked so marvellous, I practically bolted. But still the aura of Carla, and Carla's wishes, which were beginning to seem to be communicating themselves telepathically, held me put.

Then Carla appeared. I hadn't seen her before, that evening. The dress was lionskin, and it looked real, despite the anti-game-hunting laws. Her hair was a smooth auburn waterfall that left bare an ear with a gold star dependent from it. I just went into the cooking area and uncorked a bottle and drank most of it straight off.

They both had good appetites, though hers was better than his. She'd eaten a vast amount since she'd been with me, presumably ravenous after that long fast. I was the waitress, so I waited on them. When I reached my plate, the food had congealed because the warmer in the table on my side was faulty. Anyway, I wasn't hungry. There were two types of wine. I drank the cheap type. I was on the second bottle now, and sufficiently sad I could have howled, but I'd also grown uninvolved, viewing my sadness from a great height.

They danced together to the septophones. I drank some more wine. I was going to be very, very ill tomorrow. But that was tomorrow. Verily. When I looked up, they'd danced themselves into the bedroom and the panels were shut. Carla's cruelty had had its run and I wasn't prepared for any additions, such as ecstatic moans from the interior, to augment my frustration. Accordingly, garbed in my New Year parcel frock, hair in curlicues, and another bottle in my hand, I staggered forth into the night.

Maybe, I might have met a thug, a rapist, a murderer, or even one of the numerous polipatrols that roam the city to prevent the activities of such. But I didn't meet anyone who took note of me. Nobody cared. Nobody was interested. Nobody wanted to be my friend, rob me, abuse me, give me a job or a goal, or make me happy, or make love to me. So if you thought I was a Judas, just you remember that. If one of you slobs had taken any notice of me that night –

I didn't have to wait for morning to be ill. There was a handsome wash-room on Avenue East. I'll never forget it. I was there quite a while.

When the glamorous weather-control dawn irradiated the city, I was past the worst. And by ten a.m. I was trudging home, queasy, embittered, hard-done-by, but sober. I was even able to register the tabloes everywhere and the holoid neons, telling us all that the great day was here. The day of the four thousand and ninety. Thawday. I wondered dimly if Carla and the Prince of Darkness were still celebrating it in my bed. She should have been cold. Joke. All right. It isn't.

The door to my apartment let me in. The place was as I'd abandoned it. The window-blinds were down, the table strewn with plates and glasses. The bedroom door firmly shut.

I pressed the switch to raise the blinds, and nothing happened, which didn't surprise me. That in itself should have proved to me how far the influence had gone and how there was no retreat. But I only had this random desultory urge to see what the apartment door would do now. What it did was not react. Not even when I put my hand on the panel, which method was generally reserved for guests. It had admitted me, but wouldn't let me out again. Carla had done something to it. As she had to the call, the meters, and to me. But how – Personal power? Ridiculous. I was a spineless dope, that was why she'd been able to negate me. Yet – forty-one medics with a bevy of tests and questions, some of which, apparently, she hadn't got right, ate from her hand. And maybe her psychic ability had increased. Practice makes perfect.

. . . *What befalls a soul trapped for years, centuries, in a living yet statically frozen body?*

It was dark in the room with the blinds irreversibly staying down and the lights irreversibly staying off.

Then the bedroom door slid wide, and Carla slid out. Naked again, and glowing in the dark. She smiled at me, pityingly.

'Tacey, darling, now you've gotten over your sulks, there's something in here I'd like you to clear up for me.'

Dichotomy once more. I wanted to take root where I was, but she had me walking to the bedroom. She truly was glowing. As if she'd lightly sprayed herself over with something mildly luminous. I guessed what would be in the bedroom, and I'd begun retching, but, already despoiled of filling, that didn't matter. Soon I was in the doorway and she said, 'Stop that, Tacey.' And I stopped retching and stood and looked at what remained of the beautiful black medic, wrapped up in the bloodstained lionskin.

Lions drink blood, not roses.

Something loosened inside me then. It was probably the final submission, the final surrender of the fight. Presumably I'd been fighting her subconsciously from the start, or I wouldn't have gained the ragged half-freedoms I had. But now I was limp and sodden, so I could ask humbly: 'The plant was salad. But a man – what was he?'

'You don't quite get it, darling, do you?' Carla said. She stroked my hair friendlily. I didn't shudder any more. Cowed dog, I was relaxed under the contemptuous affection of my mistress. 'One was green and vegetable. One was black, male and meat. Different forms. Local dishes. I had no inclination to sample you, you comprehend, since you were approximate to my own appearance. But of course, others who find themselves to be black and male may wish to sample pale-skinned females. Don't worry, Tacey. You'll be safe. You entertain me. You're mine. Protected species.'

'Still don't understand, Carla,' I whispered meekly.

'Well, just clear up for me, and I'll explain.'

I don't have to apologise to you for what I did then, because, of course, you know all about it, the will-less indifference of the absolute slave. I bundled up the relics of Carla's lover-breakfast, and dumped them in the waste-disposal, which dealt with them pretty efficiently.

Then I cleaned the bedroom, and had a shower, and fixed Carla some coffee and biscuits. It was almost noon, the hour when the four thousand and ninety were going to be roused, and to step from their frost boxes in front of seven-eighths of the world's Spatial-viewers. Carla wanted to see it too, so I switched on my set, minus the sound.

Next Carla told me I might sit, and I sat on a pillow, and she explained.

For some reason, I don't remember her actual words. Perhaps she put it in a technical way and I got the gist but not the sentences. I'll put it in my own words here, despite the fact that a lot of you know now anyway. After all, under supervision, we still have babies sometimes. When they grow up they'll need to know. Know why they haven't got a chance, and why we hadn't. And, to level with you, know why I'm not a Judas, and that I didn't betray us, because I didn't have a chance either.

Laziness, optimism, and blind stupidity.

I suppose optimism more than anything.

Four thousand and ninety-one persons lying down in frozen stasis, aware they didn't have souls and couldn't otherwise survive, dreaming of a future of cures, and of a re-awakening in that future. And the earth dreaming of benevolent visitors from other worlds, father-mother figures to guide and help us. Sending them buzz-whuzzes to bleep, over and over, *here* we are. *Here. Here.*

I guess we do have souls. Or we have something that has nothing to do with the brain, or the nerve centres, or the spinal cord. Perhaps that dies too, when we die. Or perhaps it escapes. Whatever happens, that's the one thing you can't retain in Cryogenic Suspension. The body, all its valves and ducts and organs, lies pristine in limbo, and when you wake it up with the correct drugs, impulses, stimuli, it's live again, can be cured of its diseases, becoming a flawless vessel of – nothing. It's like an empty room, a vacant lot. The tenant's skipped.

Somewhere out in the starry night of space, one of the bleeping buzz-whuzzes was intercepted. Not by pater-mater figures, but by a predatory, bellicose alien race. It was simple to get to us – hadn't we given comprehensive directions? But on arrival they perceived a world totally unsuited to their fiery, gaseous, incorporeal forms. That was a blow, that was. But they didn't give up hope. Along with their super technology they developed a process whereby they reckoned they could transfer inside of human bodies, and thereafter live off the fat of the Terrain. However, said process wouldn't work. Why not? The human consciousness (soul?) was too strong to overcome, it wouldn't let them through. Even asleep, they couldn't oust us. Dormant, the consciousness (soul?) is still present, or at least linked. As for dead bodies, no go. A man who had expired of old age, or with a mobile on top of him was no use. The body had to be a whole one, or there was no point. Up in their saucers, which were periodically spotted, they spat and swore. They gazed at the earth and drooled, pondering mastery of a globe, and entire races of slaves at their disposal. But there was no way they could achieve their aims until – until they learned of all those Cryogenic Suspensions in their frost boxes, all those soulless lumps of ice, waiting on the day when science would release and cure them and bring them forth healthy and *void*.

If you haven't got a tenant, advertise for a new tenant. We had. And they'd come.

Carla was the first. As her eyes opened under the crystal, something looked out of them. Not Carla Brice. Not any more. But something.

Curious, cruel, powerful, indomitable, alien, deadly.

Alone, she could handle hundreds of us humans, for her influence ascended virtually minute by minute. Soon there were going to be four thousand and ninety of her kind, opening their eyes, smiling their scornful thank-yous through the Spatials at the world they had come to conquer. The world they did conquer.

We gave them beautiful, healthy, moveable houses to live in, and billions to serve them and be toyed with by them, and provided them with extra bodies to be frozen and made fit to house any left-over colleagues of theirs. And our green de-polluted meadows wherein to rejoice.

As for Carla, she'd kept quiet and careful as long as she had to. Long enough for the tests to go through and for her to communicate back, telepathically, to her people, all the data they might require on earth, prior to their arrival.

And now she sat and considered me, meteoric fiery Carla-who-wasn't-Carla, her eyes, in the dark, gleaming topaz yellow through their copper irises, revealing her basic flammable nature within the veil of a dead woman's living flesh.

They can make me do whatever they want, and they made me write this. Nothing utterly bad has been done to me, and maybe it never will. So I've been lucky there.

To them, I'm historically interesting, as Carla had been historically interesting to us, as a first. I'm the first Slave. Possibly, I can stay alive on the strength of that and not be killed for a whim.

Which, in a way, I suppose, means I'm a sort of a success, after all.

Northern Chess

Sky and land had the same sallow bluish tinge, soaked in cold light from a vague white sun. It was late summer, but summer might never have come here. The few trees were bare of leaves and birds. The cindery grassless hills rolled up and down monotonously. Their peaks gleamed dully, their dips were full of mist. It was a land for sad songs and dismal rememberings, and, when the night came, for nightmares and hallucinations.

Fifteen miles back, Jaisel's horse had died. Not for any apparent cause. It had been healthy and active when she rode from the south on it, the best the dealer had offered her, though he had tried to cheat her in the beginning. She was aiming to reach a city in the far north, on the sea coast there, but not for any particular reason. She had fallen into the casual habit of the wandering adventurer. Destination was an excuse, never a goal. And when she saw the women at their looms or in their greasy kitchens, or tangled with babies, or broken with field work, or leering out of painted masks from shadowy town doorways, Jaisel's urge to travel, to ride, to fly, to run away, increased. Generally she was running from something in fact as well as in the metaphysical. The last city she had vacated abruptly, having killed two footpads who had jumped her in the street. One had turned out to be a lordling, who had taken up robbery and rape as a hobby. In those parts, to kill a lord, with whatever justice, meant hanging and quartering. So Jaisel departed on her new horse, aiming for a city in the north. And in between had come this bleak northern empty land where her mount collapsed slowly under her and died without warning. Where the streams tasted bitter and the weather looked as if it wished to snow in summer.

She had seen only ruins. Only a flock of grayish wild sheep materialised from mist on one hand and plunged away into mist on the other. Once she heard a raven cawing. She was footsore and growing angry, with the country, with herself, and with God, while her saddle and pack gained weight on her shoulders with every mile.

Then she reached the top of one of the endless slopes, looked over and saw something new.

Down in a pool of the yellowish-bluish mist lay a village. Primitive and melancholy it was, but alive, for smoke spiralled from roof-holes, drifting into the cloudless sky. Mournful and faint, too, there came the lowing of cattle. Beyond the warren of cots, a sinister unleafed spider web of trees. Beyond them, barely seen, transparent in mist, something some distance away, a mile perhaps – a tall piled hill, or maybe a stony building of bizarre and crooked shape . . .

Jaisel started and her eyes refocused on the closer vantage of the village and the slope below.

The fresh sound was unmistakable: jingle-jangle of bells on the bridles of war horses. The sight was exotic, also, unexpected here. Two riders on steel-blue mounts, the scarlet caparisons flaming up through the quarter-tone atmosphere like bloody blades. And the shine of mail, the blink of gems.

'Render your name!' one of the two knights shouted.

She half smiled, visualising what they would see, what they would assume, the surprise in store.

'My name is Jaisel,' she shouted back.

And heard them curse.

'What sort of a name is that, boy?'

Boy. Yes, and not the only time.

She started to walk down the slope toward them.

And what they had supposed to be a boy from the top of the incline, gradually resolved itself into the surprise. Her fine flaxen hair was certainly short as a boy's, somewhat shorter. A great deal shorter than the curled manes of knights. Slender in her tarnished chain mail, with slender strong hands dripping with frayed frosty lace at the wrists. The white lace collar lying out over the mail with dangling drawstrings each ornamented by a black pearl. The left ear-lobe pierced and a gold sickle moon flickering sparks from it under the palely electric hair. The sword belt was gray leather, worn and stained. Dagger on right hip with a fancy gilt handle, thin sword on left hip, pommel burnished by much use. A girl knight with intimations of the reaver, the showman, and (for what it was worth) the prince.

When she was close enough for the surprise to have commenced, she stopped and regarded the two mounted knights. She appeared gravely amused, but really the joke had palled by now. She had had twelve years to get bored with it. And she was tired, and still angry with God.

'Well,' one of the knights said at last, 'it takes all kinds to fill the world. But I think you've mistaken your road, lady.'

He might mean an actual direction. He might mean her mode of living.

Jaisel kept quiet, and waited. Presently the second knight said chillily: 'Do you know of this place? Understand where you are?'

'No,' she said. 'It would be a courteous kindness if you told me.'

The first knight frowned. 'It would be a courteous kindness to send you home to your father, your husband and your children.'

Jaisel fixed her eyes on him. One eye was a little narrower than the other. This gave her face a mocking, witty slant.

'Then, sir,' she said, 'send me. Come. I invite you.'

The first knight gesticulated theatrically. 'I am Renier of Towers,' he said. 'I don't fight women.'

'You do,' she said. 'You are doing it now. Not successfully.'

The second knight grinned; she had not anticipated that.

'She has you, Renier. Let her be. No girl travels alone like this one, and dressed as she is, without skills to back it. Listen, Jaisel. This land is cursed. You've seen, the life's sucked out of it. The village here. Women and beasts birth monsters. The people fall sick without cause. Or with some cause. There was an alchemist who claimed possession of this region. Maudras. A necromancer, a worshipper of old unholy gods. Three castles of his scabbed the countryside between here and Towers in the west. Those three are no more – taken and razed. The final castle is here, a mile off to the northeast. If the mist would lift, you might see it. The Prince of Towers means to expunge all trace of Maudras from the earth. We are the prince's knights, sent here to deal with the fourth castle as with the rest.'

'And the castle remains untaken,' said Renier. 'Months we've sat here in this unwholesome plague-ridden wilderness.'

'Who defends the castle?' Jaisel asked. 'Maudras himself?'

'Maudras was burned in Towers a year ago,' the second knight said. 'His familiar, or his curse, holds the castle against God's knights.' His face was pale and grim. Both knights indeed were alike in that. But Renier stretched his mouth and said to her sweetly: 'Not a spot for a maid. A camp of men. A haunted castle in a blighted country. Better get home.'

'I have no horse,' said Jaisel levelly. 'But coins to buy one.'

'We've horses and to spare,' said the other knight. 'Dead men don't require mounts. I am called Cassant. Vault up behind me and I'll bring you to the camp.'

She swung up lightly, despite the saddle and pack on her shoulders. Renier watched her, sneering, fascinated.

As they turned the horses' heads into the lake of mist, he rode near and murmured: 'Beware, lady. The women in the village are sickly and revolting. A knight's honour may be forgotten. But probably you have been raped frequently.'

'Once,' she said, 'ten years back. I was his last pleasure. I dug his grave myself, being respectful of the dead.' She met Renier's eyes again and added gently, 'And when I am in the district I visit his grave and spit on it.'

The mist was denser below than Jaisel had judged from the slope. In the village a lot was hidden, which was maybe as well. At a turning among the cots she thought she spied a forlorn hunched-over woman, leading by a tether a shadowy animal, which seemed to be a cow with two heads.

They rode between the trees and out the other side, and piecemeal the war camp of Towers evolved through the mist. Blood-blotch red banners hung lankly; the ghosts of tents clawed with bright heraldics that penetrated the obscurity. Horses puffed breath like dragon-smoke at their pickets. A couple of Javelot-cannon emplacements, the bronze tubes sweating on their wheels, the javelins stacked by, the powder casks wrapped in sharkskin but probably damp.

At this juncture, suddenly the mist unravelled. A vista opened away from the camp for two hundred yards northeast, revealing the castle of the necromancer-alchemist, Maudras.

It reared up, stark and peculiar against a tin-coloured sky.

The lower portion was carved from the native rock-base of a conical hill. This rose into a plethora of walls and craning, squinnying towers, that seemed somehow like the petrification of a thing once unnaturally growing. A causeway flung itself up the hill and under an arched doormouth, barricaded by iron.

No movements were discernible on battlements or roofs. No pennant flew. The castle had an aura of the tomb. Yet not necessarily a tomb of the dead.

It was the camp which had more of the feel of a mortuary about it. From an oblique quarter emanated groanings. Where men were to be found outside the tents, they crouched listlessly over fires. Cook-pots and heaps of accoutrements plainly went unattended. By a scarlet pavilion two knights sat at chess. The game was sporadic and violent and seemed likely to end in blows.

Cassant drew rein a space to the side of the scarlet pavilion, whose cloth was blazoned with three gold turrets – the insignia of Towers. A boy ran to take charge of the horse as its two riders dismounted. But Renier remained astride his horse, staring at Jaisel. Soon he announced generally, in a herald's carrying tone: 'Come, gentlemen, welcome a new recruit. A peerless knight. A damsel in breeches.'

All around, heads lifted. A sullen interest bloomed over the apathy of the camp: the slurred spiteful humour of men who were ill, or else under sentence of execution. They began to get up from the pallid fires and shamble closer. The fierce knights paused and gazed arrogantly across with extravagant oaths.

'Mistress, you're in for trouble,' said Cassant ruefully. 'But be fair, he warned you of it.'

Jaisel shrugged. She glanced at Renier, nonchalantly posed on the steel-blue horse, right leg loose of the stirrup now and hooked across the saddlebow. At ease, malevolently, he beamed at her. Jaisel slipped the gaudy dagger from her belt, let him catch the flash of the gilt, then tossed it at him. The little blade, with its wasp-sting point, sang through the air, singeing the hairs on his right cheek. It buried itself, where she had aimed it, in the picket post behind him. But Renier, reacting to the feint as she had intended, lunged desperately aside for the sake of his pretty face, took all his own weight on the yet-stirruped leg and off the free one, unbalanced royally, and plunged crashing to the ground. At the same instant, fully startled, the horse tried to rear. Still left-leggedly trapped in the stirrup, Renier of Towers went slithering through the hot ashes of a fire.

A hubbub resulted – delighted unfriendly mirth. The soldiers were as prepared to make sport of a boastful lord on his ears in the ash as of a helpless girl.

And the helpless girl was not quite finished. Renier was fumbling for his sword. Jaisel leaped over him like a lion, kicking his hands away as she passed. Landing, she wrenched his foot out of the stirrup and, having liberated him, jumped to the picket to retrieve her dagger. As Renier gained his knees, he beheld her waiting for him, quiet as a statue, her pack slung on the ground, the thin sword, slick with light, ready as a sixth long murderous finger to her hand.

A second he faltered, while the camp, ferociously animated, buzzed. Then his ringed hand went to the hilt of his own sword. It was two- to three-thirds its length from the scabbard when a voice bellowed from the doorway of the scarlet and gold pavilion: 'Dare to draw upon a woman, Renier, and I'll flay you myself.'

Gasping, Renier let the sword grate home again. Jaisel turned and saw a man incarnadine with anger as the tent he had stepped from. Her own dormant anger woke and filled her, white anger not red, bored anger, cold anger.

'Don't fear him slain, sir,' she said. 'I will give him only a slight cut, and afterward spare him.'

The incarnadine captain of the camp of Towers bent a baleful shaggy lour on her.

'Strumpet, or witch?' he thundered.

'Tell me first,' said Jaisel coolly, 'your title. Is it coward or imbecile?'

Silence was settling like flies on honey.

The captain shook himself.

'I never yet struck a wench –' he said.

'Nor will you now, by God's wounds.'

His mouth dropped ajar. He disciplined it and asked firmly: 'Why coward and why imbecile?'

'Humouring me, are you?' she inquired. She strolled toward him and let the sword tip weave a delicate pattern about his nose. To his credit, having calmed himself, he retained the calm. 'Coward or imbecile,' she said, drawing lines of glinting fire an inch from his nostrils, 'because you cannot take a castle that offers no defenders.'

A response then. A beefy paw thrust up to flick the sword away from him and out of her hand. But the sword was too quick. Now it rested horizontally on the air, tip twitching a moment at his throat. And now it was gone back into its scabbard, and merely a smiling strange-eyed girl was before him.

'I already know enough of you,' the captain said, 'that you are a trial to men and an affront to heaven is evident. Despite that, I will answer your abuse. Maudras' last castle is defended by some sorcery he

conjured to guard it. Three assaults were attempted. The result you
shall witness. Follow, she-wolf.'

And he strode off through the thick of the men who parted to let
him by, and to let the she-wolf by in his wake. No one touched her but
one fool, who had observed, but learned nothing. The pommel of her
dagger in his ribs, bruising through mail and shirt, put paid to his
flirtation.

'Here,' the captain barked.

He drew aside the flap of a dark tent, and she saw twenty men lying
on rusty mattresses and the two surgeons going up and down. The
casualties of some savage combat. She beheld things she had beheld
often, those things which sickened less but appalled more with
repetition. Near to the entrance a boy younger than herself, dreaming
horribly in a fever, called out. Jaisel slipped into the tent. She set her
icy palm on the boy's forehead and felt his raging heat burn through it.
But her touch seemed to alleviate his dream at least. He grew quieter.

'Again,' she said softly, 'coward, or imbecile. And these are the
sacrificial victims on the altar of cowardice or imbecility.'

Probably, the captain had never met such merciless eyes. Or,
perhaps not so inexplicably, from between the smooth lids of a young
girl.

'Enchantment,' he said gruffly. 'And sorcery. We were powerless
against it. Do you drink wine, you virago? Yes, no doubt. Come and
drink it with me then in my pavilion and you shall have the full story.
Not that you deserve it. But you are the last thrown stone that kills a
man. Injustice atop all the rest, and from a *woman*.'

Abruptly she laughed at him, her anger spent.

Red wine and red meat were served in the red pavilion. All the seven
knights of the Towers camp were present, Cassant and Renier among
the rest. Outside, their men went on sitting around the fires. A dreary
song had been struck up, and was repeated, over and over, as iron
snow-light radiated from the northern summer sky.

The captain of the knights had told again the story Cassant had
recounted to Jaisel on the slope: the three castles razed, the final castle
which proved unassailable. Gruff and bellicose, the captain found it
hard to speak of supernatural items and growled the matter into his
wine.

'Three assaults were offered the walls of the castle. Montaube led
the first of these. He died, and fifty men with him. Of what? We saw

no swordsmen on the battlements, no javelots were fired, no arrows. Yet men sprinkled the ground, bloody and dying, as if an army twice our numbers had come to grips with them unseen. The second assault, I led. I escaped by a miracle. I saw a man, his mail split as if by a bolt shot from a great distance. He dropped with a cry and blood bursting from a terrible wound. Not a soul was near but I, his captain. No weapon or shot was visible. The third assault – was planned, but never carried through. We reached the escarpment, and my soldiers began falling like scythed grain. No shame in our retreat. Another thing. Last month, three brave fools, men of dead Montaube's, decided secretly to effect entry by night over the walls. A sentry perceived them vanish within. They were not attacked. Nor did they return.'

There was a long quiet in the pavilion. Jaisel glanced up and encountered the wrathful glare of the captain.

'Ride home to Towers, then,' she said. 'What else is there to do?'

'And what other council would you predict from a woman?' broke in Renier. 'We are *men*, madam. We'll take that rock, or die. Honour, lady. Did you never hear of it in the whorehouse where you were whelped?'

'You have had too much wine, sir,' said Jaisel. 'But by all means have some more.' She poured her cup, measured and deliberate, over his curling hair. Two or three guffawed, enjoying this novelty. Renier leapt up. The captain bellowed familiarly, and Renier again relapsed.

Wine ran in rosy streams across his handsome brow.

'Truly, you do right to reprove me, and the she-wolf is right to anoint me with her scorn. We sit here like cowards, as she mentioned. There's one way to take the castle. A challenge. Single combat between God and Satan. Can the haunting of Maudras refuse that?' Renier got to his feet with precision now.

'You are drunk, Renier,' the captain snapped.

'Not too drunk to fight.' Renier was at the entrance. The captain roared. Renier only bowed. 'I am a knight. Only so far can you command me.'

'You fool –' said Cassant.

'I am, however, my own fool,' said Renier.

The knights stood, witnesses to his departure. Respect, sorrow and dread showed in their eyes, their nervous fingers fiddling with jewels, wine cups, chess figures.

Outside, the dreary song had broken off. Renier was shouting for his horse and battle gear.

The knights crowded to the flap to watch him armed. Their captain elect joined them. No further protest was attempted, as if a divine ordinance were being obeyed.

Jaisel walked out of the pavilion. The light was thickening as if to hem them in. Red fires, red banners, no other colour able to pierce the gloom. Renier sat his horse like a carved chess figure himself, an immaculate knight moving against a castle on a misty board.

The horse fidgeted, trembled. Jaisel ran her hand peacefully down its nose amid the litter of straps and buckles. She did not look at Renier, swaggering above her. She sensed too well his panic under the pride.

'Don't' she said to him softly, 'ride into the arms of death because you think I shamed your manhood. It's too large a purge for so small an ill.'

'Go away, girl,' he jeered at her. 'Go and have babies as God fashioned you to do.'

'God did not fashion you to die, Renier of Towers.'

'Maybe you're wrong in that,' he said wildly, and jerked the horse around and away from her.

He was galloping from the camp across the plain toward the rock. A herald dashed out and followed, but prudently hanging some yards behind, and when he sounded the brass, the notes cracked, and his horse shied at the noise. But Renier's horse threw itself on as if in preparation for a massive jump at the end of its running.

'He's mad; will die,' Cassant mumbled.

'And my fault,' Jaisel answered.

A low horrified moan went through the ranks of the watchers. The iron barricades of the huge castle's mouth were sluggishly folding aside. Nothing rode forth. It was, on the contrary, patently an invitation.

One man yelled to Renier across a hundred yards of gray ground. Several swelled the cry. Suddenly, three-quarters of the camp of Towers was howling. To make sport of a noble was one thing. To see him seek annihilation was another. They screamed themselves hoarse, begging him to choose reason above honour.

Jaisel, not uttering a word, turned from the spectacle. When she heard Cassant swearing, she knew Renier had galloped straight in the iron portal. The commotion of shouting crumbled into breathings, oaths. And then came the shock and clangour of two iron leaves meeting together again across the mouth of hell.

Impossible to imagine what he might be confronting now. Perhaps he would triumph, re-emerge in glory. Perhaps the evil in Maudras' castle had faded, or had never existed. Was an illusion. Or a lie.

They waited. The soldiers, the knights. The woman. A cold wind blew up, raking plumes, pennants, the long curled hair, plucking bridle bells, the gold sickle moon in Jaisel's left ear, the fragile lace at her wrists, and the foaming lace at the wrists of others.

The white sun westered, muddied, disappeared. Clouds like curds forming in milk formed in the sky.

Darkness slunk in on all fours. Mist boiled over, hiding the view of the castle. The fires burned, the horses coughed at their pickets.

There was the smell of a wet rottenness, like marshland – the mist – or rotting hope.

A young knight whose name Jaisel had forgotten was at her elbow. He thrust in her face a chess piece of red amber.

'The white queen possessed the red knight,' he hissed at her. 'Put him in the box then. Slam the lid. Fine chess game here in the north. Castles unbreachable and bitches for queens. Corpses for God's knights.'

Jaisel stared him down till he went away. From the corner of her eye, she noticed Cassant was weeping tears, frugally, one at a time.

It was too easy to get by the sentries in the mist and dark. Of course, they were alert against the outer environs, not the camp itself. But, still too easy. Discipline was lax. Honour had become everything, and honour was not enough.

Yet it was her own honour that drove her, she was not immune. Nor immune to this sad region. She was full of guilt she had no need to feel, and full of regret for a man with whom she had shared only a mutual dislike, distrust, and some quick verbal cuts and quicker deeds of wrath. Renier had given himself to the castle, to show himself valiant, to shame her. She was duly shamed. Accordingly, she was goaded to breach the castle also, to plumb its vile secret. To save his life if she could, avenge him if not. And die if the castle should outwit her? No. Here was the strangest fancy of all. Somewhere in her bones she did not believe Maudras' castle could do that. After all, her entire life had been a succession of persons, things, fate itself, trying to vanquish her and her aims. From the first drop of menstrual blood, the first husband chosen for her at the age of twelve, the first (and last) rape, the first swordmaster who had mocked her demand to learn and ended setting wagers on her – there had been so many lions in her way. And she had systematically overcome each of them. Because she did not, *would* not, accept that destiny was unchangeable. Or that what was merely named unconquerable could not be conquered.

Maudras' castle then, just another symbol to be thrown down. And the sick-sweet twang of fear in her vitals was no more than before any battle, like an old scar throbbing, simple to ignore.

She padded across the plain noiselessly in the smoky mist. Sword on left hip, dagger on the right. Saddle and pack had been left behind beneath her blanket. Some would-be goat might suffer astonishment if he ventured to her sleeping place. Otherwise they would not detect her absence till sunrise.

The mist ceased thirty feet from the causeway.

She paused a moment, and considered the eccentric edifice pouring aloft into overcast black sky. Now the castle had a choice. It could gape invitingly as it had before Renier the challenger. Or leave her to climb the wall seventy feet high above the doormouth.

The iron barricades stayed shut.

She went along the causeway.

Gazing up, the cranky towers seemed to reel, sway. Certainly it had an aura of wickedness, of impenetrable lingering hate . . .

White queen against bishop of darkness.

Queen takes castle, a rare twist to an ancient game.

The wall.

Masonry jutted, stonework creviced, protruded. Even weeds had rooted there. It was a gift, this wall, to any who would climb it. Which implied a maleficent joke, similar to the opening doors. *Enter. Come, I welcome you. Enter me and be damned within me.*

She jumped, caught hold, began to ascend. Loose-limbed and agile from a hundred trees, some other less lordly walls, one cliff-face five years ago – Jaisel could skim up vertical buildings like a cat. She did not really require all the solicitous help Maudras' wall pressed on her.

She gained the outer battlements in minutes and was looking in. Beyond this barrier, the curtain, a courtyard with its central guard – but all pitch black, difficult to assess. Only that configuration of turrets and crooked bastions breaking clear against the sky. As before, she thought of a growth, petrified.

The sound was of ripped cloth. But it was actually ripped atmosphere. Jaisel threw her body flat on the broad parapet and something kissed the nape of her neck as it rushed by into the night.

Reminiscent of a javelot bolt. Or the thicker swan-flighted arrows of the north. Without sentience, yet meant for the heart, and capable of stilling it.

She tilted herself swiftly over the parapet, hung by her fingers, and dropped seven feet to a platform below. As she landed, the tearing sound was reiterated. A violent hand tugged her arm. She glanced and beheld shredded lace barely to be seen in the blackness. The mail above her wrist was heated.

Some power which could make her out when she was nearly blind, but which seemed to attack randomly, inaccurately. She cast herself flat again and crawled on her belly to the head of a stair.

Here, descending, she became the perfect target. No matter. Her second swordsmaster had been something of an acrobat –

Jaisel launched herself into air and judging where the rims of the steps should be, executed three bold erratic somersaults, arriving ultimately in a hedgehog-like roll in the court.

As she straightened from this roll, she was aware of a sudden dim glow. She spun to meet it, sword and dagger to hand, then checked, heart and gorge passing each other as they travelled in the wrong directions.

The glow was worse than sorcery. It was caused by a decaying corpse half propped in a ruined cubby under the stairs. Putrescent, the remnants gave off a phosphorescent shine, matched by an intolerable stench that seemed to intensify with recognition. And next, something else. Lit by the witch-light of dead flesh, an inscription apparently chiselled in the stone beside it. Against her wits, Jaisel could not resist studying it. In pure clerical calligraphy it read: MAUDRAS SLEW ME.

One of Montaube's men.

Only the fighter's seventh sense warned Jaisel. It sent her ducking, darting, her sword arm sweeping up – and a great blow smashed against the blade, singing through her arm into her breast and shoulder. A great invisible blow.

The thought boiled in her – *How can I fight what I cannot see?* And the second inevitable thought: *I have always fought that way, combat with abstracts.* And in that extraordinary instant, wheeling to avoid the slashing lethal blows of a murderous nonentity, Jaisel realised that though she could not *see*, yet she could *sense*.

Perhaps twenty further hackings hailed against her sword, chipped the stones around. Her arm was almost numbed, but organised and obedient as a war machine, kept up its parries, feints, deflectings, thrusts. And then, eyes nearly closed, seeing better through her instinct with a hair's-breadth, dancing-with-death accuracy, she paid out her blade the length of her arm, her body hurtling behind it, and *felt* tissue part on either side of the steel. And immediately there followed a brain-slicing shriek, more like breath forced from a bladder than the protest of a dying throat.

The way was open. She sensed this too, and shot forward, doubled over, blade swirling its precaution. A fresh doorway, the gate into the guard, yawning unbarred, and across this gate, to be leaped, a glow, a reeking skeleton, the elegant chiselling in the stone floor on this occasion: MAUDRAS SLEW ME.

'Maudras!' Jaisel shouted as she leaped.

She was in the wide hollow of the castle guard. In the huge black, which tingled and burned and flashed with colours thrown by her own racing blood against the discs of her eyes.

Then the darkness screamed, an awful shattering of notes, which brought on an avalanche, a cacophany, as if the roof fell. It took her an extra heart-beat to understand, to fling herself from the path of a charging destruction no less potent for being natural. As the guard wall met her spine, the screaming nightmare, Renier's horse, exploded by her and out into the court beyond the door.

She lay quiet, taking air, and something stirred against her arm. She wrenched away and raised her sword, but Montaube's ultimate glowing soldier was there, draped on the base of what looked to be a pillar trunk. A lamp, he shone for her as the circulatory flashes died from the interior of her eyes. So she saw Renier of Towers sprawled not a foot from her.

She kneeled, and tested the quality of the tension about her. And she interpreted from it a savouring, a cat's-paw willingness to play, to let out the leash before dragging it tight once more.

The corpse (MAUDRAS SLEW ME inscribed on the pillar) appeared to glow brighter to enable her to see the mark on Renier's forehead, like the bruise caused by some glancing bolt. A trickle of blood where formerly wine had trickled. The lids shivering, the chest rising and falling shallowly.

She leaned to him and whispered: 'You live then. Your luck's kinder than I reckoned. To be stunned rather than slaughtered. And Maudras' magic waiting for you to get up again. Not liking to kill when you would not know it. Preferring to make a meal of killing you, unfair and unsquare.'

Then, without preface, terror swamped the hollow pillared guard of Maudras' castle.

A hundred, ten hundred, whirling slivers of steel carved the nothingness. From the blind vault, blades swooped, seared, wailed. Jaisel was netted in a sea of death. Waves of death broke over her, gushed aside, were negated by vaster waves. She sprang from one edge and reached another. The slashing was like the beaks of birds, scoring hands, cheeks; scratches as yet, but pecking, diligent. While, in its turn, her sword sank miles deep in substances like mud, like powder. Subhuman voices squalled. Unseen shapes tottered. But the rain of bites, of pecks, of scratches, whirled her this way, that way, against pillars, broken stones, downward, upward. And she was in terror. Fought in terror. Terror lent her miraculous skills, feats, and a crazy flailing will to survive, and a high wild cry which again and again she smote the darkness with, along with dagger and sword.

Till abruptly she could no longer fight. Her limbs melted and terror melted with them into a worse state of abject exhaustion, acceptance, resignation. Her spirit sank, she sank, the sword sank from one hand, the dagger from the other. Drowning, she thought stubbornly: die fighting, at least. But she did not have the strength left her.

Not until that moment did she grow aware of the cessation of blows, the silence.

She had stumbled against, was partly leaning on, some upright block of stone that had been in her way when she dropped. Dully, her mind struggled with a paradox that would not quite resolve. She had been battling shadows, which had slain others instantly, but had not slain Jaisel. Surely what she supposed was a game had gone on too long for a game. While in earnest, now she was finished, the mechanism for butchery in this castle might slay her, yet did not. And swimming wonder surfaced scornfully: am I charmed?

There was a light. Not the phosphorus of Montaube's soldiers. It was a light the colour the wretched country had been by day, a sallow snow-blue glaze, dirty silver on the columns, coming up like a Sabbat moon from out of nowhere.

Jaisel stared into the light, and perceived a face floating in it. No doubt. It must be the countenance of burned Maudras, the last malicious dregs of his spirit on holiday from hell to effect menace. More skull than man. Eye sockets faintly gleaming, mouth taut as if in agony.

With loathing and aversion, and with horror, the skull regarded her. It seemed, perversely, to instruct her to shift her gaze downward, to the stone block where she leaned powerlessly.

And something in the face ridiculously amused her, made her shake with laughter, shudder with it, so that she knew before she looked.

The light was snuffed a second later.

Then the castle began, in rumbling stages, to collapse on every side. Matter of factly, she went to Renier and lay over his unconscious body to protect him from the cascading granite.

He was not grateful as she bathed his forehead at the chill pool equidistant between the ruin and the camp of Towers.

Nearby, the horse licked the grudging turf. The mist had fled, and a rose-crimson sun was blooming on the horizon. A hundred yards off, the camp gave evidence of enormous turmoil. Renier swore at her.

'Am I to credit that a strumpet nullified the sorcery of Maudras? Don't feed me that stew.'

'You suffer it too hardly. As ever,' said Jaisel, honed to patience by the events of the night. 'Any woman might have achieved this thing. But women warriors are uncommon.'

'There is one too many, indeed.'

Jaisel stood. She started to walk away. Renier called after her huskily:

'Wait. Say to me again what was written in the stone.'

Her back to him, she halted. Concisely, wryly smiling, she said: ' "I, Maudras, to this castle do allot my everlasting bane, that no man shall ever approach its walls without hurt, nor enter it and live long. Nor, to the world's ending, shall it be taken by any *man*." '

Renier snarled.

She did not respond to that, but walked on.

Presently he caught up to her, and striding at her side, said: 'How many other prophecies could be undone, do you judge, lady Insolence, that dismiss women in such fashion?'

'As many as there are stars in heaven,' she said.

Brooding, but no longer arguing, he escorted her into the camp.